S. S. BAZINET

AREL'S BLOOD

BOOK TWO

The Vampire Reclamation Project

Renata Press
Albuquerque, New Mexico

Published by Renata Press
Albuquerque, New Mexico
renatapress.com

Visit the author's website
ssbazinet.com

ISBN-13: 978-1-937279-12-7

*For all those who enjoy a journey
into the light.*

Acknowledgments

I have so many people in my life who have helped to make this book possible. My appreciation and gratitude goes out to all of my family for their continued, loving support. Regarding the book's content, Laura Christine has been my editing guru and guiding light. Gene has been an invaluable blessing as a copy editor. Anna Marie and Julia Ann have also been extremely helpful with their thoughtful support and additional copy editing. Gabriel is forever cheering me on!

One

Arel's gut was on fire, searing his tissues, consuming his energy. But he was familiar with fever and pain. When he was a child, misery was his constant companion. He'd learned that he couldn't cope with it. He endured it. Now he had to go a step further, he had to ignore it. Carol was in trouble. Her life was on the line, and his mind was issuing orders. *Go back to her bedside! Help her!*

But how could he obey those orders? Tim was literally dragging him down the hospital corridor, putting distance between Arel and Carol's room. Arel struggled against the iron grip Tim had on his arm, but he couldn't successfully battle Tim's mass and strength, especially in his weakened condition. At six-foot-three, Tim was four inches taller than Arel. He also had the beefed-up body of a pro ballplayer. Arel came from an English lineage. He bore the slender, genteel frame of an upper-class bloodline. Still, he had to do something to get Tim's attention. He glared up at his captor and barked out a hoarse appeal. "Tim! You have to let me go back to help!"

His croaky-voiced order seemed to backfire. Tim stiffened his jaw and stepped up his forward pace. Arel continued to resist, but spasms of pain were gripping his gut, making his knees want to buckle. The hospital-green walls were closing in on him. The antiseptic smells had a suffocating effect. He couldn't manage enough air. He took short, gasping breaths, trying to get a little oxygen. His pleas came out in breathless spurts. "You're supposed to be my friend! Why won't you listen to me?"

Tim finally gave him a quick, scowling glance as they neared the end of the hallway. That's when Arel noted that Tim was puffing away too. It was a small victory. Maybe Arel was putting up a better fight than he thought. But his triumph was useless, wasn't it? He had no choice but to follow as Tim slammed through a pair of swinging, hospital doors. Luckily, his forced march ended when Tim came to an abrupt stop a few feet beyond the doors.

As Arel tried to catch his breath, he noticed that Tim was scanning the busy waiting area that adjoined the hallway. He saw the person Tim was searching for. A blond-haired man sat in a corner of the room. When Tim waved to him, the man acknowledged the gesture and stood up.

Tim urged the man on in a weary voice. "Michael, get over here fast. Arel is really going nuts."

Arel took the opportunity to jerk free from Tim's grasp, but a bout of dizziness made him brace himself on his knees. "Don't get Michael involved," he huffed. "He doesn't know anything about childbirth."

Tim shot him an imploring look, but he didn't reply.

Michael's face was calm and serene as he walked over to join them. Only his eyes showed any reaction to the situation. They flickered with concern when he looked at Arel.

Tim's face relaxed a little. "Please talk some sense into this guy," he begged.

His request made Arel come to attention. He stumbled forward and grabbed Michael's shirt. "Michael, tell Tim to stay out of this. Carol needs me."

"I don't think so," Tim countered. "Arel's upsetting her. They had to toss him out of the birthing room for her sake and his."

Arel tightened his grip, forcing Michael to look at him. "I was a little nervous, that's all. The bottom line is that I can help."

Tim ignored Arel's comments and continued on with his full disclosure of facts. "Arel fainted twice trying to help."

Arel's face went flush with humiliation, but he couldn't deny the truth. When he was under extreme duress, he passed out. It was one of his body's defense strategies. He shut out the world and all its pain by losing consciousness. How many times had the world gone black when he was really upset? How many times had his friends, Tim and Kevin, intervened when his body was making a quick trip to the floor?

10

As time passed, he was making headway, gaining control over his physical response, but this wasn't one of those times. Still, he looked back at the hospital doors with resolve. "I don't care how many times I faint. I can't bear the thought that Carol is suffering."

Arel's statement was filled with all the passion he could manage. His lungs were heaving in and out like a broken bellows. Why did a hospital always make him feel like he was a mountain climber who couldn't catch his breath? He slowly released Michael's shirt, giving himself time to get more oxygen. "Listen, both of you. Just give me five minutes. I promise to make everything better."

With his hands out in front of him, Arel gave the men a gesture to remain where they were. Tim didn't move, but he squinted back as if he was viewing someone who was headed for a padded cell. Michael maintained a look of concern.

Arel didn't care what they might be thinking. He backed up a couple of steps and turned towards the doors leading to the birthing room.

He couldn't let Carol down. It was a rock solid intention, but he was having trouble navigating. He couldn't keep his gait steady, and his vision blurred. It didn't matter. He'd force his body to do what he wanted.

He wouldn't abandon a person he cherished. The thought spurred him on when he had no reserves left. Before he got very far, Michael snagged his arm.

"Arel, you'll never make it to Carol's room in your condition. You have to calm down or you know what could happen."

Michael, an angel who had taken on physical form, was a couple of inches shorter than Tim. His frame was lighter and less muscular, but he had a definite air of strength and vitality. Yet he'd never been anything but Arel's gentle friend and mentor. He had also shared his untainted blood with Arel, offering him a way to escape the curse of being a vampire. Yet the gift could also be a curse when Arel's negative emotions were in play. If Arel lost control, his physical vessel was put at risk.

Michael was very aware of the danger that Arel faced. "Before you can help anyone, take a moment and—"

"How can I take a moment when I know what can happen in childbirth? So many things can go wrong. I've studied the facts for months."

Michael's crystal-blue eyes filled with understanding. "I know what you're saying, but that doesn't mean Carol is in danger."

"You didn't hear her! She's in terrible pain!" Arel's brain was yelling out orders, demanding that he do something before it was too late. He had to find a way to save Carol from some horrible fate. Unfortunately, it was everything he could do to remain upright.

Michael came to his aid, taking hold of him, and leading him in the opposite direction. "You don't want Carol to see you like this, do you? Let's go find a place where you can get yourself together."

It was a reasonable request, especially with the world spinning and Arel's legs feeling like they forgot how to walk. "Okay, but just for a few minutes."

"Yes, yes, for just a few minutes." Michael's voice had the tone used by mothers when their child has lost touch with all that's safe in the world. "But you also have to find a way to relax a little. Your body is overheating."

Arel tugged at his collar. "I know. This place is a death trap. There's no air. And they keep the thermostat at about a thousand degrees." He was rambling on in his croaky voice, not making sense. He could hear himself saying crazy stuff, but his brain had taken a bad turn in the birthing room. "I had a vision, Michael! I saw Carol hemorrhaging. There was so much blood. It was everywhere. In the end, the doctor couldn't save her."

As he related the vivid images, he stopped in the middle of the hallway. Searching out Michael's eyes, he was able to stand up straighter and reinforce his point with more steadfastness in his voice. "That's why I have to go back. I figured out how I can help. Remember when Kevin was in the hospital, and I kind of sucked up all the negative energy in the room? I'll do that now. I'll get rid of whatever might hurt Carol."

"My friend, I think you've had enough negative energy already. That's why you're in this condition, but it's not your job to try to fix everything. Carol wants to do this on her own. Try to respect that."

"After what I saw happening to her?"

Michael let out a knowing sigh. "Your vision resulted from your worries and the negative energy you've taken on. It's clouded your reason. If you keep going like this, you know the consequences."

"I don't care about me! It's Carol who's important!" Blurting out the words, Arel turned and started to stagger down the hall. He barely got three feet when his gut flared again, sending out a shooting pain that crippled him in his tracks. He sunk to the floor, barely able to move.

No, not now!

Arel's gut was a fiery repository for all his fears and nightmares. He'd been fueling those terrors all day, letting a lifetime of misery prove that he couldn't trust that things would work out. Minute after minute, hour after hour, he obsessed about how much danger Carol might be in. He should have been more prudent about the adverse effects he was having on his own wellbeing, but he was in full blown fight mode. Like a soldier, he battled to protect the life of a woman who'd been there for him in his darkest hour.

At the beginning of Arel's transformation, Michael's blood became a powerful purging agent that targeted Arel's psyche. Arel soon learned how much pain he'd hidden from himself. He was overwhelmed by so many agonizing memories surfacing so fast that he nearly despaired. Carol was the first person to befriend him in that challenging time. Michael was around long before Carol, but Michael was an angel, he didn't count.

Yet, in Arel's eyes, Carol was almost as caring. She was kind and sweet and utterly forgiving. Even when he lied and deceived her, her heart was open and always ready to see the best in him. Of course, there were reasons why he needed to deceive Carol in the beginning. He couldn't tell her the truth about himself. In fact, he never told any of his new family the whole truth, that he had been a vampire, that he was well over a hundred years old even if he looked like a young man. He didn't need to. He wasn't a parasite who lived on blood anymore. He wasn't a simple human being either. After Michael's contribution, Arel had some amazing and very potent abilities. Even if he was still unsure about using those gifts, he had to find a way to help Carol, no matter what the cost.

I can do this for her. I have to do this.

He tried to force back the pain as he groveled on the hard tile. He knew it was a hopeless effort when another massive wave of fiery heat made him cry out.

Michael was instantly there to help him. "Arel, please, you have to stop thinking the worst."

When he looked up and caught a glimpse of Michael's face, he knew he needed to heed Michael's advice. Normal people didn't have to worry about killing themselves with an emotional eruption. He did.

"Clear your mind," Michael whispered. "Let everything go, at least for the moment."

"How?" Arel's eyes were imploring, fluid orbs in a wasteland of dry, unbearable heat. Once his gut engaged, once it started heating up, it became its own master. "You know I haven't learned how to control any of this."

With Michael helping him up, Arel got to his feet and staggered to the wall. He fell against it, hugging the cool surface, hoping for some relief from the heat that was overwhelming his body.

Michael tried his best to reverse what was happening. His soothing blue energy could be a powerful, healing balm that counteracted Arel's escalating temperature. But things were moving too fast, and then there was the other problem.

"Arel, you have to let me in. You need to trust me."

Arel blinked back with wide, staring eyes. He'd been determined to handle the situation himself. He'd walled himself off from the angel's earlier efforts. Now, with his smoldering core headed towards a full-blown firestorm, his mind was paralyzed with fear. Trust was a word that made no sense. "I think it's too late," he whispered as he thought about the first time he'd had this problem and how he'd almost incinerated himself.

"Don't give up now," Michael said in a strong, encouraging tone.

Before Arel had a chance to reply, a loud voice called out to them from the other end of the hall.

"Arel, Michael! Great news! It's a boy!" Tim shouted out his announcement as he jogged over to where they stood.

Arel could barely acknowledge Tim's presence or hear what he was saying. He was trying to resign himself to the lethal force he harbored in his core. It threatened to have its way once and for all.

"You're not passing out again, are you?" Tim asked as he grabbed Arel's shoulder. He administered a brisk slap to Arel's flushed cheek. "Arel, pay attention! There's a new baby boy in the world!"

The younger man's stinging blow and eye-to-eye contact were enough to finally interrupt Arel's raging emotions. In the small pause that followed, he blinked back, trying to focus his attention on something besides his misery. "What?"

"It's all over, Arel. Carol had the baby!"

Tim shouted out the message a second time as if he was talking to someone who was hearing impaired. His insistent voice penetrated the buzzing in Arel's ears. Coming back to reality for another brief moment, he mumbled out a couple more syllables. "Baby?"

Tim shook Arel's shoulder again. "Yes, that's right, Carol had a little boy, and they're both doing great."

Arel took several quick breaths. As he did, Tim's message became a drizzle of rain on the hot, glowing coals in his gut. The dread that fed his inner fires was slowly replaced by a sense of surprise and wonder. After a long moment of concentration, he raised his eyes enough to look at Michael. "She did it. She really did it."

Michael smiled. "Yes, she did."

Arel slumped in relief as a sudden joy started to surface. This was his dream come true. His panic had been in vain, just like Michael said. Nothing was going to destroy a member of his family. It was just the opposite. His family was growing. A child was now a part of it.

As Arel's mind shifted, as relief began to dissolve his fears, his body responded. The pain eased as his gut began powering down. His physical vessel could be like that, on the brink of catastrophe one moment and able to reverse its course in the next. "Can I see Carol? Can I see the baby?"

He took a step forward, but his body was still weak and his leg gave way. Fortunately Michael and Tim were old hands at keeping him upright. They were quick to each grab an arm.

Tim gave Michael a teasing look as they walked slowly down the hallway. "Can you imagine what it would be like if Arel was having a baby?"

The question made Michael's steady gaze go wide. His voice was barely a whisper when he responded. "No, I can't imagine that."

Two

Kevin shifted his weight trying to get comfortable in a hospital chair that was too small for his stocky, six-foot-four frame. The chair creaked, but it still refused to accommodate a man of his size. His movements only made the baby he was holding fidget and stretch. His newborn son was so little, the tiniest human being Kevin had ever seen. They were complete opposites. Kevin had been quite a formidable bruiser when he played college ball. Since then, he'd put on a good twenty pounds. So how was he supposed to know how to handle a fragile infant?

He glanced up at Carol with pleading eyes. His pretty wife was sitting in her hospital bed, wearing a faded hospital gown. Her blond hair was wispy and unattended, but she never looked more beautiful to him. She would certainly be a wonderful mother, but would he measure up in his role as a father? When she looked back at him, he had his doubts. "I don't know if I'm holding the baby the right way. What if I drop him?"

Carol gave him a nurturing smile, already in her mommy role. "Honey, you're doing fine, isn't that right, Peggy?"

His sister, Peggy, sat across from them. When their eyes met, Kevin gave her a hopeful look. "What do you think, Peg?"

"Just pretend he's a football," Peggy teased. Her face was lined with fatigue after hours at the hospital. Only her voice maintained an assertive tone. "But, seriously, big brother, you did a great job as Carol's coach."

Kevin hadn't expected praise, but it was certainly helpful. "Thanks. When it's your turn, Tim will be the perfect partner."

Peggy slowly got out of the chair and ran her hand over her pregnant belly. "I feel like I swallowed a beach ball, but I'm not too worried about the whole thing as long as Arel isn't around."

Peggy's sharp remark was followed by the sound of someone clearing his voice. When Kevin looked up, he saw Arel, embarrassed and contrite, waiting timidly just outside the room. Tim and Michael were his back up, standing behind him.

"Arel, I didn't see you there," Peggy blurted out. Her scowl was quickly replaced with a sheepish smile. "Sorry, I didn't mean that comment to sound too harsh."

Kevin gave Arel a welcoming wave. His friend had done his best while Carol was in labor, but the poor guy kept passing out. Of course that wasn't a surprise. Arel never adjusted well to new circumstances. On the plus side, Kevin looked like a pro next to Arel. "Look who's here, Carol," he said with a smile.

Carol's opinion about Arel was obvious. She lit up when she saw him. "Come in," she called out with enthusiasm. "And that goes for Tim and Michael too."

Arel clearly heard her, but he didn't move. He clutched at the doorjamb with white-knuckled fingers. "Really? Can you forgive me?"

"There's nothing to forgive," Carol replied in an understanding voice. "You were just worried, weren't you?"

The question seemed to give Arel permission to move quickly to her bedside. "I was very worried," he said as he closed the space between them. Like an off-balance sailor in stormy seas, he grabbed hold of the bed rail and steadied himself. "I didn't realize how tough having a baby could be. You should be so proud of yourself."

Carol reached out to him. "Thank you."

"Women know what to do," Peggy insisted as she stepped forward. She targeted Arel with a questioning frown. "What about you, sweetie? Are you okay now?"

Kevin sucked in a breath. He hoped Peggy wasn't going to start grilling Arel. She meant well, but she could be a little overbearing. "Arel looks okay, right Arel?"

Arel's face reddened again as he let go of the bed rail, pushed his shoulders back, and adjusted his body into a more self-assured stance. "Yes, of course I am."

Tim walked over to Peggy and took her hand in his. "I think Arel would like to see the baby."

17

Arel looked back eagerly. "Yes, if it's okay with Carol and Kevin."

"Of course," Carol said. "We all know that it's the moment you've been waiting for."

Everyone in the room laughed. They all understood that Arel had waged an eight-month campaign prior to the baby's birth. His focus had been on the health and wellbeing of mother and child. Now his vigilant watch was at an end.

Arel walked over to where Kevin sat. With his hands clasped behind his back, he looked over Kevin's shoulder and smiled. "He's so small."

"I know," Kevin agreed. He was happy that he wasn't the only one who seemed to notice the size of the baby. He pulled back the blanket a little so Arel could get a better look. "Have you been around many newborns before?"

Arel cleared his throat. "This is my first, up close that is."

"Well, let me introduce you formally. Arel, meet your new godchild."

Arel grabbed the back of the chair. "Me? You want me to be his godfather?"

"That's right," Carol said. "And do you know what we named your godchild?"

Arel shook his head. "You and Kevin have been very secretive about names."

Carol gave Arel another affectionate smile. "His name is Ariel. It's a little different than your name, but it's basically the same."

Kevin glanced back at Arel. "Carol told me that it's the name of an angel."

Carol sobered and smoothed out her bed sheet. "Kevin and I have talked about it, and we feel that you've been our angel. If it hadn't been for you, we might not have gotten through everything."

Arel hesitated. "I didn't do that much."

"Oh, come now, that's not true," Tim said as he moved in closer to check out the baby too. When he looked up, he pounded Arel's back in a friendly but solid manner. "We've all heard the stories about Hotel Arel and how you took care of these two through thick and thin in those early days."

Arel seemed to take the enthusiastic body blows with a minimum of discomfort. "Thanks, but I was just being a friend."

"You've been the best friend," Carol said. "So, dear friend, would you like to hold Ariel?"

Arel's golden eyes flared with momentary confusion. "Hold the baby?"

Peggy pointed to a chair. "Maybe you should sit down first."

"Yeah, relax," Kevin said. "Carol and I want you to get used to this type of thing in case we need a babysitter one of these days."

Arel quickly seated himself, breathing in deeply as if he was readying himself for a marathon. "This is all so unexpected. I'm going to be a godfather . . . and a babysitter?"

Michael stood behind Arel, looking pleased. "Would you ever have imagined all of this a year and a half ago?"

Arel gasped in some air. "No, not at all."

"I'm really glad things have turned out like they did," Kevin said. He remembered a very different Arel. When they had first met, Arel was extremely sensitive and guarded. Just the simple act of Peggy putting her hand on his had been a violation. He reacted with horror, as if her hand had the power to burn him. Afterwards, when Arel tried to shut them all out, Peggy's stubbornness came in handy. She made sure that the others remained adamant in their commitment to help him. It wasn't easy to convince the frightened man to widen his self-contained circle of trust. It had taken time and patience on all their parts to finally come together as a family. Yet, here Arel sat, no longer skeleton-thin, but handsome and flourishing. He had also proven to be the best of friends when Kevin went through a very rough patch of his own.

"Here you go," Kevin said as he handed over his newborn son to Arel. "It's nice to know that my boy will always have someone he can depend on."

* * *

Arel couldn't stop staring at his godchild. He was used to adults, including himself, who all had their fixed routines and ways of thinking. The child in his arms eclipsed that world and brought in a feeling of new possibilities and new ideas about life. And the baby seemed so at ease. He slept so peacefully after his transition from the sheltered confines of his mother's womb to the outer world. Even though he was being passed around from person to person, he didn't seem to notice. Such a constitution was to be envied.

What kind of soul feels so comfortable with the world?

He glanced back at Michael, wanting some answers. Who *was* the soul who'd volunteered to incarnate in place of the original, intended one? Was this child someone Arel had known before, in one of his other lives? When he queried Michael before the child's birth, Michael wouldn't divulge any information.

The angel seemed just as tight-lipped about the matter now. He avoided Arel's eyes and touched one of the baby's small fists, making it react enough to open slightly, exposing long, delicate fingers. "Quite a miracle, isn't he?"

"He's perfect," Arel whispered back. He looked up at Kevin. "And he's lucky. He has you and Carol for parents."

Kevin smiled. "Thanks for believing in me these past months."

"Of course," Arel mumbled, but he was focused on the child he was holding. He noted every twitch and movement the baby made. "Oh look, I think he might be waking up."

The baby yawned and straightened his body out in a stretch. His miniature face became more animated. After he yawned a second time, his eyelids began to flicker ever so slightly. With a seemingly momentous effort, they managed to open just a crack. With another try, they lifted, exposing two grey-blue eyes.

Arel smiled. "That's strange. I think he's really looking at me, and with some degree of clarity." He had read about babies and knew that it took time for them to be able to distinguish details at first. Yet this incredible child was definitely giving it a good try. The baby stared back at him with unwavering attention. His gaze had a powerful, almost primitive quality that reminded Arel of the gaze of a fierce bird.

But there's more to what he's doing.

The child was observing him in a manner that indicated an unexpected talent, as if he could see past Arel's physical body and look at his very soul. As they continued to stare at each other, their minds merged for just a moment. In that brief space of time, knowledge was passed from one to the other. Arel's earlier questions were answered. He knew the soul who was looking back at him.

Oh no! It can't be! Oh hell, tell me he's not who I think he is!

Arel had to tighten his jaw to keep from crying out as the child's true identity triggered a terrible pain in his chest and closed off his airways.

Why? Why is this soul haunting me now? What did I do to deserve this misery?

In the next instant, the connection was broken. The baby closed his eyes and fell asleep again, leaving Arel gaping at his future. There would be no new beginning for him after what had been revealed. An untainted soul had returned from the dead, and Arel wanted no part of him. When he could finally breathe, he looked up at Michael with anger and hurt. "Take him," he ordered quietly.

After Arel handed the baby off to Michael, he knew he had to leave. "I'm sorry, but I'm really tired," he announced. He avoided making eye contact as he made up an excuse. He told the group something about his bad nerves and having to have some time to himself. It was true, but it was a gross understatement of the truth. Bad nerves? His whole body was sick.

Arel made his way to the parking garage alone. He insisted that Michael ride home with Peggy and Tim. He had no time for angels who allowed such a thing to happen. His only thought, his only salvation, was to get away from the hospital. He had to flee from the infant who brought back so much pain from Arel's own childhood.

Arel wasn't feverish anymore. Once in his car, he was stiff with cold. He drove out of the parking garage with gritted teeth, trying to contain the downward spiral his emotions were taking. But it was no use trying to fight facts or the past. By the time he reached the interstate, the cold hand of fate clawed at his chest and tore open old, chilling wounds. Luckily, traffic was light, and he would soon reach the exit he wanted to take. He had to put distance between himself and the baby. It probably wouldn't help much, but he had to do something, *anything* to try to numb what was happening. Yet, a heavy blanket of darkness was gathering around him. No matter what Michael or his friends said about having a normal, happy life, he would never find peace. He'd never escape the worst curse of all, being alive and knowing that his past was swiftly catching up with him.

Three

Peggy let out a heavy sigh as she climbed the stairs. It was good to be home and on her way to bed. "I'm exhausted."

Tim followed her up the stairs. "Carol was in labor for a long time," he said quietly. "You stayed with her through most of it. It's no wonder that you're feeling worn."

"I wanted to be there if Kevin flaked out."

"I hope you haven't overdone it."

"I'll be fine after a good night's sleep." She grabbed the handrail to help herself up the last two steps. As she made her way down the hall, she looked back at Tim. Little furrows of stress spoiled his usually smooth brow. His broad shoulders were slightly bent. Obviously, he was really tired too. "Are you getting anxious about our baby?" she asked as she ran her hand over her large, round belly.

"I'd be lying if I said no, but I think it's normal to be a bit nervous."

"At least you're not like Arel." She rolled her eyes. "He was horrible in the birthing room."

"In all fairness, he was concerned," Tim said as he took her hand and led her into the bedroom.

She let out another sigh. "Arel was nuts. I mean I love him dearly, but—"

Tim put on a serious face. "He's wondering if he can be there for you too?"

"What? After the way he acted today?" Her tone was high-pitched and filled with alarm, but when she saw the mischief in Tim's eyes, she started to laugh.

Looking only slightly contrite, Tim pulled her close and kissed her gently but with some degree of passion. "I love you, Peg."

It was what she needed. When she had a tough day, he always found a way to distract her from her worries. "I love you too." As she thought about their relationship, Arel came to mind again.

"Do you think Arel is really alright? He looked weird when he left the hospital."

"He's probably totally wiped out too."

"I hope he got home okay." She pulled away from Tim and walked over to the window. The rambling rancher next door was dark except for a light in the front room. She felt a little better knowing Arel was probably sitting in his favorite recliner and relaxing. She closed the curtain. "Maybe Arel needs somebody. An understanding woman might help him to unwind a little."

"Maybe, but I can't imagine him ever having kids."

She giggled. "Arel would never make it through his wife's delivery. But maybe one of these days, we could help him find someone."

"Peggy, please."

She turned and gave Tim a pleading look. "But I really care about him. He deserves to be happy like us."

"Of course he does, but that's his choice."

"I helped Carol and Kevin find each other."

"Yes, but Carol and Kevin are normal. Arel is—"

"He's special. That's what he is." She walked back to where Tim was standing and put her hands on his chest. She enjoyed the feel of his solid, masculine body. "That's why we have to keep our eyes open for someone just as special."

Tim sighed. "I guess, but you're forgetting what that person would be up against. I have no trouble admitting that Arel is caring and even nurturing to a fault, but he's also . . . what's the word I'm looking for?"

"Intense?"

Tim nodded. "He can also be extremely moody, excessive, overly passionate, the list goes on."

"Alright, I get the picture."

Tim bent over and nuzzled her neck. "Good, now, can we go to bed?"

She closed her eyes and felt her weariness settle in deeper. "I can't think of anything I'd like more."

* * *

Abrigail sat on the white linen sofa, letting her sparkly, blue gaze travel around the living room. The upper level of Arel's suburban house had undergone significant changes since Michael's arrival. Dark walls and carpets had given way to a lighter, more modern look. The décor reflected Michael's preferences, and Arel had been willing to indulge his angelic friend's wishes. Besides, Arel could always retreat to the lower, below ground level if he needed more conservative surroundings.

"You look very contemplative, Michael," she said as she turned her attention to her fellow angel. He sat in a chair by the window. A few gardening books littered the side table next to him. "I'm glad I dropped in to check on you. I take it that the hospital event didn't go very well."

Michael's face remained calm, but there was a flicker of concern in his usually steady eyes. "Arel is very unhappy at this point."

Abrigail sat back and allowed herself to appreciate the moment more fully. When she took on a physical body, she wasn't used to its heaviness. It took awhile to adjust to being contained in something as dense as flesh and bone.

Michael gave her a knowing glance. "It's just the two of us. You don't have to manifest a form if you'd rather not."

Abrigail smiled back. "I need the practice. Besides, after the initial transition, it can be fun to experience reality in this way. And I want to be ready if Arel needs someone tangible to hang on to. Remember when he was dying and needed company? He wanted a soft place to lay his head. He might need that type of comfort again after today."

"Yes, when Arel handed the baby over to me, he gave me a wounded look, the kind you give to someone when they deliver you to the executioner."

"But he was doing so well up until now."

"One of the biggest problems is that his energy is very low. He's exhausted, and when he's this tired, he has very little ability to stay balanced even when it comes to smaller challenges."

"Would it have been easier if you told him about the child's soul ahead of time?"

Michael's head jerked up. "And give him months to worry?"

"I see," she said as she looked away and studied a beautiful bronze that sat on a long side table against the far wall. It depicted a strong, masculine angel watching over a child. The bronze reminded her of Michael. He had been in the trenches of physicality for a long time. He knew a lot more about the human psyche than she did. "How can I help?"

Michael's face brightened a little. "Gabriel is fielding this one."

"Really? That should be interesting. Gabriel isn't always what you'd expect an angel to be, not when he's in physical form."

"Hopefully, the role he adopts will be just what Arel needs."

"So you're not involved at all?"

"Arel doesn't want to talk to me right now. In fact, every time he senses my presence, he only becomes more agitated and angry. It's best if he thinks I'm not around."

For a few minutes, neither spoke, but Abrigail continued to study her friend. With his strong, striking features, he projected a sort of commander-in-chief energy, and rightly so. In other realms he was accustomed to directing his legions. Now, sitting quietly, he hid his true nature very well. He appeared to be an ordinary human who was simply Arel's faithful friend. "I'm surprised that Arel still blames you as often as he does."

"He can't help it. The fear overloads his circuits. He needs someone to blame when he can't handle his emotional swings."

Abrigail's eyes sparkled playfully. "In other words, you let him shirk responsibility now and then."

"He's barely coping at times like this."

"Was it a mistake to give him your blood?"

Michael's response was immediate and assured. "I've always believed in him. That will never change."

"One thing that's consistent with Arel is the way he likes to run off when he's unhappy. If you'd like, I can check on him for you."

"Certainly. Give it a try."

"I'm detecting a bit of doubt on your part. What's going on?"

"He can still be very defensive when he's upset."

"Right, so you're saying that he's heavily shielded."

Michael smiled but didn't reply.

Abrigail raised her chin and sat up straighter. She wanted to help if she could. "Oh well, I'll try to reach him anyway."

This time Michael gave her a look of appreciation. "I hope you can get through."

Abrigail shut her eyes and let her mind drift away from her physical form. Instead, she focused on her etheric wings. They were spread out behind her and acted like energetic antennas, searching for any information that might help. When she found Arel's energy signature, she hesitated, softening her own vibration so she didn't come on too strong. Arel could be very aware of an angelic presence after being around Michael. She had to reach out to him slowly, tuning into his energy field with a degree of caution. The last thing she wanted was to threaten Arel and make him feel more insecure. Finally, she pressed on and made contact. She pulled back immediately. "Oh goodness, he is upset," she said with surprise. While she was being very careful with Arel's energy state, her own was now slightly off-kilter. She had never felt that kind of shock from a human's aura before. It was akin to what an animal felt when it touched an electrified fence. "And he's much more powerful than I remember."

"Sorry, I forgot to warn you about his newest trick. But it's not intentional. He's not consciously aware of what he's doing."

She gave herself a little shake, helping her energy to return to a relaxed state again. "I hope that Gabriel can find a way to help."

The faintest trace of a smile crossed Michael's lips. "If there's a way, Gabriel will find it. Of that, I'm sure."

"Oh come now, Michael. I know you. You're still watching over Arel too. If you get a chance to help him, you will."

Michael's smile widened. "Of course."

Four

L ow clouds obscured the moon and allowed darkness to cover the empty farmland on either side of the two-lane road. Arel didn't know where the highway was taking him, and it didn't matter. With a great amount of effort, he was finally able to rein in some of his angst. He made a decision that helped lessen the pain he felt at the hospital.

From now on, I can't let myself care about anything or anyone.

Whenever he did care or let his emotions get involved, he ended up worse off than before. Michael was to blame. The angel convinced him to take another chance on life. And where did that get him? His heart was eventually so battered and bruised, he actually died. Michael had to resuscitate him.

Dammit, I soldiered on. I agreed to come back and try another round of torture.

The Mustang was flying down the highway at a speed that far exceeded the limit. He didn't notice. His foot, pressed hard against the accelerator, was powered by the same need that sent him fleeing from the hospital.

Wherever I end up has to be better than where I've been.

He decided he'd give himself the new start he needed, one that didn't involve angels or babies.

What a relief it is not to have to think about anyone else.

He loosened a button on his shirt, lowered the driver's-side window, and inhaled deeply. The fields were still damp and sweet-smelling after a recent rain. An earthy aroma filled his nostrils. The city air didn't have that wonderful fragrance. It reminded him of the farmland and meadows that surrounded his childhood home in England.

Damn, what a hellish place that was.

He quickly closed the window, vowing to shut out any thoughts associated with the past. He wasn't quick enough. That one, deep breath opened inner floodgates and a barrage of images flowed in. Smell had that power. It was connected to a part of the brain associated with memory and feeling. No matter how much he wanted to forget everything but the road and the present moment, he was instantly transported back in time to a place he swore he'd never visit again. The home where he grew up was vividly portrayed in his mind's eye, and he hated every bit of its grey, aging stone and crumbling mortar.

The depressing dwelling sat on land that had been in his family for six generations before him. It was a large, foreboding place with thorny bushes and heavy vines covering most of the exterior. The interior with its high-ceilinged rooms and musty air was even more depressing. It was cold and damp most of the year and always suffered from a shortage of natural light.

There was only one person who could bring warmth to that hateful house.

His breath caught on the thought, and he had to clutch at the steering wheel with shaky hands.

Concentrate on the road! Don't think about him.

He pressed harder on the accelerator, increasing his speed, but he couldn't outrun the image of Aldwin.

My brother!

Aldwin was thirteen years older than Arel. He was tall, fair and charming. He was the coveted firstborn son, and he had a confident, talented personality to go along with the position. He excelled in whatever he put his mind to. When Aldwin came home from university and graced the house and his family with his presence, he looked like a youthful prince.

Arel was more of a misfit foundling. Skinny and awkward, he ran about like any child, but he often missed seeing a rock or a stair and was forever left with skinned knees and bruises. He wasn't winsome or fair-haired. He had a mop of unruly, black curls which his nanny never successfully tamed. Even now, Arel scowled when he thought about the woman's rough treatment, how she yanked and pulled at his hair with no regard for the pain she caused. She knew her charge wasn't a valued member of the family. It was her excuse to abuse him whenever she wanted.

The old biddy was probably hand-picked by my mother.

Arel was an unwanted child, the unexpected baby who shouldn't have been conceived. His mother never forgave him for embarrassing her with his presence. How dare he show himself at a tea party, reminding her friends that she'd been careless and allowed herself to have a child when she was supposed to be past that sort of situation?

Arel didn't fare much better with his father. The man was already invested in Aldwin. He didn't have time or patience for his scrawny, second child. But Arel accepted his role in the family. Someday, he knew things would change. Aldwin told him so. Whenever Aldwin visited, he always made time for his little brother. Those special times were Arel's happiest. "Teach me everything," he often pleaded. "Please, I want to be just like you!"

Aldwin's response was to tousle Arel's curls and laugh. "Of course, I promise."

His brother's promise was like a Christmas star in Arel's fanciful daydreams. He pictured a time when his request would be granted. He would be transformed into an older version of himself, one that looked like Aldwin. He'd finally be tall and handsome too. Maybe he would even be wanted. But his starry vision was lost to fate on a Friday late in spring. It wasn't the kind of day a boy of seven should have to face, but it came anyway, not with bells and Christmas whistles for celebrating, but with someone's screams. It was still early morning, and the cries woke Arel out of a deep sleep. For a long moment, he didn't move. He wasn't able to do anything but lie very still as the sounds filled his young mind with their message. Someone was in terrible pain. Was it his mother? Was she being torn apart by some monster?

When the screams finally died away, they were replaced by loud sobbing. Arel's mother, that person who usually had such a sharp tongue and a callous, sullen expression when she looked at him, was clearly broken in some way. He had to find out why. Even if she didn't love him, she was his mother, and he had a duty to her. Aldwin was schooling him in such matters. His brother taught him about bravery and being a true English gentleman.

Remembering his brother's encouraging face was enough to spur him on. His frozen state was replaced by urgency and movement. He crawled out of bed and crept from his room. Cautiously, he ventured down the long, wide hallway, letting the sound of his mother's grief draw him forward. When he got to the broad staircase, he stopped. No matter what Aldwin had taught him, he froze again. A deep, inner-knowing told him that he was making a mistake. If he went forward, he would suffer for it. A feeling of dread grabbed hold. It invaded his small body with a warning so dark and frightening that he wanted to cry out, but he wouldn't be a coward. He wouldn't let Aldwin down, no matter what.

It took all his courage to reach out and take hold of the mahogany spindles, to stand on tiptoe and peer over the railing. A long moment passed before he could make sense of what he saw. When he finally understood what was happening, Arel knew why his mother's heart was breaking. He knew why she would never be the same. What he saw so clearly below in the great hall made his body go weak again and his knees shake.

"Aldwin!" His whisper went unheard as he continued to stare downwards.

Only the night before, his brother had stopped by Arel's bedroom. They laughed together as they made plans for Arel to learn the ways of a proper horseman. As Aldwin was leaving, he gave Arel a broad, easy smile. "Father said you've been banned from the stables, but we'll go there tomorrow after my ride. I'll teach you how to act so you don't make the animals nervous."

Now, far below, Aldwin lay on the massive, oak table that sat in the middle of the entry hall. Guests often put their hats and gloves on the table's broad surface. But its function had changed. Aldwin's body rested on the place where hats were supposed to go. His blond hair was fanned out over the dark, varnished wood like a halo. A patch of his hair was matted with blood.

Arel wouldn't let himself make any sound. He held on tight to the balusters and to the hope that his mother was mistaken in her sorrow. Aldwin was clearly injured, but he'd soon wake up. His eyes would open, and he'd smile again.

Don't cry mother. He's going to be fine.

The thought helped to rouse Arel's body into action. He descended the aging stairs slowly, knowing their weaknesses, their squeaks and creaks. He tried so hard not to make a noise as if he'd somehow defile the solemn atmosphere. It filled the lower hall and drifted upwards, blanketing him in a grey, dismal fog of despair. Yet

30

he couldn't give in to it. He had to hold on to the courage that Aldwin insisted he had inside of him.

Brother, help me to be as brave as you said.

When he arrived at the landing, he glanced at his mother. She was weeping silently now. Her eyes were red and vacant, not seeing anything but the cruel hand of God who took her son.

Mother?

He almost called out to her, but he knew he didn't exist in her world. He could have been a ghost as he made his way across the large expanse of stone and mortar floor. Even though the weather was warming outside, the large hall lacked any warmth. Its chill was a sharp instrument that could penetrate flesh with ease. It invaded his frail body, settling in his bones. He shivered uncontrollably as he took the last few steps to where his brother lay. He clenched his teeth to keep them from chattering. When he raised his eyes and stared at his brother's face, it was pale and ashen. In a moment of acute clarity, the truth couldn't be denied. That's when his child's heart shattered into a thousand pieces.

My brother is really dead!

Everything inside of him rebelled at the thought. He still couldn't accept it. Instead, he reached out for Aldwin's outstretched hand and held it tight. It was even colder than his, but he wouldn't let go of it. Tears streamed freely down his cheeks. "Please, brother," he cried out, "I need you."

"Get away from him!"

A voice shouted out from behind him. It filled the hall like the bellow of some wounded beast.

Arel glanced back to see that it wasn't a beast that yelled at him. It was his father who shrieked out in madness and rage.

"Father?"

The man had been sitting in the shadows, head on chest. Up until Arel made his presence known, his father was mute and stoic in his vigil. Now, he was standing erect and rigid. All reason in the man was swept away by the enormity of what he'd lost. His perfect child, his golden boy who'd grown up tall and strong and capable, his beloved son who was everything to him, was dead. "How dare you touch my boy!" he yelled at his second son. He moved forward wielding his cane.

31

But Arel couldn't let go of Aldwin's hand. His brother was the only one who ever cared for him or protected him. He prayed for his brother's help.

What should I do, Aldwin? Tell me!

But Aldwin didn't help him. Instead his father's cane came down on his back. There was such force behind the blow that it broke his connection to his brother and brought him to his knees. The pain was excruciating, driving out the numbing coldness, but he still couldn't move. He could only writhe in agony as the blows kept coming.

"Why didn't God take *you*?" His father shouted each time he brought down the cruel, wooden stick.

After that, Arel didn't remember anything. The next day, he woke up in his bed, broken and forever altered. His childhood and his dreams of a beautiful world had been stripped away, leaving him alone and unprotected from what was yet to come. It was only later that he understood that everything changed the instant that Aldwin was thrown from his horse. As soon as his head struck the corner of a stony wall and he closed his eyes for the last time, a curse descended over the lives of those who loved him. It settled on the great hall where his body lay on the table, leveling them all with its darkness and desolation.

* * *

"Bloody hell!" Arel yelled out as he came back to reality. His childhood trauma was quickly put aside when the Mustang's tires hit rock and gravel on the rough shoulder of the road. He fought for control as the car headed for a ditch. Luckily his reflexes were good even in his miserable state. He braked fast and swerved enough to get back on pavement. But the Mustang was clocking seventy, and he had to pay attention.

It took a few minutes for his heart to calm down as he stared doggedly at the road. He had every intention to stay focused on what he was doing. He succeeded in part. He was able to keep the car where it belonged, but his mind wasn't as easy to direct. His recent recall of his brother's death flashed repeatedly in and out.

Why can't I forget it all?

With Michael's blood and the angel's help, Arel thought he purged most of his past. In a hellish transformation, he faced horrors that seemed impossible to release and found a way to release them. But he hadn't addressed his brother's role in his life. He managed to skirt around that issue. Now, he didn't have that option. Aldwin was back from the dead. His soul looked at Arel through the eyes of a newborn baby.

I guess I'm supposed to be happy to have him back.

It was just the opposite. He realized how much hatred he still harbored in his heart. It was a seething resentment that was beaten into him. As his father caned him, each blow drove home a message. Each blow taught him that he was the one who should have died.

"Damn you, brother! I hope you rot in hell for leaving me to that bastard's punishment!"

The surge of temper that fueled his profanity and ill will didn't make him feel any better. Deep down, he knew it wasn't justified.

Aldwin didn't leave me on purpose.

Arel couldn't deny the truth. Aldwin was good and pure, the best brother anyone could have wanted. Their father was right in mourning his loss.

And he was probably right in loathing me. What did I bring to the table?

Arel was clearly an inferior throwback. Michael had said otherwise, but the truth was evident. Didn't Tim accuse him of acting crazy that very night? Didn't Peggy, one of his biggest supporters, speak about him in the same way? And now, looking back on his performance, he knew they were right. He was always fainting or acting like a child having a tantrum. Even now, what was he doing? He was running away from a beautiful, little baby! How insane was that?

Aldwin was wrong about me! I'm an idiot and a coward who has no business being alive.

That's when another decision was made. Maybe his father didn't succeed in killing him, but Arel could make his father's wish come true now.

"Is that what you want, Father, my life?" he shouted as he took his hands off the steering wheel. "God knows I'm ready to die!"

"Arel, watch out!"

His rant was cut short. A loud voice, Michael's voice, shouted out in his head. At the same time, a movement caught his eye. A motorcycle came out of nowhere. It swung out in front of the Mustang. No tail lights, no warning.

"What the—"

Arel grabbed the wheel again and slammed on his brakes. The car swerved as he tried to stay out of the path of the bike. But the motorcycle swerved too. It was out of control, crisscrossing the highway in front of the car. The Mustang narrowly missed clipping the cycle with its front fender. The bike kept going.

"God no!" Arel watched the bike go airborne. The side of the road had a steep drop-off, and the bike went flying over it. The Mustang was in trouble too. It didn't take flight like the cycle. It stayed earthbound, hurdling over the side of the road, still going much too fast. No amount of braking could save him this time.

"Oh hell!" He screamed out the words and braced for impact. A concrete structure was coming up fast. The car was heading straight for it. For the briefest of moments, just before he hit the wall, Arel glimpsed Michael. He felt the angel's hand push his head sideways just before the airbag exploded to life. If it hadn't been for Michael's intervention, Arel's nose would have been broken. But he didn't think about his good fortune. When everything stopped moving, he sat in a heap, dazed and in a state of shock. His heart was in his throat, and he couldn't swallow or move. When his body finally regained some semblance of control, he automatically battled the air bag. But it wasn't his own situation that made him frantic to free himself. He kept seeing the motorcycle and its driver sail off the side of the road.

The guy is probably dead!

After fighting the airbag out of the way and unbuckling his seatbelt, he was able to open the car door and climb out. He stood gulping in the night air and thinking about how to get help.

"Michael! I need you!" He called out for angelic aid as he tried to still his shaky legs. They were almost useless, making him cling to the car for support as he made his way around to the other side. When he was on the side facing the field, he scanned the darkness.

"Michael! Somebody could be dead!" His voice was almost as weak as his legs. He needed his friend to be there for him, but his surroundings were as devoid of heavenly help as the devil's kitchen.

Holding his hand to his heart, trying to keep the vessel inside his chest, he focused his attention on the path that the motorcycle had taken. Luckily the moon was in a patch of clear sky, and he could see well enough. He made his body go forward, stumbling over rocks and furrows. When he finally glimpsed a metal carcass resting in the field, he held his breath. There was also a body not far from the bike. It was as motionless as the vehicle.

"Oh no!" As Arel approached the still form, his mind flashed to Aldwin. He pictured his brother lying so still on the oak table. Only now, when he looked down, he saw a boy who was lying face up on Illinois farmland. Like Aldwin, his hair appeared blond and wavy. Thankfully, there was no blood to indicate a head wound.

Please, no, this can't be happening. I'm looking at a person who probably doesn't even shave yet.

He dropped to his knees and tried to feel for a pulse, but his hands were trembling so badly that he couldn't feel anything. When he put his head to the boy's chest, he thought he heard something, but there was no rise and fall to indicate that the boy was breathing.

"Oh lord, don't let him die too—" He didn't know much about CPR. He'd only seen it performed in movies. After another shout for Michael and no answer, he started a running dialog with himself. "Stay calm! You have to stay calm." His hands flailed about as he tried to think about what he was supposed to do. Finally, he opened the boy's mouth and put his own over it.

You have to hold his nose.

He repeatedly tried to give the breath of life. There was a problem. He was breathing in and out so fast that he sucked back the air he was trying to give. He stopped, feeling incompetent again.

You don't have time to doubt yourself! A person could die if you don't get it together.

When Arel started the life-giving technique again, he was calmer, more determined. This time he performed the action correctly. There was a slight rise in the boy's chest. After a few more breaths, the boy moaned. The weak utterance made Arel fall back in joy and relief. He'd never imagined that a moan could be music to his ears.

Could it be true? Did I bring him back?

He couldn't take his eyes off the boy's chest. Every rise and fall was a miracle. When the boy started coming around, Arel's elation soared to a whole new level. The boy was going to make it. "Thank goodness," he said aloud. He leaned in closer. "It's okay," he whispered. "Everything is going to be fine." After a moment, he sat back on his heels and allowed himself a better look at the person he had saved.

He's so young and innocent. There's so much of the child left in him.

When the boy's lids flickered open, he stared at Arel with grey-blue eyes. They were the same color as the newborn's eyes, the same color as Aldwin's eyes. For an instant, Arel wanted to run away again, but this time it wasn't an option, especially when the boy tried to move and cried out in pain.

"Stay still," Arel cautioned as he rubbed at his brow. What could he do? He remembered his cell phone. "I'll call for help."

He stood up quickly and retrieved his phone, grateful that he could hand his recent charge over to proper medical authorities. His hopes soon dimmed. He couldn't get a signal. "Dammit!" He repeated his protest as he tried different locations in the field and back on the road. After spending precious minutes on the highway and not seeing any cars, he hurried back to the boy.

"I'm sorry, we must be in a dead zone or my battery is going."

"So cold," the boy stuttered back.

Arel hadn't noticed the temperature, but he was freezing too. "I'm sorry." He took off his jacket and quickly covered the boy. "I have a blanket in the trunk of my car."

He started to get up to retrieve the cover, but the boy reached out.

"Wait!" The boy's tone was insistent. "If something happens to me, if I don't make it—"

"No, don't talk like that." He knelt down again and took the boy's hand. At least it wasn't lifeless as Aldwin's had been. He tried to smile and offer comfort. "You're going to be fine."

The boy's grip tightened on his. "I'm glad you're here. Don't leave."

"Don't worry, I won't." Arel felt something stir inside as he listened to himself saying the words. He wasn't a wounded child anymore. He was the older one now. He was the adult who could offer strength to a person who needed his help.

* * *

The night sky was a beautiful backdrop for the moon as it sailed in and out of wispy cloud banks. It was a chilly night, but Michael and Abrigail didn't feel the cold. They were in their etheric bodies.

Abrigail's form brightened as she studied the two people in the field below.

"Arel is taking such care with our Gabriel. And Gabriel is doing a perfect job of playing a young, injured man."

Michael gave her a broad smile. "Gabriel told me that he's going to call himself Carey while he's in physical form."

"Interesting name."

"It's a simple one. Gabriel doesn't want Arel to discover his real identity."

Abrigail gave herself a little shake as she recalled her earlier encounter with Arel's energy shields. "After his vision about losing his brother, I think Arel wants a flesh and blood connection."

"It was a defining moment in Arel's life. He's never been able to get over the effects of that loss."

"Arel was a beautiful child. All that he wanted was someone to love him."

"Yes, but on a deeper level, he was afraid of truly opening himself to anyone."

"What do you mean?"

Michael shifted his focus to some denser clouds that were swallowing up the moon again. The farmland below was quickly shrouded in an intermittent darkness. "The trauma of that past life, when Arel was burned at the stake, left him with deep issues of trust and safety."

"I see." Abrigail let out a sigh. "But his brother, Aldwin, loved him. It was a difficult role to play, to die like that and leave Arel to their father's cruelty."

"That's true, but even if Aldwin had lived, Arel would have probably grown up with a certain amount of bitterness. Aldwin would always have been the son who was wanted, and Arel would have judged himself as the one who was never loved."

Abrigail's energy was animated with curiosity. "You've done a lot to help him change those beliefs. I'm rather surprised that he had such a reaction to Carol and Kevin's baby. After remembering his brother's death, he even wanted to end his life."

"When Arel's feeling of being the inferior, worthless son takes hold, he can lose himself in the pain. His faith in himself slips away. But Aldwin's death was part of a greater plan."

"Something tells me that Gabriel might find a way to hurry that plan along."

"He can be very creative, and he likes a challenge."

Abrigail laughed when she thought about how stubborn Arel could be. "Then our fellow angel should love his current assignment."

* * *

Arel pushed a lock of wavy, blond hair out of the boy's eyes. His patient was shaking worse than ever, clutching at the blanket that Arel had retrieved for him. The thin picnic throw was hardly enough to keep a person warm, and the temperature was still dropping. "Do you think you have any serious injuries? Maybe I could get you to my car. It might be warmer."

The boy grimaced back. "No . . . don't think I could make it that far. I'm so cold . . . freezing."

"I wish I knew how to help you."

Arel clasped his hands together and rubbed them briskly, trying to get some circulation going. It was a hopeless gesture. The cold, night air and the stress of the accident had him shivering as violently as the boy.

Why can't I get my damn internal furnace going when I need it?

He was trying his best to force himself into some kind of emotional tantrum. He brought up images from the past. He forced himself to think about memories that should have made him angry. He needed something to fire up his gut, but nothing worked. Even thoughts about his brother and his father left him in a state of limbo. But he had to do something to warm the person in his care.

"Maybe my body heat would help," he offered as he carefully gathered the boy into his arms. The boy responded at once, grabbing hold of Arel's shirt and trying to get closer. It was a survival instinct on the boy's part. If allowed, bodies know what to do. They seek out warmth. Hearts have a similar need for connection. As Arel felt the boy shivering in his arms, he understood the boy's desperation from a deeper level. Wanting someone to be there when one is cold and hurting was a familiar feeling. His entire childhood had been desperately cold and painful. There was no warm, swaddling blanket to welcome him into the world. There weren't any happy people gathered in a hospital room celebrating his birth. His nursery was set up away from his parents' room where his hungry cries wouldn't disturb them. He grew up without the knowledge that a child was supposed to be warm, was supposed to be loved.

Perhaps the cruelty I suffered would have been more bearable if I hadn't learned that it didn't exist for everyone. But even a very young child observes his environment and learns what's going on around him.

When Arel was old enough, he realized there was another child, another son named Aldwin. Unlike him, this boy was carefully tended, carefully loved and nurtured by his parents and the servants who followed their lead. Arel tried to be like his brother so that he'd be loved too. Of course that didn't happen. He'd never be like Aldwin.

"Aldwin was perfect like Carol's baby." He let the statement slip out with no feeling behind it.

The boy trembled again. "What . . . what did you say?" he asked in a ragged gasp.

Arel held him closer, wondering why there was no warmth to give the person in his care. He knew he was capable of giving. Before Carol gave birth, he cared so much that his gut was on fire. Afterwards, he was all smiles and happiness when he found out that mother and child were fine. His heart was working beautifully until the baby looked up at him. Now his heart felt frozen in a block of memory that refused to thaw.

The boy obviously didn't understand what Arel was feeling. "I'm lucky, aren't I?" he said in an almost cheerful tone.

"What do you mean?"

"That you're here."

The statement made Arel laugh, but there was bitterness in the sound he made. "You're lucky because you didn't kill yourself like my brother."

"Your brother?"

"Yes, he was like you. He did things with no thought of fear, like you on that bike. Unfortunately, a high-strung horse bolted at a gate and threw him into a wall." He paused. "My family wished it had been me instead."

The boy blinked up at him. "But if you died, I wouldn't have you here to help me. I might have died too."

Arel frowned. The boy had a valid point, but it didn't seem to help much. It didn't change the past.

"What is it? What's the matter?" the boy asked.

What could Arel say? Even if it meant that he wouldn't have been there to save the boy, he wished he had died instead of Aldwin.

After long moments of silence, the boy seemed to understand what the problem was. He let go of Arel's shirt and let himself fall back unto the ground. He pushed off the blanket defiantly. "I'm sorry that I've been such a burden." His voice was resigned, as if he was used to being abandoned to the elements. "I'm fine now. Don't worry about me."

The moonlight drifted out from behind a cloud. Once again, its powerful rays spotlighted the boy. He was wearing a windbreaker that was faded and stained. His jeans had holes in the knees, not the designer kind, but holes that came from too much wear. His sneakers were falling apart.

A flush of shame was the first warmth that Arel felt since the hospital episode. Carol and Kevin's child would grow up feeling secure in the world. Yet, here in this field, a boy was hurt and cold. He obviously came from a different world, a world of want and neglect. This boy had learned not to expect anything from anybody. Someday, he'd be bitter and filled with resentment.

Just like me.

Arel tried to breathe, but his lungs barely took in any air. He felt sick and inadequate until another thought saved him.

But it doesn't have to be that way. Here and now, I have a choice. Maybe I don't value my own life, but what about another person's life? This young man is hardly more than a child. He needs somebody to care.

Arel was suddenly tired of his anger. He was tired of thinking about death. There was a new baby in the family, and there was a young man who needed his help. What was he willing to do about it?

"You're not a burden," he said, haltingly at first. He scrambled in a sea of confusion, trying to find his way back to new possibilities. Then he let go of trying and some words slipped out on their own. "From now on, you have a friend if you want one."

"Are you sure about that?" the young man asked. His blue eyes, already filled with pain, came alive with a flicker of doubt. "I don't want somebody handing out charity."

Arel's gaze rallied in response, going from dull and fretful, to golden pools of compassion. "I understand that, but this has nothing to do with charity." And he meant what he said. In fact, the idea that he could change the young man's direction in life gave him new hope. For the first time since he'd fled from the hospital, his body quickened and his heart beat faster. When he looked up at the moon, it seemed brighter. Its silver light was suddenly more radiant, like it was there to clear away the gloom that he'd harbored for so long.

Arel reached out for the blanket. "Let's try to get you warm, okay?"

His suggestion was met with silence, and Arel knew he had to also restore the boy's dignity. "Besides, if we huddle together, I'll be warmer too. We're both cold."

The boy finally complied with a sigh of exhaustion. "Whatever."

Arel held him close again and watched as the boy fell asleep. Even in his slumber, he was trembling.

"I'll do my best to be there for you," Arel whispered. His words sparked something in his chest. At first, a small, fiery sensation stirred in his heart, but as he continued to think about how to help the young man, the warmth grew in strength and intensity. Even his limbs began to feel a measure of heat. "You're not going to be cold anymore if I can help it."

Soon Arel could feel the boy's heart beating as surely as he felt his own. It reminded him of the times when he'd felt Michael's heart. The young man's vessel was surprisingly similar.

* * *

Abrigail remained close to Michael as they continued to observe the scene below. They both smiled when Arel's heart shifted into a warming mode.

"That's Gabriel's signal, right?" she asked.

Michael's energetic form expanded. "Yes, it is."

Gabriel, an angel in the guise of a young man, had been waiting for Arel to set aside his judgments and lower his shields. It was an opportunity to give Arel's heart a much needed infusion of love. Gabriel's energy would hopefully also add a new element of ease and worthiness.

"Arel needs all the help he can get in the challenging times ahead," Michael said.

"More storms?"

"I'm afraid so. Arel is still at the beginning of his journey."

Abrigail paused, hoping Arel's future wasn't as difficult as his past. "But things are moving in the right direction."

Michael's response was enthusiastic. "Yes, especially after tonight."

"I'm impressed with Gabriel's performance. He had a very good sense of what was needed when Arel became obstinate. He turned Arel's attitude around very quickly."

Michael returned to observing the scene below. "That's true. Maybe I've been going about all this the wrong way. I'm usually trying to help Arel. But watching him with Gabriel, I'm beginning to think that he loves being the one who comes to the rescue."

"Except in the birthing room. From what I've gathered, he doesn't exactly excel when it comes to being a good coach." Abrigail paused, noting that Michael seemed suddenly very quiet. "Michael? What is it?"

"Nothing really. I'm just reflecting a bit."

"You're thinking about Gabriel on that motorcycle, aren't you?"

Michael's energy turned playful. "Gabriel has some hidden talents I've never seen before."

"Did you notice his face when he was flying down the highway? Even in human form, he literally glowed."

"I agree."

"Maybe he'll let you borrow his bike," Abrigail teased.

"I might give it a try."

Abrigail was a little taken back. Michael was known for his courage, wisdom, and total dedication to angelic virtues, but she never thought of him traveling the highway on a Harley. "Remember your body. Make sure that you wear a proper helmet," she advised with motherly caution. "The old one that Gabriel was wearing bounced off when he hit the ground."

Michael laughed again. "I'll be careful, and I'll also make sure that Arel doesn't know about my extra-curricular activities. He has a certain image of me now, and I don't want to confuse him."

"Regarding Arel, I have a question. He called out repeatedly for your help, and you ignored him. What are you going to tell him when you see him?"

"He wouldn't believe me if I told him how difficult it was to stand aside and to do nothing so that Gabriel could step in."

Abrigail felt the tinge of sadness in Michael's reply. "Strange, isn't it? Humans believe that angels don't have real feelings and concerns. If they only knew, I think they'd be very surprised."

"You have to remember that most humans don't even understand themselves."

"Indeed," Abrigail replied as she watched Michael. His energy streamed out from him in great waves of light. It was directed at Arel and Gabriel, warming the air around them. She nudged him, sending sparks of light splintering in all directions. "I remember how Arel used to refer to himself as God's lab rat. Does he still do that?"

Michael sighed quietly. "Not quite as often."

Five

Arel came awake with a groan. The sun was directly in his line of vision. He shielded his eyes and glanced around. Where was he? Why was he in a field? He moaned again when memory kicked in. For a split second, he saw a motorcycle flying through the air.

Where's the kid I saved?

He jerked upright and then relaxed again. The person he was looking for was standing a few yards away. "There you are. Thank goodness, you look better," he said with relief. The rider who'd sailed across the landscape appeared to be a little older in the light of day. Arel estimated that the young man was eighteen or nineteen years old. His face was still very youthful with only the slightest hint of a beard. His hair was also darker than Arel had thought. It was more of a light brown than blond.

The boy walked towards him. "Yes, I feel pretty good thanks to you."

Arel got up slowly, noting the stiffness in his back. Sleeping on the ground wasn't his idea of fun. Some stretching helped. "I was really worried last night. I thought you might be seriously hurt."

"I think getting thrown from the bike was a shock, but I'm okay now."

"You look surprisingly good after what happened."

When the boy walked over, his movements were perfectly normal. There was no sign of injury. Arel suspected that Michael might have had something to do with the boy's rapid recovery. But that didn't excuse the angel from ignoring him when he called for help.

The boy paused in front of him. "I checked my bike, and it's a little banged up, but it's okay too. I thought I could ride into town and send back a tow truck, if that's alright with you. Or I could take you with me if you want to ride on—"

"No, a tow truck will be fine." Arel had no desire to experience the motorcycle firsthand. "And please, be more careful from now on."

"Yeah, sure." The boy looked down and rubbed the dirt with his worn shoe. "I'm sorry about your car."

Arel hadn't thought about the Mustang until the boy mentioned it. "Oh yes, my car."

"I think it's a goner."

"Yes, I think so too," Arel said as he walked over to the vehicle. It was listing at an odd angle. After smashing into the concrete wall, the car looked more like an accordion than a sporty automobile. He'd been very lucky to get away without a scratch.

The boy came over too and extended his hand. "Again, I'm sorry. Hope there aren't hard feelings. Is there some way I can help pay—"

"No, I have insurance. It's okay," Arel said as he shook hands. The boy was barely able to clothe himself. He didn't need the burden of paying for a car. "But thanks anyway."

Arel returned his gaze to the Mustang. On a couple of occasions, it had served as a means of euphoric escape. Now it was ready for the scrap heap. He was able to force his eyes away from the wreckage, but a part of him felt a moment of deep regret. His beautiful car was indeed a goner, but he couldn't indulge in the matter. Instead, he pulled out his wallet. "I'm glad that you're safe. That's what counts. Let me give you my card, in case you need anything. And here's some money for gas or whatever."

The boy shook his head. "No, that's not—"

"Please, take it, I insist. Consider it a gift," he said as he pressed the card and some bills into the boy's hand.

The boy let out a gasp. "A hundred bucks! Nobody ever gave me a gift like this."

"Just be careful from now on."

"Sure, I promise. Maybe I'll see you again someday."

"I'd like that."

The boy looked suddenly shy as he stepped back. "Better get going," he said in a quiet tone. He turned and started jogging towards his bike. As soon as he reached it, he jumped on and turned to wave. After he got the cycle started, he took off slowly at first, then revved the engine and roared down the field. He hardly slowed down when he found a suitable place to get back on the road. The bike threw back bits of the muddy field as it climbed a shallow embankment.

"Slow down!" Arel knew the boy didn't hear his shout, but he couldn't help but yell when a tinge of fear for the young man's safety took hold. "Crazy kid. I hope he's careful." He barely had the thought when he realized he didn't even know the boy's name.

Six

Carol walked into the living room feeling a little sleep deprived but content. Everything in her world had changed so suddenly. It was hard to believe that Kevin was sitting on the sofa holding their baby. It was a wonderful scene that made the long months of being pregnant worth every minute. Kevin was being a great dad, and their child was perfect as he dozed peacefully, securely wrapped up in a blanket. Only a small arm had escaped its confines and was draped over the side. She smiled as she came over to join them. "How did my two men do while I was napping?"

Kevin looked up and gave her a puzzled frown. "You're awake already? You must have only slept for ten minutes."

"I couldn't help it. I couldn't sleep after I started thinking about how lucky I am."

Kevin corrected her. "How lucky *we* are."

"That's right. We're a family now."

"Yes we are."

"There's only one thing that could make everything even more perfect."

"What's that?"

"Arel, of course. I can't believe I'm home from the hospital, and he hasn't phoned once. Do you think he's okay?"

Kevin stared at the baby. "He's incredible."

"Arel?"

Kevin laughed. "I'm talking about our son, Ariel."

Carol sat down next to him, adjusted the baby's blanket, and let out a sigh. "What about Arel? He was calling us three times a day before the baby was born, now nothing."

"He's giving us space."

"Arel? Are you kidding? He loves being involved. He paid for the whole nursery."

Kevin paused for a moment and shrugged. "Peggy would tell us if something was wrong. She's always tuned into Arel when he's in trouble."

"I guess you're right. I'm being silly." She cuddled up close to him, watching him finger the baby's small fist. It was waving unsteadily as the newborn started waking up. After a moment, the baby's face contorted into a frown. He let out a small cry.

Kevin winked at her. "It's feeding time, Mom."

Carol felt a small shiver of alarm as Kevin handed her the baby. "Already? I just fed him an hour ago. How could he be hungry again?"

Kevin gave her a self-conscious smile. "Sorry, my mother said she couldn't keep up with my appetite either."

Seven

Arel's flight into farm country was petal-to-the-metal fast. Getting back to Chicago wasn't nearly as easy. He had ended up far from city conveniences. Luckily, there was a town located about seven miles away from the accident site. The small community did have a towing garage for the Mustang. It didn't have a car rental service. Arel was left with few options when it came to getting back home. He refused to call his friends just because he'd gotten himself into another mess. Instead, he found out that an afternoon bus could ferry him to a town with a rental service. While he waited for the bus, he made inquiries. He asked people around town about the young man on the motorcycle. No one recognized the boy's description.

The bus he finally boarded had to make several stops before it arrived at the larger community. It was almost evening by the time he got the keys to a rental car. Still, he was grateful to be going home. His nerves were frayed after his unexpected journey to hell and back. On the plus side of things, he had found some clarity about the painful memories he'd avoided for years. Plus, he played the Good Samaritan. All in all, it was a good trip. But the best part was getting back to his home in the Chicago suburbs.

It was late when he pulled into his driveway and got out of the rental car. His only desire was to get some sleep. He walked towards the house, glanced at the garage doors and hesitated. His beloved Mustang was probably still sitting on some muddy lot, waiting for insurance adjusters and the dump. He'd never see his car again.

Just forget it and be grateful nobody was seriously injured.

A sharp wind whipped open his coat and sent a chill through his body. It was another cold night, but at least he wouldn't have to sleep outdoors in the elements. But what about the young man he had helped? Would he sleep in a warm bed? Would he have the means to feed himself in the days to come? They were questions that didn't have answers, and there was nothing he could do about it.

* * *

Peggy frowned as she stepped away from her post at the window. She'd been checking on Arel's house all evening. With Michael being away for a couple of days, it was empty, but she hoped Arel would come home soon. She turned to Tim who was already in bed. "Where is he? Why won't he answer his cell phone?"

Tim glanced up briefly from the book he was reading. "Honey, we've already talked about all this."

"I know, but I'm frustrated."

"It's ten o'clock, Peg. Let's go to sleep. You need your rest. You look tired again."

"You're probably right. It's just strange, that's all."

Tim put his book on the side table and crossed his arms. "I know how you feel, but we should let it go for tonight and see if Arel shows up in the morning."

Peggy walked over to the bed and uncinched her robe. It didn't fit properly anymore. The belt was tied way too high. She was having a hard time feeling comfortable with her very pregnant body, and she was a little anxious about the baby's birth. Perhaps that was the reason Arel's behavior was getting on her nerves. She was out of patience. She scowled at Tim as she climbed into bed. "I don't have any horrible feelings about Arel's welfare, so I guess he's fine. Still, it's confusing. After all his carrying on over Kevin and Carol's baby, why would he disappear as soon as the baby is born?"

Tim shrugged. "Who knows? That's what I was trying to tell you when you suggested your matchmaking scheme. I don't think Arel is ready to have a relationship. He's too unpredictable."

"Fine, I'm going to forget about the whole matter and go to sleep." Shifting her round belly, Peggy was just getting comfortable when she heard something outside. A moment later, a car door slammed shut. "Tim, did you hear that? It might be Arel. Maybe you should check it out."

"If you say so." Tim pushed back the covers obediently and climbed out of bed. When he got to the window, he squinted as he reported his findings to Peggy. "There's enough moonlight to see a car in Arel's driveway, and Arel is walking towards the house. Still, I wonder—"

Peggy went on instant alert. "Wonder what? What is it?"

Tim hesitated. "I don't recognize the car that Arel is driving. It's not the Mustang."

"Does he look okay?" she asked in an anxious voice.

"Yes, I think he's fine."

"Thank goodness."

Tim started back to bed. "See, I told you not to worry."

Peggy shut her eyes tight, hoping to fall asleep without any more thoughts buzzing around in her mind. "I still say it's weird."

"It's Arel. Weird is normal."

Eight

The sound of someone calling out his name brought Arel out of his deep, dreamless state. "No, go away," he moaned as he turned over and looked at the clock. He'd been in bed for nine hours, but he felt like he needed another nine.

"Arel, are you awake? Where are you?"

He recognized Peggy's voice. It seemed to be coming from the foyer. Her tone was loud and demanding, a sure sign that sleep was a lost cause. "Why did I give her a house key?" The question repeated in his mind as he rubbed at his eyes, trying to get his bearings.

"Arel, please, answer me! Are you okay?" Peggy called out again.

Arel forced himself into a sitting position. "Be right out."

"Take your time." It was Tim's voice. Even though it was masculine in nature, it was softer and more comforting.

"Coming." Arel managed to sound civil as he dragged himself from the bed. He was still fighting his lethargic state as he stumbled to the hall. He stopped to yawn and blink himself fully awake. A scowl quickly settled in. Was something wrong? The house felt strange, and he didn't know why. But he didn't have time to think about it. He had guests waiting.

"My heavens," Peggy gasped as soon as she saw him. "What happened to you? Your clothes! Is that mud?"

Arel looked down at his slacks and shirt. They were beyond ruined. The field where he performed emergency life support had been muddy in spots. Afterwards, he hadn't cared about his appearance. He was too weary to care about anything when he got home. He fell into bed without changing. Now he realized how out of character he must seem. "I had a little accident," he confessed.

Tim frowned. "Is that why you're driving a rental?"

"Yes, the Mustang is . . . is . . . it's a goner." He used the young man's words.

"You mean it's totaled?" Tim asked.

"Yes, totally totaled," Arel replied.

"What?" Peggy's eyes went wide with fright as she rushed over to him. "No wonder I was so worried!" she cried out as she gave him a fierce, bear hug.

Tim let out a sympathetic whistle. "It was a really nice car. Sorry about that."

"Who cares about a car?" Peggy asked as she released Arel and stood back. "Are you sure you're alright? Look at those dark circles under your eyes. And your hair—" She pushed her fingers through his dark curls.

Arel knew why she was alarmed. When he was unshaven and his hair was unattended, he could have a wild, haunted look, one that would have gone nicely on a gothic novel cover. "Peggy, stop worrying."

"Why didn't you call us?" she asked.

Arel took hold of her hands. "You don't need to be burdened in your condition. I'm fine."

Peggy gave his clothes another sweeping look. "Fine? I don't think so. You look like a guy who got trampled in a cattle stampede."

"Maybe, but with a little sleep, I'll recover. However, now that you're here, would you do something for me? Call Carol and Kevin. Tell them that I want to come over and see the baby later, if that's okay."

Peggy's tight shoulders dropped a couple of inches. "Oh, that's a good idea. I think they'd love to know you haven't forgotten them."

"No, of course I haven't," Arel said with another yawn. "Sorry, but I have to get some more sleep."

"No kidding," Tim added.

"We'll check back later," Peggy insisted.

"Thank you for your concern," Arel said as he began his trek back to his bedroom. Halfway there, he stopped. "Have you guys seen Michael around?"

Tim shrugged. "He told us that he'd be out of town for a couple of days."

"What? He's gone?" Arel's gut flared instantly at the thought of angel abandonment, but he refused to yield to his anger. Recently, he'd done quite nicely without Michael's help. If the angel wanted to run off, it didn't matter. "I see. Thanks for telling me. Maybe in the future, he'll be courteous enough to leave me a note."

Nine

Carol and Kevin Bailey lived a few streets away from Arel. The young couple had followed Peggy and Tim's lead and decided on the same neighborhood when they bought their home. The three-bedroom bungalow wasn't as big as Arel's large rancher or the Werner house, but it suited the young couple.

Arel noted the door wreath as he walked up the winding, flagstone path. Carol was doing a good job making the home her own. Kevin wasn't as interested in house matters, but he kept the lawn cut and beds tidy. Now, standing on their porch, Arel was glad for them both. They'd had their troubles, but they looked happy enough when their baby was born.

I hope they can keep it that way.

He paused at the door long enough to admire the wreath again, fingering the silk daisies that Carol had added.

Relax!

He gave himself the mental order, hoping he didn't look too self-conscious after running out on the new parents. At least his physical appearance was back to normal. He was freshly showered, with his facial accents neatly trimmed. Glancing down at himself, at his Armani shirt and custom-made, Italian trousers, he realized that he'd never let go of his proper, strict upbringing. He was taught to dress well and maintain his manners. Even now, he realized that he wanted to be like Aldwin.

When the door opened, Carol welcomed him in. She looked petite and pretty in a silky, floral print outfit. Its soft colors complimented her green eyes. Her glow of motherhood was brighter than ever. Arel hoped he could match her enthusiasm and truly let go of the memories surrounding his brother's death. He had let go in some respects. He had a change of heart when he allowed himself to care about the kid on the motorcycle. Thinking about the young man's grin as they shook hands was enough to ease his face into a smile when Carol reached out to him.

"It's so good to see you," she said as she gave him a hug. When she let him go, she took his hand. "Now come with me. Kevin and the baby are waiting to see you."

As Arel followed her to the living room, he couldn't help but express his feelings. "Motherhood agrees with you, Carol. You're more beautiful than ever."

She paused and looked back thoughtfully. "Thank you, but I've been a little worried. Peggy told us about the accident. I hope you're okay."

"It was just some crazy thing. I love to take a drive every once in a while. I got carried away and things happened. But it's behind me now, and that little guy is what's important," he said pointing towards the sofa where Kevin was holding the baby.

Kevin looked up with a proud father's expression on his face. "Hi, old buddy. Come over and get acquainted with little Ariel."

Arel felt his jaw tighten, but he ignored it and sat down next to Kevin. "I still find it hard to believe you named him after me."

"Yep, we did, but you've been missing out on all the fun," Kevin said. "You have to get used to holding him. I'm getting to be pretty good at it."

Arel nodded. "I guess I have some catching up to do." His voice was steady, but he could feel his body tense. What if he held the baby and freaked out again like he had at the hospital?

Kevin didn't seem to notice Arel's uneasiness. He was already plopping the baby down into Arel's lap. "Here you go. As Ariel's godfather, you two need to get to know each other."

Arel took a deep breath as he held the newborn for a second time. Their eyes did meet again, but there was no unusual connection, no fear or past memory recall. The whole hospital episode was like a bad dream that faded in the light of day. Maybe that's all it was. How could he be sure of something as elusive as the identity of a person's soul?

Kevin was all smiles. "Look at the little bruiser, Arel, isn't he something?"

"Yes, you're right." Arel found himself smiling too, watching as the baby's tiny hands and fingers flailed at the air, like he was directing some flighty, musical score. He reached out to touch one of the child's hands and carefully stroked his soft skin. A shock of bewilderment surged through him when the small fist suddenly opened and took hold of his finger.

"Look at that," Carol beamed. "He likes you."

"Yes, you might be right," he agreed as the baby's tiny fingers tightened even more. "He's got quite a grip."

Kevin puffed out his broad chest. "That's my boy."

Arel gave him a thoughtful glance. He remembered all the bone-crushing handshakes he'd suffered when he first met Kevin. Now, even at such a young age, Kevin's son's tenacious hold was impressive. As he waited for his finger to be released, he felt a new sensation, a warm feeling that was spreading onto his slacks. A moment of panic followed when he realized what was happening.

Carol was quick to notice the mild state of shock registered on his face. "Is something wrong?"

"The baby, I mean, Little Ariel. . . uh—" He stumbled over the words and glanced down.

"What?" Kevin asked, looking curious.

"I think he . . . um . . . had an accident."

Kevin burst out laughing. "You're kidding."

Carol blushed. "Kevin isn't the best with diapers yet. Sorry about that." She stared at Arel's expensive slacks. "We'll pay for the cleaning bill."

"Yeah, sorry. I'm all thumbs," Kevin said as he got up to correct the situation. "Come here, Junior."

Kevin's attempted intervention met with resistance. The baby wouldn't let go of Arel's finger.

"It's okay," Arel said with as much composure as he could muster. "I'll just hold him for a bit."

"Are you sure?" Kevin asked.

Arel shrugged again, trying to smile and not quite succeeding. "It's not a real problem, right?" But his mind was quickly reminding him about the world of nature. His brows narrowed with a strange realization. The baby was marking him, like an animal marks his territory, claiming him as its own, and he couldn't do anything about it.

As they waited, an awkward silence took hold. Arel knew he had to break it quickly and put the new parents at ease. "I think I have a solution to the diapering problem. Show me what to do. It's probably the only way I'll be safe when I hold my godchild."

Carol's face melted into a smile. "You're probably right. Kevin's having a tough time of it."

"Hey, it's not that easy," Kevin added as he helped Arel to stand up. "Changing station is this way."

As Arel followed Kevin into the bedroom, with the newborn cradled in his arms, he saw a little of his future unfolding. He was being inducted into a whole new realm of duties. It included chores he never contemplated before. How capable would he be around such a tiny human being? It was a frightening undertaking, yet he was determined to excel. After all, he was the baby's godfather, and he would do everything he could to prove himself worthy of that honor. Running away was no longer an option.

Ten

Sipping morning tea in Peggy's kitchen, Carol put her cup in its saucer and frowned. "I don't know why, but after the baby has his two o'clock feeding, he won't go back to sleep like he did the first few days. Kevin and I have tried everything to comfort him, but when he keeps crying and fussing, we both panic."

Peggy swirled the small amount of tea remaining in her cup and smiled. "So you call Arel?"

Carol bit her lip, but then she smiled. "It's an old habit. You know how much Arel helped us when I was first pregnant. I guess we thought that we just needed to hear his voice."

"I don't think he knows much about newborns."

"Oh, but you're wrong. I think he's been on the internet exploring everything he can learn about the subject. So when I called, and I was so upset, he insisted on coming right over."

"Really?"

Carol gave Peggy a nod of contentment. "He's wonderful. He's discovered this technique for quieting crying babies. And it works."

Peggy laughed. "I bet that poor little guy is just tired and naturally goes back to sleep."

"I thought so too, that first night."

"Arel's been at your place since then?"

"He's made three house calls so far. He's like some kind of baby whisperer. I swear, Kevin and I do the same things that Arel does, but he's the only one who knows how to get the baby back to sleep."

"I was wondering about why he can't get rid of the circles under his eyes. How long does he stay?"

"He's there for hours." Carol giggled as she reached down into her purse and pulled out some photos. "I printed these out this morning. Kevin got up to check on the two of them and couldn't resist taking a few pictures."

Peggy let out an overly loud laugh as she glanced at the shots of the would-be baby expert. "Oh my goodness, look at Arel. He's sound asleep on the floor. And look how he's got one hand draped over the baby in his infant seat." She gave Carol a baffled look. "Why doesn't he put the baby back in his crib?"

"He says that if he tries, Ariel, I mean Ariel Jr., wakes up. It seems they've got some kind of bond going."

"Ariel Jr.?"

"Yes, we needed to add the junior part. It's getting too confusing with Arel and Ariel's names being so similar."

"I love the name, Ariel. It's perfect. Tim and I are still working on a name for our baby." Peggy looked at the pictures and laughed again. "You have a good thing going, the perfect name and a built-in baby whisperer."

"I know. I feel a little guilty, but at least I'm functional now that I'm getting some sleep."

Peggy looked a bit guilty too as she finished off a third biscuit. She washed it down with the last bit of her tea. When she glanced at Carol, her eyes were teasing. "So what you're saying is that I have a built in nanny next door. I'll have to remember that if we have problems."

Eleven

Arel was stretched out in a recliner in the living room. He needed a nap. He'd been on baby duty the night before, again. The sound of pots, banging in the kitchen, woke him up. He grabbed for the recliner handle and forced the chair into an upright position. "Who's there? Tim? Peggy?" As he called out he tried to get a kink out of his neck.

"No, it's me. I'm trying to tidy up a bit. Sorry if I woke you."

Arel's eyes blinked open at once, flickering about the room. Could it be? Was that Michael's voice answering him? Of course it was. For years, he had listened to the angel's deep, resonant tone. It was almost as familiar as his own voice. But he'd almost given up on hearing it again. Without delay, he sat up and abandoned the recliner. He practically ran to the kitchen. He couldn't contain his excitement. "You're back!"

Michael gave him a friendly glance as he picked up a pot out of the dish drainer. "Yes, I am."

"I can't believe it," he said as he rushed over to where the missing angel was standing. He stared at Michael for a long moment with grateful eyes. He even reached out and grabbed Michael's shoulder. "Where have you been?"

The question danced around his brain, fueled by the thought that his best friend, his father substitute was really there again. The feeling didn't last. It was quickly replaced by a need for an explanation. "Do you know how worried I've been?"

Sure, he'd been flippant at first, telling himself he didn't care about the angel's absence, but that feeling waned after a couple of days. Michael was his touchstone, his teacher, and his most trusted ally. How many days and hours had he agonized over the idea that Michael wasn't returning. Now, seeing him again should have been reason for a happy reunion. And it was, but he couldn't contain the other side of things. He harbored a deep-seated feeling of angelic neglect. It rushed to the surface so fast he couldn't contain his frustration.

"Haven't you heard me calling you?" he yelled as he grabbed the pot out of Michael's hand. He slammed it down on one of the stove burners.

Michael seemed unaffected by his mood and remained mute as he moved to the table. He began to straighten the place mats, taking great care to align each one perfectly with the table edge.

Arel crossed his arms and watched him. He knew he shouldn't act like a peevish child, but Michael was also at fault. It wasn't befitting Michael's role as a guardian and reliable comrade to ignore him. Yet Michael seemed oblivious. He continued to arrange the placemats.

It was too much for Arel. He exploded a second time. "What are you doing? Why are you adjusting placemats instead of telling me what's going on?" He was suffering from lack of sleep and now he was on the receiving end of Michael's indifferent attitude. "Can't you see how upset I am?" Needing to demonstrate his point, he grabbed one of the mats off the table and sailed it across the room.

Michael gave him a look of surprise. "I know how you like everything to be very neat. I was trying to be helpful."

"Michael, please, you've been gone for over a week and a half. I thought you deserted me."

"You know I'd never do that. I was giving you some space, letting you get used to the baby. I know it was a shock to find out—"

"Then it's true?" Arel blurted out the question in a rush of anticipation. "Is the baby connected to Aldwin?" Before Michael could answer, Arel held up his hand. "Never mind. It doesn't matter now. I know that." He'd made peace with the whole idea of souls and babies being connected to his past. He wanted to move on. He needed to stay focused on the present.

Michael smiled. "So you're alright with everything?"

"Why would you ask? You can read me like a book. You know me better than I know myself."

"Yes, perhaps." Michael walked out of the kitchen and continued on into the living room. He took a seat on the sofa.

Arel frowned as he followed him. He didn't appreciate the angel's casual attitude. In fact, it scared him. Why wasn't Michael showing more concern for what he'd been going through? Had something changed between them? Had he pushed Michael too far at the hospital? He sat down on the recliner again and tried to quiet himself. His blood pressure was headed upwards so fast his head was starting to pound. He rubbed at his brow. "Anyway, let's get back to my original problem. When I called for you on the night of the accident, where were you? I needed your help."

"You seemed to do fine on your own."

"You have an answer for everything, don't you?" His anger wouldn't back down even though he was trying his best to be reasonable. Finally, as he sat back in the recliner, he realized that Michael was telling him something that might be important. "What did you say?"

"You handled the accident very well."

He glanced at Michael and then averted his eyes to the arm of the chair. The recliner was covered in an ivory-colored linen. He fingered the textured surface beneath his hand, noting the minute ridges as he considered Michael's compliment. "You really think that I did okay?"

"Yes, you did an amazing job when you helped that young man."

"Do you think that he's alright? I couldn't find him after the accident."

"I'm sure he's fine. Besides, didn't you give him your card?"

"Ha! I was right. You do know everything that's going on, admit it."

"I know some things." Michael paused and stared at him with intense, penetrating eyes. "But I don't know everything."

An uneasy feeling in Arel's gut told him that something was up. "What are you getting at? We're not discussing the accident anymore, are we?"

Michael stiffened ever so slightly. "We need to talk."

The statement was delivered in a quiet, contained tone, but it sent Arel's body into instant freeze. He couldn't move or reply. The first time Michael told him that they needed to talk, Arel learned that his heart was failing, that he might not have much longer to live.

Michael gave him a warm, confident smile. "It's not something to get upset over."

Arel heard Michael's statement, but his mind was already reading between the lines. "Oh no, what now?" As feeling returned to his limbs, he stood up and started to pace. "I should have known it would come to this. Life is just starting to make sense again. The biggest problem I have is little Ariel Jr. waking up and crying every night."

"I'm very happy to hear that you're feeling good about everything."

Arel glared back. "I don't want to hear about your happiness. We've been through this before. You don't say, 'We have to talk,' unless it's bad news."

"There was unfortunate news that first time. However, on the second occasion, the whole thing about your soul dying—"

Arel paled and grabbed for a side table for support. "You're not back to that, are you? I thought we had that subject straightened out."

"Your soul cannot die," Michael said sternly. "You came up with that thought on your own."

Arel pulled away from the table and looked back. "Are you sure? I don't remember."

"I'm sure."

"At least that's a relief. After all the hell a person goes through, it seems wrong to think that it's all for nothing."

"I wanted to talk to you about learning to control your emotions."

"My emotions? Is that what this is about?"

"You were very upset at the hospital before and after the baby was born. I just thought that you might want some help in learning how to deal with such intense situations."

Arel eyed Michael wearily. Was the angel telling partial truths and leaving something scary out? "So there's nothing for me to worry about?"

Michael smiled back. "I just thought you might like some help in dealing with things that overwhelm you."

Arel threw up his hands and smiled too. "Of course I would. Do you think that I enjoy feeling like I'm going to self-destruct? We should have had this conversation ages ago. It would have saved both of us a lot of trouble."

"Wonderful, because I want to—"

"There's just one problem," Arel interjected.

"What problem?"

"The problem is that I've been feeling very strange lately. I'm sure you're aware that a lot of things from my childhood have been coming up."

"Yes, you've faced a very difficult part of your past. That's another thing to feel proud about."

"Whatever," Arel said as he began to pace again. "What I've realized is how limited my life is. I've always tried to be what my parents wanted. Like you said, I have to have everything so neat. But there's a reason for that. I'm trying to control things when I feel they're out of control."

Michael's frown deepened. "Go on."

"So in a way, it's not self-control that I need, but less control. I need to live life to the fullest."

"And how would you like to do that?"

Arel felt his strength return and walked over to the sofa. With a hopeful smile, he sat down next to Michael. "I want to show you something," he said as he leaned forward. He snatched up a newly purchased DVD from the coffee table. "I just watched this movie about Mount Everest, and the whole idea of mountain climbing interests me. If I try something like climbing, I'd have to manage my emotions like you're saying. At the same time, I'd break out of my shell, my small world. I'm sure you'll agree that it's the perfect solution."

Michael's eyes were steady, but his voice wavered slightly. "You're planning on climbing Mount Everest?"

"Maybe, someday, when I'm not chained to a diaper pail." He glanced at Michael, waiting for a positive comment, but the angel remained silent. "Well what do you think? It's a good plan, right?"

Michael's eyes remained focused on the DVD. "Learning control while you're climbing in unstable snow conditions, well, that could be—"

"What? What's wrong?" Arel stood up again. "You have that look on your face."

"What look?"

"Like I'm crazy or something. Admit it. You hate my idea, don't you?" He didn't give Michael a chance to respond this time. He didn't need negative feedback. "Why is it that I can't just do something I want to do? Why is it that you always have an agenda about my life?"

"I'm concerned about you. You do believe that, don't you?"

"What's your point?"

"Let's go back to the incident at the hospital. I got a glimpse, you might say, into your energy field."

"I see," Arel said, trying to contain his temper. Maybe he didn't want a father figure after all, not if Michael was going to try to always manage his life. He walked back to the recliner and fell heavily into its confines. "And what did that glimpse tell you."

"At the hospital, your love and desire to help were corrupted by all your fear. As you already know, when that happens, the energy can become very destructive. You survived the incident, but it was a very close call. Unless you learn to direct the energy, you might not survive the next one."

"Direct the energy? What an interesting concept," Arel sneered back. "And how do I do that? I have your blood fueling my feelings. When my emotions get triggered it's like trying to put a lid on Mount Vesuvius."

"It doesn't have to be that way. Your feelings are remnants from your past, but they're still simply feelings. You have to stop identifying with them. You have to empty yourself of everything that doesn't serve your best interest."

"And how much time do I have to accomplish this goal you have in mind? You and I both know that I'm failing when it comes to putting aside my feelings. So you're right about my surviving. As I see it, my chances are slim at best."

"But you do have a chance. That's the point. If you listen to what I'm telling you—"

"I'm tired of listening. First, I listened to my brother, then my father, and now you!" Arel paused, shutting his eyes, pushing back the resentment that was lurking just beneath the surface. "I appreciate what you've tried to do, but if I'm probably going to die anyway, I'd rather take my chances on Mount Everest. I know that sounds ridiculous, but I want to do something original for a change, something that's my idea and mine alone."

"And I want that for you too, but it's not that simple," Michael said quietly. "Even if you do survive a mountain challenge, sooner or later, you'll have to confront this thing that we've started."

Arel let out a huff of dissent, digging in his heels, needing to direct his own life for a change. "Then it'll have to be later."

Twelve

Arel was into the first mile of his pre-dawn jogging. The sky was bathed in milky darkness with only the first bands of color beginning to show. Most people were still asleep in their beds. But he was too excited about training. The thought of adventure, of conquering snowy heights made his thirty pound pack easier to shoulder. Wouldn't it be a glorious thing to strike out in a direction that nobody in his family had ever investigated? Aldwin might have known a lot about the activities of a gentleman, but he didn't know anything about scaling a mountain.

I'm carving out new territory, big brother!

His one misgiving involved Michael. After their little chat, Arel knew he was stepping outside the recommended course for his life. Not that Michael was pushing his agenda. That wasn't Michael's style. He even wished Arel a good run before Arel left the house.

What was he doing up at that hour? He's flesh and blood. Doesn't he ever sleep?

Michael had been around for years, but Arel never caught him dozing. That was the trouble with Michael. He was a mystery. He dressed like a regular guy, and he tended his garden like a person who simply loved plants. He occasionally played ball with the guys.

But he's not like a normal human being.

Michael was more like the sun. He was always a source of warmth, a nurturing element that didn't deviate from day to day. He didn't have a personal agenda. Instead, his attitude was always compassionate and kind. When he went missing, the house felt diminished. It didn't have that lightness that Michael radiated wherever he went.

And I am thankful that he's been there for me.

As Arel pounded the pavement, he acknowledged how much Michael had done to help him. He had no problem with being forever grateful to the angel. The curse of being a vampire was a thing of the past.

But I'm always arguing with him, and I want to know why.

He jogged down the quiet street wanting clarity. He didn't like to be constantly bucking Michael's suggestions. It was just the opposite. He never enjoyed conflict.

So what is going on?

He couldn't come up with a satisfactory answer until the sun started to rise. Its rays were so dazzling, he found himself squinting and shying away from its brilliance. That's when he had his answer. Michael, like the solar orb, lived in his own stratosphere. He peacefully sailed across his piece of space, oblivious to what it was like to know pain and suffering.

That's why I'm constantly battling with him. His damnable blood wants me to sail too, but I can't change that fast. I need a break.

He was doing his best to keep up with his emotions and the constant barrage of the past re-surfacing. But if he needed a diversion, that was okay.

I made a good decision. I'm sure of it.

In fact, just the thought that he might be wiser than an angel gave him more energy. He started running rather than jogging, enjoying his own company for once.

Michael is right about one thing. I need to give myself more credit.

The thought was enough to loosen up his muscles. His body was suddenly lighter. He increased his speed. After the first block, houses moved by swiftly. The sun had its place in life, but he wasn't like the fiery orb. He needed to be alive in his own place, down on earth. He had to create a life where he could be comfortable.

Angel blood or not, I'm still very much a human being with definite limitations.

"Really, Arel? Are you making excuses again, like you did with me?"

A feminine voice, speaking so clearly in his mind, sent shock waves through his argument. He stopped abruptly, blinking at the sun again, afraid to move or turn away. "Justina?"

"Yes, my love, it is. I've been trying to get your attention for so long. Why have you pushed me aside? I wasn't an angel like Michael.

I was flesh and blood. I was the woman you swore you loved with all your heart. Yet it's been so long since we've spoken."

"Justina, you're dead!"

Arel heard a soft laughter, tinged with sadness. It was followed by Justina speaking to him again.

"And you've made sure I stayed dead, haven't you? I've never had a real place in your life or your heart since that horrible day, my last day on the earth."

Arel shut his eyes, knowing he was hallucinating. Sure he'd relived memories before. He even heard Michael's voice in his head. But like Justina pointed out, she wasn't an angel. She wasn't alive. How could he hear her?

Justina seemed to understand his dilemma. "Whether you like it or not, you're more capable now. You're able to access so much more than what normal eyes and ears perceive, but you don't seem too happy about it." She laughed again. This time her sadness was buoyed by accusation. "I feel you shutting the door I'm standing in. You want to keep me dead, don't you?"

"My beloved Justina, my only wish is to keep you safe! That's why I've behaved like I have."

"You're not making sense. What does safety have to do with anything when I'm dead?"

"You wouldn't understand. Just know that I'll always love you, and I'll always do whatever I have to do to make sure you don't suffer anymore."

"But Arel—"

"I'm so sorry, Justina, but you have to trust me. You also have to stay away from me. I wish that it was different, but I can't talk to you, now or ever."

As soon as he made himself clear, Justina was gone. Any remnants of her words vanished with her. It had to be that way. He had faced a past life of being burned at the stake. Recently, he had come to terms with parts of his brother's death. Those were his victories, but he couldn't deal with Justina. There was too much guilt surrounding her memory. Michael insisted that there was more to the story than he was allowing himself to see, but the facts he remembered were horrifying. On that gruesome night when Justina died, they had had a terrible fight. It ended with him kneeling over her. His hands were covered in her blood. If there was more to it, he couldn't go there. Her death was and always would be his responsibility. The guilt he suffered over it would always be his burden. He would never contest that fact. He couldn't and he wouldn't run away from it either. He'd once been given the gift of love, of having a beautiful woman in his life. He destroyed that gift. It would never be his again. He didn't deserve it. Yet if he dwelt on what had been between himself and Justina, it would paralyze him completely. He'd be no use to himself or anyone. His only option was to force what had happened back into the past. His decision to train would help him forget what couldn't be changed. Michael told him that he needed to live in the moment.

He's right about that.

As Arel breathed deeply, rhythmically, as he focused on the beautiful morning unfolding in front of him, he began to feel better. He tuned his ears to the sound of birds waking up. He let his vision fill with images of baby Ariel and how serene the infant was when Arel sang to him in the middle of the night. Carol and Kevin's happy faces came to mind. And Tim and Peggy's too. He had to keep the good things in his thoughts, nothing else.

Think about the now! Think about the now! There's only the now!

The new mantra started working. He was able to run even faster. For a brief instant, he felt the pain of Justina's visit ease a little. He'd have to settle for that and make it enough.

Thirteen

The Bailey kitchen was filled with the aroma of fresh-baked cookies as Peggy, Tim, Carol and Kevin sat around the kitchen table.

"Oh goodness, I love your baking," Peggy said as she finished her second oatmeal raisin treat. "You're amazing, Carol."

Carol beamed back her appreciation. "I followed the recipe on the oatmeal box, that's all. But I'm happy that you like them."

Peggy brushed a crumb off her lip. "Let's keep this little gathering quiet. Remember, Arel has us on a sugar lockdown."

"Well, he's right about the excessive sugar," Tim said thoughtfully. "But I can't resist these darn things."

"We all know that he's right about things in general," Peggy said as she grabbed a stray raisin and greedily popped it into her mouth. "It's just that a person has to have some balance. As far as Arel himself, the problem is that he can only give advice. Sometimes, he seems clueless when it comes to caring for himself."

Carol nodded. "You mean the way he's insisting on this plan to conquer the seven summits?"

Kevin took a long drag on his coffee and reached for a cookie. Just as he was about to take a bite, he paused. "A little climbing is fine. But I think Arel could get himself killed. We've all seen him in action, tripping over things when he's upset."

"And fainting!" Peggy added.

Tim shrugged. "He does seem to be accident prone."

Peggy began to stir her tea anxiously. "That's why I called this meeting. Ever since he started getting in shape for mountain climbing, I've been getting the worst feelings about what could

71

happen to him. I'm also having nightmares about him tripping off the side of some mountain ledge. I've tried to say things to him, to warn him about what I'm feeling, but he just ignores me."

Carol patted her arm. "You know we believe in your intuition. If it weren't for you, we would never have been able to be there for Arel in the beginning." She glanced around at the little group. "Now, look at all of us. We love him dearly."

"I remember the early days," Kevin complained. "We were his slaves. Remember your dishpan hands, Tim? You must have washed a thousand pots in those early days."

"I remember more than that," Tim added. "I was also washing windows and painting Arel's bedroom."

They all laughed as they reminisced about the two men helping out Arel when his health was failing.

"Sorry about that," Peggy said as she sat back, looking satisfied after her last cookie. "You and Tim got the tough stuff. He was very sweet with Carol and me."

Carol held up her hand. "Whatever happened early on, happened because Arel was sick and hurting. But I think we would all agree that he's more than made up for what we did for him. He has a heart of gold."

They all nodded in unison.

"He's made a lot of great meals for us," Tim said patting his stomach. "And he was there for Peggy when she was first pregnant and having mood swings."

Peggy blushed. "I have no trouble admitting it. I was a real pain, but he never quite lost his patience. He came close a time or two. I thought he might pull out some of that thick, dark hair of his."

Kevin put down his coffee mug. "Hey, don't feel bad. I had to listen to Arel's moaning and groaning when he started working out the first time, remember? Coaching him was sheer hell. I'm lucky to have any hair left after that ordeal."

After the laughter died down again, Tim cleared his throat. "All joking aside, does anybody know what we can do if he actually goes for Everest? We can't tie him down."

"I guess we can pray for a miracle," Carol suggested.

"I think that's what it's going to take," Kevin said with a frown. "He's one of the most stubborn people I've known."

Everyone laughed again, making Kevin's frown deepen. "Did I say something funny?"

"Sorry, Kev," Tim said, still grinning, "but that's exactly what Arel says about you."

"I see. Well, maybe I am stubborn, but that quality might come in handy. I'm going to think of something I can do to help Arel before he goes traipsing off to scale a peak. That's a promise."

Fourteen

rel stretched out in the chair as he surveyed the hospital waiting room. It had been a little more than five weeks since baby Ariel's birth. Now it was Peggy's turn to have her baby, but he wasn't involved personally. He had given up on the idea of coaching a mother-to-be. One of the contributing factors to his relaxed state was his new passion for running. At first, his desire to train harder was fed by neediness. He had to put Justina out of his mind. If he kept focused on his morning runs, it helped. As the days and the weeks passed, he thought about her less and less. Gradually, he moved into a place of happiness, even euphoria. He'd read about "runner's high." He agreed with others who experienced it. When he ran, consciously syncing mind and body with the task, his worries slipped away. He entered a space where nothing existed but the feeling of movement and freedom. It was an intoxicating state that made him want more. He refused to miss a day's run. He was preparing himself to climb a mountain, but the thrill of running became its own reward. Sure he sometimes overtaxed himself physically. Ace bandages and a steadfast determination kept his body going. When he wasn't running, he liked to read about mountain climbing and related topics. He surrounded himself with an exciting world of information that made his future look exhilarating. But running was already a joy in itself.

As Arel sat across from Michael in the waiting room, he was still high on life just reliving his morning run. They hadn't spoken much since their last serious discussion. Still, Arel had proven his point about striking out in his own direction. He felt rather proud of himself. "You've been so right about living, Michael. It can be wonderful."

Michael looked up from his book. "Yes, I'm glad your regimen is working for you."

"Are you sure? Because I want you to understand that I feel better than ever."

Michael returned his focus to the book he was reading. "That's good."

Arel sat up straighter. Michael was being overly quiet again. "This is why I don't like to talk to you about things that matter."

"What do you mean?"

"You have this way of making me feel like an idiot. But, don't worry, Michael, you're simply out of touch with my world. From my standpoint, I'm being responsible whether you think so or not." He leaned in closer and lowered his voice to a whisper. He needed to bring a little levity to the situation. "Your baby bird is leaving the angelic nest, friend."

"The nest?"

"Yes, that place where you want to keep me so I'm always safe. But the truth is that I'm getting on with who I am. I'm not that broken guy you started helping years ago." He cleared his throat and crossed his arms over his chest. "Strange, isn't it? I feel so at ease. After all of your dire words of warning, look at me. Except for a pulled muscle now and then, I'm the picture of health."

Michael studied him for several moments. "About your body, I—"

"Stop!" For the first time that day, Arel was annoyed. He didn't need the angel upsetting the blissful world he was creating for himself. "Are you starting again? After what I just said? I just told you that my body is fine. Now, let's change the subject."

Michael put his book aside and crossed his arms too. "What would you like to talk about?"

Arel smiled. "Aren't you a little surprised about how well I'm doing with Peggy being in labor?"

"You do look very calm."

"I'm concerned about her, but it's like a rerun on TV. Carol was fine, so I figure you were right, a body knows how to handle childbirth." He eased himself down in the chair. "This is actually a relief, a little time out from everything. With my daily workouts, my extra training routine, trying to help with baby Ariel and the twice weekly dinners for the kids—"

Michael gave him a curious look. "Kids?"

"You know, Carol, Kevin, Peggy, Tim."

"You're referring to them as 'kids' now?"

"It seems appropriate. I've become their father figure in some ways. And as far as actual years go, I am their senior." He laughed, but lowered his voice again. "Can you believe that I have almost a century on them?"

"I have more than that," Michael said with a wink.

"That's right, you do. No wonder you're always so serene. Age does that, doesn't it?"

"I was kidding. I don't think in terms of aging."

Arel jerked upright. He had never contemplated the idea of Michael and the passage of time. "Whether you believe in aging or not, you must be ancient in earth years. Come to think of it, you're probably the oldest person on earth."

Michael relaxed his arms and adopted an upright, commanding posture. "My body isn't that old."

"Yes, but if we go deeper and examine who you really are—" Arel began to study Michael fixedly. "I mean people take on different personalities with each lifetime, but your kind are always the same. With that idea in mind, you're older than Methuselah, a lot older. He lived to be what? A thousand, give or take a few years." As he spoke, his voice picked up in volume. "But you, you're what? A million years old?"

A couple of people on the other side of the room glanced up at Arel's announcement and stared at Michael.

"You might want to keep your voice down," Michael suggested.

Arel leaned forward again. "Just how old are you? Were you an angel for some caveman? What was he like? Did you help him discover fire?"

"I don't think that's important."

Arel squinted back, letting his mind explore new areas that he found intriguing. "But the idea of being around for so long might be very relevant. Maybe I'm wrong about age and serenity. Maybe you're so old that I get on your nerves. Maybe that's the real reason you disappear off and on, right? I'm like a baby to you, a very, very young baby, and I tire you out just like Ariel Jr. does with me."

Michael glanced around at the gawkers who were still looking at him. "You might have a point."

"Geez, I'm sorry." Arel pulled back and scratched his head. "I've always thought of you as someone wise, but also someone in their prime. Now, considering the facts, I'm getting a new spin on things."

"I think you're getting the wrong idea about—"

"Can you deny that you're older than dirt?"

Just as Michael was about to field the question, Tim came walking towards them. Michael gave Arel a relieved smile. "Excuse me," he said as he got up to greet Tim.

Arel jumped up to join them. "Is the baby here?"

Tim nodded. "Peggy had a girl, six pounds nine ounces." His large frame was slightly bent as he spoke, and his eyes didn't have their usual clarity. "She and the baby are both doing fine."

Arel beamed back a happy grin in spite of Tim's drained appearance. He couldn't help it. For him, this particular birthing process had been a breeze. "That's wonderful! But what about you? How did it go with the coaching?"

Tim swallowed hard. "I was almost as bad as you."

"But at least you didn't get yourself kicked out of the birthing room."

"No, but it was close a couple of times. By the way, would you call Carol and Kevin and give them the news? I need to get back to Peggy."

Arel nodded. "Yes, I know that they really wanted to be here, but with the new baby, you know."

Tim paused. "Thank you both for your support. Knowing that you were close meant a lot to Peggy and me."

Arel's grin widened. "No problem." He looked at Michael and patted his back. "But I don't know about this guy. He was getting a little squirmy just before you came out to tell us the news."

"Really?" Tim studied Michael more closely. "Are you okay, Michael?"

"I'm fine," Michael said as he turned to get his book from the seating area.

Arel moved closer to Tim. "He never complains. Very commendable under the circumstances."

Tim focused with fresh attention. "What circumstances? He said he's fine."

"It's nothing I can talk about. But just between us, go easy on him. He's had a lot on his mind for a very long, long time."

* * *

Arel stood in the doorway of Peggy's hospital room. Everything felt repetitive after being in an identical doorway just weeks earlier. The big difference was the way he felt. "I can't believe I'm actually getting used to this place," he said to Michael who was next to him.

Tim smiled and waved them both into the room. "Peggy, we have visitors."

Peggy was preoccupied with the small bundle in her arms, but she smiled when she saw her friends. "Arel, Michael! Look at our sweet, little girl."

Arel quickly walked over to her bedside. "Congratulations!"

"Thank you," Peggy said quickly. "Isn't she the cutest, and she's just waking up."

Michael stood behind Arel. "What an exquisite child. I'm so happy for both of you."

Arel leaned in to get a better view. "Yes, she's beautiful, just like her mother." The newborn was pink-skinned and delicate, with a bit of light, wispy hair. When she opened her eyes, they were bright and expectant, but there was no sign that she knew Arel and vice versa. The only thing he observed was a very new and very tiny, human being. "What name did you decide on?"

"Her name is Sara," Tim said as he reached out and adjusted the baby's blanket, covering a small foot.

Peggy sucked in a breath. "For a while, I was afraid we were going to have to call her Baby Girl. We finally decided on a name while I was in labor." She let out a small bout of laughter. "What a relief."

The baby tensed immediately, as if the sound of Peggy's voice had struck a raw chord. A moment later, she screwed up her face and let out a piercing, adamant wail.

Peggy's face registered alarm too. "What's the matter, little Sara? Did mommy scare you?"

Tim stepped in quickly. "It's okay, Peg, all babies cry." He looked at Arel. "Isn't that right, Arel? Little Ariel, Jr. cries all the time, doesn't he?"

Arel started to answer, but the baby's screaming escalated in volume, drowning out his words.

"Don't cry, sweetie," Peggy pleaded as she began to rock the infant. It didn't help. The baby was in full chorus and refused to be silenced.

Tim leaned over the bed, trying his best to assist Peggy, but she looked like she was ready to cry too.

Arel was accustomed to little Ariel, Jr.'s cries, but baby Sara took the act of bawling to a new volume level that he found almost alarming. He put a hand on Peggy's shoulder and gave her his most encouraging smile. "I think we better let you all have a little time to get acquainted. We'll come back later."

Peggy glanced up, a look of panic taking over her petite features. "Thanks, maybe we do need a little time to ourselves."

"If you need anything, you know where I am," Arel said as he gestured to Michael and began to move towards the door. As they made their way down the hospital corridor, Arel quickly recovered his composure. Sara's vocal expressions matched Peggy's. He glanced at Michael. "Like mother, like daughter, right, Michael?"

Michael nodded. "Yes, indeed, both mother and child have very powerful voices."

"Poor Peggy, she looks like she needs some rest." Arel gave Michael a playful smile. "You look a little tired too. I'll get you home so you can get your beauty sleep or whatever it is that you do to renew your energy."

Michael returned a pleading look. "You're enjoying this age business."

Arel avoided Michael's eyes, but his own were bright with merriment. "Indeed I am. It seems I'm dealing with both ends of the spectrum. New life and babies on the one hand, and on the other, the geriatric side of things. I'm in the company of an elder who probably tended to the first humans who inhabited earth. No wonder I feel like I constantly have my hands full."

Michael gave him a good-humored sigh. "Believe me, I know that feeling too."

Fifteen

Peggy sat in the nursery staring forlornly into space. It was three in the morning as she dabbed at her cheeks with a tissue. Motherhood wasn't at all what she thought it would be. She imagined cuddling a sweet cherub who smiled contentedly back at her. Instead, two-week-old Sara was screaming like a banshee. Tim nearly wore out the carpet trying to soothe her. When the room finally quieted and Sara fell asleep, it felt like a miracle, one that Peggy had been praying for. She was afraid to move, scared that her miracle might be just a dream and Sara would start crying again. Happily, Tim was able to ease the baby back into her crib.

"It's okay, honey," he whispered when he turned his attention to Peggy. "You need to go back to sleep. You look exhausted."

Peggy let him help her out of the rocker and lead her out of the nursery. He was right about her being physically worn. More than that, her nerves were also beyond frayed. The tears started up again when she got back to their bedroom. "My own baby hates me!"

Tim shouldered her over to the bed and held back the cover so she could climb in. "The doctor told us that some babies simply cry alot."

"But she howled for two hours!"

Tim leaned over and kissed her cheek. "This is just a temporary situation. Sara will outgrow this stage before we know it."

She gripped the edge of the blanket as she looked back at him. Her handsome husband, usually so strong and virile, was staring back with wary eyes and wrinkles in his brow that she never noticed

80

before. "I don't know, Tim. Maybe there's something wrong. I seem to upset her."

"It's got nothing to do with you. She cries with me too. Some babies are just very sensitive. It takes time for them to adjust to the world." He grinned at Peggy.

"Why are you smiling like that?"

"Can you imagine having someone like Arel for a baby? Even now, as an adult, he can go ballistic if someone spills juice on his rug. I know he tries to act calm, but if you look at the tension in his face, he's screaming inside, louder than Sara."

Peggy smiled too. Tim was right. Arel could have an "it's the end of the world" attitude about even small problems. "I guess you have a point. Some people do have a tougher time adjusting. On the other hand, he does have a way with Carol and Kevin's baby. Why can't he calm our Sara down?"

"Maybe when you put two sensitive people together, it doesn't always work."

Peggy reached out for Tim's hand. "Thank you for all your help. You succeeded where Arel failed. You got Sara back to sleep."

Tim chuckled. "I guess I'm a bit of a baby whisperer too."

"You're more than that. You're not only the best husband in the world, but now you're the best father around."

Tim put his hand over hers and squeezed it gently. "Just remember that I'm always here for you and Sara. Now shut your eyes and dream about how much I love you, okay?"

"Okay, but there's just one more thing."

"What's that?"

"I had another one of my visions when I was doing the laundry. I got a flash of Arel. He was hurt and in terrible pain."

Tim squeezed her hand again. "Honey, he's fine. I'll admit he wasn't okay when you first started having those feelings about him, but he's changed."

"I know he has, so why am I so afraid about what might happen to him?"

"I think it's your mothering instinct. Worrying about Sara has heightened your need to care for those you love. And let's face it, for all his wisdom concerning other people, Arel can still act a little immature."

"You're right. A couple of times, when I've been up with the baby just before dawn, I caught a glimpse of him running down the street. He's like a crazy kid out there, pushing his body to the limit and beyond."

"I think he gets a little boxed in with all the family stuff that's going on. He just needs an outlet that gets him out of the house for awhile."

The thought of Arel trying to cope with diapers and regurgitated milk, made her giggle. "First Carol and I had all our problems with being pregnant. Now, he's got two babies in his life. For a bachelor, I guess that's a lot to take in. Still, I worry about the mountain climbing thing. What if he goes through with his plans?"

"Don't forget that Kevin is determined to get through to him, to help him reconsider."

"Do you really think he can? Arel won't listen to me."

"Kevin is working on a plan. He's secretly doing some running himself, and you know that he excels at that type of thing."

"What good is that going to do?"

"Arel's been getting pretty cocky about what good shape he's in. Kevin wants to clip his wings a little, take a little of the wind out of his sails before he treks off to Nepal."

"Kevin's not going to damage Arel's self-confidence, is he?"

"That's not his intention, but we don't want Arel thinking he can scale a twenty-nine thousand foot mountain, do we?"

"No, we certainly don't."

Sixteen

Arel stood jogging in place as he waited for Kevin. The younger man had insisted on joining him for a run. He looked at his watch again. "Where is he?"

He hated waiting around. It gave his mind time to wander, to find subjects that could disturb his equilibrium, that tranquil state he'd been nurturing each time he ran.

"Hey! Arel!" Kevin came around the corner and waved at him.

He frowned back. "Finally, you're late."

"Two minutes late," Kevin called out. "I had to change a diaper."

"Or you overslept." Arel tried to use a teasing tone as the younger man joined him, but the wait, even though it was short, was irritating.

"So let's go already," Kevin insisted as he groaned out a yawn.

As they started jogging, Arel realized how much he valued his time alone. His morning runs gave him an opportunity to breathe in life while forgetting everything else. He'd never felt so comfortable with himself before. He glanced over at Kevin. "You look tired, but you were the one who wanted to join me at this early hour."

"You're right, it is a little early," Kevin chuckled. "Still, you seem pretty chipper."

"Tell that to your sister." Arel let out a huff of annoyance as he picked up the pace. "Every time I see her, she has a worried expression, and she gives me a lecture on acting responsibly."

"Aw come on, Arel, you know Peggy. She's just worried, that's all."

"Do you feel the same way? Do you think I'm making a fool out of myself because I'm thinking about mountain climbing?"

"I'd never think of you as a fool. You're blowing Peggy's way of expressing things out of proportion."

Arel slowed to a stop. "Oh really? When I spoke with Carol, she said that you all agree with Peggy."

"Listen, can't the rest of us offer you advice? You do it with us all the time. Anyway, if I do give you a few tips, consider it another training lesson from your old coach."

"That's fair, I guess. But before you say anything, let me prove that I'm perfectly capable of taking care of myself. In fact, I'll race you. And since you're not as prepared, we'll make it a short race, say three blocks."

"What's that going to prove?"

"I want everyone to know that I'm fine, more than fine. There's nothing for anyone to worry about. No matter what Peggy thinks, I'm very careful."

Kevin gave him another appraising once over. "Okay, if you insist. But can I give you one suggestion?"

Arel jogged in place. "If you have to, go ahead." He was trying his best to appear open, but he felt his original irritation increasing. His body was getting more anxious. Why was he surrounded by do-gooders who clearly saw him as incapable of making good decisions for himself? First, there was Michael, then Peggy and Carol. Now Kevin was making it clear that he didn't trust Arel's judgment. "What invaluable information would you like to give me?"

Kevin's eyes filled with the same concern that Arel saw in Peggy's eyes. "Please, Arel, just lighten up a bit and take it easy, pace yourself."

"Really? This from the guy who nearly killed me when I really was out of shape."

"Believe it or not, I knew just how far to push your body without going too far. That's what a good coach is all about. He has the know-how to gauge a person's abilities and weaknesses."

"Yes, maybe, but I'm not that beginner any more. I'm coaching myself."

Kevin put his knuckles on his hips and stepped back. "What about those pulled muscles you've had? When I was your coach, you might have had a sore body, but you never injured yourself."

Kevin's point had some validity, but Arel was tired of trying to explain himself. "When I'm running, I feel great. That's the bottom line. So stop talking and let's race a few blocks. I'll make it quick and easy on you. We can stop at the entrance to the park."

"Whatever. If you want to race, I'm game."

Kevin's words were like the signal gun sounding in Arel's ear. He took off running. At first they ran side by side, but he soon quickened his pace and pulled ahead. He needed to have his own space so he could go into running mode. It worked. As he pushed for more speed, he began to feel the lightness he valued. He wasn't only leaving Kevin behind, he was leaving all his naysayers in his dust. It didn't take long to finish off the first block.

Only two more to go.

He pushed harder. His legs sent out pain signals, letting him know that his body wasn't totally healed from his last bout of overexertion. Yet, he hardly paid his legs any heed. His mind reveled in the fact that Kevin was falling further behind.

Just a block and a half to go.

He wasn't having his normal runner's high since the race was a short one, but he was feeling vindicated. When the race was over, Kevin could go home and tell everyone that all was well.

And maybe I'll get some peace. No, it's more than that. I'll beat a real athlete. Kevin is in his prime. He's played college ball. He's as fit as they come.

It was an exhilarating thought that made him demand even more from his body. The next block flew by, and Kevin was a good ways back.

I'm doing it. I set a goal and no one is going to stop me from achieving it.

"I said you should pace yourself!" Kevin shouted out.

Arel glanced around and saw the younger man suddenly come alive. Going into a sprint, Kevin began to gain ground.

"Dammit," Arel cried out as he forced his body into overdrive. There was no way that he was going to let himself lose now. It wouldn't be fair after all the work he'd done.

Come on! Move!

In spite of being pushed to its limits, his body complied and gave him what he asked for as he leapt over a tall curb and started across a street. His lungs were heaving, but overall he was running well. He wasn't expecting his hamstring to grab as he approached the other side. When the pain seized his leg, he was going too fast to correct the situation. With the curb in front of him, he began to fall. Throwing both hands out, he couldn't stop his forward motion.

"No!" he yelped as both of his shins slammed down on the edge of the concrete. An excruciating pain in both limbs followed. For a moment he saw stars. When he tried to move, the pain immobilized him.

Kevin arrived a couple of moments later and crouched down beside him. "Holy moly, you really went down hard!"

Arel could only grit his teeth as he tried to respond. Finally he got out two words. "Call Michael."

"Of course I will, but I think you need to go to the emergency room."

Seventeen

Arel arrived back home on crutches. Going the distance from the driveway to the front door seemed an impossible challenge. As he hobbled forward, he fought the debilitating pain that came with each step. Michael and Kevin were hovering on either side. Peggy rushed over from her porch and greeted him like a returning war veteran.

"Oh, you poor baby!" she cried when she looked down and saw the splints and bandages on both of his legs. "I knew there was something to the visions I've been having."

"It's okay," Arel managed, but he was lying. He only suffered from hairline fractures, but he felt like a cripple.

Kevin brought Peggy up to speed on the situation. "You're not going to believe this, but Arel is allergic to every pain med they tried. Even topical creams cause his skin to react violently. So we can't give him anything, not even an aspirin."

Once inside the house, Arel slowly made his way to his bedroom. "Please everyone, go home. Michael can take it from here."

Peggy lingered a few feet behind him. "Are you sure, sweetie? I'll stay if you want."

"No, I think I just need some rest. Thank you anyway."

* * *

A soft knock on Arel's bedroom door brought him out of his pain stupor. When Michael let himself in, Arel glared up at him. "I bet you're happy about this. You didn't want me to do any climbing from the start."

Michael came over to the side of the bed and reached out to touch Arel's shoulder. "That isn't true."

Arel pulled back reflexively, but his movement sent his legs into spasms of pain.

Michael stepped away. "I'm sorry. I truly am. I would never want to see you hurt in any way."

Arel's jaw tightened. Having someone like Michael around was hard. Michael indulged in truthful words and wise advice. On the other hand, Arel was constantly forced to consume a heaping helping of crow. "As usual, I'm being stupid . . . saying ridiculous things." After a moment he looked at Michael with repentant eyes. "Can you do something to heal my legs?"

"I've tried to help several times. But your body isn't responding."

"My body? How can it have anything to do with your helping me? I give the orders, don't I? So please, do something to get me on my feet again."

"The physical part of a person has its own sense of who it is, and it can take action when it feels threatened."

"Are you saying that my body did this to me?"

"You haven't exactly been its best friend."

Arel thought about the morning run, and how he'd been so determined to win, no matter what. "So you're saying it's punishing me?"

Michael paused and stared at him. "Everyone needs to respect their bodies. That's what I'm saying."

"Well, dammit, my body better get with the program because I'm not backing down. I make the decisions about what I do and don't do." As his voice became obstinate and more determined a fresh bout of pain shot through his legs. He winced and stubbornly held his ground, clenching his fists and his teeth.

Michael hesitated. When he spoke, his tone was kindly but firm. "I'm being your ally when I tell you this. It's not wise to go up against the vessel that makes it possible to live on this earth."

The words, delivered in a kind and gentle tone, triggered a deep reservoir of bitterness. "It's wrecked everything! I was doing so well. This is a total setback."

"Maybe this isn't a bad thing. While you're recuperating, you'll have time to work on what we were talking about before you started training."

Arel's bitterness turned to wrath. "That's the last thing I want to do! You may not have wanted this to happen, but secretly you see it as an opportunity. All you can think about is the damnable process! I went through hell reliving the nightmare about Aldwin and my father. I want a reprieve! I want a normal life! Haven't I earned that?"

Michael's gaze never wavered, but he didn't respond. He didn't need to. Arel already knew what was needed, and it terrified him.

"Why doesn't it ever stop?" As he asked the question, Arel already knew the answer. He could feel it in his gut. Dark, horrible memories were swirling in their closeted chamber. They wanted out.

Michael carefully put a hand on the bed. "Dear friend, it's not up to me. Some part of you wants to rid itself of the pain that you're holding on to. It's like having dirt in a wound. The wound is going to fester until you stop and clean it out."

"I don't care," Arel said with clenched teeth, trying not to move for fear of his legs going ballistic again. "I know what this is about, and I won't go there."

Michael let out a sigh. "Justina has come back, hasn't she?"

Arel swallowed, but the sudden lump in his throat couldn't be dislodged. "Michael, please, I'm begging you. Don't bring her into this."

"Is that what you want, to shut it all out, even if facing what happened that night will make the pain that you're in go away?"

"Yes, that's what I want! A hundred times, yes!" Arel lifted his gaze to meet Michael's. "Please don't mention her again."

Michael nodded. "I promise."

Eighteen

It had been nearly a week since Arel's accident. With Michael's help, he relocated to his downstairs bedroom, deserting the one in the upper portion of the house in favor of his old haunt. There were no windows there, only darkness and quiet. A bedside lamp illuminated the beautifully furnished room with forty watts of soft light.

The king-sized bed was pillowed, with silky, black sheets and a lavish down comforter. Arel sat propped up on top of the fine bedclothes. He still couldn't stand anything to touch his legs. He didn't dare move them. If he did, he was punished with sharp, stabbing spasms.

Even if his rational mind told him that Michael was on his side, Arel felt like he was in the trenches again, at war with Michael's blood. The angelic stuff was on the march. He could feel it coursing through him, searching his very cells for what he'd hidden away, trying to ferret out those dark memories that he couldn't face. He would have had more strength to fight the assault except for the fractures in his legs. The physical damage seemed minimal, but the unrelenting pain was always there pounding at his energy reserves, never letting him rest.

I can't give in to my body or the blood!

His mind weaved in and out of the throbbing minutes and aching hours searching for freedom, wanting to fly away from everything, wanting to avoid what lay before him. But the pain wouldn't be denied its due. It always won out in the end and brought him back to his past.

"Don't you know I can't deal with what's being asked?" he shouted upwards, targeting Michael with a rush of frustration and self-pity. "I'm sorry," he whispered in the next breath, feeling ashamed of himself.

I'm blaming him for my sins. I'm at fault!

But what could he do? How long could he go on, unable to walk or even move without his nerves screaming in anguish? How long could he hang on to his resolve to keep the darkness in his gut in its place? The truth was obvious. It was only a matter of time until the pain would break him, just as his father had broken him with his cane. Sooner or later, he'd have to face what he'd done to Justina. But at least she hadn't been in his head. That was a small comfort.

Instead, he began having flashbacks about her. Nighttime was the worst. Their time together invaded his dreams, turning them into nightmares when he relived those unbearable moments of holding her lifeless body in his arms.

"Don't fall asleep. Don't fall asleep," he repeated as the hours of darkness caught up with him again. There were no windows to expose him to the call of night, but his internal clock was ticking, telling him that he wouldn't be able to stay awake forever. As he was starting to lose the battle, as his eyelids began to close, a knock on the door brought him back to a full, waking state.

"Michael, if that's you, go away. I'm too exhausted to talk."

A voice answered from the other side of the door. "It's Abrigail. Can I come in?"

He tightened his fists and sighed. He hadn't seen the pretty angel in a long time. He only felt her buzzing fleetingly around the edges of reality. "If you must."

The door opened a few inches, and Abrigail's face beamed back a smile. "Hello, dearest, I wanted to say how sorry I am about your accident."

He returned a frown, not trusting her completely, but he waved her towards him anyway. "Finally, someone besides Michael to really talk to."

Abrigail tiptoed over and stopped several feet from the bed. "I remember when your heart was in trouble. You enjoyed my company. I thought that I might stay with you now."

As Arel stared at her, his vision blurred and so did Abrigail's face. He thought he caught a glimpse of Justina. She looked just as she had when he first met her. It was a good memory, one that held only brightness and delight. But he couldn't let himself indulge, even in the good memories. He rubbed at his eyes and blinked a couple of times until Abrigail was smiling at him again.

"Should I sit over in the corner?" Abrigail asked.

"No, come here. I want to feel your hand on my forehead like before. It helps with the fever. A few hours ago I could feel my temperature soaring."

Abrigail moved forward reluctantly. "Are you sure?"

"Of course."

When Abrigail reached out and then hesitated, Arel blinked back with confusion. "What's going on? Are you scowling at me?"

"Nothing, nothing's going on." Taking a deep breath, Abrigail carefully lowered her hand to his forehead. As soon as she established contact, she jumped back. "Oh my!" She squeaked out a little cry of discomfort as she stared at him with wide, sparkly eyes.

Arel had never seen an angel look so flustered except for the time Peggy's shrill voice made Michael lose his balance. The tall, confident angel ended up flat out on the floor with a very surprised look on his face. "Abrigail, what happened? Are you okay?"

Abrigail adjusted the silky, white dress she was wearing, smoothing out non-existent wrinkles. "I'm fine. It's just that I'm not used to being in physical form and then being—"

"What? What are you trying to tell me?"

"Dearest, would you please lower your shields?"

"My shields?"

"It's not you. It's me. Even in physical form, I'm very sensitive to energy, and you have a little field of protection around you."

"Michael never said anything."

"He's made adjustments to your recent . . . expressions. I should too, but it would be easier if you simply trusted me."

"Maybe I am defensive. Since I injured my legs, I've had to be careful."

Abrigail stepped closer a second time. "You look so tired. Is it the memories about Justina again?"

"Why do I have to keep thinking about her?"

Abrigail stared back with concern creasing her flawless features. "We've talked about this before, quite a while ago, remember?"

"Yes, of course, it was when I was first going through this hellish transformation."

"Are you sure it's the blood this time, or is it that you haven't let Justina go?"

"I thought I had, in some ways."

"But you never let yourself find any resolution."

Every muscle in Arel's body tensed and his legs retaliated. He held on to the sheet. "I can't forgive myself if that's what you mean."

"You always have a choice."

"No, I don't!"

"But Justina wouldn't want to see you like this, would she?"

"Of course not. She made it clear that my happiness was as important as her own. She was too innocent to understand that she was dealing with a monster."

"You told me that you loved her."

"Of course I did. When we were first together, all the hurt and pain I suffered at my father's hand disappeared. Being with Justina changed everything. For a time, our world seemed beautiful and perfect."

"And you didn't want that world to end."

"No, but it did vanish, all because of me. I'm the guilty party. I hate the pain that I'm in, but I know I deserve it."

"Tell me what happened that last time that you and Justina were together."

The request, so simple and direct, immobilized him with a searing truth. No matter how hard he tried to bury the details of the night in question, he'd never succeed.

Abrigail took his hand in hers. "It's okay. I'm an angel, remember? Even if you have judgments about what happened, I don't."

Abrigail was right. It was time to confess his sins. His jaw tightened, and the words began to trickle out in a whisper. "The evening started out like so many that we shared. Justina was totally enjoying herself. Neither one of us could have expected how violently it would end." He closed his eyes and let the gates of memory open wide. "Oh god, forgive me for that night."

* * *

"I love you! I love you! I love you, Arel!" Justina's lilting voice sang out, filling the candlelit room with her joy! She spun round and

93

round, dancing, leaping in the air, joining the flickering light and shadow, caught up in her own ecstasy.

"And I love you," Arel whispered back.

"Say it louder!" Justina was swirling in front of him. She sent him kisses every time she came near him. Her face was so young. It glowed with eagerness and unrestrained excitement. "Tell me what's in your heart!" she cried out. "Shout it from the rooftops!"

He tried again. "I love you." This time there was passion in each syllable, but his volume was still lacking. It was his way. He learned to be very quiet early in life, to stay hidden in the shadows, not to sing out his intention.

Justina gave him a petulant look, the kind a child has when she doesn't get a piece of candy, but then she laughed. "Dance with me! Let's enjoy ourselves!"

He blinked back, but he couldn't move. When people around him got excited, a warning went off. Excited people were dangerous. They lost their temper and beat you.

"Arel, please, you never want to play with me! Now get up and dance, please!"

Justina was holding out her skirt as she continued to enjoy her delight. He strained to enjoy the music that poured out of her heart, but he was a deaf man who didn't have that capacity.

"Arel! Aren't you happy?"

He turned away, red-faced, clutching at the arm of the chair. Justina was in one of her exuberant moods, wanting more from him than he knew how to give. That's when he realized how different they were. Justina was still the innocent child. They were close in physical age, but his own childlike qualities had been lost long ago. He didn't know how to play or dance.

"You're brooding again," she said as she came over and sat down in his lap. Her face and her body were rigid with sudden anger and disappointment. "I think you're getting bored with me."

It was becoming a frequent argument on her part.

"No, of course I'm not," he managed, but his voice was weak. Each day he was failing more and more. He tried his best, but he felt old and arthritic when he tried to stretch out to meet Justina's needs. They had been together for months, loving one another. They often lost themselves in expressing that love physically. But those times didn't involve time and space. When they returned to reality, he was his broken self again, not only broken but also cursed.

94

"You say that, but how can I believe you," she continued. Her brows were closing in on themselves as her sulkiness deepened. "I gave you everything. I trusted you with all that I am."

It was true. Justina handed over her virtue so easily. And he had done the same. Both were virgins when they met. They were both untested instruments of lovemaking. Yet he knew how to be tender with her, how to worship every ounce of her flesh and anoint it with his complete adoration. In that one area, he was pure and innocent.

"You made me think you'd always love me. I thought we'd be married soon," she cried out. Her voice was louder and filled with more need. "Why did you lie to me?" She screamed out the question and raised her hand as if to strike him.

He winced sharply, shutting his eyes, thrown back into a familiar feeling, a knowing feeling that life always brought pain.

"I'm sorry," she whispered, suddenly ashamed of herself. "I love you! And I want you to love me!" She threw her arms around his neck and held him tight. "Please don't do this to me. Tell me that we'll always be together."

He tried to speak, to tell her that she was the only thing in the world he had to live for, but the paralysis was there again. Justina had always been so sweet, so kind. Now she wanted to hit him. What had he done to spoil such a beautiful soul? The answer came at once. He was a parasite, a parasite that pretended he could leave that part of himself at the door. He'd been a fool to think such a ridiculous thing. When he took Justina that first night in his bed, when he robbed her of her maidenhood, he corrupted her. Maybe he never sucked her blood, but he took something from her that she could never get back again.

"Aren't you even listening to me?" Justina asked. She sat up, swiping at her tears, glaring at him. Her eyes, so bright a few minutes earlier, were filled with hurt and outrage. "Arel, tell me that I haven't been a fool."

He tried to answer again, opening his mouth and choked on the bitter truth of what he'd done to her. When he looked away with shame, she began shaking him. She grabbed his shoulders in her small hands and aggressively tried to force him to speak. But the only part of him that could still respond was his heart. It had been shattered after his brother's death, but having Justina in his life mended it in some way. Her love put the pieces back together enough for him to feel again, to think that life had some redeeming part to it. Now, he could feel the vessel falling apart. As it did, waves of loathing and self-hatred flooded every muscle and cell in his body.

"Don't turn away from me," Justina yelled again, forcing him to look at her.

In spite of her outrage, she was still so beautiful, a rose in the tempest he created. The beautiful flower was being battered by his utter inability to still her fears. As his heart was collapsing into ruin, it rallied one last time. He had to free Justina from the destructive force that he was. He had to give her a chance at a better life. He croaked out the only words that he knew to give her.

"Please, let me go, Justina. Find someone who—"

"Liar!" She stood up, targeting him with a wild, flaring stare. "After all the times you said you loved me! You tell me to move on?"

"I didn't mean—"

"I know what you mean! I see the disgust in your eyes!"

"No, I blame myself—"

"For what? For getting involved with a lowly dressmaker? You, a man of station, lowering himself? What am I to you? A whore?"

As she shouted out in bitterness, his body trembled, growing weaker and more pathetic. His fingers dug into the velvet upholstery. He used every bit of strength he had left to fight back. "No! You're wrong!" Again, his voice was raspy and breathless. He'd lost his ability to argue like a normal person. "I'll always love you."

"But not enough to marry me, is that it?"

"I can't marry you!" Finally, he had enough breath to yell back. No matter how much his body shook, he had to find a way to show Justina what he really was, a crippled leech who would destroy her if she stayed with him. He had to find a way to make her despise him for her sake. "This has all been a mistake."

She stared back at him, shocked by the unfamiliar hardness in his face. "What are you saying?"

"If you think our relationship was more than it was, I'm sorry." He made sure that his tone was cold even though he knew what his words would do to her. They punished her heart, her tender vessel of love, with as much cruelty as his father's cane had punished his seven-year-old back. But he couldn't help it. For her well-being, he had to sever their bond. He couldn't think about himself now. He couldn't think about his own heart being destroyed. He couldn't think about anything but being strong and unbending for her sake.

Struck by his sudden betrayal, she stumbled back and sank to the floor as if his pronouncement took away all the strength in her body. "I can't believe that you mean that," she gasped.

He could see what he'd done to her, but he was committed now, to ending everything. He wouldn't have the strength to hurt her like this again. He looked away, studying the wallpaper, the faded birds flying in a sky that was gray with age. "You'll find someone who deserves you, but it's not me."

"But I can't love anyone else," she sobbed.

"You're still so young. What do you know about love?" he asked, making himself laugh at her. "You're just a child, a child who wants something that I can never satisfy."

She was quiet now, unmoving. She sat on the floor as if she'd been frozen to the spot by his terrible declarations.

When he finally went to her and tried to help her up, she glared at him, pushing him away. "No! Don't touch me!" she screamed. "You've taken everything from me! I have nothing left to live for!"

* * *

As Arel finished relating the story to Abrigail, he knew he'd made a mistake. To go back to a time when he broke the heart of the only woman he had ever loved was too much. How had he managed to live with the pain as long as he did?

Abrigail gently pushed a lock of hair from his eyes. "I'm not here to rekindle your pain. I asked about that night because I want you to let go of it. You did your best. You thought you were freeing Justina. That's why you said the things you said."

He looked away. "My ignorance, my loathful words killed her!"

"That's completely untrue!" A voice called out, but it wasn't Abrigail's voice rebuffing Arel's declaration. This person sounded younger. "I should know. I was there."

He turned back to where Abrigail was standing and saw another visitor. "Justina!"

A pretty, young woman stood next to Abrigail. "Yes, my darling. It's me," she said as she stepped closer.

Was he going completely insane? Had Michael's blood and his battle with the past driven him crazy? "I don't understand—"

97

Justina's face brightened. "All these years I've tried to reach out to you, but you wouldn't let me, except for that one time when you were running." She turned to Abrigail. "Finally, this wonderful angel helped me to breach the wall of guilt that you've held on to for so long."

Justina hadn't changed at all. Her golden-blonde hair was pulled back and cascaded down her shoulders. Her blue eyes were sparkling in the dim light as if they brought their own source of illumination.

"I'm dreaming again. Or am I hallucinating?" he asked haltingly.

"I don't have much time, my love," Justina said. "We have to talk, please."

Arel stared back, not knowing how to respond. It was clear that she needed him to listen to her.

Justina reached out for his hand. "My body died, but we're so much more than just the physical. Still, your self-blame was so complete that it's kept a part of me tethered to you and the life we shared. Now it's time for both of us to move on."

"Move on? When I know what I did?"

Justina looked down with a frown. "You wanted to leave me, to abandon me, didn't you?"

"Abandon you?" Her words were like a horrible, cutting blade that sliced open the festering wound that Arel harbored deep within. "I loved you!" he shouted. "I was trying to do what was best for you!" As soon as the words were out, he regretted them, just as he regretted yelling at Michael.

Justina leaned in close, putting her arms around him and pulling him to her. "I know that now. I know the truth."

"It doesn't change anything. What I wanted doesn't matter. I killed you," he said despairingly. "How can I forgive myself for that?"

"But you didn't."

Arel shook his head. "Don't say that. I can't let you say that."

"I took my own life, my darling," Justina said in an insistent voice.

The words terrified him, made him push her back so that he could look at her with hard, unflinching eyes.

"No, it's not true! I'm the one who's responsible!"

"Remember this?" Justina reached in the pocket of her dress and retrieved a man's cut-throat razor. "It was yours, but I used it."

His eyes lost focus for a moment, refusing to acknowledge what she offered him.

"Look at it," Justina pleaded. "Look at what you've been running from."

"No!" Arel pulled back in revulsion as he stared at the hideous object being thrust in his face. The implement with its long horn and pearl handle, had a cutting edge that was sharp and deadly. "I'm begging you!" He turned away, trying to hide from what she was forcing on him.

Justina pressed on. "It was perfect for its task. It's unfortunate that I was so good at what I did."

"Stop it!" Arel put his hands over his ears. "It didn't happen that way!"

Justina smiled, pulling his hands down and bringing her eyes in line with his. "We're not the lost children that we were when I died. It's time for the truth," she said with conviction.

He wanted to resist her, but he was helpless, just like he was on that night when she died. He hated her for what she was doing to him again.

"Dearest Arel, I was so young. I was so impetuous. Then after my death, you tried to save me from my sins, tried to protect me from the punishment of taking my own life, but it's over now. I killed myself. You couldn't do anything. It happened so fast. I was too rash, too hysterical."

After almost a hundred years, he was forced to listen to what had actually happened. "I tried to stop you," he whispered in defeat, remembering how he ran after her when he realized what she was going to do. "But I failed!"

When he grabbed the razor from her hand, it was too late. Justina had acted so swiftly, so forcefully, with the despair of one whose heart was broken. Her wound was deep and fatal. He tried his best to help, clamping his hand over her slender throat, praying that she wouldn't die, but her blood poured out from her in a flood of grief, slipping through his fingers.

"I'm sorry," Justina said, releasing him, letting him fall back on the pillows.

He lay there trying to breathe. He was like the young man who'd been thrown from the motorcycle. There was no oxygen. There was nothing to sustain him. Even Michael's blood was stagnating, pooling in his arteries, unable to navigate his body. His heart was languid, felled by the thought that all his suffering had been for nothing.

"How could you do such a thing? I loved you," he said in a barely audible voice. "I loved you enough to spare you from my dark, ugly world. But you trampled on my gift. You destroyed yourself. You sent yourself into the world of the damned."

Justina shook her head. "You shouldn't have taken my sin on yourself. No matter how much you pretended that it was your fault, it wasn't."

His eyes went dark. Something snapped inside of him, making him gasp and gobble up the air again. He'd been holding on for so long, trying to save the love of his life. Now, knowing it was a worthless farce, everything started to move again. His heart started pounding, readying itself for his rage. His hand flew out and grabbed her wrist. "What choice did I have? I couldn't save you in this life, but I wouldn't let myself think that you were burning in hell in the next!"

His fury poured out of him, like the blood that had emptied out of Justina. Better the guilt of thinking that he killed Justina physically than thinking that he was responsible for her burning forever in Hades.

"But I'm not damned," she said quietly. "After my suicide, I was in the darkness at first, but it was the darkness that I made with my despair. After a time, I received the help I needed to find my way back to the light."

Justina backed up, making him release her. "Just know that I've never stopped loving you. Forgive me and forgive yourself," she whispered as she faded away.

He frantically searched the room, but only Abrigail remained. The angel stood very still by the side of his bed.

"Justina is right. It's time to forgive yourself and her," she said quietly.

Suddenly he hated Abrigail and life itself as his anger gave way to a caustic resentment. "Forgiveness? Now? Has all the misery and the pain been for nothing? And the love that Justina and I shared, was it worthless?"

"You have to decide how to make your experiences worthwhile. You have to give them meaning."

"How? Everything Justina and I had seems so ridiculous at this point."

"Give yourself the gift of understanding," Abrigail said as she went to the door. As she was about to leave, she pointed to something on the bed. "Justina left you something that might help."

His eyes glazed over with fresh hatred as the door closed, but then he looked at where she'd been pointing.

"Oh god, no!" The razor that killed Justina was laying a few feet away on the soft, black comforter. He didn't know how it could be real, but when he reached out for it, it was cold and hard in his hand.

"So is this the answer?" he shouted out.

Justina's soft laughter echoed in the room. "No, of course not, but I want you to do something for me. Please, hold it to your own throat."

"Why? Am I supposed to kill myself too?"

"Trust me, please. Just do as I ask."

He grabbed the razor, ready to fling it into oblivion. He was tired of stupidity, his own and Justina's. Yet he couldn't let go of the damnable thing. Somehow Justina invaded his body and began forcing the blade towards him. He couldn't stop his hand as it traveled to his throat. Before the blade made contact with his skin, it stopped moving.

"Trust me," Justina whispered again. "Open your senses and let yourself understand what I felt."

He couldn't refuse her or what was being asked of him. He still loved her in spite of everything, but he let out a huff of laughter. "I hope you know that trust isn't one of my strong points."

Justina laughed too. "Then be brave for me."

With a final heavy sigh, he surrendered and allowed his body to connect with the tainted object. As it rested against his throat, it gave up its secrets to him. He knew that it held Justina's feelings in its steely form. Her energy had permeated the blade and imprinted it with her last moments.

"My lord, Justina, we were so alike. You felt totally alone in the world. How could that be possible? You were so beautiful, so desirable. I would have thought you had countless beaus on your doorstep. But you didn't see yourself that way, did you?"

"We were mirrors for each other, my darling," Justina said with a note of sadness. "I was too young to even know who I was. Everything revolved around you. You tried to give me a chance for a better life, but all that I knew was that my world was gone the minute you rejected me."

"You deserved a beautiful life. I wanted so much to give that to you."

"We both threw our lives away," she replied. "But now, you've been given a most precious gift, another chance at happiness."

* * *

Peggy's shriek brought Tim out of a dreamy sleep. Her loud cry of alarm sent him into an instant state of panic. "What is it? The baby? Is she alright?" He rubbed at his eyes. "Peggy?"

"A nightmare! I just had the worst dream!" Peggy answered as she sat up. "It's Arel! He's in danger! Quick, go over to his house! Now!"

"Why? What's going on?" he asked as he threw back the covers.

"Never mind, just go!"

Tim didn't stop to reason. Peggy sounded so frightened. With her orders still fresh in his ears, he ran out of the room, through the hall and down the steps.

Is she right? Is Arel in trouble again?

He barely paused as he grabbed his keys on the foyer table. He was catching Peggy's dread that something had happened to Arel. Once outside the house, he realized he was in his bare feet. It didn't matter. Arel was his friend, a friend who'd proven himself repeatedly when Peggy or Carol or Kevin needed help.

Hell, he's family now.

When Tim got to Arel's front door, his fingers shook with cold and dread as he tried to open the lock. Finally, he worked it successfully. Letting himself in, he paused to think about where Arel was sleeping.

I think it's the lower level.

He hastily took to the stairs, nearly tripping when he almost missed a step. Once he was at the bottom and through the door that led to the rest of the lower level, he headed for the bedroom. He didn't knock before going in. He slammed open the door and looked around the dim room. "What the—"

Arel was sitting on the bed, holding a razor to his throat and talking to himself.

"Are you nuts? Drop it!" Tim usually prided himself on being calm. Now he yelled out his shock and anger in a loud, but anxious voice. When Arel continued to stare at him with the razor still in hand, he took action. "I said drop it!"

Bounding across the room, he delivered a hard blow to Arel's arm. The razor went flying. Thankfully Arel didn't look injured in any way. "What is wrong with you?" he blurted out in shock. He never imagined Arel would try to take his own life. He was more of a run-away-from-the-world kind of guy.

Arel stared back with questioning eyes. "Tim? What are you doing here?"

Tim let out a breath of outrage as he realized how close his friend had come to harming himself. "Don't you know we all care about you? Why would you try to do something like this?"

Arel narrowed his brows and sat up straighter. "You think I want to kill myself?"

Tim backed away and glanced around. "Why else would you be holding that razor? And where did the damn thing go?" he asked as he began to search the floor. "I thought you knew you could talk to me or Kevin if you had a problem." He got down on his knees and looked under the bed. He could feel his frustration building. "I always knew you were excitable, but this is crazy." He got up, still in searching mode, but scratching his head. "This is the strangest thing. I saw you with a razor."

There was a soft rapping on the bedroom door. "I heard voices," Michael said, interrupting Tim's search.

"Thank goodness you're here," Tim said quickly. "Arel has crossed the line this time."

* * *

An hour after Tim's explosive entrance, Arel stared vacantly into space. Tim had finally gone home, but only with the promise that Michael would stand guard over Arel. It wasn't going to be as easy to appease Peggy. Michael was on the phone with her, and her concern was being stated in a loud, demanding voice that Arel could plainly hear. Michael didn't try to argue with her. He stood at attention, looking tall and steadfast as he held the phone tight to his ear. When he was given instructions about being Arel's caregiver, he stiffened as if he was a private in boot camp. When he did respond, his replies were short and crisp.

"Yes, Peggy, I promise to stay with him . . . no . . . I won't leave him for a minute . . . right . . . I'll keep you informed . . . yes, I know that the first forty-eight hours are crucial . . . no . . . I won't take my eyes off of him . . . I'll report back tomorrow . . . Good night."

Arel breathed a sigh of relief when Michael hung up the phone. "What a mess this is," he said with disgust.

Michael came over and stood by the bed. "Yes, it is."

"You know I wasn't going to do anything to myself, don't you? You believe me, right? Peggy and Tim have some crazy idea—"

"They care about you."

"They see me as the person in the family who is always going mad."

Michael offered a weak smile and an explanation. "Peggy dreamed that she saw you with the razor. Tim saw you holding it."

"Those things might have happened, but Peggy and Tim misinterpreted them."

"Peggy's your friend. You might think that you're handling your own problems, but every thought, every word, every pain that you feel, or any human feels, creates a field around them. Perhaps, you did put out a cry for help. You've just been through a lot tonight."

"Yes, including the fact that the love of my life just informed me that I've been a fool all this time. Why shouldn't I be screaming, but I wasn't trying to kill myself."

"I know."

"You know all of it, don't you? All these years you've been trying to tell me about that night, but I wouldn't listen."

"You wanted to protect the woman you never stopped loving."

"But my efforts never helped her. All my guilt and shame, it's all been for nothing."

"Can I talk to you about a couple of those issues?"

Arel grimaced at the prospect. "Like what? What can you say that can make my foolishness any better?"

"Time is the first thing I'd like to discuss. Remember our discussion about how old I am?"

The tension in Arel's shoulders eased a little. "Yes, for once we had a chat that I found enjoyable. I hope I wasn't too irreverent."

"No, not at all. I'm happy that you were enjoying yourself."

"At your expense?" Arel felt a tinge of embarrassment creeping in. "I'm sorry."

Michael grinned back. "I'll survive. Besides, I don't share your view of time. For me, there are only moments. I can access moments in what you call the past and the future. I can be present with any of them just like I'm present with you now in this moment. For me, there's no such thing as getting older from that point of view."

"Great, what's the future got in store for me? Do I get my wings someday or do I go down in flames?"

"That's for you to decide. The 'now' moments that I'm talking about are always shifting and changing with every decision you make."

"Michael, I already have a throbbing headache, and you're making it worse."

"Sorry, let me get to the point I wanted to make. It's about the guilt that you've felt over Justina's death."

Arel rubbed at his temples and squinted back. "Yes, go on."

"Your guilt is based on what happened after you tried to convince Justina that you weren't the right person for her. But if you go back to that moment when you were pushing her away, your only motive was love. You loved her so much that you didn't want her to get hurt by staying with you."

"Yes, that's true. So what? It was a stupid move."

"But you didn't know that when you told her those things. You were willing to sacrifice your own heart in favor of her future happiness. If you look at yourself in that moment, trying to do your best, what do you really have to feel guilty about?"

"I never thought of it that way." Arel picked at a piece of lint on the comforter. "I guess I thought my best wasn't good enough."

"It's harder for humans to see things like I do. But maybe this will make it easier. Would you judge a baby for not walking when it's a month old?"

"No, of course not, but I'm still left with the feeling that I wasted so many years of my life being misguided."

"You did what you did for love, and love is never wasted. Even when it's misguided, it can still shine through darkness. When Justina crossed over, she was in a despairing state, but your connection to her was strong. Your love was a constant source of hope that helped her find her way back to herself."

"Really?" Arel's legs were throbbing again, but Michael's words helped the pain ease. "Because if I think that in some small way, I was there for her, then I don't mind being a fool."

Michael sighed. "I never think of you that way."

"That's because you can't. You only see the best in people."

Michael laughed. "Just because I see things differently, I'm not blind."

"So what do you call a person like me?"

"You're a friend. You're also a person who's passionate to the point of being willing to damn yourself to save another. You're a person who's capable of great love because you've known what it's like not to be loved. Now, Justina is asking you to love yourself too."

Nineteen

For two weeks after Arel's supposed suicide attempt, he found himself at the center of a parade of concerned visitors. Peggy and Carol took turns coming over during the day. Kevin and Tim stopped in after work. Questions were always being asked about Arel's frame of mind. It wasn't easy, but he was slowly convincing his friends that he was okay. As he proved to everyone that he was mentally stable, the constant visits were finally tapering off. His physical woes were going away too. His legs were healing. He'd even begun taking short walks every day.

"So why is my doorbell ringing?" he mumbled as he made his way to the foyer. It was noon, with the sun shining through the windows. When he opened the door, Peggy stood waiting on the sunlit porch.

"This isn't a social call, sweetie. I have some mail for you," she announced. "It was in my box by mistake. I thought it might be important. It has a London return address."

He stared at the letter Peggy was holding out to him. "London?"

Peggy thrust the letter into his hand. "I better get back to Sara. She's starting to wake up."

He got in a quick thank you as Peggy rushed off, but he suddenly didn't feel as okay as he thought he was. He studied the elegant, embossed envelope for a long moment before he closed the door. With his hand starting to tremble, he let out a shout. "Michael, come here! I need to talk to you."

He hadn't thought about his nemesis, William, for quite a while, not since he'd heard William's voice that one time, calling to him. Now, he was sure he was holding a tangible connection to the man he never wanted to see again. There was no name on the envelope, only a post office box, but that was the way William functioned.

"What is it?" Michael asked as he walked into the foyer.

Arel waved the envelope at him. "It's from William. He's found me," he said as he ripped open the envelope, retrieved the contents and started to read.

Michael waited patiently. Finally, he spoke up. "Do you want to tell me what the letter says?"

Arel's fist slowly closed, crumbling the note he was holding. "William is coming to New York in three weeks. He wants me to meet him there."

"How do you feel about that?"

Arel snorted out a breath. "I want to kill the bastard the moment I see him again."

"You hate him that much?"

"I only wish I had been strong enough to take him out the last time that I saw him."

"I thought you didn't like violence."

"I don't, but sometimes a person has to make an exception."

Michael hesitated before he commented. "Maybe you won't understand what I'm going to say, but hate and love are often two sides of the same coin."

Arel glanced up and stared back. "No, I understand it perfectly. I loved William. He was like another brother. He could be a cad with others, but he always protected me. I trusted him completely. And what did I get for that trust. He cursed me and made me a monster like himself."

"But you're not that monster anymore."

"No, but he is. Maybe that's the reason I was saved from what I'd become. The purpose of your blood is finally dawning on me. The real monster has to be stopped."

Michael backed away, letting his eyes become very focused and clearly dismayed. "That's a dangerous road to go down. Are you sure you want to allow yourself to think in those terms?"

"All I know is that William will never hurt another person again if I can help it."

Twenty

Arel sat in the living room recliner and forced himself to smile at the baby in his arms. Ariel Jr. was already a very robust and weighty child who knew what he wanted. The baby had disposed of his gel teether ring in exchange for Arel's finger. Now, he was happily gumming away with his new chewing treat. Arel tried to pay attention to his godchild, but his mind constantly circled back to William and to Michael's comment. The angel definitely made it clear that it wasn't a wise move to seek revenge on his former friend. But maybe it wasn't revenge that Arel intended.

I just don't want anyone else to suffer like I have.

At least that's what he kept telling himself. He also tried to be attentive to his guests. It was Saturday night and everyone had been invited to Arel's house for dinner. He'd made plans for the gathering before he knew about William's letter. Now, it wasn't easy to pretend that he was carefree and happy during their visit, but he did a pretty convincing job. After a pleasant meal and fresh strawberry shortcake for dessert, everyone moved to the living room. It was their normal routine. Peggy and Tim sat on the sofa with baby Sara cuddled in her father's lap. Carol and Kevin sat together on the loveseat. There was the usual small talk.

"Better be careful, Arel. Junior is teething early," Kevin advised as he watched his son's interaction with his godfather. "He's got a pretty strong set of jaws."

Arel barely paid Kevin's advice any attention, but he did try to stay focused on the baby. "Thank you for including me in his life."

Carol laughed. "Little Ariel adores you, and you know it. You came through for him and for us during those first few weeks."

Arel nodded, but an attack of sadness spoiled the moment. What would the future bring? Would he be around to see his godchild grow up? Or would William find a way to ruin his new life too? He recoiled at the thought.

Not this time.

Peggy locked on to him and gave him the once-over. "Is there something the matter? You seem a little quiet."

Arel was just about to deny that anything was wrong when Ariel, Jr. clamped down on his finger with the gusto of a sumo wrestler enjoying a cheeseburger. It was a surprisingly, painful experience, but he suffered quietly, not wanting to alarm his petite, redheaded watchdog. "Uh, no," he insisted as he retrieved the gel teether and quickly offered it to the baby. Fortunately, the bright colors got the little boy's attention. Arel used the distraction to dislodge his finger from the baby's strong gums.

"You're just getting back to normal physically," Carol chimed in. "Don't overdo, please. Let Kevin hold the baby."

Carol's offer was followed by a loud, crashing sound.

"Sorry," Michael called out. "The roaster got away from me."

Tim glanced towards the kitchen. "Maybe we should give him a hand in there?"

Arel was too distracted to think about kitchen duties. As he handed the baby to Kevin, he sighed. "I'm sure Michael's fine. We have a deal. I fix the dinner, and he cleans up."

Kevin groaned. "Some deal. Do you realize how many pots and pans you use when you cook? I never understood the term 'scullery maid' until I became your indentured servant."

Arel blinked back. "Was I really that bad?"

"Yes." Kevin and Tim both voiced the affirmative and then laughed.

Arel realized that they were trying to be funny, but there was a pleading undertone to their accusation. "I'm sorry about that."

"Don't pay them any attention," Carol said as she gave Kevin a warning look. "I'm sure the guys were happy to help out."

Peggy quickly shifted the conversation to a more pleasant subject. "Your dinner was delicious, sweetie. Thank you again. And you look wonderful. I think I speak for all of us when I say we're relieved that you're over your—" She paused, looking a little uncertain about how to go on.

Arel quickly managed to find a tone of calm and composure. "My momentary flight into insanity? I keep telling you it was all a misunderstanding."

Peggy blushed. "Just so you're alright now." Her deep brown eyes took on a focused, thoughtful gaze. "You are, aren't you?"

"Why wouldn't I be? I have my health, my family, and I'm taking a vacation."

"A vacation! Really?" Carol asked. "That's great as long as it's not to some mountain in Tibet."

"I'm going to New York. I'll stay at a nice hotel and take in the sights. I'm also meeting an old acquaintance. I hope that meets with everyone's approval." Arel made his announcement sound as lighthearted as possible. His deception seemed to work.

"Perfect," Peggy said as she took Tim's arm. Squeezing it, her face glowed with satisfaction. It was clear that she saw herself as a minor heroine in getting Arel back on track.

"So you're going to take a bite out of the Big Apple?" Tim queried.

"I thought I'd like to explore it a bit," Arel said.

"Just make sure that it doesn't take a bite out of you, Arel. You meet all kinds in a big city like that," Kevin cautioned.

"I'll remember that." Arel tried to maintain a smile when he thought about his upcoming trip. He knew all about something or someone wanting to take a bite out of him. A selfish fiend named William had already exercised that license.

How would William feel if he were on the receiving end of things?

The sound of more pans clanging in the kitchen brought Arel out of his reverie. A pang of guilt followed. He looked at Tim. "Maybe you're right about Michael. Excuse me while I make sure he doesn't over do."

Michael came out of the kitchen before Arel got very far. He was drying his hands on a well-worn apron. "Well, that's the last of the lot," he announced.

Arel gave him a look of surprise. "I was coming in to help you."

Michael's eyes sparkled brightly. "That was very considerate of you, but the kitchen is spotless."

Kevin let out an amused laugh. "You timed that perfectly, Arel."

Twenty-One

Arel wasn't in New York. He stood on a dusty street where cattle ponies were tied to posts. A saloon named Trails End was close-by. His mouth was dry, but he didn't need liquor. His situation called for stronger measures. He was clothed in cowboy attire, complete with checkered shirt, a leather vest, and a .45 colt strapped to his hip. With his hand stationed over his holster, he was ready to settle an old score.

"This is the end of the line, Will!" he yelled out to the man he was facing.

William was wearing a gun and holster too. His face was serene. He even smiled. "Don't be an idiot, Arel. You know you can't win. I'm a better man than you."

Arel went for his gun, but he wasn't fast enough. William's draw was so quick that his hand was a blur. He got off a shot before Arel could take proper aim. The bullet from William's gun hit Arel with such force that he flew backwards and slammed to the ground. Blood poured out of his chest. As he lay dying, he shut his eyes, but he heard Michael calling out to him.

"Arel, wake up! You're having a nightmare."

It took a moment for Arel to come awake. When he did, his chest hurt. For a moment he wondered if his heart was physically acting up again. "What a hell of a dream," he moaned. "I couldn't sleep, so I caught the end of an old western movie on TV late last night. It must have triggered my nightmare."

Michael stepped back, giving Arel time to calm himself. "You're probably still tired, but there's a young man waiting to see you in the living room."

Arel made himself sit up enough to get a look at the clock on his bedside stand. He couldn't believe it was already eleven. His previous training schedule was a thing of the past, especially when he was falling asleep at dawn. "A young man? Who?"

"His name is Carey, and he says that he knows you."

"Never heard of him. He's probably a kid selling magazines." Arel started to do a neck roll and froze. "Dammit, my neck is stiff as hell." He'd been awake for less than a minute, and he was already in a bad mood. But he gave himself some slack. He'd just been shot through the heart by the man he thought he could better. He eyed Michael without moving his neck. The angel was the only one he dared to complain to with his friends watching him so carefully. "I guess this is going to be another one of those trying days."

Michael motioned for him to stand up. "You've been in quite a state since you got that letter from William."

Arel carefully inched out of bed and winced when his neck caught again. "Damn that hurts! Must be a nerve."

Michael reached out for Arel's shoulders and began to massage them. "What about a little assistance with the situation? I have some friends in mind who could help you to prepare for your meeting with William."

"More of your kind? What can they do?"

"We know more about the ways of humans than you might think. Let them surprise you."

The thought of a surprise made his tension escalate. "Ow! Easy does it, Michael. You're not massaging a heavyweight like Kevin."

"Sorry, I thought I was being careful."

"You don't know your own strength."

"Try to relax."

"How? Do you know that I hardly slept all night? When I did fall asleep, I had horrible dreams." He tried another neck roll. This time he succeeded in completing the circular movement. "Anyway, getting back to this person who wants to see me, tell him I don't need more magazines and send him on his way."

"I don't think he's selling anything, but he does seem sincere. It might be important for you to talk to him."

"Fine, like I don't have enough on my mind." He walked over to the closet, slid back the doors, and inspected his wardrobe. Each shirt and every pair of slacks was perfectly hung and organized according to color. The arrangement usually offered a bit of comfort.

At least a part of his world was in order. But what difference would an orderly closet make when he met William?

Michael paused on his way to the door. "Are you okay?"

Arel yanked a charcoal button-down from its hanger and felt his shoulders tighten again. "Just let me get dressed. We'll talk later."

If his dream was at all prophetic, Arel needed to prepare himself for New York. He'd been thinking strictly in terms of what he'd do to William. He hadn't thought about the possibility that William might be a threat he couldn't handle. He rubbed at his chest, soothing the area where he'd been shot in his dream. That's when his anger kicked in again. Dream or no, William was the one who was going down this time.

But first, I have to get rid of this Carey person.

As Arel walked to the living room, he searched his memory for the name and came up with a big zero. It didn't matter. The only thing he could concentrate on was New York. He was having trouble making Michael see his viewpoint about William, but maybe Michael's friends would propose something valuable that he could use.

These guys better be experts in vampire control.

"Hi again."

A familiar voice interrupted Arel's thoughts when he got to the living room doorway. When he looked up, he was shocked to see the young man from the motorcycle accident. "It's you!" Arel blurted out in surprise. He hadn't expected to ever see the kid again. Now, there was an instant recall of the helpless feeling he'd had at the scene of the accident they shared. Arel's first thought was that the person lying on the ground was dead. Happily, things worked out and now the boy was back. It made him smile as he came forward. "How are you?"

"I'm fine." The boy flushed with embarrassment as if he could read minds. When he spoke, he looked down at the carpet uneasily. "Bet you never thought I'd come here when you gave me your card. But I had to stop in and thank you again. Ever since that night, you've kind of been my hero."

"Really? I didn't—" Arel had to pause when his neck caught again. He frowned reflexively. "It's a nice compliment, but—"

"Don't worry. I'm not here to bug you." The boy avoided eye contact. "I just wanted to stop by and show my appreciation."

Arel held his head at a slight angle to keep it from catching as he gestured for his visitor to stay put. "Wait a minute. Your name is Carey, right?"

Carey shifted his weight. "Yeah, and you're Arel? Anyway that's what your card says."

"Yes, sorry, I forgot to introduce myself." Arel started to smile and winced instead.

"Is something wrong?"

"Arel has a stiff neck," Michael explained as he came over and started to rub Arel's shoulders again.

Arel attempted another smile. "I'm happy that you decided to visit. I didn't know where to find you after the accident. I asked around in the nearby town, but nobody had any information about you."

"I was just passing through the area."

"Where are you from?"

"Here and there," Carey shrugged. "I'm sort of the wandering type. Anyway, your friend said you have a tight schedule so I better get going."

"Oh, you mean this guy?" Arel eased himself out of Michael's massage. "He exaggerates."

Carey started to edge his way towards the foyer. "No, he's right. I don't want to overstay my welcome."

"Please, don't worry about that." Arel studied Carey's attire, noting that the young man's clothes hadn't improved since his motorcycle accident. They were worn and wanting. Physically, Carey appeared even thinner than before and had hardly any color in his face. "What about lunch before you go? I had a dinner party last night and there are lots of leftovers. Do you like fettuccine?"

Carey returned a puzzled frown and laughed. "Fetta-what?"

"It's Italian food."

"Spaghetti is great, but—"

"I insist. You can try out my cooking and let me know what you think."

"Okay, I guess I could stay a little longer," Carey said with another shrug. After a long moment of hesitation, he walked over to Arel and held out his hand. "You sure are a nice guy."

As Arel shook Carey's hand, he grabbed the boy's forearm too, needing to reinforce the meaningful experience they'd shared.

Carey pulled back, cringing.

Arel released Carey's arm at once. "I'm sorry," he said looking down at where Carey's sleeve ended. A bit of discolored skin was showing. "What happened to you?"

Carey averted his eyes as he tugged at his sleeve and tried to cover his wrist. "I guess I'm accident prone. But nobody knows that better than you."

"Yes, things do happen." But Arel wasn't buying the accident excuse. After growing up with an alcoholic father, he suspected that Carey was covering up more than his discolored arm. He also knew that he had to be careful if Carey was trying to hide something. The boy's eyes were already shifty as if he was ready to bolt. "Anyway, I promised you lunch. And there's dessert too. Do you like cake and ice cream?"

Carey hesitated as a slow grin brightened his young face. "I am a sucker for sweets."

"Then follow me to the kitchen, and I'll get those leftovers out."

Thirty minutes later, Carey had wolfed down his lunch and then enjoyed seconds of the fettuccine, heavily buttered Italian bread, and a large salad. While he was eating, he opened up a little to Arel, explaining how much he loved his bike and adventure. He smiled a lot when he talked about his dreams. His youthful ideas of exploring new places and "seeing the world" were delivered in a hopeful tone.

While Carey talked, Arel found himself nodding, but he had reservations about what Carey's future would bring. Dreams and reality were two very different things, especially if Carey came from an abusive home. While Carey was having his ice cream and cake, Arel excused himself to talk to Michael. "We'll be right back," he said as he ushered Michael to a hall bedroom. Once he shut the door and was sure they wouldn't be overheard, he gave Michael an inquiring frown. "Give me the scoop? What happened to Carey? Has someone been abusing him?"

Michael hedged. "It's not a matter that I feel I can talk about. He's entitled to his privacy."

"Fine, but you have to agree that his arm is hurting, right?"

"Right."

"Well, I want you to help him. He needs to know that somebody cares about him, and not just when he's had an accident. He might leave this house and never come back. If that happens at least he'll know people can be there for him. It'll provide him with a better foundation about life."

"You're very passionate about this."

"Yes, I've been alone. A friend can be like a lifeline that keeps you hanging in there." As soon as Arel said it, he thought about William, and what a guiding force his former friend had been until he turned into Arel's worst enemy. "If I can just steer Carey in the right direction, he'll have a better chance."

"I'll help if I can. But how are you going to convince him to let me do that?"

"I don't know. I'll have to think about it."

Michael's eyes lit up with enthusiasm. "There is another option. You could help him. He already trusts you."

"Me? What can I do?" Arel paused remembering his ability to absorb negative energy.

Michael smiled. "I'm talking about your ability to be a conduit for healing. That's what I am."

"Michael, please, what do I know about such things?"

"You have to trust yourself, or you can take my word for it."

"I don't know that I'm capable of either of those things."

"How about this? Leave it up to Carey. If he decides that he wants some help, he can also decide who helps him."

Arel sighed. "Fine, I can agree to that. I just hope your faith in me means something."

* * *

Arel sat on the sofa, staring at Carey. He tried to choose his words carefully. "So what do you think? You've had an accident, and you hurt your arm. Would you be willing to let Michael try to help you? He has a gift for healing."

Carey was slouched down in the recliner, rubbing his full belly and looking satisfied. "When you say 'gift for healing' are you talking about that hocus pocus stuff you sometimes see in weird movies?"

Arel smiled indulgently. "Some of it is hocus pocus, but I think there's more to it in certain cases."

"Like in your case?" Carey asked with more enthusiasm. "I was pretty banged up after my accident, but with your help, I was fine the next morning."

"Me? I don't know about that—"

"I think you're right, Carey," Michael cut in. "As Arel's friend, I've had the same idea for quite a while."

Carey narrowed his brows thoughtfully. "Well, my arm has been a pain when I'm riding for a while. I guess if Arel is willing, I could give this thing a try."

Arel rubbed his neck and gave Michael a now-you've-done-it look, but Michael was sitting with legs stretched out in front of him, content with himself. "I don't know what to say. I mean I'd love to help if I can—"

"Really, you'd do that for me?" Carey asked as he studied Arel with watchful eyes.

It was a challenge that Arel couldn't turn down. He had to learn to believe in himself if he was going to go up against William. Still, as he stood up, he hesitated for a long moment before he proceeded. He prayed silently that Michael's faith in him was justified as he went over to where Carey was sitting. "Don't expect too much," he said as he pulled over a footstool and took a seat.

Carey ignored the remark and sat up. His gaze ignited as if he was waiting for an exciting movie to begin. "This is kind of fun."

Arel put his hands over Carey's arm and tried to sound enthusiastic too. "Good, I'm glad you feel that way." Suddenly there was a lot on the line. Carey thought of him as a hero. Would he be able to live up to that title? He didn't feel like he had any outstanding abilities. Michael's blood had just the opposite effect on him. His performance in the hospital came to mind. He wanted desperately to help, but that didn't happen. Instead, he passed out. Now, he felt a bout of wooziness taking over again. Was he going to faint in front of Carey?

Michael came over, put a steadying hand on Arel's shoulder, and smiled at Carey. "Arel usually needs a moment to compose himself."

"Of course," Carey chirped back. "But he sure came through for me the first time."

Arel swallowed hard. Michael's hand was helping a little, but the room was closing in fast as he tried to summon some super power that would help Carey. He was also trying to remember the Hippocratic Oath, to do no harm. His most powerful intention was to be more like Michael. Maybe it all worked because there was a flash that sliced through his field of vision. When it hit his brain, everything went laser bright. The world spun out of control. Caught up in a swirling vortex, he ended up in a dream state again. Happily there were no guns involved, just a wispy place that reminded him of those tales about clouds and angels singing. It was a short escapade into the heavenly realms that ended as quickly as it began. When he opened his eyes, he didn't know if he fell asleep or perhaps he fainted. What he did know was that Carey was smiling back at him.

"Thanks, Arel! My arm feels better," Carey announced.

Speechless, Arel leaned back with relief and nearly fell off the footstool. Luckily Michael was still there and stopped him from experiencing a very embarrassing moment. After that, his mind was a blank wasteland unable to rally a single thought.

Carey was still smiling as he stood up. "Thank you for everything, but I have to get going."

Michael became Arel's mouthpiece. "Thank you for stopping by. Let me see you out. In fact, maybe you can show me your bike. It sounds like a nice machine."

"Great," Carey said with fresh eagerness. When he got to the door, he waved. "Good bye, Arel."

"Goodbye." Arel managed to stay upright and get out one triumphant word. To put meaningful sounds together felt almost impossible. But another sensation was clear enough. His body was actually vibrating. As he came back to himself, as his mind started up again and his body calmed down, a question surfaced. Had he really helped Carey this time? He didn't know. He didn't have enough of himself to check Carey's arm. But the young man did leave looking happy. Maybe that was enough.

* * *

Michael's gaze lingered on Carey's motorcycle. It was an aging, seen-better-days model. Still, his fellow angel, Gabriel, alias Carey, had imbued it with a youthful energy that gave its failing chrome just a bit of shine. "Maybe I'll give your bike a try one of these days."

Carey laughed. "I don't think Arel approves of my mode of transportation, but I've had some good times on it."

"You certainly enjoyed yourself the night you had your run in with Arel."

Carey's grin widened. "How many times do I have a chance to be a wild child?"

"You did play the role of a rebellious kid very well. Abrigail and I almost forgot your true identity."

"I had to be your opposite, didn't I?"

"It worked. Arel is totally committed to helping you."

"Yes, I could feel his desire today, but he didn't deliver much when it came to healing my arm."

Michael hedged for a long moment. "Arel's not aware of what he's capable of doing."

Carey leaned in. "For a guy who has the potential to light up a few city blocks, he gave me about twenty watts of power."

Michael's smile deepened. "You're lucky your arm isn't smoking. Arel hasn't worked much with his healing abilities. He's kind of approached it all from the more negative end of things. He has no control when it comes to the energy he can tap into. That's why I wanted him to practice on you. I figured that between us, we could manage a mistake."

"No control? Wow, I guess you're right about my arm. I'm glad he added the 'do no harm' part while he was praying."

"He's in touch with the right values, most of the time."

Carey rubbed the front fender of his bike with part of his t-shirt. "That's a plus."

"Thanks for volunteering to help him learn a little more. He's been rather reluctant when I've tried to get him involved. He says he has more important things to concentrate on."

Carey glanced up. For a moment, his gaze matched Michael's concern. "You mean William and their meeting in New York."

"Yes. There are going to be some challenging times ahead. But for now, I better get back to him."

"Yes, I think Arel zapped his brain a bit. He has a lot of resistance. The energy was there, but he didn't trust himself enough to allow it to flow properly. I think it backed up on him."

"I agree. I'm hoping our friends can help him ease some of his issues."

* * *

Peggy stood at her front window. She was partially obscured behind a curtain as she watched the activity in Arel's driveway. "Tim, come over here," she urged.

Tim put his paper aside, stood up and joined Peggy at her post. "Are you spying on people again?"

"Oh hush. You know you're curious too."

Tim glanced out the window. "Who's Michael talking to?"

"Some skinny kid, but his back is turned. I can't get a good look at his face. I wonder if he's one of Michael's friends."

Tim leaned forward and sighed. "That bike's pretty beat up, but it looks like fun."

Peggy glanced back at him and saw the longing in his eyes, a bit of envy that came from remembering his own days aboard a motorcycle. "You miss your youthful escapades, don't you?"

"I don't think about them much. I have a different life now, a much better one with you and the baby."

"Really? Are you sure?"

"Of course." Tim pulled her away from the window and smiled. "What about you? I go off to work every day. You're home all the time. Is that tough?"

"I love being able to be with Sara, but I guess I get scared. I want to be a good mom, but I think I'm losing touch with who I am."

"You? My unflinching Queen of the Beasts?"

Peggy smiled too as she remembered the title she was given as a bossy, young girl. "When I was that person running around the neighborhood, voicing myself at every turn, I felt a sense of freedom. Now life is moving by too fast, and I can't keep up. When I'm sitting in the rocking chair in the nursery, I don't want anything more than a few extra hours of sleep."

Tim gathered her in close enough to rest his head on hers. "Personally, I feel like everything is just right. And you could never lose touch with who you are. You're too strong. Sara has a wonderful role model."

"I hope so."

"You'll always be the spirited woman I married. That will never change."

Peggy let out a heavy sigh and pulled back. "I wish Kevin said things like that to Carol."

"Why, is something going on with the two of them?"

"I don't know, but Carol can look disappointed when they're together. I don't think Kevin has a clue about how to support her when she's upset."

"He loves her. And he's a great dad."

Peggy stared at the floor and fidgeted. "I know all that, but he needs to talk to Carol more. You know my brother, communication isn't his strong point."

"I thought they were doing great after the baby was born."

"The baby isn't the problem. It's more about Carol feeling lost at times. I think she needs Kevin to be more attentive when she goes off course."

"If you want, I could take him out for beer and talk to him."

"No, he might think that he's not measuring up, like he did before when Carol was pregnant."

"That was a tough situation."

Peggy grimaced. "Yes, and Kevin was a big dope and took his negative feelings out on himself. Then Carol got the wrong idea and left him. I don't want that to happen again. That's why I've kept my mouth shut. Kevin will take everything I say as criticism."

"You never know, they might figure things out."

She reached up and adjusted Tim's shirt collar. "Thank the stars that Arel seems to have a way with both of them."

"I think Arel is trying to forget all of us for a while."

She laughed. "Well, it's understandable. When I think about how strange it must seem to be a bachelor one minute and have babies everywhere the next. On the other hand, he thinks and worries too much when he's left to himself."

Tim leaned down and kissed her forehead. "He's not the only one who worries."

"I know, but sometimes I can't help it. But I'm trying not to jump to conclusions anymore, like thinking that Arel wanted to kill himself. I'm sorry if I even had you convinced about seeing him with a razor in his hand. But Michael insisted that Arel was okay."

"I must have been half-asleep and suggestible. I never found any razor, and I searched every inch of that room."

She laid her head on Tim's chest again. "Thank goodness the whole thing is behind us."

"Yes, it is. Now please, try to have some faith in everybody. If you can do that, I think you'll start feeling like yourself again."

"You're right. I'm going to make a real effort to picture Kevin stepping up to the plate. As for Arel, he'll be on vacation soon, staying at a nice hotel and taking in a Broadway play. So I don't have to think about him."

Twenty-Two

"**O**h great," Arel said in a complaining tone. Kell, his new angelic teacher had arrived. "No disrespect intended, but are you the best that Michael can do?"

Arel had been looking forward to meeting some new kinds of angels, ones who had known battle, angels who were familiar with ways to combat evil. After his recent nightmare about William shooting him through the heart, he needed angels who wore armor and carried flaming swords. Okay, that was asking for too much, but Kell didn't even inspire confidence. In his corporeal form, Kell was more of an angelic slob. He wore baggy, faded sweatpants and a stretched out t-shirt that said, "Give me a job." He wasn't tall or powerfully built. He was average height, with dark hair and black eyes that drifted as he listened to Arel. Michael said that the sorry angel also served as Tim's etheric guardian.

Poor Tim! But at least he isn't aware of angels or what his personal angel looks like.

As Arel settled into his disappointment, Kell's expression remained placid. He finally spoke in a quiet, unassuming voice. "No disrespect intended, but are you in any shape to benefit from what I have to offer?"

Arel immediately assessed himself. "I had a little accident a while back, but all in all, I'm fine."

"Good, than let's begin," Kell said as he stepped forward. As soon as he closed the distance between them, he stuck out a slender finger and gave Arel's chest a tap.

Arel had been so busy thinking about how to get rid of Kell that he wasn't ready for the slight shove. The next moment, he was toppling backwards. Luckily, he was standing in front of the couch and had a soft landing for his floundering body. Kell's action was a shock that immediately bruised his tender ego. "What's that supposed to prove?" he protested.

Kell stepped back again. "If you're going up against an opponent, you have to know your weaknesses and how to overcome them. When you looked at me, you assumed certain things. That mindset made you unaware and unprepared."

"Yes, but you're an angel who has powers. It's easy for you to push people around."

"Don't worry, I'm staying within the normal parameters of the physical form that I'm in. But it was easy to catch you off balance. It was also an effective way to demonstrate my point. Don't make judgments too soon." He paused. "So tell me what you want to accomplish."

"I'm meeting someone. When I do, I have to be able to take charge of the situation."

"Excellent. Playing the victim role isn't in your best interest."

Arel stared back with a bit more optimism. Kell seemed to understand the situation. "So how can you help me?"

Kell gave him the faintest smile. "I can show you how to stop resisting. It's as simple as that. When you stop resisting your opponent, you free yourself from what he's doing."

"I guess that's true, but what if my opponent strikes out like you just did?"

Kell came forward and offered his hand. "Stand up, and I'll show you."

Arel gave Kell a warning look as the angel helped him into a standing position. This time he leaned forward and readied himself for another push.

Kell shook his head. "No, let's reverse roles. This time it's your turn. I want you to really give me all you've got. Don't hold back."

It's seemed like a simple request. "Really? Are you sure? I might be stronger than I look."

"No problem, but let's make safety a priority. I'll stand in front of the couch this time."

After they changed places, Arel shrugged. "I don't want to hurt you." It was true. He had no desire to harm anyone except William.

But the invitation to push around an angel felt kind of good. He had suffered so much trying to deal with Michael's blood. This was an opportunity to release a little of his frustration. Leaning forward again, he reached out with both hands and lunged. At the same instant, Kell moved out of the way. Arel missed his mark and went headlong into the couch again. When he stood up this time, his patience was wearing thin. "Are you enjoying yourself?"

Kell assumed an apologetic stance. "Sorry, but you asked what to do if your opponent strikes out at you. I just gave you a possible solution. Now let's get down to work."

"What kind of work?"

"The easiest kind, doing nothing." Kell walked over to the center of the room and sat down, lotus style, on the floor. "Since your legs are still healing, you can sit in a chair?"

"Hold on. I thought Michael said you're some kind of martial arts master. Aren't you going to show me something practical?"

"I'm familiar with the disciplines, but that's not what you need."

"Listen, Kell, you don't know what William might do if—"

Kell laughed. "It's okay, really. Take a seat."

Arel felt his spirits drop another notch as he obeyed Kell and walked over to his favorite wing back chair. He sat down trying to dispel the feeling that he was wasting time. "Now what?"

"Sit and breathe. That's all there is to it."

"But—"

Kell closed his eyes. "I've taught many others before you. Just sit."

"Why? I already know all about meditation. This is nothing new. I need—"

Kell's hand shot up and cut him off. "Just sit and breathe. Very simple."

Arel's jaw tightened as soon as he shut his eyes. The nightmare was back, playing out the scene where he was shot. William was standing over him, gloating. He opened his eyes and started to get up. "This isn't helping. I can't—"

"Sit!" Kell's order was immediate and sharp. It's deep, resonant tone struck Arel's chest in the same place as William's bullet. Again he felt like he was falling. He grabbed hold of the chair arms to steady himself.

Kell's voice deepened and became more resolute. "William doesn't matter. The past and future don't matter. You only have this moment. In this moment, you can be at peace. There's nothing more."

Still clasping the chair, Arel tried to reason with Kell. "Who cares about this moment? I have to—"

"Sit!"

"Listen, you're an angel, you don't understand my—"

"Sit!"

"Okay, but explain to me why—"

"Sit!"

"I'm not some poodle, Kell. You can't keep telling me to—"

"Sit and breathe, please!"

It was that last word, please, that made Arel pause. When he looked back at Kell, the angel's eyes were open and direct, but they were also filled with concern and compassion. So why was he fighting someone who was there to help him? Kell was one of the good guys, like Michael.

Poor Michael! What a hard time I've given him.

Michael had been devoted for so long and yet Arel still balked repeatedly at most of his suggestions. Kell had a more direct, more adamant approach, but each of them was trying to be his friend. The thought made something in him collapse. His chest felt lighter.

Maybe it's time that I listened.

Arel sat back in his chair and let out a sigh. As he closed his eyes, Kell's words echoed in his mind. "In this moment, you can be at peace."

Could it be that simple?

He wanted to agree with Kell, especially when he realized how tired he was. Lack of sleep and constant worry were taking a toll.

Can I sit here, relax and trust that life is safe? I wonder—

A searing pain hit his gut with the answer.

No! William gave you the same advice as Kell and Michael. He was a friend too, but what happened when you listened to him? Do you remember that night?

Time shifted backwards before Arel could brace himself against the memory that surfaced. The room where he sat faded away. It was replaced by a room in William's London apartment. The room was poorly lit by the flames that leapt about in a fireplace. They were both young men and best friends. William was crouched down in front of him, smiling, and telling him that all would be well.

There was an unspoken exchange of faith and brotherhood between them. Everything that seemed troubling or frightening in Arel's life was magically dissolved in William's pale eyes. For the first time in more than a dozen years, that bruised and broken vessel that Arel called his heart was being nurtured. William's care and devotion was binding up its wounds.

Arel had wanted someone he could trust again ever since his brother's death. He'd felt so small, so diminished by the pain he'd experienced. He'd lost faith in finding his way back to himself. He needed a beacon, a guide who could help him navigate life without the terror that he normally felt. William's compassionate assurances brought his long pilgrimage to a close. William offered new hope that life could be good, that it could offer more than beatings and humiliation. The feeling was so glorious that Arel gave himself to it completely. When William asked for his trust, he surrendered it willingly. His reward was a perfect moment. All was well and good. Fear didn't exist in that moment.

But that moment passed. The one that followed was its opposite. Arel's brief acceptance that goodness and brotherhood existed was followed by one all-encompassing fact. He'd been deceived. William wasn't a light in the storm. He turned into the storm itself. He transformed into a monster, a vampire who wanted Arel's blood.

Arel fought back as William fed on him. He begged William to stop what he was doing, but William was too strong. He wouldn't listen. Finally, as Arel gasped out what felt like his dying breath, William stopped. He cut his own wrist. He forced his blood on Arel. The man kept smiling, saying he was giving Arel the best gift anyone could give another. All the while, Arel knew it was a treacherous lie that William was using as an excuse for his wrong doing.

Arel nearly choked as he swallowed the dark liquid that flowed from William's vein. He was barely able to think about what was happening to him. But as he stared at William's glowing eyes, it was clear that he was looking at a monster. And that monster had cursed him too.

Arel prayed that he wouldn't survive. Yet, he did survive. Only now, his normal world was swept away. He might have known his father's wrath, but it remained an outside force. William's cruel curse, his tainted blood, invaded Arel's body and there was no way to stop its effects.

Every cell in his physical being battled to survive the onslaught, but none were strong enough to survive unscathed. Countless, inner lives screamed out in agony as each one was scalded in the liquid acid of betrayal. The torture seemed unending. Each second became an eternity. The pain only stopped when Arel was completely consumed, when he'd lost himself to the hideous scourge that now lived inside of him.

Afterwards, he lay gasping for breath and loathing the fact that his lungs were still working. He lay in ruins, a shell of seething hatred and resentment that had no power to reverse what William had done.

"Arel, come back!"

As Arel remained half-unconscious in William's flat, a voice called to him from far away. He was too weak to answer it, but it wouldn't stop calling to him. He was exposed and raw, barely able to understand what the voice was saying, but it kept ordering him to obey.

"Arel, open your eyes!"

Finally, he was able to do as he was told. When his vision cleared, Kell was hovering over him. Michael was there too. He tried to speak to them, but nothing worked. Later, he woke up in his bed with Michael keeping watch over him. He was hot with fever, as though his bowels and body were fired by the burning embers of William's fireplace. When he realized his voice had returned, he let his rage have its way. "I hate him, Michael. I hate William with all that I am."

Michael frowned. "You have to let go of that hate, or you won't survive. Your physical vessel is sustained by a positive life force and hate is a powerful impediment."

"After what I just experienced?"

"I'm sorry that the memory was so real."

"How could I have been thrown back there again? Your fellow angel was guiding me. I was listening to Kell as he dispensed his demands. Next thing I know, I'm in a living hell."

"Kell hoped to help you find some measure of peace."

"And I listened to him! I let down my guard and trusted him!"

"Yes, you did, but not with much conviction. You've been like a captain at the helm of a ship. All these years, you've been preparing the crew for a fight. When you relaxed, it was as if the captain let go of the wheel and stepped out for dinner. Your body responded like a battle-ready unit. It released the memory stored in your cells and replayed a long ago confrontation. It proved to you, its captain, that you can't leave the helm."

"My body is always doing what it wants."

"We've talked about this before. Bodies have their own consciousness in some respects. When you store all your fears in their cells, they react."

"I'm sick of the fevers, the fainting spells, and all the other ways my body screws up."

"I agree."

"You do?"

"Yes, that's why I'd like you to work with Carol's angel, Grace."

"What's her specialty? I've already had the equivalent of an angelic dog trainer. Do you know how many times Kell told me to 'sit'? If I hadn't had that nightmare and lost myself in the past, I'd probably be begging for a biscuit right now."

Michael smiled. "I'm glad you haven't lost your sense of humor."

* * *

Kell sat on Arel's lower-level, living area couch. When Michael joined him, he clasped his hands and paused hesitantly. "Arel is quite a volatile soul."

Michael sat down in the wing back chair that Arel had occupied earlier. "At least his fever is going down, and he's recovering."

"He's a bit . . . a bit lacking in any kind of emotional mastery."

Michael sighed. "Mastery? That's a tricky subject. On the other hand, he's come a long way, and he certainly tries his best."

"Trust seems to be a major hurdle. I was able to help a little. He started to respond to the energy I was sending. I hoped that he would calm himself, but he shifted gears so fast. Once his memories were activated, I couldn't do anything to slow things down. He's capable of throwing up some very powerful shields when he should be allowing us to assist."

"I thought I was making progress in that area. I also thought Arel might be able to ease off his anger long enough to see a different way out of his situation."

Kell shrugged. "Maybe you're expecting too much. We both know how strong a human's attachment to a negative state can be."

He paused, letting some small facet of mirth creep in. "Arel really wanted me to be a combative type, with fiery sword and all that stuff. I think he wanted a more imposing type of angel."

Michael laughed. "You do look very impressive when you're in your formal wear."

Kell changed dramatically when he smiled back. His rather plain features came alive, taking on the powerful, animated look of a true heavenly warrior. Chiseled by authority and power, his face glowed with a beautiful light that matched that of a small sun. The next moment, he returned to a more ordinary appearance. "I remember a time when golden armor and a drawn sword could impress even kings. When they saw me, they stopped fighting long enough to think about their deeds. Sometimes they decided to stop destroying each other. But mankind is beyond such simple parlor tricks. I purposely adopted a very humble dress for my interaction with Arel."

"I agree. He doesn't need to be encouraged to take up arms."

"Most definitely not." Kell gave Michael a thoughtful glance. "He's been nursing his rage for a hundred years. How can we help him to let go of that kind of momentum? We don't have much time. He's going to meet William, the object of his wrath, in a few weeks."

"Arel does have hidden strengths. When he uses them, he surprises me."

"But Michael, what if Arel can't see beyond his destructive emotions? What if his worst fears are projected onto William? Can either of them survive that kind of negative encounter?"

"The future is fluid. Let's hope that it doesn't come to that kind of exchange."

There was a long pause before Kell spoke again. When he did, his face was filled with a puzzled frown. "I'm curious about something. I understand that Carol's angel, Grace, is going to try to help Arel. Didn't he have a problem with her a while back?"

Michael hesitated. "Yes, but Arel doesn't remember what happened. When he was first trying to deal with my blood and all the chaos that resulted, he made friends with Carol online in a chat room. After some time, their friendship made him uncomfortable. Instead of simply communicating with her and expressing his feelings, he came up with another idea. He decided to visit her in her sleep by using an out-of-body technique. His intention was innocent. While Carol was dozing, he thought he could give her suggestions about each of them going their separate ways. But nothing went as planned when his astral body appeared in Carol's bedroom. Grace, acting as Carol's guardian angel, had one duty in mind. She was there to protect Carol. By assuming a very frightening, dragon-like form, Grace tried to scare Arel off. She not only succeeded, she inadvertently nearly scared him to death."

"He doesn't have a great track record with us, does he?"

"No, I'm afraid not."

"I know that Grace is very good with helping people understand their relationship to their body. I also understand that Arel doesn't remember his encounter with Grace. However, his body will remember Grace. Won't that be a problem?"

"I think Grace wants to make up for what happened before. Perhaps she can use his body's reactions to her. If Arel feels anxious when Grace visits, it might prompt him to learn better ways to interact with his body. He knows he needs those skills when he goes to New York to meet William."

Twenty-Three

Two days after his session with Kell, Arel was scheduled to meet his second angelic helper. Fortunately, he'd recovered quickly and felt quite normal again. Still, after what he'd experienced with Kell, he was a little nervous as he walked to the foyer to answer the bell. He was surprised by the plump, matronly woman who greeted him. She was dressed in a crisp, linen pant suit, and she could have easily blended in with the ladies at an ice cream social.

"Michael told me that you're Carol's angel," he said as he welcomed her in.

"Yes, I'm Grace." Her voice was cheerful and a bit high pitched. "And Michael's told me all about you too."

He paused expectantly. "Really? What did he say?"

"Oh let's not go into that," she said as she reached out to him and gave him a motherly hug.

He jumped back instinctively, realizing that her close proximity made every muscle in his body tense and his heart pound. In spite of Grace's maternal attitude, an alarm went off in his gut.

Grace gave him a knowing look and quietly continued into the living room. "Sorry, I didn't mean to make you uncomfortable. Are you ready to get started?"

Arel eyed her cautiously as he walked over to a chair located in the furthest corner of the room. When he thought about his sudden uneasy reaction, he reminded himself of why Grace was there. He needed more control of his body. "Thank you for coming," he said trying to appease himself more than Grace. "I appreciate your help."

She sat up and put her shoulders back in a gesture of pride. "I love what I do."

"Isn't that how angels have to feel? It's your job to love everything and everybody."

"We might have a wider range of responses than you imagine," she said giving him a wink.

Arel's heart sped up again. "Sorry, but I'm not interested in your range of responses. Just tell me more about what I can do to control my body." He paused and thought about a particular reaction that he hated, fainting dead away in front of people. "Bodies are a real pain in the—"

"Your body is a divine creation," Grace stated with authority. "It's up to you to help it stay attuned to that blueprint. If you hamper or diminish the body's capacity to work properly, you're responsible for its reactions."

Arel scowled impatiently. "Did Michael tell you the problem I'm facing? It's about more than my body—"

"Yes, I know about William. And I gathered that you need to manage yourself if your meeting with him is going to be successful."

Arel thought about fainting in front of William and cringed. "Fine, let's just get this over with."

"A little enthusiasm on your part would help."

Arel slumped down in his chair and stared into space. "Enthusiasm? I'm afraid that's asking too much."

Grace let out a little huff. "I see we have a lot of work ahead of us. So let's not dally. First of all, I'd like you to pick a part of your body that you want to work with."

"What do you mean?"

"Just do as I say. Choose a part of your physical form that you can connect with."

Arel held up a slightly crooked pinky. "What about this?"

"Perfect, now grasp that finger and hold it firmly. Bring all your attention to it."

Arel let out his own heartier huff, but he obeyed. "Now what?"

Grace stood up, walked over to him and placed her hand over his. "You have to focus. Put some energy into connecting with what's hidden in that physical part of yourself."

Her touch sent a powerful wave of energy through Arel's hand and into his finger. The surge traveled all the way to his gut and immediately ignited a flash of memory. It wasn't about William, but it was so miserable that he cried out. He was being slammed against a wall. He heard his finger crack when he used his hands to protect himself from his father. The images were violent, and it took all his self-control not to whimper like a child.

Grace let go of him. "That's the first part," she explained. "Now we have to clear that energy."

Arel was still reeling, still disengaging from his father's clutches as Grace backed away. It took a moment to come back to the quiet living area he now occupied. His gaze swept over its beautiful paintings and sculptures as he tried to convince himself that he wasn't a small boy anymore. When he finally succeeded, he sat up more attentively. He was curious about what he'd felt. "I had all those memories in my little finger?" His curiosity turned to panic with his next thought. What if he took hold of his brain and focused on what was stored there? He'd be rendered catatonic in an instant.

Obviously able to read his mind, Grace laughed. "Don't be ridiculous."

Arel blinked back. "I'm not. I'm thinking ahead."

"Well stop it. Let's concentrate on your finger. I'm trying to teach you to release the cellular memories that you have stored there. By letting go of them, you can restore the body to its natural state of peace."

"Peace, now? Every time I meet with your kind, I'm reliving earlier miseries."

"You wanted to face this man from your past in an up-to-date and capable manner. Right now, that kind of interaction is impossible if you don't let go of things that make you fearful."

Arel swallowed her advice like a bitter potion. "Okay, what's next?"

"It's all about staying with your body and letting it know it can depend on you. Next you have to learn to view the memory without the emotions. You'll be telling the body that you're in control and that the body is safe now. You'll bring it up to date, so to speak. After that, the body will be willing to let the memory go."

Arel's brow narrowed in concentration. How hard could it be to make his smallest finger release a memory? Five minutes later, he was sweating profusely. No matter how he tried, the pain he felt was melded to his flesh. Finally, he looked up at Grace with annoyance. "Somehow, working with Michael seems easier than working with you or Kell."

"Michael indulges you. He's a little like training wheels on a child's bicycle. I'm teaching you how to be independent."

"Maybe I need some indulging."

Grace gave him a reluctant smile and put her hand on his again, but she didn't activate the memory this time. After the initial sizzle, he felt a light, airy sensation go through his finger, making it feel like he could move it more freely than before.

"Bodies filled with memories that are negative will resist and contract from life," she explained. "You need your body to be your ally, not a handicap. A calm, serene mind and a healthy, happy body will enhance your power, your ability to stay in control in any situation. Now try it again with your hand. Then eventually, you can release all of your painful body memories."

Arel stood up and moved past her. "No, I don't think so."

Grace's bright eyes widened in surprise. "Why would you hold on to that kind of pain? It only serves to remind you of the cruelties of life. You don't need that reminder."

"Maybe I do, not where my father is concerned, but with William, it's different. He pretended to care, to be the brother that I lost. That was just before he cursed me! My body needs to remember that. It needs a healthy dose of fear when it goes up against that kind of cruelty." He turned and glared back at her. "Angels don't understand the concept, Grace, but sometimes we have to fight fire with fire."

Twenty-Four

The shades were drawn in Carol and Kevin's bedroom, leaving the room in relative darkness. Arel sat in a corner with a dim floor lamp nearby. It provided enough light for Arel to be able to read to Carol. She was sick with a stomach flu. Kevin had gone to the drugstore to get some medicine, and he had asked Arel to keep watch in case the baby woke up. Arel was only half way through a short chapter when Carol fell asleep.

Thank goodness I was able to work my magic with an adult.

He seemed to have an ability to calm fussy or sick babies. His small victories in helping them were heartening. Maybe some of Michael's caring nature had rubbed off on him. It was an encouraging thought, especially with his recent failures with Kell and Grace.

Helping Carol fall asleep was especially gratifying. When he first learned of her particular condition, he balked. The idea of staying with someone who could throw up at any moment was a scary prospect. When he cared for Kevin on an earlier occasion, there had been a number of terrible episodes of vomiting. Kevin even missed the commode twice. It was Arel's first introduction to service, and it left a lasting impression when it came to tending people with sick stomachs.

As he watched Carol dozing, he noted how a few wisps of her blonde hair stuck out from under the covers. He knew he cared deeply about her welfare. Of course that was a proven point after being there for her when she was giving birth.

Or at least I tried to be there for her.

Since Carol was sleeping, he got up and started out of the room. He wanted to check on the baby. He was almost to the door when Carol let out a little moan. He peeked back in to see if she was waking up.

Oh hell, not this again.

He hated seeing auras, but Carol's was glowering back at him. Her energy body was normally bright and clear, composed of multi-layered colors. Now it had transformed in some respects, especially around the center of her body. The small storm of angry red and black energy was menacing to observe. It had to do with the stomach bug that she had.

Poor thing. I hope she feels better soon.

He shouldn't have let himself connect with her misery. His own stomach did a momentary lurch. He looked away at once. Compassion was one thing, taking on another person's problem was another. In the past, he'd had some dangerous encounters with other people's energy. His most recent was with Carol when she was in the hospital. His most recent was with Carol when she was in the hospital. He was almost a goner that time.

The thought was followed by another that was more positive. This was a perfect opportunity to learn more control. Surprisingly Kell's instruction to quiet his mind hadn't been dismissed, even after the disaster Arel experienced. However, Arel was working independently, especially after Grace's remark about training wheels. He hoped she knew he was quite capable of helping himself.

The idea of being the captain of his ship was appealing. If he really put some determination behind his self-directed program, he could do just that. He could learn to steer his vessel with a firm and steady hand. When he went to New York and entered enemy waters, he'd be an adept master of his body and emotions. At least that was the plan. Carol's loud groan interrupted his thought and made his stomach lurch again.

Don't go there. It's not your problem.

Yet, he couldn't just leave, could he? On how many occasions had he been hurting as a child? How many times had he suffered all alone? If only someone could have been there to make it better, the world would have been so much brighter.

He looked back at the bed and saw that Carol was fighting the covers. She was trying to escape her wretchedness as it continued to punish her, even in her sleep.

Michael said I have the power to heal. He insisted on it when Carey came to visit. Maybe I can help Carol.

It was a lofty idea. Unfortunately, he hadn't practiced Michael's method. Yes, he had managed to help the babies, but he didn't try to do anything in those cases. He simply loved them with every fiber in his being. Now, he felt confused about what to do. Was love the answer? It didn't seem like enough, or was it? Did he have enough love to help Carol?

His mind rambled on and took a turn off course. If he was so loving, how could he hate William so completely? When he pictured the man, he wanted to kill the fiend. That kind of reaction had nothing to do with being good-intentioned.

In the middle of his inner dialog, Carol moaned and thrashed around in the bed again. He reacted without thought this time. He said the first thing that came to mind. "I'm so sorry that you're suffering, dear friend. I wish I could help you."

His words acted like a trigger, setting off a response in his gut. "Oh no," he moaned too. "I can't let this get out of control!"

He knew what was happening as soon as he felt a tremendous vacuum-like force within his core. The problem was how to stop it. It was another one of those tricks that Michael hadn't had time to teach him. Or maybe Arel refused to make time. He hadn't wanted to face that part of himself. It seemed like an overwhelming task that he didn't have the time to work on.

Now, the autopilot process in his gut was acting on its own, suctioning out the horrid, dark mass around Carol's solar plexus. As her dark energy joined his own energy field, he felt a wave of extreme nausea hit his stomach.

Stop! Don't do this!

He issued orders and tried to reverse what was in motion. Nothing worked. As he battled against himself, Carol's angel, Grace, appeared out of nowhere. Her entrance was so sudden, he jumped. "Grace, you scared me!"

Grace was in her ethereal form with a brilliant glow about her. She even had wings. They were spread out like great rays of the sun. The energy that she projected was that of a caring granny, but the power coming off of her made him think that she could turn into the Terminator if she wanted to.

"What are you doing?" she demanded as she protectively took her place between Arel and her charge.

"I don't know what happened. I was trying to help."

"You were doing a lot more than that," she corrected. "And I thought that you were learning to control yourself. But I will not allow you to do anything that might harm Carol."

"Give me a break." He was amazed at how miserable a case of the stomach flu could be. He'd been immune to normal bugs and viruses for as long as he could remember. Now, he was sure he was turning a nice shade of green.

Grace studied him for a long moment. "Oh my, I don't think you did yourself any favor."

He couldn't reply. His hand was clasped across his mouth. He was headed for the bathroom when he heard Kevin's car pulling into the garage.

Oh, thank heavens, I can go home and be sick.

He barely waved at Kevin when the young man came through the door. On his way out, he delivered a brief apology as they passed each other. "Sorry, I have to go."

He managed to hold off the inevitable until he was safely back in his house. He practically flew down the lower level stairs. He ran from the entrance to the bathroom. Once there, he went down on his knees. As he clung to the toilet, he thought about Kevin's previous bout of flu and knew why people called the bathroom fixture a porcelain god. He was ready to worship the damn unit if it would allow him to rid himself of the bile rising up in his throat, if it would accept his offering of the nauseating stuff in his stomach.

As he waited to vomit, as his stomach churned and his head ached, he realized he was bonded with the ills of humanity again. It was horrible to admit, but his former vampire condition had had its perks. Never once had he needed the cold surface of a toilet to soothe his brow.

Michael appeared in the doorway. "You don't eat, remember? You don't have anything in your stomach to throw up."

He panted out a response. "Then how can I feel like this?"

Michael put out a hand to help him up. "It's all about energy."

He used the angel's offering to pull himself up to a standing position. Swaying with misery and a splitting headache, he got out a pleading sentence. "Explain what you mean."

Michael smiled and put his hand to Arel's stomach. "Goodness, your shields are down for a change. I think you'll be better soon."

As Arel felt the angel's energy quiet his stomach, he knew a master captain was at the helm. "I guess I need training wheels after all."

Michael stepped back. "What do you mean?"

"I don't know what happened. I wanted to do what you do, but of course it didn't work out like I planned."

"So you took on the energy behind Carol's virus."

"Poor woman, I'm grateful that I don't normally experience this sort of thing." He stumbled over to the sink and splashed his face with cold water. "I guess Grace would think it was cheating to have you bailing me out, but I'm grateful."

"Remember that you always have that option. All humans can ask for help, and it'll be given gladly."

Arel grabbed a towel. "Speaking of Grace, I swear, she looked at me like I was still a vampire."

Michael began to laugh as he walked towards the living area.

Arel trailed after him, dabbing his face with the towel. After Michael's kindly healing help, he tried to hide the fact that Michael's sense of humor never seemed appropriate. Maybe Michael was right when he said that Arel always missed the point. Still, his curiosity was peaked. "What's funny about the way Grace sees me?"

Michael took a seat in the library area and gazed back thoughtfully. "In a way, you are still a vampire."

Arel's hands went limp, letting the towel fall to the floor. "No! After all I've been through, you can't tell me something like that."

"Please, let me finish," Michael said, reigning in any sign of levity.

Arel used the wall and furniture to rubber-leg his way to his wing back chair. How could Michael call him a vampire? The word itself was an offense. It was right up there with the word, parasite. And a parasite was a despicable organism that Arel couldn't abide. He kept his eyes on Michael as he fell heavily into the comforting confines of the chair. "Go on, explain yourself."

Michael took his time, clearly not wanting to aggravate the situation. "You're not physically what you were, but psychically you're very capable of draining another person's energy."

Arel blinked back, unappeased. "I know all that, but you never referred to that ability as being a vampire."

"I'm sorry. It's just a word. It's not something you need to dwell on."

"To me, being a vampire means being the lowest of creatures, sucking the blood of helpless victims."

"We both know you're not that kind of vampire."

Arel ran his hand over the smooth leather on the arm of the chair. "Do you know what William said when we were still friends? His view of humanity was that we all feed off of each other's energy. I guess I didn't pay much attention to the concept."

"William was right, but you can be a sort of super-sized version of what he's talking about. That's why Grace looked like she did. She knows what you're capable of doing."

"But I didn't want to hurt Carol. I felt sorry for her."

"And Grace understands that, but as your power grows, you can do things that are detrimental. She broke the connection between the two of you before you could do real harm."

"That's just great. Every time I try to give myself a break, you come up with something that scares the hell out of me."

"You don't have to fear your—"

"What am I, some kind of loose cannon? Tell me all, Michael! Is it safe for me to be with people?"

Michael gave him the hands up gesture to calm down. "Most of the time people naturally shield themselves. In your case, you tend to keep your shields up with the general populace. But in this instance, Carol trusted you and was open to your help. As a proper healer you can allow the light you can channel to help another. The problem happens when you get involved personally and try to take on another's negative energy."

"I guess my feelings did get triggered."

"Be easy on yourself, you're learning."

Arel blinked back with stark, darkened eyes, looking and feeling like an innocent bird of prey that just ingested a poisoned mouse when its only intention was to feed its young. "Dammit, I'll be more careful next time and double up on my own shields."

"There'll come a time when you won't need them. Kell was trying to help you to control your energy field. Once you can do that, you'll know how to use your abilities in ways that are in line with what's best for yourself and for all concerned."

"Sounds like another huge project. I'll use the shields. It's safer all around."

"They do have their down side."

"I know." Arel recalled with dismal clarity the many times that he shielded himself so heavily that he rendered Michael powerless to help him. "When will I get to that place where I don't have to worry about all this stuff that you're trying to teach me? Do you see me ever being what you want me to be?"

"It's not what I want that counts."

"That's not an answer. What is this process that I'm going through? You never explained what—"

"Because I don't know. What I can tell you is that your physical form will be able to channel much more energy or you might say 'power' than would normally be possible."

"So it's my physical form that's different."

"Yes, but when any aspect of a person changes, the other parts have to keep up. The greater the power, the greater the awareness needed to control it. That's your challenge. Your perception of who you are has to keep up with your abilities so that you can use them wisely."

Arel grabbed for his stomach. "That's a horrible responsibility."

"It's also a gift. Believe in yourself, the true you. When you asked for my blood, that's what you wanted. That's where your strength lies."

"I just wanted my life back. I didn't have any grand ideas about who I am."

"Perhaps, but maybe you should give it some thought. The truth is that every human being has a chance at greatness. If they could see themselves as the Creator sees them, they'd be very surprised."

Arel felt his jaw tighten. "I don't have time for the Creator's vision of me. New York is right around the corner."

Twenty-Five

As the days passed, Arel couldn't help himself. He kept thinking about Michael's comment. Supposedly, his body had changed. Yet, when Arel gazed in the mirror, there was no indication of an outward change. His build was still slender and inadequate compared to the impressive bulk of men like Tim and Kevin. Michael had also used the word, 'greatness', in regard to what a person could achieve. Was there anything of that quality that he might discover in himself?

It was pretty impressive to remember being burned at the stake and still be able to forgive the ignorance of my persecutors.

He had also experienced amazing, heavenly visions, but those flights into loftier realities slipped away as quickly as a dream. Michael explained that Arel still had too much fear to really hold on to them permanently. It took control and power to achieve such feats.

That was the problem. The airy stuff that Michael talked about and that Arel experienced in brief moments didn't seem nearly as real as the world that his nemesis, William, inhabited. His one-time friend lived in a very concrete reality, a reality where he simply took what he wanted. William plucked the apple from the tree or dispatched a life with ease. To deal with William, Arel knew that he had to be just as tough.

If he could turn the tables on William, what a twist that would be. If he could use the power that Michael talked about to best the monster at his own game, maybe the man would scurry back to London forever.

It was a wonderful thought, and for an instant, Arel saw himself as a very different type of person. He saw himself as a warrior. Even if he'd always abhorred violence, if he allowed himself a bit of leeway, the feeling that stirred in his bones felt natural. He even smiled.

"I can stand up for what I want. If need be, I can fight for what's right," he said in a loud, assertive voice.

His body seemed to be listening. It immediately hardened with anticipation. Why did he have to always worry about being the nice guy? Nice guys could be fools. They were naïve and allowed people like William to call the shots. Sometimes life called for strength and even force. So why did he insist on being so meek?

When he got into bed and turned off the light, he had a final thought before falling asleep. Maybe his greatness meant being the toughest guy around. It was the only thing some people respected.

* * *

Hovering above a muddy and fouled field, Arel's attention was riveted on the carnage below. The stench of a battle filled his nostrils. His ears were assaulted by the yells of those who fought and the moans of those who were dying. Visually, he was horrified by the hacked-off limbs and the bloodied condition of the felled bodies that littered the ground.

I must be having a nightmare!

He'd had some radical thoughts before bedtime, but he wasn't prepared for a medieval combat zone. His first idea was to control the dream, to wake himself up, but the ferocity he observed drew him in. He couldn't take his eyes off what was happening. It was so real, so striking and shocking in every detail.

The more he focused on the conflict, the more his lens of perception zoomed in. He felt himself getting closer and closer to the action. The battle was far from over. There were still a thousand men and more fighting. Large numbers of foot soldiers and a scattering of knights on horseback were all massed in a grisly struggle.

In the middle of it all, he saw a warrior who stood out. In full battle armor, he sat astride a magnificent, black stallion. With a grim determination, the knight urged the beast on. Maneuvering through the hordes of fighting men and the fallen, man and beast worked as a team. The horse was a courageous comrade, attuned to the will of his

144

master. He was almost as valiant and fierce a fighter as the one who rode on his broad back. Rearing at the mounted enemy, he was striking blows with his powerful forelegs. When chance brought another horse or rider close, he used his teeth to punish the enemy.

Arel had never witnessed such a potent connection between animal and human. He had to wonder what such a union felt like. There was so much strength in both man and horse. Their bond called to him like an intoxicating drug. A deep desire was present in his own gut as he attuned himself to the grand horse as it advanced and to the knight who pressed on obstinately.

The knight himself battled with sword and shield, slowly cutting his way through the ranks of those who opposed him. He was felling the enemy mercilessly as if they were merely wheat in the field.

As Arel watched the knight fight, a cruel energy pulled him into the battle, into the clear knowledge that he wasn't an observer any more. Arel now sat astride the black stallion. Instead of watching the action, it was his arm that was striking the blows. All around him, the faces of men stared back at him. Some were filled with wrath, others with fear. He knew his own face was filled with a controlled rage.

His body was strong and his arm had the strength to wield his sword with little effort. He brought it down on a man's helmet with such might that the metal gave in. It struck bone and beyond. He heard the sound of a man's skull being destroyed, but he didn't pause to notice when the man fell to the ground. He was already looking for the next one who would feel his wrath. His horse, Frick, was also pushing forward with his sixteen hundred pounds of muscle and outrage. His loud, bellowing screams and deep roars added to the terror of those in his path. His breath came in great snorts, and his eyes were bright and wild with purpose.

That purpose was dictated by his master, a knight whose iron will was all-consuming. His power and focus were absolute and untainted. There was no doubt, no sense of weakness. He thought himself a man divinely appointed, bent on defeating any who would not bow to his deity.

After a few minutes, the knight's will was so one-pointed that it swallowed up Arel's scattered thoughts. Its power was absolute, not merging with his will, but blotting it out. In their unholy union, as he was baptized with the name of Cuthbert, Arel lost himself to a force that was pure and brutal.

Numb to the misery around him, his sword felt so natural, so much a part of him, that each swing of its bloody blade was filled with an extension of his fury, his need to silence those who dared to oppose him. Countless men cried out as they fell under his righteous instrument of death, but their screams fell on uncaring ears.

* * *

As the battle drew to a close and night was coming on, Cuthbert knew he was victorious. The field had been reduced to a hundred, perhaps less, and many were running for their lives. As he watched the rout, he realized that he was tired. Frick was tired. In a moment of careless celebration, he shut his eyes and breathed in the sickening smells with a sigh of exhaustion.

The high, pitched shriek of Frick brought him out of his worn state with a jolt. The horse's shriek wasn't a scream to battle, but a scream of pain. His terror was instantly felt by Cuthbert too. Man and rider were tuned into each other completely. Frick's cries of misery breached Cuthbert's thick shield of unfeeling ruthlessness. His fortified heart took a terrible blow when he realized a lance had been driven deep into his fearless steed. Tearing through hide and flesh, it sunk itself deep into the horse's lungs, making him gasp for air.

Cuthbert felt his own breath cut short. He'd had Frick since he was a boy. When he first saw the beautiful colt, Cuthbert knew that his god had given him a gift. They were meant to serve a greater cause as a unit. They learned to fight and grow strong together. Cuthbert knew the soul of this great beast, and it knew his.

Now Cuthbert could feel Frick slipping away from him. The great horse's body was quivering with weakness. But even in the throes of impending death, Frick performed one last service to his master. He held steady long enough to go down on his forelegs, allowing Cuthbert to dismount. But he couldn't hold the position for long. As soon as the knight was clear, the mighty stallion let himself roll over on his side. His breath was heaving and coming slower now.

Cuthbert refused to believe he was losing Frick. Throwing off his helmet, he knelt down at the horse's head, too sick to speak. Frick stared back at him with eyes that held a wild look of shock and pain. His gaze changed for only the slightest instant when he saw his master's face close to him. In that singular moment, they beheld each other with the great love that had always passed between them.

* * *

Bryan, a knight clad in armor and rigid resolve, wasn't far from Cuthbert when he saw the black horse, Frick, go down. It was a blow that struck his heart too, for he knew how much his friend loved his mount. Yet he also knew that Cuthbert was acting foolishly, kneeling by the animal instead of staying aware of the danger around him. It was a fault that Bryan had never witnessed in his friend's unbending nature.

"Cuthbert," he bellowed, "watch out!"

There were still a few of the enemy close by who had also seen the knight lose his mount, seen him distracted by the event. He was an easy target.

Bryan shouted out for help from a fellow comrade, Miles, who was also close by. "Over there!" he yelled as he pushed his lagging horse forward, urging him into a gallop. He quickly closed the distance between himself and his grieving friend. He arrived just in time to drive his sword into the back of a man readying his arm to throw a lance at Cuthbert. Miles arrived a minute later. Together, they formed a defensive alliance around the dying horse and their desolate friend.

* * *

As the day gave way to evening, a heavy cloud cover obliterated the stars and the light. The battlefield lay in darkness as a damp, bitter cold settled over the dead and the ones crying out in pain. Stripped of his armor, Cuthbert started searching for his men, the ones who were stricken but still alive. He refused a torch to light his way. He couldn't let anyone see his sorrow over Frick's death. The heaviness he carried in his heart and body were only for him to know.

Stumbling over the rough, freezing ground, peering at the bodies that lay scattered everywhere, he couldn't stop the emotions that flowed out of him. Every face that stared back at him was seen through a prism of tears. Somehow the stallion's death had torn away the icy veil that usually stood between the battle and his heart. The sounds of men moaning in misery and the foul stench of bowels ripped open added to his grieving state. When the moon broke through the clouds, he was able to see the men more clearly, his own and the enemy's. Most were young and unseasoned, grist for the mill of battle. Some, in their death looked like boys who had been wrenched from their mothers. Others wore masks of horror. They hadn't been prepared to meet their maker on this day. Some of the men on the field were still alive. They were the most frightened, their eyes were pleading for help, despairing that it would never come. Most were too far gone, and Cuthbert knew that they were right to despair.

Occasionally, he stopped to give comfort to those who were dying before moving on. As he examined the spoils of victory, he began to catch the sickness, the hopelessness that surrounded him. All the fuel of adrenaline was gone. He was spent and empty. If Frick were alive, he would have climbed on the horse's broad back and ridden away from it all as he often did after a battle. He'd refresh himself with the clear knowing that what he'd done was correct and true. Now, as he walked among the hundreds who lay like useless chaff on the ground, he felt tied to them, weighed down by their wasted bodies.

The clouds came together, blotting out the light again. He thought about Bryan and Miles. The three of them had always provided friendship and comfort for each other in the worst of times. He called out their names. When he heard one of them answer, he used the sound as a beacon. Forcing his legs to move towards it, he started to run. He'd only gone a few yards, when his foot caught the edge of a body. Falling forward, he came down in a great crash. The surprise of the fall was followed by an unwelcome sensation. Pain, sharp and cutting, filled his chest.

By chance, he had come down on a dagger. Clasped in a dead man's hand, its length was now buried in his breast.

* * *

When Cuthbert opened his eyes, he saw Bryan's face, full of sadness, staring down at him. Miles was kneeling close by. Both of his friends were grief stricken, unable to believe that such a fate could claim their friend. He tried to speak to them, to tell them that it would be alright, but blood welled up in his throat, cutting short his words. It poured out from his mouth. It was choking him.

As the darkness of death stole the faces of friends from his sight, as he felt himself being pulled from cradling arms, Cuthbert knew that he'd fought his last battle.

*　*　*

Arel woke from the dream, struggling to banish the darkness and the battlefield, but it was still so real that he couldn't move. Again, he grabbed at his chest. First, he dreamed of a bullet putting a hole in his chest. Now it felt like a dagger was embedded there. He was sick again, but he knew it had nothing to do with Carol or anyone else. This was misery that came from a life that he lived long ago.

As a crusading knight, I killed just as ruthlessly as William.

It was a shameful thought that he couldn't push away.

Twenty-Six

Arel stood by the shelves in the library area, staring at his collection of old books, books that he once loved. As a young boy, he read about King Arthur and the Knights of the Round Table. Their lives played out in his mind as he imagined their glorious exploits. But now, the idea of being that kind of warrior was repulsive. He'd been on the battlefield. He'd seen the horror of an actual battle the night before. He knew the feel of armor, the stench of open bowels and the sounds of Frick's last gasping breaths. He hadn't simply been dreaming. His experience was too tangible. He was sure he relived a past life, and it left him more depressed than he'd been in a long time.

"Arel, did you want to see me?"

Kell's voice broke into Arel's dismal mood. When he looked over at the doorway, the angel was standing there with hands on hips. He was wearing old sweat pants again, but this time his white t-shirt simply bore a small pair of gold wings.

Arel gestured him over. "Yes, come in, Kell. I want to talk about a few things."

"Does it involve your recent experience as a warrior?" Kell asked. "Michael said you had quite a bad time of it last night."

"That's putting it mildly. I relived a time when I was slaughtering boys who never knew a razor and men who didn't have a chance in hell against my hardened heart and my brutal blade."

"Try not to be so hard on yourself," Kell said. He walked over to the sofa and sat down. "Those were dark times. If you were a knight, you joined much of humanity in a more polarized view of life. Your mind judged everything from a standpoint of right and wrong.

150

With those judgments as your guide, you thought it was okay to kill without mercy. But youʼre not that person anymore."

"Really? Do you know how many times Iʼve thought about killing William?"

"Is that what youʼre planning to do?"

Arelʼs shoulders sagged in defeat. "No, not now, not after what I experienced. Killing anyone is a ghastly act. Thatʼs why I asked you here. I needed to talk to someone about the mess Iʼm facing."

"Shouldnʼt you be having this conversation with Michael?"

"No, I want some straight answers, and I donʼt know if Michael would be forthright enough. Your fellow angel, Grace, told me that Michael indulges me."

Kell smiled. "And you see me as more of a no-nonsense type?"

"Yes, something like that."

"I have a different view of Michael, but fire away. Iʼll do my best to help in any way that I can."

Arel walked over to the wing back chair and sat down. It was time for the truth, but he didnʼt know if he was ready for it. "Did Michael make a really bad mistake when he gave me his blood?"

"What do you mean?"

Arel flinched. "Donʼt give me that. I think you know what I mean. Look at me, Kell. Iʼm a sorry excuse for a human being when it comes down to it. Iʼm angry half the time, or complaining. I refuse most of Michaelʼs suggestions, and then I blame him rather than taking responsibility for myself."

"So thatʼs it? You think Michael didnʼt know what he was doing?"

"I used to believe that angels were more capable in their choices, but maybe I was wrong." He gave Kell a hard, demanding scowl. "Now I want the truth. Tell me why Michael took a chance on me?"

Kellʼs mouth curved upwards slightly. He almost smiled. But the moment passed. Instead, he stood up and walked over to where Arel was sitting. His expression was neither happy nor sad, as if neutrality was his best option. "Let me tell you a little about Michael."

Arel felt his body bracing itself for the worst. "Oh hell, is he some kind of rogue angel? Is he operating outside the guidelines that your kind are supposed to follow?"

Kell stood over him, looking taller than before. His eyes shifted from dark brown to jet black orbs that picked up the light from the lamp. They flickered brightly as he began to speak. His voice was quiet and deep. "Michael is very special."

Arel felt his body go weak, but his mind remained sharp and cutting. Scenarios quickly presented themselves. Had he been tricked again? First there was his brother, promising to be there for him. That never happened. Then there was William, acting like another brother and betraying Arel in the worst kind of way. Now, he was being told that he'd given his last bit of trust to a "special" angel. "How is Michael special?"

Kell pulled back and sighed wistfully. "I don't mean that he's better than the rest of us. We are all part of the Creator's focused energy, but it's what we do with that energy that makes each of us unique. In Michael's case, he's dared to be more courageous than most of us. He's ventured into places where no other angel dared to go, so to speak."

Arel tried to swallow, but couldn't make his throat work. "Is that a good thing?"

Kell's face softened, and he laughed. He leaned over and clasped Arel's shoulders. "Michael is a leader! He's tough. He doesn't give up on anyone. You and he have a lot in common."

Arel's eyes went wide. "How can you compare us? I'm nothing like Michael!"

Kell straightened, gave Arel a wink, and walked back to the couch. He let himself flop down on one of its soft cushions. "This might come as a bit of a surprise, but the two of you have been together for a very long time. If Michael gave you his blood, he knew what he was doing, trust me. He might be courageous, but his courage has always been tempered with wisdom."

Arel sat up straighter and released the arms of the chair, flexing his fingers to work out the stiffness. "So why does he indulge me?"

"He knows what you're up against. He may be tough, but not in the way you might think. He won't ever push you, but he'll never stop supporting you either."

"How are you or Grace different?"

"We don't have the experience that Michael has in certain areas. As I said before, he's out on the frontline. And because of that, he can be wiser at times, and also more allowing. He understands what it takes to be a human being and the challenges each of you face. Believe it or not, some of us aren't as patient as others. We definitely intend on helping you, but our understanding of your plight can be less informed."

"I'll keep that in mind, but I still want to know what you think about me meeting William." Arel studied the rug, noting a small spot that needed attention. Finally, he looked up. "Do you think I'll do okay in New York?"

"My honest opinion?"

"Yes, spit it out."

Kell shrugged. "Maybe you're not brandishing a sword, but when it comes to William, I think you want a battle." His eyes softened a bit. "Change your focus before it's too late."

Twenty-Seven

Arel pushed the baby stroller along at a leisurely pace, enjoying the temperate day. The sun was out most of the time, sailing in and out of an occasional cloud. It added just the right amount of warmth to make the afternoon a pleasant one. As he turned onto Kevin and Carol's tree lined street, he paused. The trees hadn't started to turn yet. Their leaves were still a beautiful, deep green. As fall advanced, that would soon change, just as Arel's world would soon change. He tried not to imagine the worst when it came to his meeting in New York, but Kell had given him a warning about wanting to battle it out with William.

Unfortunately, I think he's right.

At least he was prepared to face his negative attitude. Still, he didn't seem to be making much progress in changing it. He'd been nursing his hatred of William for too long. He couldn't just drop the subject in the few weeks that he had to prepare. It was a failing on his part, but, as Michael explained, to dwell on his shortcomings or any sort of negativity would only make things worse. That was one reason he was grateful to be out with the baby. The air was good for him too.

As he took in a deep, refreshing breath, he thought about Kell's compliment and half-laughed. The angel compared him to Michael, the 'special' angel.

I think Kell's starting to indulge me too.

He pushed the stroller forward again. As he neared the Bailey house, he realized that little Ariel Bailey had fallen asleep. The infant looked like one of the cherubs in a Renaissance painting, complete

154

with round, rosy cheeks. He was a teething, fussy cherub, but the fresh air and motion of the pram had lulled the little boy to dreamland. By the time Arel got to the Bailey's porch, he felt lulled into a better mood too.

"Hello, Carol? We're back," he called out softly. He didn't want to wake the baby as he carefully angled the stroller through the front door.

Carol came out of the kitchen. She greeted him with a wave, but she was wearing that "I'm not happy" face.

"Carol, what is it?" he asked in a whisper. "Did something happen while I was gone?"

She shrugged. "No, it's just—"

The small entrance area seemed to fill up with a sudden gloom as she bent over the carriage and checked on the baby.

Carol's unhappiness hit Arel's gut and gave him a jolt. "Why don't I put the baby in his crib and we can talk."

She shook her head. "No, you might wake him up. If he gets a good hour in, he'll be a happier boy. Let's go into the other room while he's napping."

Arel glanced at the pram and noted how big the child looked in the stroller. He tried to introduce a cheerier note into the conversation. "He may be named after me, but little Ariel definitely takes after his daddy."

Carol huffed out a sigh and started out of the room. "I hope that he isn't like Kevin in every way."

Arel heard the somber tone in her voice as he followed her to the living room. It was going to be one of those sessions he hated. Carol's emotional floodgates were ready to burst. Would he have the counseling resources to save either of them from the raging waters that would follow? He was barely containing his own floodgates.

As she sat down, Carol smiled. "Listen, you're going on vacation soon, I don't want to burden you."

Arel sucked in an easier breath. Those were the words he needed. "Yes, I'm leaving on—"

"But—" Carol called out the word like she was announcing bingo. It was followed by a pause as she clasped the tissue she pulled from her pocket. "But maybe before you go, you can give me a few words of wisdom."

Arel sank back into the sofa, bracing himself for a deluge. When Carol took hold of a tissue and fondled it like a lost friend, things were going to get bad.

Oh hell, I'm in no shape to hand out wisdom. That cookie jar is empty!

Arel rubbed his brow, knowing he had to proceed carefully. In the past, he'd been too direct in how he approached Carol's problems. The wrong question had unleashed all her unhappiness. Until every last drop of misery was vented, she was inconsolable. He wouldn't make that mistake again. "Can I make you a cup of tea?" he asked.

Carol's eyes lifted in admiration. "You're always so sweet. You always try to help." She barely got out the words, and her face reddened with emotion. "Why can't Kevin be like you?" There was a choking sound to her voice.

Arel stifled his next breath, but firmed up his tone. It seemed the floodgates had a hair trigger. "Carol, I bet you haven't had lunch. Let me make you some of your favorite soup."

"You really are so considerate!" Carol looked at him with grateful eyes and burst into tears.

Arel's simple statement, meant to direct the conversation towards a neutral zone, backfired. He'd have to let Carol direct things from there on out. He remained quiet and waited.

Carol managed to explain her plight between sobs. "I've been doing everything I can to handle my feelings. I really have. When Ariel was born and afterwards, I even thought things would be fine, but now—" Her last words came out in a halting shriek of wretchedness.

Arel kept his voice low. "What is it? Tell me."

"I feel so alone! You remember how it was before, when I first got pregnant."

A moment of panic set in, making Arel blurt out his next words. "You're not leaving Kevin, are you?"

"No, of course not, but if I did, he probably wouldn't notice. Kevin is living in his own world."

Arel's eyes darkened with confusion and worry. "I'm sorry," he said as he sat down next to her.

She leaned in with imploring eyes. "You're such a good friend."

Arel instinctively put an arm around her shoulders. "Please, don't cry. It's going to be okay."

Carol fell against him as she continued to sob. "I don't think so!"

Arel held her protectively, searching for the wisdom he was expected to offer. Carol and Kevin didn't always know how to communicate, but he was sure both were committed to the relationship. "Whatever's wrong can be worked out."

Carol was sobbing too loud to hear him, but after a couple of minutes, she pulled away, sniffling. "I'm sorry to be acting like this. It's just that I'm so frustrated."

Arel dived in fully now. There was no reason to hold back. "Kevin acted badly when you got pregnant because he didn't think that he'd measure up as a father. Now he looks happy when he's with the baby. I can't imagine a prouder dad."

Carol tore at her soggy tissue. "I know. I thought we were doing great after Ariel was born. But as time goes on, Kevin is getting more aloof, like he doesn't want to spend time with me. He's wonderful with the baby, but otherwise, he watches TV. I try to get him to talk, but he just mumbles something about how he's had a long day."

Arel retrieved a clean kerchief and handed it to her.

Carol took it and swiped her eyes again. "I don't know what to do." Fresh tears started down her cheeks. "Maybe he's not in love with me anymore."

"No, I don't believe that." He sat back and let his mind work on the facts. Kevin was usually easygoing, but if something was bothering him, the man could get stubborn and refuse to open up. In that respect, Kevin was Carol's opposite.

I think I know what's wrong!

Arel's face brightened as soon as he recalled his vision of himself as a knight. He and Kevin were friends in that lifetime too, but Kevin's name had been Miles. Miles was a restless soul. Adventure and purpose were his focus. The thought of settling down was the last thing he wanted.

Kevin's got some of the same patterns of behavior now.

In his current life, Kevin had remained a bachelor into his thirties. At the same time, he had been very active. He loved sports and anything that allowed him to feel fully engaged. He was definitely action-orientated.

That's why he's hopeless with changing diapers.

Carol didn't see it, but Arel smiled as he reached out for her hand. "Kevin needs an outlet," he said with certainty.

She sat up, flashing moist, alert eyes in his direction. "An outlet? What kind of outlet."

"Carol, my dear, Kevin's problem isn't you or the baby. He's simply one of those men with energy to spare. Now, I bet he doesn't even play racketball with Tim anymore, right?"

Carol nodded. "With the babies and the schedules, they can't find a time that suits them both."

"I know it doesn't seem this way, but underneath his lethargy, Kevin has a need to express himself more actively. That need can be channeled. And I think I know how. I have a martial arts instructor by the name of Kell. I think he might be able to help Kevin, challenge him a bit."

Carol set up and stared back. "Could it be that simple?"

"Kevin has trouble when he's restless, you know that."

Carol's eyes slowly filled with hope. "Then it isn't me?"

"Of course it's not you. But as your friend, I have to tell you that you need to stop constantly thinking that it is."

"I guess you're right. I've always felt that way when things go wrong. You know that."

"Believe me, I understand. We can all be pulled into past behaviors, but maybe you can stop this one from going any further. You're perfectly fine, and Kevin adores you." Arel stood up. "I'll tell you what I'll do. Before I leave, I'll have a little dinner party for you and Kevin. I'll also invite Peggy and Tim. Everyone can meet Kell."

Pausing, Arel thought about Carey. The young man would need someone he could turn to when Arel was in New York. "And I want you to meet someone else. Carey's young, and he could use a friend while I'm on vacation."

Looking relieved, Carol handed back his linen kerchief. "Of course, if he's a friend of yours, I'm sure he's wonderful too."

Twenty-Eight

Arel leaned over his desk, working on bills. He didn't want the lights to be turned off while he was away. He looked up when he heard Michael calling to him from the foyer.

"Arel, your young friend Carey is here," Michael announced. "He's anxious to talk to you."

Over the past couple of weeks Carey had visited a few times. They were welcome interruptions that gave Arel time to get to know him better.

"Coming," he called back. Bills were a distraction, but not a welcome one. Arel walked to the foyer, ready to give Carey a meal and to chat for a while. When he saw Carey, he knew something was wrong. There was a slight grimace on his youthful face. When he shifted his weight, he winced.

"Hi, Arel. I have a little problem."

Arel couldn't help but return a look of annoyance. "Did something happen on that damnable monster you call a motorcycle?" As soon as the words were out of his mouth, he regretted them.

Carey turned a bright red. "I got careless and burned my leg on the bike muffler."

"I'm sorry to hear that, but that bike could be the end of you." Again Arel's critical tone couldn't be stifled. Perhaps he was taking on more of a paternal mode than he intended.

Carey backed away. "I think I came at a bad time. Sorry."

"No, it's okay." Arel rubbed at his brow. "I'm concerned about you. Ever since that night—"

"My leg is no big deal. It's just that I thought you might need some practice with helping people. Remember you told me you were learning the ropes from Michael."

"Arel tries very hard at everything he tackles," Michael chimed in.

"Thanks for that," Arel said, "but it doesn't mean I'm any good at healing a burn." He turned to Carey and saw the disappointment in his eyes. "Oh never mind, just show me your leg."

Carey hesitated long enough to give him an apologetic smile. "Are you sure?"

Arel nodded, trying to remember that elusive quality called patience. "Yes, I'm sure," he said in a softer tone.

Carey was wearing sweat pants that were older and in worse shape than the ones that Kell wore. "I can't wear my jeans. It hurts too much," he said as he exposed his injured leg.

"Bloody hell." Arel cringed as he realized the extent of Carey's burn. A good portion of his calf was involved. The area was raw and oozing. "You might have third-degree burns. You need a doctor's attention."

"I don't want to see a doctor," Carey shot back.

"That's ridiculous. Why are you always so obstinate?"

Carey crossed his arms. "Why are you being so judgmental?"

Arel held his tongue, knowing that the things he'd heard about teenagers were one-hundred-percent correct. Carey's independent nature was always on the surface, ready to challenge any advice he was given.

"Michael, look at the mess this kid's made of his leg." Arel's tone was tinged with frustration that bordered on anger. "Tell him to let me take him to the ER."

Michael examined Carey's leg. "Arel is right, go see a doctor."

Carey quickly covered the burn and turned to leave. "Never mind. I'll be fine. I'm a fast healer."

"Just stop right there, young man," Arel ordered.

Carey returned a wounded look. "Why, so you can yell at me some more?"

Arel sucked in his frustration. "I'm sorry. I want what's best for you."

"I don't think so. You won't even try to help me."

"I would, but—"

"But what?" Carey started for the door again.

"Okay, I'll do what I can, but you have to promise me something."

Carey paused, turned around and stared back with a narrowed gaze. "What's that?"

Arel didn't like the boy's attitude, but what could he do? Carey's leg could get infected or worse. "If I can't help you, promise you'll let me take you to get proper medical attention."

Carey shrugged. "I guess."

Arel hesitated. "You're not lying, are you?"

"I said I would, isn't my word good enough?" Carey's voice was filled with resentment.

"You need more than medical attention. You need to learn some manners."

Carey's scowl deepened. "And you could be nicer, like you were when we met."

A flush of shame made Arel realize he'd forgotten that he was supposed to be the adult, the person who was compassionate and understanding. Instead he was arguing with a person who was clearly in pain and who didn't know any better. "Again, I'm sorry. Please, come over and sit down."

Carey eyed him cautiously as he took a seat in the recliner. "Can we hurry this up a little? I want to get going."

"Okay, okay." Arel pulled over a footstool and sat down across from Carey. He tried to remember what Kell had advised about confrontations. There was something about not letting his emotions rule his behavior. For starters, he had to try to keep his voice calm and directed. "With an injury like yours, I shouldn't be the one doing this. Michael could probably help you."

Carey crossed his arms again. "I don't want Michael's help."

Arel balked at the young man's unrelenting immaturity. "Fine, let's just get on with it," he said hastily. Then he noted Carey's eyes and saw the truth. Underneath the looks and the tough words, Carey was really scared.

He's just a big kid who's in trouble.

Justina's words came to mind. "We're mirrors for each other."

Am I looking at myself? Is all my constant anger at Michael and life a result of still being an emotional kid like Carey?

It was a hard concept to swallow. He'd have to think it over later. But now, he turned his attention to Carey's leg again. His anger slipped away as he inspected the injury. "I really am sorry about your leg."

"Yeah," Carey said stoically.

Arel put his hands on either side of Carey's leg. "Don't worry, I won't make it worse. I won't touch you." But when it came to the actual business of helping, he had to take some calming breaths and try to settle his nerves. When he looked up at Michael, the angel's smile was kind and encouraging. Michael had been coaching him on the mechanics of healing and seemed to have faith in him. He connected with that faith long enough to have a light bulb moment.

Michael is a mirror too! Why haven't I realized that before?

It was a powerful thought that sent his brain spiraling towards the next one. He didn't have to act like an angry juvenile forever. He had angelic blood in his veins. He could tap into the power that Michael used. If he did, he might even be able to help Carey.

Time to prove yourself!

He made sure that his shields were up as he gave himself some mental reminders.

Come on, you're just a channel for the energy. It's the energy itself that will do the work.

As he saw himself opening up to the powerful source of healing that Michael talked about, he started to lose his focus. The room disappeared, there was a swooshing sound in his ears. A moment later, he was standing on a radiant plane. The light was like that of the sun, yet it didn't blind him. Instead, he felt himself merging with it.

* * *

Michael noted that Arel's eyes took on a fluidness that made them shine like golden orbs just before he closed them. A moment later, his energy shifted. It wasn't a small shift, a ruler-sized shift, but one that astounded the angel. "Grab him!" he yelled to Carey as he took hold of Arel's shoulder.

Carey followed suit, putting a firm hand on Arel's other shoulder. His face was no longer that of an unruly adolescent. It was an angel's face, and it was suddenly creased with apprehension and alarm.

"Be prepared—" were the only two words Michael got out when the flash hit. The powerful discharge of energy made the air sizzle and threatened Michael's connection to his etheric body. It took all of his concentration to physically maintain his hold on Arel.

Carey obviously had the same problem as he tried to ground the energy that Arel was channeling. It was bright enough to illuminate the room, but that wasn't all it did. The physical forms of the two angels glowed. As the light began to dim, Michael was left speechless.

Carey was mute too. When he found his tongue, he pointed at Michael. "Your eyes are too bright."

Michael coughed and pointed back. "Yours too."

Carey, being slighter in build and being the recipient of Arel's healing session, automatically patted himself down. "Am I smoking? I feel crisp around the edges." He paused. "What about Arel?"

Michael tried to clear the fuzzy feeling in his brain as he checked on Arel who was now unconscious and spread out on the rug. His chest was moving up and down in a steady, normal manner. "I think we were able to divert most of the blast."

Carey recovered enough to move to Arel's side. "A couple of overloaded circuits, but I think he's basically fine."

"I thought so." Michael gave Carey the once-over and then scanned himself for damage. "He's not the only one who's overloaded. My body has never felt quite like this before."

Carey stood up a little too quickly and swayed back and forth, a seafarer who'd lost his sea legs. "You weren't kidding about the 'no control' part. He went full throttle from what I can tell."

Michael worked his tight jaws into some semblance of normalcy. "I don't know. We might have been spared the worst. I think he called it when he recently asked me about being a loose cannon."

"If he only knew that he could take out William with a 'healing hand'."

Michael agreed. "William would definitely know he'd been touched." He crouched down next to Arel, and waited until Arel's eyes fluttered open. They were slightly crossed.

Arel moaned and tried to focus. "Michael? Is that you?"

"How do you feel?" Michael asked as he put his hand on Arel's brow. "At least you don't have a fever."

"I feel like a grenade went off in my head."

"Give yourself a few moments."

Arel looked around anxiously. "Where's Carey? Is he alright?"

"I am," Carey answered as he came over.

Arel was still blinky. "I think I fainted. I'm sorry."

Carey smiled and pulled up his pants leg. "What do you think?"

Arel half sat up and frowned. "Where's the burn?"

Carey started laughing. "It's gone. You did it. I'm okay."

"No, that can't be. I think you have the wrong person. I don't remember doing anything. Michael is the one—"

Michael shook his head. "No, I'm sure that it wasn't me." From what he could tell, Arel's body would be fine. His own physical form would need a few minutes. His next thought was a tough one. What would Arel do with his powers in New York? It was a question that made him frown.

Twenty-Nine

William strolled through the New York hotel lobby, looking more like a British rock star than a vampire. Fair skinned, blue-eyed and tall, he wore his honey-brown hair long and loose. It complimented his high cheekbones and striking angular features. A black, blousy, designer shirt, opened low on his chest, and tight black jeans added flair to his image. Leaving most of his usual, more conservative wardrobe behind, he'd decided to make his trip to the States a tribute to his younger, wilder days.

He smiled to himself as he reminisced about his first experience in the new world. It had been many, many years ago, and he'd been so young. His passion, when allowed, was wholly unbridled in those days. He had enjoyed life in New York so much that he applied for US citizenship. He had retained dual citizenship ever since.

But his visits to the States weren't all playtime. Even as a young man, he'd had a practical side. He could be a very savvy business man. He'd made many profitable investments. Yet, he hadn't been back to New York for a long time. And the business he wanted to conduct had nothing to do with investments. It involved something much more challenging.

Luckily, I gave myself a couple of days before I meet Arel.

Arel could be a real downer on a good day. On a bad day, the guy could be hell in all its fury.

My god, I better enjoy this grand city while I can.

It was a thought that propelled him into action. Still, as he stepped out of the hotel to join the evening strollers, he knew he'd have to make a few attitude adjustments. If he was going to relive his youthful adventures, he had to let go of his normal lifestyle. He'd

165

been totally self-fulfilled and self-contained for so long that he wasn't used to looking to the outer world for entertainment. He was counting on New York to inspire him otherwise.

As he paused outside the hotel, he began to observe the crowds, letting his eyes feast upon all the possible offerings passing by. When he finally merged with the moving stream of bodies, he got a closeup feel for those who might tempt him to indulge in his old habits. He inhaled deeply and felt an undercurrent of excitement ignite and rush to the surface. Before his trip, he had actively cultivated his old hunger, allowing it to build for weeks. Now, it rippled through every cell in his body. The exquisite sensuousness was a reminder of his past.

As a young man, he might have been overly rash, but he appreciated how perceptive he was, even then. Before he became a vampire, he already understood people, their cruelty, and their stupidity. It was the reason he despised the masses, why it was so easy to transition to being a bloodsucker. But would he want to feast on humanity again? For a moment, he hesitated. To connect with those around him might not be pleasurable or desirable. No matter, he had to test the waters, didn't he?

He glanced around and let his mind open more fully. He let himself adjust to the neediness of the masses around him. It hit him in waves as he sauntered slowly down the avenue. He was surrounded by people who were anxious to get on with their evenings, who wanted to forget their miserable jobs and boring lives. They were looking for something that could satisfy their cravings. That's why they went to bars or even Broadway shows. They thought they wanted an evening out. Yet, beneath their temporary fixes, they were searching for that elusive quality called true happiness. Unfortunately, for the majority, it would always be out of reach.

Yet, they keep searching. Their hunger never goes away.

He breathed in their neediness like the night air, using it to arouse his own desires. But he wasn't looking for anything elusive. He was on vacation and wanted a bit of fun. He came to the right place. Compared to London, New York was more open, more generous in how it expressed itself. He was looking forward to indulging in its generosity.

So many of you and just one of me.

He smiled as he fingered his choker. Small, golden skulls, intertwined with carved, black-bone beads, circled his neck. He rarely wore the piece now, but it had been a favorite item in his youth. People seemed drawn to its fine detail and sinister theme. He found their interest amusing. When it came to actually dying, they didn't seem nearly as fascinated.

He, on the other hand, had spent years being an avid student of death. He prided himself on his ability to predict the way his victims would react to their impending doom. Some were terrified. Some went like lambs to the slaughter, so used to being victims, that they accepted their fate with quiet resignation.

He sighed, reminding himself why he stopped actually killing people.

They're boring. And what a chore it is to take care of the details afterwards.

Having to deal with bodies and making sure that people's deaths weren't traced back to him was too much work. The game beforehand had its perks. He knew how to play with humans, how to exploit their weaknesses and how to bring them down to a place where they all groveled and pleaded. It was a wonderful pastime when he was immature and inwardly raging at the world. But even those activities became tedious. He didn't need to lash out anymore. He had other ways of taking care of his physical and emotional needs. Blood, like fine wine, had its dealers, and his sources knew exactly how to satisfy his discerning tastes. In the past, there was an exaltation that resulted from taking a victim. Now, he was thrilled by a special acquisition at Sotheby's. His home in London was a small gallery of prized artwork.

But New York is a temptress.

He studied the excess of choices around him, hoping for something new to catch his eye, to spark his interest. If it happened, he might have to revert to the old ways. But would the old ways still work? He'd have to find out.

He took long, confident strides across the thoroughfare. It was teeming with vehicles and people. Many passersby seemed compelled to take note of his arresting blue eyes and the way he carried himself. Their interest flickered over his person as he walked by. A particularly attractive young woman stared back at him, flirting with her pouty lips, adding a bit of extra sway to her hips. He let himself enjoy her attentions and kept going.

"Sorry sweetheart," he said under his breath, aware that his good looks and avidly-honed magnetism hadn't gone unnoticed. "Even 'beautiful' gets tiresome when you've been around as long as I have."

But people couldn't help being drawn to his physical allure and that aura of power and superiority he projected. He was a delicious enticement for those lusting for something, or someone, to break the monotonous spell that gripped their every waking moment. Their hearts quickened when he doled out even the tiniest bit of consideration in their direction.

He laughed inwardly, knowing that he could certainly fulfill their needs. He could gratify their lust. He could fill that horrible ache, that blight of despair that twisted their hearts and made them desperate for any kind of attention. He could also dispose of their wills as easily as turning off a light switch. Making them his powerless pawns wasn't hard. But why would he want that? He had no use for humans or their needs. Yes, he did have a few favorites he visited, beautiful women who satisfied his physical lusts now and then. However, they were merely amusements.

But who could give him what he really craved deep down? Who could activate those hidden levels of self that he'd ignored for so long? There was one person who filled the bill. The thought darkened his mood, threatening to snuff out his excitement.

Dammit, William, don't do this to yourself. You're here to enjoy this place.

Surprised at how he let his awareness be so easily diverted, he forced himself back to the moment. There was so much life around him, and he was neglecting it all.

You're in one of the most amazing cities in the world. There has to be something here that you want.

He paused by a building, opening all his senses. He gazed at the flashes of vibrant color and listened to the honking horns. He zeroed in on an island of animated laughter that signaled someone's need to be heard. He inhaled the perfumes that were meant to arouse and seduce. He felt the pulsating bodies that nearly bumped into him, as if they wanted to be taken, wanted him to escort them to some forsaken alley. The world was alive with opportunity. It was there for his taking.

* * *

The sun had been up for hours, but William couldn't sleep. He lay awake in a lush, king-size bed, glancing at the clock as the minutes ticked by. The previous night, with all his expectations about revisiting his past, turned out to be a terrible disappointment. He made every effort to interest himself in several of the city's more promising occupants, but in the end, his experience simply reinforced what he had known for a long time.

Dammit, humanity is just plain dull. I can't be bothered.

With the blinds shut tight and the heavily-lined curtains closed, he lay in the shadowy darkness of his room feeling frustrated with himself. Mind-chatter wasn't his usual way. He knew how to focus, how to direct his thoughts in any direction he wanted. Most of the time, he chose to appreciate the moment and where he was. When he traveled he surrounded himself with the finer things in life. Now he was oblivious to his well-appointed room. Its handcrafted furniture and the spectacular marble bathroom barely mattered. He usually noticed such niceties, but nothing about his physical surroundings could shift his mood.

So what do I really want?

It wasn't a question he usually asked himself. He led a contented life and a busy one. He kept up with the times whether that meant investigating social trends, or delving into science and technology. He loved to travel, and of course he enjoyed finding new pieces of art for his collection.

My life is perfect . . . almost.

The "almost" part brought him to New York. The past few months he'd been thinking about Arel. After all the years of ignoring the fact that his former friend existed, he couldn't put the guy out of his mind.

But why? He's an idiot who despises me.

The statement was direct and unbending, but he noticed that his heart beat faster just thinking about their upcoming meeting. He observed his reaction objectively, maintaining a distance from the vessel in his chest.

Getting up from the plush bed, he stood and stretched his body, working out the tightness in his muscles. He wasn't usually tense, but there was a growing expectancy building up in him. It wasn't like the anticipation he felt when he went out exploring the city. This was a different kind of eagerness.

He walked over to the ornate, beautifully-carved mahogany dresser. Peering into its large, gilded mirror, he let out a snort of dismay.

You still can't help yourself, can you? After all these years, you still can't think about Arel without a touch of fondness. You know all his faults, yet you still give him absolution.

There was a slight flush to his normally pale skin, and he knew that his breathing was shallower than it needed to be.

You're the idiot, William, a total idiot for coming here. Arel's not worth it, and you know it.

The list of reasons why he should be bitter about their relationship was a long one. At the top of the list was the word, "sacrifice." He didn't believe in doing things for a higher purpose, yet he had done just that for Arel. In return, Arel labeled him a bastard and closed the door on their alliance. He cast William out of his life. Still William forgave him, just like he would have to forgive a child that didn't know any better. They were both very young when their lives changed drastically, but William had to be the adult even then.

He thinks I'm the guilty party. That's what's so ironic.

Maybe that was it. Every hundred years or so, he needed a refresher course in what happened when he let another person matter to him. By seeing Arel again, he would remind himself not to get soft, not to let himself care about anyone.

You'll see. He'll still be a self-centered, offensive jerk.

As he moved away from the dresser, he laughed at himself. He knew what was coming. When he met with Arel, he knew that he was willingly throwing himself in front of a bus.

So prepare yourself. When it's over, you'll be cursing yourself for coming here.

Yet, he continued to indulge his feelings. Going back to the bed, he threw himself down on its soft, pillowy surface and allowed his mind to wander. Scenes from the past ran through his mind in a bittersweet pageant. He and Arel had been the closest of friends. William thought he found someone whom he could trust and believe in. He let himself think of Arel as family.

I considered him my brother.

He let out a sigh of disgust, knowing that he was stalling. All his thoughts and feelings were a smokescreen. "Stop with all this silliness and get down to business," he ordered aloud. Sucking in a deep breath, he swept his mind clean of all he'd been contemplating. "You know the real reason that you're here."

His visit had nothing to do with his sentimental emotions about seeing a brother again. Emotions weren't a reason to act. Did an animal get sentimental or nostalgic? Emotions were the body's responses to selected input, nothing more. He didn't believe in a conscience either, not as humanity defined it. But for some strange reason, he could never let go of duty and accountability. They were part of the natural order. Unlike humanity, the animal kingdom was organized and dependable. If a wolf cub was overly aggressive and dangerous to the pack, it was dispatched by the parent. Nature was the one thing he respected, and he lived by its code.

You gave Arel the gift that made him what he is. Now you have to determine if you made a mistake.

Arel had been given a century to straighten himself out. If he was still miserable after all that time, he had to be put down, like any suffering animal.

William scowled at the thought, determined that he'd make the end quick and painless, another gift to Arel.

Or you could surprise me, Arel. Maybe you've grown up and learned how to handle yourself. If so, we'll spend some time exchanging pleasantries. We'll enjoy some laughter after all this time.

The thought of Arel being able to let go and laugh at life seemed like a stretch. Perhaps that was too much to ask. If Arel demonstrated an ability to simply handle life, William would be satisfied.

Thirty

The doorbell was on its second ring as Arel threw down a towel on the kitchen table. "I'm coming!"

Michael glanced up from where he was standing at the stove. "Do you want me to get that?"

"No, keep stirring that pot."

"Arel, sweetie? Are you sure we need five courses?" Peggy called after him as she placed hors d'oeuvres on a serving tray.

Arel paused in the dining room. "Yes, I'm sure. I want this to be a very special evening." He wore his chef's apron and a frown. Five courses was a bit much, but this might be the last dinner party he ever hosted. He needed it to be memorable.

Carol gave Peggy a teasing grin as she ferried silverware to the dining table. "I already asked him that question. You know our Arel. He wants everything to be a five-star experience."

Arel tried to smile back at her, but his face was stuck in worry mode. Carol had come to him in tears the week before. Hopefully the dinner party would provide a solution to her problem. He invited Kell to attend. If Kevin agreed to work with Kell, the young man would have an outlet for his restless spirit.

I hope Kell behaves himself.

The angel was a genius when it came to one-word sentences. But that wasn't what was needed around people who were supposed to be enjoying themselves. He sent out a silent plea and hoped Kell got the message.

Be sociable, Kell. Try to act like a regular person instead of a canine trainer.

Arel's other guest, Carey, seemed reluctant to attend the gathering. Arel had to offer generous portions of encouragement before he had agreed to the invitation. The young man was also hesitant about accepting money to buy suitable clothes. Arel overrode his protests and put a crisp one hundred dollar bill in Carey's palm. On the plus side, they'd had some good conversations after Arel's miracle work on Carey's leg. Arel even managed to introduce Carey to the idea of going back to school.

Of course, he probably won't take my advice. And Kevin might balk at the idea of working with Kell. If Kevin is difficult, Carol will be in tears again.

When the doorbell rang a second time, he massaged his temples, hoping a migraine didn't take hold. He knew his careful plans could fall apart if anybody did the unexpected. "Michael, check the bread in the oven!" He didn't mean to shout, but his loud outburst did help to vent some of his rising anxiety.

"Got it," Michael called back in a relaxed tone. "All is well in the kitchen."

He knew what Michael was actually trying to tell him.

I'm getting worked up again. I have to relax.

A tiny, cheerful thought slipped in as he reached for the door handle.

Tonight Carey will be wearing something decent for a change.

He took another breath, forced himself to smile and opened the door. Unfortunately, he went mute as soon as he saw his guest. For long moments, he didn't move.

Carey had to be the one to offer a greeting. "Hi, Arel. Am I on time?"

Arel found his tongue, but he couldn't answer the question. "Carey . . . holy hell." The rather inappropriate words slipped out before he could censor himself.

Carey smiled. "You look kind of surprised. Did you think I wouldn't come?"

"I hoped that you would, but—,"

Carey's smile widened into a grin. "How do I look? I bought a new shirt like you suggested."

"Yes, I see that."

Instead of a torn t-shirt, Carey was wearing one that looked new enough. That wasn't the problem. It was the shirt's bright, neon-orange color that shocked Arel. The words, "Easy On The Juice, Bro!" were spelled out in bold, black letters on the front. Otherwise,

Carey looked like he always did. With his hair pulled back in a haphazard, ponytail, he had on his usual torn jeans, and old tennis shoes. He was clutching his aging jacket in his hand.

Carey waited for his answer. "Well, what do you think, Arel? Do I look okay?"

"I'm sorry, Carey," Arel gasped. "I didn't realize how little a hundred dollars buys."

Carey sobered. "The bike needed some parts, but I had enough left over for this neat shirt. I know how to shop for bargains."

Arel finally managed a nod. "It's very original."

Michael joined them at the door. "I like your shirt, Carey." He clamped a hand down on Arel's shoulder. "Carey will add some spark to your party, Arel."

Carey gave Michael the thumbs up sign as he pushed past them. "Thanks, the thrift store is great. Arel should try it. He'd save a lot of money."

Arel nodded despondently. "Yes, I'm sure I would."

A voice called out before he could close the door.

"Evening, friend," Kell said as he came up the walk. "In case you didn't notice, there's a beautiful moon tonight."

Arel was stunned a second time. Instead of an overly casual guy in jogging pants and old t-shirt, Kell wore a grey, designer button-down, an expensive, dark sports jacket, and stylish, black trousers. His carefully groomed, shoulder-length hair was shiny and loose. It accentuated his flashing, dark eyes. When he smiled, his charisma was all too apparent. Almost equally shocking was his manner. He spoke to Arel in the friendliest of tones, and his smile was completely genuine.

* * *

Peggy walked into the dining room to help Carol and noticed Arel's guests standing in the living area. She quickly slipped back into the shadows.

Oh, my goodness! Who have we here?

She wore a smirk when she turned to Carol. "Come here," she ordered in a soft whisper.

Carol was busy getting some napkins out of the buffet. She stared up with a blank look on her face. "What is it?"

"Shh!" Peggy held a finger to her lips and waved Carol over. "Come here, quick!"

Doing as she was told, Carol crept over to stand beside Peggy. "Is there a problem?"

Peggy pointed to the living room and stepped back.

Carol smiled as soon as she realized what Peggy was trying to show her. "Wow, are those the guys Arel was telling us about?"

Peggy pulled Carol back and gestured her into the kitchen. "Yes, I think so, but Arel didn't tell us how cute they were."

They took turns peeking around the doorway for another look.

Peggy's face melted into a placid sea of contentment. "I think I've seen the younger one before, but not up close. He looks like a teenage Brad Pitt. He also has kind of a wild look."

Carol giggled. "I like the other one too. Look at his gorgeous, black hair. It makes him look sophisticated and mysterious at the same time."

"I agree. They're both extremely attractive. Of course the younger one has some maturing to do, but watch out world when he hits his stride."

"Spying again, sweetheart?"

Peggy jumped back, clutching her chest, and bumped into the tall, muscular man who was standing over her. "Tim Werner! I thought you were outside in the yard talking to Kevin."

"I wanted to check in and see if you needed something. It's a good thing I did, isn't it?"

"You nearly scared me to death!"

Instead of answering her complaint, Tim gently pushed her aside and glanced into the living room. "Oh, I see what the fuss is all about." He gave Peggy the raised eyebrow look. "Do I have something to worry about?"

Peggy smiled back at the teasing quality in his voice. "Of course not."

"What's going on?" Kevin asked as he joined their group. He peaked over Carol's head to check out the living area. After a moment, he shrugged. "What's the big deal? I assume those guys are friends of Arel's."

Carol let out a disgusted huff. "Kevin Bailey, you're totally oblivious."

Kevin stared back with innocent eyes. "What did I say?"

* * *

Arel returned to the dining table and sat down with a contented smile. "I just checked on the babies. They're both sound asleep."

Peggy reached out and patted his hand. "You're the perfect baby host. Converting that third bedroom into a temporary nursery was very nice of you."

Her statement was followed by a generous round of agreement from the rest of the table's occupants.

"Thanks, everyone," Arel beamed back. After a day of tension and worry about his plans, he was finally starting to relax. Everything was going beautifully. His worries about Kell and Carey faded fast as both the men mingled and became a hit with the group.

Kevin shot Arel a glance and patted his stomach. "And your dinner was great too. I love Italian, and that lasagna was perfect. Way to go."

Carol stiffened. "Yes, Arel, be proud of yourself. I'm sure Kevin's compliment is genuine. If nothing else, he does pay attention to his food."

Kevin smiled agreeably. "I sure do."

Arel's shoulders jerked to attention. Maybe he'd relaxed too soon. Carol's flaring, green eyes had been targeting Kevin all evening, and her remarks were just as sharp whenever she said anything to him.

Kevin, how can you be so unaware of your wife's needs?

Kevin had hardly paid any attention to Carol since they arrived. While Tim was often at Peggy's side, being helpful. Kevin seemed not to notice that he had a beautiful wife with him. It was the perfect behavior to make Carol revert back to feeling unwanted.

Arel knew he had to act quickly. He jumped to his feet, tapping a nearby dish with a spoon. "Attention, everyone. I want to say a couple of things. First of all, I want to thank everyone for coming. And I want to thank Carol, Peggy and Michael for helping out in the kitchen."

"Yes, thank you, guys," Tim said enthusiastically. "I'll have to admit that Kevin and I snuck out the back before Arel could induct us into service."

Arel gave Tim an annoyed look. "So that's what happened to you. But I have to admit, you and Kevin really did put your time in.

And as a sort of thank you, I'd like to give you a gift. My instructor, Kell, is not only a great meditation teacher, but he's—"

"Kell is your teacher?" Kevin asked, cutting in. "We just met him, but he has to be more than a great teacher, he must be a saint if he's working with you. Take it from one who knows."

Kell smiled. "Arel isn't that difficult, once we got over the first few hurdles."

Arel felt his face get warm as everyone laughed good-naturedly. But his embarrassment gave way to concern when he glanced at Carol. She wasn't laughing or even smiling. She was glaring at Kevin after his remark.

Arel held up his hands. "Okay, folks, I get it. I can be a little difficult at times. Now, if I can continue, I have a little gift for Kevin and Tim. Kell is also somewhat of a martial arts expert and has agreed to give you two a half-dozen lessons if you're interested."

Kevin brightened. "Martial arts? I've thought about trying karate when I was in college." He paused and gave Carol a sideways glance. "But I'm pretty busy on the home front. This might not be a good time."

"Sounds rather interesting, Arel," Tim shrugged, "but I don't have a lot of time either."

Arel gave them each a sly smile. "You can all meet here, in the empty storage room behind my downstairs quarters. That way you won't have to travel anywhere."

"Your storage area?" Tim laughed. "It looks great, like the rest of your place, minus the furniture."

"Exactly," Arel nodded. "Kell said it would be perfect."

Carol sat up straighter as she connected with Arel's pleading smile. She turned to Kevin. "Do you think you'd like to try it?"

Kevin put his arm around Carol's shoulders. "Yeah, I guess so. But you haven't looked very happy lately. I know the baby is a lot of work. Maybe I better not."

Carol softened as Kevin pulled her closer. She reached out for his hand. "Of course it's okay to accept Arel's offer." A smile crept in. "I'll have my own Jet Li."

Kevin gave her a look of surprise. "You know who Jet Li is? I had no idea."

Carol gave him an impish look. "There's lots of things you don't know about me."

Arel let out a sigh of relief when he heard her teasing tone. He'd been holding his breath again and welcomed some oxygen. There was hope for a successful evening after all.

Peggy grabbed hold of Tim's arm and pulled him towards her. "What about you, sweetie?"

"Sounds okay," Tim said dispassionately, but when he glanced at Kevin, he had the same expression that boys displayed when they signed up for the high school football team.

Arel ran his hand over the linen table cloth as he contemplated his small victory. He could cross Carol's problem off his list of problems, at least for the time being. However, his musings were cut short when Carey stood up. He'd been very quiet during the dinner. Now everyone looked at him expectantly.

"Did Arel tell you about how he saved my life?" Carey asked with a glowing smile.

The question silenced everyone at the table for a long moment.

"Saved your life?" Peggy repeated. Her eyes traveled from Carey, who was all youth and animation, to Arel, who looked instantly annoyed by the statement. "We knew he had an accident, but he never said anything about being a hero."

Kell smiled too. "How wonderful."

"Tell us all about it," Carol said as she continued to squeeze Kevin's hand.

Carey smiled at her, then directed his eager gaze at Arel. "I had a motorcycle accident out on the highway. I don't remember much about what happened after I got thrown from my bike. I guess I was unconscious for a while. But when I came around, Arel was as white as a sheet, and he was saying, 'Thank god that you're breathing again.'"

Arel sat down dejectedly. Why was Carey bringing up the accident? It was one of the scariest nights of his life. He wanted to forget it ever happened. "It was no big deal, everybody," he insisted. "Carey is exaggerating."

It was Carey's turn to be upset. He blinked back at Arel with surprise and shock. "You don't think saving my life is worth mentioning?"

"That's not what I meant," Arel stammered. "I'm referring to my efforts. I just did what anyone would do in the circumstances."

Carey's eyes widened with pain, like Arel's words were made of stone, and they'd been thrown at him. "So saving me is right up there with taking out the trash, right?" He pushed his chair out from the table and backed up. "It meant a little more than that to me." Throwing his napkin on the table, he glared at Arel. "But I guess I was wrong!"

As everyone at the table watched Carey storm out of the room, Arel was quickly getting to his feet again. He couldn't believe how fast things could escalate out of control. He knew that he often had a quick fuse, but Carey's temperament seemed even more volatile. He went from calm and grateful to insulted and furious in the space of a few moments. Of course, Carey was still so young. And the young man was also very fast on his feet. Arel had to run to keep up with him. "Carey! Where are you going?"

Without turning to answer, Carey's tone was hard, but laced with obvious hurt. "It's plain how you feel about me," he said as he reached the foyer and put his hand on the door knob. "I should never have thought you really cared. I shouldn't have come here in the first place."

Arel rushed over to where Carey stood and grabbed hold of his arm. "I do care!"

"Let go of me!" Carey shouted, trying to pull away. "Don't pretend any more. I'm nothing to you."

Arel froze when he heard the words, 'I'm nothing.' How many times had he thought the same thing as a boy? Cowering under his father's blows, he felt like he didn't matter. Now as he held Carey's arm, he thought about the horrible bruise that he'd seen there.

Still resisting him, Carey was twisting the locked door handle. "Leave me alone. I want to leave."

"Look at me, please," Arel said with a new sense of urgency.

Carey finally turned to face him. "Why?"

Arel paused, his hand trembling on the young man's arm. He was losing Carey all over again, not to an accident but to the blow that he inadvertently visited on his young friend. "You're very important to me. You have to believe that."

"Then why did you make the way you saved me sound so crappy?"

"That's just me being me. It has nothing to do with how you should feel."

"That doesn't make any sense. How can you be my friend and not agree that it was important to save my life?"

179

As they argued, the rest of the dinner party had gathered close. Tim stepped forward. "He has a point, Arel. You were a hero. But if you don't put any value on your efforts, what's Carey supposed to think?"

Arel paused as he began to question his actions on that fateful night of the accident. When he thought that Carey was in danger of dying, he cared deeply. The young man, for whatever reasons, became his only focus. For a few minutes, he knew that he'd have done anything to help him. But afterwards, he didn't think of himself as a hero.

Moving closer, Kevin gave Arel one of his 'you sure put your foot in it this time' smiles. "Sometimes you're a little dumb for such a wise person."

Arel looked back, totally confused. "What am I missing here?"

Kevin shrugged. "You're so afraid to acknowledge that you're a good guy, Arel,"

"Do you really believe that?" Arel asked. He had never thought that he was good. He simply did what he thought was needed or helpful.

Kevin nodded, "Yeah, I do."

"So do I," Tim added.

Arel tried to understand the foreign concept, but then he let it go. Carey's feelings were the only thing that mattered. When his gaze met Carey's, it was filled with an earnest plea. "Saving your life was the most noteworthy thing that I've ever done. I still thank God that I could help. Can you forgive me if I took anything away from that?"

For a moment, Carey stood motionless. Finally, he gave Arel a spontaneous smile. "You were really cool."

Arel let out a gasp of relief. "Yes, absolutely."

Carey laughed. "I was like one of those stunt guys. You know, the way I flew off my bike."

Just remembering the episode made Arel pale. "It was like something out of a movie." Mentally, he added the words, 'a horror movie.' He gestured Carey back towards the dining room. "Do you want me to tell the whole story?"

Carey gave him a sideways glance. His steel-blue eyes pinned Arel with their intense need to be validated. "You won't leave anything out?"

Arel felt his chest tighten. Carey's trusting eyes and his willingness to give life another chance were activating a feeling he wasn't familiar with. Glancing over at Kevin and Tim, the two new fathers, he realized that Carey was becoming the son he'd never had. How could he say 'no' to a gift like that?

* * *

At the end of the evening, as Arel closed the door on the last of the evening's guests, he was glad that Carey remained behind. The young man sat on the sofa finishing off an extra-large piece of peach cobbler. He was happily flicking off the crumbs that were on his shirt.

"I wouldn't do that," Michael corrected as he was passing through. "Arel is very picky about the furniture."

Overhearing his remark, Arel walked into the living room with a forced smile on his face, determined to prove he could be a forgiving type of parent. "Leave Carey alone, Michael. He's our guest."

Giving him a surprised look, Michael stopped for a moment. "But I thought that you told me—"

"Never mind. There are a lot more important things in life than a little upholstery fabric."

Smiling, Carey sat up straighter and held out his plate to Michael. "Hey Michael, could you take this to the kitchen?"

After a quick glance at Arel, Michael took the plate. "Of course."

Carey grinned. "Good job, old buddy."

Arel's smile faded. "Uh, Carey, that's not an appropriate way to talk to Michael."

Carey sat up with a flush of embarrassment. "I guess I'm just so anxious to talk to you." Looking towards the kitchen, he put his hand to his mouth. "Sorry Michael!" Next, he turned back to Arel, still excited. "By the way, your friends are great."

Arel nodded. "I could tell that they really liked you too."

"Yeah, they told me to visit any time. That was nice."

Arel started to sit down on the opposite end of the sofa and paused to collect several crumbs off his seat. "Carey, you know that I'm leaving for New York, right?"

"Yeah, I know." Carey's voice became dull and indifferent as he fidgeted, drumming his fingers on the sofa arm.

Arel glanced up. "Something on your mind?"

Carey instantly gave him a fierce look, like he was taking aim at big game. "Take me with you!"

Arel held up his hands. "Absolutely not!"

"Why? I have family in New York. I could see them."

"Then I'll buy you a plane ticket. You can fly."

Carey's eyes went wide and pleading. "I want to go with you! Besides, you're just going to meet a friend. I could help you drive and get you there faster. Then you can drop me off and go on with your holiday."

Arel rubbed his temples, thinking about his 'friend.' William was a fiend, a scourge on the human race. There was no way he would let Carey anywhere near him. "I'm sorry, but I can't take you with me. I'm driving to New York because I want some time alone to think and enjoy the ride."

Carey frowned. "Okay, if you say so. I'll take my bike."

Arel's headache started up in earnest. He had to hold the line with Carey. "I said I'd fly you there."

"No, thanks," Carey said in a sulky tone. "I just thought we could spend some time together. You almost had me convinced that you might enjoy my company. Stupid idea. Besides I'm like you, I love the open road, flying down the highway on my bike. It'll be fun."

Arel swallowed hard at the thought. "The damn thing is falling apart. You won't get out of the state."

Carey shrugged. "You old folks are so cautious. If it falls apart, I can hitch a ride. I've done it in the past."

"I see," Arel said as they stared at each other. Carey wasn't going to give in. If this was what it was like to have a son, he didn't like it. But he knew he had to be firm. When a person assumed a parental role, he couldn't let the person in his care bully him. "Do what you want," he said as he gave Carey a final uncompromising look. "I'm going to bed. Michael will show you out."

As Arel walked out of the room, he felt shaken about Carey's obstinate plans, but what more could he say?

"Sweet dreams, Arel," Carey called after him.

* * *

Arel's bedroom was a perfect, slightly cool temperature. His bed was comfortable. He was tired after a long day and ready for a restful repose. Sleep should have come quickly, but every time he shut his eyes, he had visions of Carey out on the road alone. There were so many reasons why the kid shouldn't do what he intended to do.

He's reckless. His bike is falling apart, and it'll probably break down in the middle of nowhere. If he starts hitch hiking, he could run into the worst of humans.

Soon the thoughts were escalating into full blown scenarios. He saw himself sitting in a theatre watching a movie called, "So Many Ways To Die." Carey had the starring role, and he was also doing all the stunts. Needless to say, the film didn't have a happy ending.

Still, he couldn't take Carey with him, could he? William would be waiting in New York. He had to protect Carey by keeping him far, far away from his old nemesis.

It was three in the morning when Arel finally fell asleep. Unfortunately, he visited the movies again, this time in his nightmares.

* * *

Michael and Carey watched Arel from the corner of the room. Shedding their corporeal forms, they glowed like the softest of nightlights. They didn't want to be seen if Arel woke up. Michael smiled at Carey. "You played the role of an offended teenager perfectly. I'm constantly amazed at how authentic you can be."

For an instant, Carey's glow escalated way beyond nightlight wattage. "Thanks, it's nice to get some feedback."

"Believe me, Arel gave me plenty of feedback before he went to bed. To him, you're quite the challenge."

"I've been studying young people for a long time. It's not hard to mimic their behavior once you realize that the teen years are all about independence and challenging authority."

Michael watched Arel restlessly thrashing about in his bed. "Do you think you were a little hard on him?"

Carey hesitated briefly. "I had to find a way to strengthen our bond, and insisting on him being a hero did get his attention. He responded even better than I hoped." He smiled. "I wonder if he'll let me call him dad someday."

"I don't think he's quite as ready for parenting as he thinks."

Carey agreed. "That's true, but that's not Arel's biggest problem at the moment."

"You mean William? There wasn't much time to prepare Arel for their meeting."

"His old friend has changed a lot since Arel knew him."

"Yes, I know." Michael moved closer to Arel's bed and noted Arel's tight knit brows. They practically formed a solid line of anxiety. "I was hoping Kell could show Arel how to adopt a bit of emotional detachment."

"Emotional detachment? Are you kidding?"

"I know that's a stretch, but if he takes you with him, you'll have a couple of extra days to help him."

"What do you suggest?"

"He needs to stay as positive as possible."

Carey grinned. "So I should try to lighten him up?"

"Indeed. He also needs to process more of his background with William. I'm hoping that he'll remember our discussions about not being a victim. If he could release some of his anger, things would go a whole lot smoother."

"Michael, please. I think your boy is really stuck when it comes to the idea of betrayal."

"True, and he can also be very stubborn too. No matter what, he might still refuse to take you with him."

As they talked, Arel began to yell in his sleep. "You're going to kill yourself, slow down!"

Carey smiled confidently as he continued to send Arel disastrous scenarios. "Don't worry. He'll take me with him."

Thirty-One

Arel greeted the first day of his journey to New York with a scowl. It deepened as he threw a worn duffel bag into the trunk of his new, deep-blue Mustang coupe. After the last evening's argument with Carey, he woke up worried about what the young man thought about him. He hoped he hadn't driven Carey away by being too adamant about the trip. Now, as the morning progressed, he wasn't worried at all. Carey had been waiting on his doorstep at seven o'clock sharp. The kid was like glue.

"This is going to be fun!" Carey's voice was pure enthusiasm as he climbed into the Mustang's passenger seat. "We'll have a road party."

Arel slammed the trunk down hard. "I can't believe you talked me into letting you come," he grumbled as he came around to the driver side. He got behind the wheel, put on his seatbelt and gave Carey a censuring glance. Carey couldn't see his disapproving face. He was playing with the radio. "Carey? Are you paying any attention to what I'm saying?"

Carey's answer wasn't a verbal one. A blaring explosion of heavy metal filled the small space and blasted Arel out of any kind of composure. He jumped so forcefully, he knew he missed a couple of heartbeats. He gave Carey a fiercer look. "Would you mind? I like to think when I'm driving. If you want music, you can put on one of my stations."

"Sorry." Carey leaned forward, turned off the radio and smiled indulgently. "Did you bring some snacks? How about that leftover lasagna? I don't mind if it's cold."

Arel let out a sigh, trying to find that small bit of patience that could get him through the thought of Carey eating a tomato based dish in his new Mustang. His leather seats were probably safe, but would his floor mat recover if Carey ground in the red sauce with his shoes?

"Arel, did you hear me?" Carey asked in a louder tone.

Grasping the steering wheel, Arel reminded himself of what was important. He had to be the easygoing parent he'd never known. Still, he wanted to be on his way. "You just had breakfast thirty minutes ago, remember? We'll stop somewhere after we're on the road for a couple of hours."

"Bummer," Carey whispered as he reached for the radio dial.

He pushed Carey's hand away. "Let me, I know where the good stations are."

Carey grinned back. "Try 108.2 FM, it's got lots of oldies. They'll probably bring back nice memories from when you were my age."

Arel continued to inhale slowly as he adjusted the radio tuner. "How's this?" he asked, bringing in a classical station.

Carey laughed. "Geez, Arel, I didn't know you were around that long ago."

Arel put on his sunglasses and started the engine. "You have no idea."

* * *

As the Mustang cruised down the interstate, Arel was actually enjoying the drive. The city traffic was behind them, and they were traveling through mostly rural, farming communities. The open scenery was peaceful and calming to his body. The soft music in the background added an element of tranquility. All was going well until Carey turned off the radio, crossed his arms and drilled into him with his grey eyes. He groaned inwardly. "Carey, I can't help it if you're bored."

"Who's bored? I thought we could talk."

"What do you want to talk about?"

"Tell me about this guy who you're going to see. You knew him before you moved to the States, right?"

"I don't want to talk about him." Arel's eyes remained fixed on the road. He was trying to remind himself about maintaining a serene

186

body, but his jaw tightened. "Instead of talking about me, we can continue with our discussion about your education and going to college."

"I'm taking some time off," Carey countered. "I'm tired of school. And why won't you talk about this person you're meeting? What's his name?"

"Fine, his name is William, and he's someone that I knew, period."

"Wow, you're not an open book, are you? So tell me what it's like to grow up in England. I bet it was really exciting."

"I had a mother and father, like everyone else. Other than that, there's not much to tell."

"What were you like when you were my age? Before you got so grumpy?" Carey's voice had a teasing tone to it.

Arel let a small smile replace his serious expression. "I wasn't as talkative as you. I guess I was the quiet type. I liked philosophy and literature. I liked to read."

"And your friend, was he like you?"

"Carey, please."

"What difference is it going to make if you talk about being a friend with somebody?"

Arel glanced over again. Refusing to discuss William was only making Carey more curious. A little reverse psychology seemed called for if he was going to satisfy the young man's inquisitive nature. "In many ways, we were opposites. We did share one quality. I guess we were both loners. We met at a pub near the university we both attended. For some reason, we struck up a conversation."

"Did he like art and stuff?"

"He liked science and studying the natural world."

"And you?"

"I wanted to think there was more to life than the physical. I studied philosophy. William insisted on cold, hard facts."

"It all sounds kind of boring," Carey sighed, but the next moment he sat up straighter and pointed to a road sign. "Hey, can you take the next exit? It's lunchtime."

Arel looked at the clock. "It's ten in the morning." As soon as he announced the time, he blushed a bright red. Carey was rail thin. He probably never got enough to eat. "Never mind, we can stop."

Arel barely had time to pull into a parking lot and turn off the engine before Carey was getting out of the car. "Thanks, Arel," he said, clutching a twenty dollar bill that Arel had given him. When Carey turned and jogged to the diner, there was a lightness to his steps. His attitude was obvious. The young man's life was perfect as long as there was food around.

If only it was that simple.

When Arel was Carey's age, life was a mountain to climb. Just getting through a day was a tremendous effort. As the years passed, and he made his way through university, things didn't improve much. He liked to escape by going to taverns and drinking himself senseless. That's when he first saw William.

Like Carey, William had an appetite too, a voracious appetite. But it wasn't food that made his face bright with desire. William was always hungry for knowledge about what made things tick. He studied the movement of a beetle or the flight of a bird with equal fascination. When Arel got to know William better, he learned that the one aspect of the world that William had no use for was humankind. He despised people. Even the women he slept with were simply an outlet for his lust.

But lucky me! I was the exception to his "people suck" rule. When William saw me that first night in the pub, he studied me with the same interest that he had for a woodland creature.

It was an uncomfortable moment for Arel. He was drinking copious amounts of ale, trying to blot out life. To be scrutinized by William wasn't a welcome gesture. His first response to William was to get angry with him, to warn him off. But William didn't return any animosity. He stared back with curiosity. He treated Arel like some frightened animal, remaining very still as Arel swore at him. It was a very strange encounter, with Arel finally calming down. Afterwards, William kept his distance, quietly drinking and filling in notes in the small journal he had on hand. It would take a couple of more encounters for them to start talking.

When they became friends, Arel was amazed at how at ease William was, especially around women. While Arel was painfully shy, William was more than self-assured in his approach. Women loved his blue eyes and his winning smile. They willingly gave themselves to him when he shepherded them away to dark corners. His charm traveled ahead of him when he arrived at parties. He left the young and uninitiated breathless when he said goodbye. He was also a master manipulator.

He knew all the tricks, everything that the ladies wanted to hear, and I was the bumbling dullard who watched from the sidelines.

It was one of the many issues that they argued about. William said that Arel was ridiculous to think that women weren't interested in him. He insisted that Arel's eyes drew women in with their mysterious, brooding light. "You're a real devil," William once announced. "You tease women with your looks and attitude. Why don't you share yourself a little?"

He thought William was crazy to make such statements. Now, he realized how little he knew about himself in those days. He and William were close in age, but Arel was a complete novice when it came to interacting with the fairer sex.

I must have looked and acted like an older version of Carey.

Their friendship ended when William made Arel a vampire. After that fateful night, he shunned William, refusing to be a part of his appalling downfall.

I've hated him ever since that day.

A tapping noise brought Arel back to the moment. He straightened up and stared through the side window. Carey was on the other side smiling back at him. Arel gave him a weak nod. "Good, you're back."

"Yeah, I am," Carey said in a hesitant tone. "Hey, Arel, roll down your window."

Arel did as he was told. "What is it?"

Carey moved to the side, and a young woman came into view. "I brought someone with me," he said in a cheerful tone.

Arel stared mutely at the girl. She had a pinched face that gaped out from a mass of lovely, auburn hair. She looked too frail and thin to shoulder the backpack that was slung over her shoulder.

"Arel, this is Annabel," Carey explained. "She needs a ride."

The girl could barely manage a meek smile. "If you could take me with you, mister, I'd really appreciate it."

Still maintaining his silence, Arel waved politely at the waif, but he signaled to Carey. "Can I talk to you alone?" he asked as he quickly got out of the car.

"Sure, what's up?" Carey asked.

"We'll be right back," Arel explained as he grabbed Carey's arm and moved him away from the car. "This isn't a good idea. We don't know anything about this girl. She's probably a runaway," he whispered.

Carey's face crumpled into a mask of concern. "But Arel, she's hungry, and if we don't help her, she's going to have to get a ride with who knows. If you don't want to get involved, just give me my stuff. I'll travel with her and try to at least take care of her."

"Dammit, Carey," he moaned back, knowing that the young man would carry out his ultimatum. "You're putting me in an impossible spot here."

Carey simply stared back at him, but he didn't argue.

"Fine," Arel muttered after a long pause. Reaching into his pocket, he pulled out another twenty. "Go get her some food," he ordered. "I'll get her settled in the back seat."

"No, you go," Carey insisted. "I'll stay with her."

It seemed like a better solution. He didn't know this strange girl. Better to let Carey keep her company. "Very well, I'll be back shortly."

* * *

Carey watched Arel walk into the store and turned to his fellow angel. "Welcome aboard, Annabel. Did Michael tell you why he wanted you here?"

Annabel's pale face brightened. "I get the feeling that I'm here to observe and to also adjust to being in a physical form. This is the first time that I've had the chance to be in a body for any length of time."

Carey noted how well she played the lost, young woman. She even dimmed down the sparkle in her eyes to a dazed glimmer when Arel was present. "Great job, so far. It took me a while to get the hang of it."

"You were very convincing when you talked to Arel just now."

He grinned. "Thank you, I'll take that as a compliment."

"Is it hard to make yourself get on Arel's nerves?"

Carey's grin got even wider. "This is between you and me, but I'm actually having fun, especially since it's for his best. He needs a distraction when he gets caught up in his negativity. At the same time, he does need to understand his relationship with William. It's a kind of balancing act, distraction versus helping him to come to grips with himself and his emotional backlog."

Annabel's large, thoughtful eyes filled with unease. "Michael says he's rather unstable."

"If by unstable, you mean totally unpredictable, then you're right. Even before William came into his life again, Arel almost self-destructed a couple of times. And then there are his healing abilities, that's a rather interesting subject. He's working on control, but—" He paused, staring down at his leg with slightly furrowed brows.

Annabel gave him a puzzled look. "What are you trying to tell me?"

"Sorry." He sucked in a breath and smiled again. "Let's just say that at this juncture, it's best that you don't test those abilities."

* * *

As the afternoon hours rolled by, Arel found himself glancing frequently at the rear-view mirror. Carey and his new passenger, Annabel, were definitely enjoying each other's company. Carey was particularly animated. He seemed to love entertaining Annabel with funny stories, jokes, plots from movies and a thousand other bits of meaningless information. Annabel seemed delighted by his recital. The shy wisp of a girl looked too frail to stand upright in a strong wind. Yet she responded with loud, obnoxious laughs every two minutes.

Arel's mind was reeling from her noisy reaction and Carey's constant chatter. The only positive part was that Carey was no longer bugging him. On the other hand, he could forget trying to think about anything. His cognitive abilities shut down after the first hour of listening to his back seat passengers.

Oh, thank goodness.

The interstate exit that he was looking for came into view. He'd made reservations at a very nice motel. Now, the thought of a quiet, private room was right up there with finding out that Santa had whisked William off to the North Pole.

"We're here," he announced as he pulled into the motel parking lot. He had to say it twice to get Carey's attention.

"Sorry, Arel," Carey said as he leaned forward, draping his hands over the passenger seat. "Did you want something?"

Arel quickly opened the center console. After a brief search, he found what he was looking for, a set of car keys. "These are for you," he said as he held them out to Carey.

"For me, really?"

"Yes, and there's something else." He took out his wallet and handed some bills to Carey. "Here's some money for one of those pre-paid cell phones. Buy one tomorrow when we stop for gas."

"Great, but why the keys and phone all of a sudden?"

"Just common sense. We need to be able to reach each other, and if I lock myself out of the car or some other crazy thing, you'll have a spare set."

Carey stared wide-eyed at the keys and the cash.

"Put them in a safe place, just in case," Arel added.

"Whatever you say."

"Now let's get settled in for the night." Arel opened the car door and climbed out. As he stretched out the soreness in his shoulders, he felt some relief about Carey's future, but not his own. What if something fatal happened to him in New York? William wasn't a gun-toting bad guy, like in Arel's dream. But William was a killer who couldn't be trusted. If Arel didn't make it back to Chicago, his car would belong to Carey. The young man would also have some financial security. Arel left a note in the glove compartment. It stated that if Arel had an accident, Carey would get his car and also the money that Arel put in a bank account for the young man.

Thirty-Two

Arel stood in the doorway of his motel room staring vacantly as he watched Carey toss his duffel bag on one of two queen-sized beds.

Carey beamed back at him. "This is great. We're bunking together."

Arel winced. "I don't understand it. I called the motel earlier and reserved an additional room for Annabel." His tone was distant and wounded, but he couldn't help it. Nothing was going right. He walked over to the second bed and sat down heavily. "Now they tell me that they're fully booked."

Carey looked up. "Gosh, I'm sorry. I guess you wanted to be by yourself. If it's a problem, the diner is open all night. I'll just sleep in one of the booths."

Seeing Carey's eyes dim with the thought that he was a burden was enough to shift Arel into a more positive mood. When was he going to stop acting like a selfish child? "Don't be ridiculous. I'm just surprised, that's all. Is Annabel happy with her room?"

"She looked thrilled. I don't think she's ever stayed in a place like this before." Carey's eyes traveled over the spacey interior of the room. "It's the best motel I've ever been in, too. Really classy."

"Yes, it is nice." Arel tried to sound a little more enthusiastic. He had to admit that the room was pleasant. Recently renovated, there were plush sofas and granite table tops. The bath area was beautifully tiled with a natural stone.

"I'm glad you decided to let me come along," Carey said as he threw himself on the bed and bounced. "Yep, traveling with you makes me feel like I'm living the good life. So what do you want to do? After dinner, I'll make sure to come back early. I thought we could play cards. You can teach me poker. Michael gave me a deck to bring along. He says that you're a whiz."

"I don't know about that." Arel got up and grabbed the plastic bucket from one of the tables. "I'm getting a headache. I better go get ice, I might need it later."

Bouncing back off the bed and onto his feet, Carey quickly grabbed the container out of Arel's hand. "I'll do it. I want to be helpful. Don't you know that?"

When Arel looked at Carey's eyes, he could see that the young man didn't feel the weariness that he felt. Carey looked like he was ready to go dancing.

"Yes," he smiled back, unable to resist Carey's youthful passion. "I know you do. I appreciate it."

* * *

It was eleven before Arel could convince Carey to go to sleep. When he finally decided to heed Arel's pleas, he dozed off immediately. They had played cards all evening. Carey's aptitude for poker was surprising. He was already better than Tim or Kevin. Of course, that wasn't saying much. Unlike them, Carey was immediately attuned to the game. He was so good that Arel had to actually pay close attention to his own game. When he won almost all of the hands, he realized that he'd enjoyed showing off a bit. Nevertheless, he was careful to tell Carey how well he did for a first-timer. Now as he listened to the soft, even sound of the young man's breathing, he was ready to get some sleep himself.

He turned off the lamp on the nightstand and stared up at the ceiling. Instead of drifting off, he began to rehash the trip so far. His first thoughts were about his passengers. The two kids, and they really were just that as far as he was concerned, were boisterous but their rowdiness was innocent. Under any other circumstances he could have enjoyed their continuous banter. But the trip wasn't about stories or jokes or music. It was about William.

When we met that last time, it was by accident on a cold, rainy night so long ago.

He didn't want to remember their last meeting, but when he closed his eyes, it felt vivid and real once again.

194

* * *

London's early spring weather was chill and miserable. Arel hunched over as he rushed along the ill-lit streets. With rain coming down in driving sheets, a nearby pub seemed liked a perfect place to stay until the weather let up. Once inside the vestibule, he took off his coat and shook off the worst of the wetness. When he looked up, William was staring back at him from just inside the main part of the tavern.

"Well, well," William said with a sly smile. "Look who it is. I think that you've been avoiding me."

Arel bristled with disgust and started for the door. "We have nothing to say to each other."

William quickly came forward and threw his arm over Arel's shoulders. "Stay a while."

"I said that I'm leaving!"

"Don't be ridiculous. We should chat." William smiled at him, but his tone was laced with annoyance as he half dragged Arel to the back of the establishment. Settling on a quiet spot in the corner, he pushed Arel into one of the chairs. After that, his eyes softened, their blueness going from irritation to indulgence. "You're such a pitiful creature. I should have never wasted my gift on you. But since I have, you owe me. Stay for a while."

Arel couldn't contain his outrage. "Owe you? You ruined my life!"

William blinked back innocently. "What life? You had no life."

"You bastard! How can you act so calm about what I'm going through?"

"You're creating a scene. Sit back before we have a problem," William ordered.

Arel realized William was right. Everyone was staring at them. He sullenly remained in his seat, forced to listen to William make small talk. But he knew what was really going on. William's eyes were focused on the parade of women that passed by their table. It was like a living menu at his disposal, and William was deciding on what he wanted that evening.

Arel grabbed one of William's lapels and tried to pull him closer. "You can't keep doing this. It's wrong. Don't you see that?"

William didn't take his eyes off of the feast in front of him, but he did sigh as he pushed Arel's hand away. "What are you talking about?"

"It's wrong to kill!" Arel voiced the words in a hoarse whisper.

"Why?" William asked the question as blamelessly as a three-year old who'd thrown the cat down the stairs. "A wolf doesn't worry about its needs."

"You're a human being, not an animal."

"Don't ask me to behave like a human being." William's eyes went dark. "Read your history books and learn what human beings are all about. I don't torture and maim. I don't destroy everything that's beautiful in this world."

"No matter what you think about people, you have no right to end their lives."

"Says who? You?"

"It's a basic law. Thou shall not kill."

"That's your law, not mine."

"Don't you feel it at all? Don't you ever feel guilty about what you do?"

William's eyes glowed brighter. His voice was quiet but firm. "No."

For a moment his answer hung in the air like a raised curtain of darkness between them. Then William let it drop, a soulless barrier that separated them. There was no heartfelt pain behind William's killing. When he sucked the warm blood from his victims' helpless bodies, it was done with no shame whatsoever. There were no human values, no godly decrees in him. There was nothing beyond his judgments about those he deemed unfit to inhabit the world.

Arel's eyes narrowed. "No matter what excuses you use, you're wrong."

William leaned in. "Why don't you relax and try to enjoy yourself for once in your life? You're part of this too, you know."

Arel's body went instantly hot, not from the overly warm temperature of the pub, but from the rage that lived in him. Normally, he kept it contained. Now he felt it taking over his body and his mind as his bondage became very clear. He was William's eternal victim. He was the one who drank from the depraved font of the devil and took its blood into his own body. He would always be a carrier of the demonic energy that knew only destruction. He was trapped forever.

"Do you have any idea how much I hate you for what you've done to me?" As Arel spoke, his hatred escalated. If he had a knife he would have thrust it into William's heart then and there. For all his preaching about the sin of taking a life, killing William was his only desire. Closing his fist and clenching his teeth, he tried to hold on to some sense of right and wrong, but he couldn't. It was everything he could do not to spring into action.

William clearly felt his fury, but he reacted slowly and patiently. For a long while, he studied Arel as if he was a flightless bird. "Poor Arel, always the long suffering soul," he said in a rare moment of gravity. "I thought my gift would give you strength, but you're more pathetic than ever."

"At least I'm not a monster!"

William's eyes bore into Arel's like firebrands, burning him with their reproach. "You have no idea about what I've done for you," he said bitterly, as if he touched upon an inner secret that he detested. His tone was sharp and harbored a fierce resentment, but after a moment, the hostility seemed to fade. It was replaced by an amused smile as he sat back. "Now stop behaving like an idiot."

Watching William smile again as he returned his attention to the activity around him, Arel thought he'd go mad. It was incomprehensible that William could be so indifferent to his plight, so able to toss aside the fact that he snatched Arel's life from him. "I'll never forgive you for what you've done." His voice was low and ominous. "Never!"

William glanced at him for only the briefest instant. His face was young and untainted, without a hint of remorse. "Of course you won't." He took hold of his glass and turned it slowly, pensively. "You're the ungrateful bastard, but you can't see that at all. I guess you never will."

William's soft, accusing tone was the last straw for Arel. His life had become a constant, hellish battle. He was forever forced to fight the fiendish impulses that surged through his body, never able to rest or find any peace. Yet William sat there, with his air of disappointment, calling him ungrateful.

He half-stood, his eyes blazing as his wrath reached an intensity that made the world go red. "If I never see you again, it'll be too soon," he stammered, trying to hold himself back, grasping the table so he didn't reach out and try to strangle William. He needed to remove himself from the scene, but he could only pant like a mad dog as he felt his body gather itself up for the kill.

William remained oblivious to Arel's mood, or perhaps he chose to ignore it. Instead, he spun his glass too fast, spilling the liquid. Meanwhile, Arel tried to get his feet under him, tried to manage his body as it shook with anger. When William looked up, he seemed perturbed, as if he was tired of a child being willful. He began to make little shooing gestures as he laughed. "That's right. Run away from big, bad William. Run away and get a grip, before you have a fit."

Arel barely contained his murderous feelings as he exited the table, but he heard William's parting words as he moved through the crowd. "We'll meet again, my friend. I promise you," William called out to him.

Those were the last words that passed between them. They never saw each other after that.

Now, Arel lay in his motel bed, feeling like he revisited London and revisited a mindset bent on killing someone. It made him wonder about the real reason that he dreaded his scheduled meeting. Was he really worried about protecting his new life, or was he afraid that he was still capable of murdering William?

I didn't act on my feelings in the pub. At least that's a plus.

Or was it? Maybe he didn't attempt to kill William because he'd fail at the task. William had been stronger than he was. Arel knew it in his bones.

But if that's changed? If I'm the stronger one now . . . .

Was a part of him like Cuthbert, ready to mow down his old friend on a field of battle? Michael's unadulterated blood was flowing in his veins. Yet it clearly hadn't completely rid him of his dark nature.

Who am I really? Carey called me a hero, but there's a flip side to that title. Am I a villain disguised as a nice guy?

The questions churned over and over in his mind until he was sick of not finding any answers. He returned his focus to William's sins. No matter what, William was a self-proclaimed monster. How many people had he killed? How many had fallen victim to his unforgivable deeds?

Arel realized later that he should have never gone down that path of inquiry. His overactive imagination kicked in with nightmarish images. He began to see red again, but this time he had visions of blood. How much blood had William sucked from his victims? The more he thought about it, the more he felt himself drowning in the appalling scenarios that ran through his mind. His imagination was still running wild with the bloody horror show when he finally fell asleep.

* * *

Peggy woke up yelling and trying to escape her nightmare. Still breathing fast, she sat up. The images from the dream were so vivid.

Tim had heard her cry and quickly turned on the light. "Honey, what's wrong?"

"A nightmare!" she gasped as she locked on to Tim's steady gaze. Seeing him remain so composed helped a little.

Tim sat up too and pulled her close. "It's okay, I'm here."

As he tried to soothe her, she couldn't help but repeat the same phrase over and over. "It was so horrible!"

Tim rocked her gently. "What did you dream?"

"It seemed so real! I've had some really bad nightmares, but never one like this."

Tim held her so close she could hear his heart beating as she clung to his pajama top.

"Can you talk about it?" he asked

"There was so much blood. It was everywhere." She paused and reached for a tissue. "I'm so worried about Arel. He was running, like a person trying to escape a flash flood, but he couldn't escape. The ghastly river was too fast. Soon he was swimming in the awful stuff. He tried to breathe, but he didn't have enough strength. It was too much for him."

"You're right, that was a bad one."

"What if it's more than a nightmare? I feel like Arel is in trouble again, really big trouble."

Tim laughed, then quickly caught himself. "Sorry, but he's on vacation, Peg. You're just a mother hen when it comes to Arel. You're always very protective."

She stared at him, trying to swallow back the fear that had her heart beating at twice its normal rate. "Please Tim, I know in every fiber of my being that it's more than that this time. Arel's face was so twisted in pain."

199

Tim leaned against the headboard and didn't say anything. After a couple of minutes, he let go of her. "I believe you," he said as he threw back the covers.

She watched him get out of bed and go to the closet. "What are you doing?"

"I'm getting dressed and going over to Arel's house. He probably made his New York hotel reservations online. You know how much he loves that computer of his. I can check it and get the information I need."

"But why?" She was suddenly worried that Tim might be in her nightmares next. "Whatever he has himself mixed up with is really scary."

Tim turned and gave her a reassuring smile. "I'll be fine, but if you're right, I have to go to New York. I have to help Arel if he's in trouble."

"But it's the middle of the night. And what about work?"

"I'll take a couple of sick days. And if I get started now, I'll have a better chance of booking a plane ticket for tomorrow."

She pulled the blanket close. "Call Kevin. I don't want you doing this alone."

Thirty-Three

On William's second night in New York, it was three in the morning before he got back to his hotel. As he burst into his room, he didn't think he'd ever done anything as disgusting and vile as what he'd done that night. His only thought was to get in a shower and cleanse away the aftermath. Tearing off his clothes, he was grateful that no blood had stained them. If it had, his three hundred dollar shirt would have gone right in the trash.

"Lord almighty, Arel, even if you are doing okay, I might have to rethink this idea of getting to know you again. If this is your idea of how to live, heaven help us both."

He walked briskly to the bathroom sink and washed his hands three times. Next he brushed his teeth repeatedly. A long soak in the shower finally calmed him down. Still, as he exited the bath, his stomach was queasy. He had to take deep breaths as he put on a robe and made his way to an elegant, Queen Anne wing back chair. Once seated, he found himself staring into space, wondering if he could ever understand the person he came to New York to see.

Arel was a damnable mess from the start. Why did I get involved with him?

In those first days, as they became friends, Arel reminded him of one of the Romantic poets. He had a deeply emotional makeup and a longing for the beautiful in life. That said, Arel didn't have an attachment to nature. He spoke of the stars, but he wasn't one to take long walks in the woods or admire a rose. He was content with works of art and a painted garden in the museum. There was also a good deal of Existential angst in his makeup. He expounded on noble ideas. If Arel had a stage to act on, he would have delivered a soliloquy on virtue. On the other hand, he was shy and introverted

201

with golden eyes that were still anxious from the cruelties of childhood. His winsome face looked drawn and forlorn, like he couldn't trust in the future.

And yet, I let him into my world. No, to be fair, I welcomed him into my world.

He sighed, knowing his own weaknesses and how open he was when he met Arel. Perhaps Arel represented something better to William, something purer and more innocent. Arel wasn't just another grasping, greedy, good-for-nothing like those whom William had known so well in his life.

"And after my gift, he was a poet who took to drinking the blood of rats!"

William spit out the word, rats, like it was a swear word. He was still grimacing at the thought that he had sunk that low too. But he had. Wanting to know Arel's world a little better, what Arel thought and how he handled life, William had decided to try out Arel's feeding practices. It wasn't easy to actually go through with the horrid chore when he faced his meal.

He'd found a prime, home-grown, New York rodent in a filthy back alley. Littered with trash and putrid garbage cans, the setting was an affront in itself. He should have had the sense to turn back then. Instead, he cornered the revolting creature and snatched it from its hiding place. The damnable thing almost bit him before he could kill it.

William's breath came out in a huff as he remembered the struggle he'd had. The large, wild rats of New York seemed immune to his ability to mesmerize his victims. After he succeeded in killing it, he forced himself to act quickly. Slitting its throat, he held its dirty, hairy body to his lips and took the first mouthful of blood. That's when his mind exploded in disgust. He knew he had defiled himself. He tried to spit out what he'd taken in, but it was too late. He'd been too eager to experience what his old friend experienced. When he saw a flea on his hand afterwards, he almost lost it, then and there.

"Never, never have I felt so dirty," he whispered in a seething anger, scratching at his hand, staring at it to make sure the flea hadn't had its way with him.

Oh god, Arel, you have to be insane to feed on rats. I was such a fool to think you could handle what I gave you.

Thirty-Four

Arel's eyelids were at half-mast, trying to avoid the bright stream of sunshine peeking through the drapes. Towards morning, he fell into a more restful sleep. He knew it had something to do with Carey's breathing. It wasn't a snore, but it had a peaceful, deep resonance that helped him return to sleep after his bad dreams. When he stretched out and thought about the coming day, he was ready to go.

Where is Carey?

The bed next to his was empty. He looked around the room and called out anxiously. "Carey?"

"Coming!" Carey called back. A moment later, he came out of the bathroom looking freshly showered. He was dressed, but his hair, still uncombed, was wet. Its normal waviness had been replaced by damp curls that framed his face.

For a moment, Arel thought his fellow traveler would make a good angel if he wasn't so irreverent at times, and so stubborn. "You shouldn't have let me sleep in," he said, looking at the clock. "We're behind schedule."

"You were pretty beat last night."

"I guess I was. But I feel good this morning. We should—"

A light knock on the door cut him off. He glanced at Carey. "That must be Annabel. Tell her that I'll be ready soon. In the meantime, go get a bite to eat. There's money in my wallet."

Carey smiled. "Sounds good to me."

Arel got out of bed, grabbed some clothes from the closet and moved towards the bathroom. He paused and gave Carey a pleading look. "Please get all the snacks you need at the convenience store next door. I need to make it to New York by late afternoon."

Thirty-Five

The last thing Kevin thought he'd be doing that morning was boarding a plane for New York. Tim had arranged everything the night before, but sheer luck made it possible to get tickets at the last minute. Still, Kevin had mixed emotions about their trip. Were the two of them on a wild goose chase? Or were they two guys going to face some dangerous challenge like the heroes of old? While Carol wished them well, Peggy's send-off portended the latter. She got in his face and demanded an oath of gallantry.

"Keep Arel safe!" she insisted as she waved goodbye. "But make sure that you're careful! I want you and Tim back in one piece."

Kevin frowned as he settled back in his window seat and buckled his seat belt. *Why do I let her make me mad?*

His sister had always been resolute and strong, loving the role of being a tomboy when they were kids. Now, at only five-feet in height, she still lived up to her childhood nickname, Peggy Leggy, Queen of the Beasts. Acting as the sovereign ruler of their childhood world, she drafted him into being her personal warrior when she was still in pigtails. It was a dangerous and painful duty for a kid, especially when Peggy incensed bullies who were older and bigger than he was. He wasn't a coward, but he got fed up with the resulting black eyes and Peggy's attitude. She took him for granted instead of thanking him. As he stared out the plane window and thought about New York, the old resentments were making themselves known again. He had no problem helping out Arel, but he did have a problem with his sister telling him what to do.

"Are you okay?" Tim asked.

Kevin knew he was wearing a scowl. "Yeah, sure." What could he say to Tim? His best friend worshipped his sister. "Does Arel really need us? Peggy seems so fired up, but she's always like that once she gets a bee in her bonnet."

"I kind of see her point, Kev. That was really a creepy vision that she had."

"I guess, but—" He leaned over next to Tim's ear and lowered his voice. "What the hell could a river of blood have to do with anything? It doesn't make sense."

Tim rubbed his face with both hands. "I don't know, and I'm too tired to think about it. I've been up since two. Maybe we should forget about the vision and make some plans. Once we're in New York, things could get interesting."

"I hope they're not too interesting."

Tim sighed. "With Arel, you never know."

"When we get to his hotel, do we tell him that we're there?"

Tim straightened in his seat and laid his head back. "Let's wait and see."

"Arel's going to freak if we surprise him."

"Ten to one, he faints," Tim said with a laugh.

Kevin began laughing too. "One minute, Arel's the wise one and the next, he's out flat on the floor in one of his faints. But somehow he draws you in, and before you know it, you're doing stuff you never planned on."

"Like chasing him to New York?" Tim asked. "I hate to admit it, but that was my idea. Sorry you got roped into it."

"Really? It wasn't Peggy?"

"No, she just had the dream. I'm the one who opted to chase after Arel."

Kevin took a deep breath and felt his stomach settle. Hearing that Tim was responsible for their trip changed things. His resentment gave way to the thought of adventure. "Maybe we should think about the positive side of this trip. I can use a couple of days off, can't you?"

Tim laughed. "Listening to Arel moan about us sticking our noses in his business doesn't sound like a vacation."

Kevin crossed his arms and let a tranquil drowsiness take over. "That settles it. We won't let him know we're around."

Tim gave him a nod, looking sleepy too. "Agreed."

* * *

When Kevin walked into the New York hotel where Arel was staying, he knew the idea of a vacation was going to be expensive. His brows were tightly knit when he nudged Tim. "I wonder how much these marble floors and big-ass chandeliers are going to cost us?"

Tim sighed. "Cost isn't going to be a factor if we can't get a room. When I checked last night, they were totally booked."

Kevin patted Tim's shoulder. "You did a great job getting us here. Let me find out if something opened up."

Tim nodded. "It's worth a shot."

Kevin took another look around as they walked up to the reception desk. "Arel has good taste. I'll give him that."

Huge flower arrangements on fancy tables gave the area a bright, cheery atmosphere. Ten minutes later, when the person at the desk told Kevin that there was a last minute cancellation, he learned what good taste did to the wallet. After he paid for a room and was walking to the elevators with Tim, he was suffering from sticker shock.

Tim seemed to understand his blank expression. "We'll split the expense and hope we only have to stay one night."

Kevin tapped the elevator button a couple of more times. "I know we're not telling Arel that we're here, but dammit, I hope he appreciates having friends who care."

Tim shrugged. "Maybe it's payback. Remember, Arel did help you and Carol when you were afraid she'd lose the baby. He did insist that you two move into his spare bedroom. You said he ran a five-star establishment."

Kevin did remember and smiled. "Right, I'll stop complaining. By the way while you were checking out some brochures, I asked about Arel and found out that he isn't here yet. We'll have some time to settle in before we begin phase two."

"Smart thinking, Kev."

"Thanks, I'm kind of getting into this whole thing. Fancy hotel, a spy game, we're like a couple of James Bond characters."

Tim moved forward when the elevator door opened. "I hope we can make the grade."

Kevin's smile widened. "The reception guy's going to ring our room when Arel arrives. I told him that we're here for a surprise family reunion."

"He's going to do that for you?"

Kevin let a few people exit the elevator and gave Tim a smirk. "I guess I have an honest face. Plus, I slipped the guy fifty bucks for being considerate."

Thirty-Six

The second day of travel was easier than the first. Arel was getting used to being confined in a small space with two energetic youths. Actually, Annabel wasn't very energetic, but she seemed to find Carey fascinating. As they laughed back and forth, Arel found himself joining in their conversations, even arguing with them when he noticed them lamenting the generation gap.

"I can enjoy almost any kind of music too," he insisted. "The only reason I had for turning Carey's station off, was my need to think. I have some important matters that have me preoccupied."

Carey immediately straightened up. "What important matters? Tell us. Maybe we could come up with some good ideas."

Arel glanced in the rearview mirror. Carey looked like an overeager canine just savoring the idea of his next task. "Relax, Carey, I don't want to talk about it. Besides, I want to go over what we're going to do once we arrive in New York. As I said, I'll let you drive the last leg—"

"You already explained everything," Carey complained. "But I don't know why you insist that we drop you off at Central Park."

"I told you. I want you to have the car. That way, you and Annabel will have transportation. I'll use taxis. But be careful. I'd like to see the Mustang again," he said with a smile that included a hint of a warning.

"But why can't we take you to your hotel?"

Arel kept his eyes on the road. "As I explained, this is a vacation, and I might seem a bit selfish, but I need complete privacy. End of story."

* * *

With the afternoon waning, Arel waved goodbye to Carey and Annabel as they pulled away from the curb. He stared after them, but the Mustang was soon lost in traffic. He was in New York City and he should have felt a little excitement, but instead, he felt a gloomy layer of sadness settle in. He had just severed the last connections to people who mattered to him.

Why do I let myself be like this? I've spent the last couple of days with two kids who did nothing but have a good time. Why can't I?

Why couldn't he be more like Carey and Annabel? Why didn't he think positively for five minutes after they left? The thought made him take a deep breath and loosen his jaw. He felt more alive just pulling his shoulders down from his ears.

I'm perfectly able to handle myself. I just have to believe it.

He stared at the oncoming traffic, stuck out his hand and hailed a cab. It passed him by, but a second cab stopped. He put a weary foot forward and got in. After giving the driver the name of his hotel, the cab sped away from the curb. He glanced at the passing scenery, still wondering why he wasn't capable of being enthusiastic about the amazing city he was in.

Because, in reality, I'm old!

He suddenly felt weighed down by his age and the memory of living for so many years back in Chicago. During that time, his house wasn't a home. It served as a self-imposed prison. He barely ventured out. But the curse wasn't responsible for his solitude. The world scared him. People scared him.

When I first met William, he couldn't believe what a stick in the mud I was.

The thought of William made him steel himself for what was coming.

Now, I have to meet the bastard again!

His hand clamped down on the arm rest as the cab took a corner too fast. It brought his attention back to the moment. He was doing it again, wasting his energy on negative thoughts.

Kell had a point about control. I'll save my anger for later.

Once he got to the hotel, he started to feel a little better. Since he might not survive his trip, he'd decided to splurge a bit when he looked for a nice hotel. He wasn't disappointed with his choice. The lobby was spacious, bright, and quite lavish. Beauty was expressed in its well-appointed furnishings and golden color scheme. He particularly liked the wide, circular stairway leading to a balcony above. The second story walls were a palette for large murals. They depicted tranquil, pastoral scenes that were comforting. He smiled when he thought of what Carey would say if he saw the place.

Maybe I'll take him on a real vacation if this one doesn't do me in.

When he got to his room, he liked the light airiness that was grounded in dark woods. He particularly enjoyed the beautiful, wood-paneled wall behind the king-size bed. The mixture of traditional and modern furniture helped him relax even more. Maybe he'd become too fixed in his normal habitat. Getting out into the world felt expansive. If he wasn't there to meet William, maybe he could have enjoyed himself.

Thirty-Seven

Kevin put the phone down in the cradle. He walked over and sat down across from Tim. "That was the hotel guy I paid off. Arel just checked in, but I'm starting to feel a little strange about the whole thing. Arel is here to meet an acquaintance as far as we know. No big deal. But we're acting like its life and death."

Tim lowered the paper that he was reading. "We're here as backup, nothing more. Let's just keep that in mind."

"I hope we make good spies. It looks easy when you're watching it in the movies, but in real life, it could be tricky."

Tim put his paper aside. "We'll find a place where we can keep an eye on the elevators without being too obvious."

"So we're on stakeout duty?"

Before he had a chance to comment, Tim's cell phone rang out with Peggy's ring tone. After answering it, Tim began to frown.

"What's going on?" Kevin asked in a whisper.

Tim waved him off as he continued his conversation. "You did what? You told him everything? No? He doesn't know about the dream?"

Kevin leaned in. "Told who?"

Tim stood up and began to pace. "Okay. Don't worry about it, sweetie. We'll handle it on our end. I love you too. Bye."

Kevin crossed his arms when Tim finished the call. "Out with it. What did Peggy tell you?"

Tim's frown became a scowl. "It's Carey. He called Peggy to let her know that Arel got to New York, and that he's alright. It seems that Arel loaned him the car until it's time for the return trip."

212

"Okay, that's good. So what's the problem? You sounded worried about something."

"Peggy told Carey where Arel is staying."

"You're kidding. How is Carey going to explain how he knew where to find Arel? He'll blow our cover."

"Peggy told him about us and how he has to stay out of sight. She didn't say anything about the nightmare she had. Anyway, Carey asked to see us. He's going to come to our room sometime this evening."

"Great. Now we have to worry about a kid too."

* * *

Standing in a parking lot, Carey pocketed his new cell phone and smiled at Annabel. "Peggy just called back and said that Kevin and Tim know I'm in the loop. I'm supposed to meet them later tonight."

"You seem to be fitting into Arel's world very nicely."

"I wouldn't say that yet. After he meets William, things could blow up if you know what I mean."

"Sorry, I guess I don't."

"It means that Arel could really lose control of himself. If that happens, it might be a very tough situation to handle."

"It's a shame that people get lost in their emotions." Annabel glanced around at the impressive buildings and all the coming and going that surrounded them. "Being part of things on a physical level is so incredible. There's so much to take in."

"In Arel's case, his mind is fixated on William. But we have succeeded a little. Happily, his mood is better than it was before the trip."

Annabel blinked back. "I don't know. When we were with Arel, his darker feelings seemed very close to the surface."

"Being moody can be the norm for Arel."

"Do you think he'll be able to have a peaceful meeting with William?"

Carey paused and scuffed the pavement with a worn sneaker. "I suppose that depends on how he deals with the memories that William brings up. Handling the past isn't Arel's strong point."

"Is there anything we can do?"

"You can help, but you won't need your body for what I have in mind. I'd like you to check in on him. If he should decide to nap—"

"I understand," she said quickly. "I'll make sure he's as peaceful as possible."

"It's very nice having you along." Carey held up his hand. "Now give me five."

Annabel's green eyes sparked with confusion. "Am I supposed to respond to you in some way?"

"Indeed you should," he said playfully. He held up her hand and tapped it gently.

Annabel stared back with surprise. "Why did you do that?"

"It's a gesture that people use. It means that we're confident about what we can accomplish."

"Where do you learn all of these things?"

"You need to notice the small details around you when you're in a body. It makes your performance more believable."

Annabel frowned. "There's so much to learn. I'm glad you helped me understand the kind of laughter young people use when they like one another. I think Arel was really distracted by our exchanges in the car."

"Arel was ready to throw us out of the car. But our banter gave his body a slight reprieve. He couldn't indulge in his anger over William as much."

"His obsessive focus isn't a good idea. Doesn't he know that he's putting a lot of stress on his physical vessel?"

Carey hesitated. "Michael, Grace and Kell have all tried to help him to 'lighten up' as they say, but Arel doesn't agree with their advice. He feels that a serious, even grim, approach is more powerful, especially when it comes to William."

"It sounds like Arel is going into this meeting with a dangerous agenda."

"Yes, he is."

Thirty-Eight

Kevin and Tim positioned themselves in an out of the way corner, close to Arel's room. It seemed the best way to keep an eye on his movements. As evening advanced, Kevin adjusted his position in his seat and stared at Tim doggedly. "In a place like this, you'd think the chairs would be more comfortable."

Tim looked up from the tourist literature he was reading and gave the hall a quick sweep. "Hopefully we won't have to stay here much longer. On the plus side, we're lucky that the maid service finished most of the rooms earlier. I don't want to look suspicious hanging around here."

Kevin picked up the brochure that Tim had already scanned. "I wish our wives were here. Carol is always on me to do something with her. There's tons of stuff to do in New York."

"There are great places in Chicago too."

"Yeah, I guess, but I don't think about stuff like that when I'm at home."

"Peggy and I can watch the baby for you guys if you want to get out more."

Kevin tossed the pamphlet aside. "I don't know what Carol expects from me. She's always complaining that I don't communicate. With the baby, everything revolves around him. What am I supposed to talk to her about, baby food?"

Tim snorted. "Feelings, old man. Women always want to talk about feelings."

"What do I know about that stuff? I love Carol and our son. Isn't that what's important?"

"Yes, of course. But you have to tell her that."

Kevin tried to get comfortable again. "I go to work, and I do what I can to help when I get home. I hoped that was enough."

"Nope," Tim said adamantly. "Women need reassurance."

"I don't have the knack like you do. Maybe Arel is wrong about me. Maybe I should have stayed a bachelor. That way Carol wouldn't always feel let down."

"Arel has faith in you, and so do I. You'll learn. It just takes time."

Kevin bristled. "You don't seem to have this problem."

"What can I say?" Tim asked with a laugh. "I'm more in touch with my feminine side."

"Oh that's great, I guess I'll have to try that next."

"Shh!" Tim put his finger to his lips. "I think Arel's leaving. He just came out of his room."

They sat at the far end of the hall, opposite the elevators. Getting up, they quickly moved around the corner and out of sight. Waiting in silence, they gave Arel time to lock his room and walk to the elevators.

"Come on," Tim said as he crept forward. He looked around the corner as the elevator doors were opening.

* * *

After Arel got settled in his hotel room, he'd climbed into bed. His intention was to rest for a few minutes before preparing for his meeting with William. Instead, he'd fallen asleep and slept soundly for a couple of hours. When he woke up, he couldn't believe how deep he'd gone. Panic set in when he glanced at the clock. "Oh hell, I'm going to be late."

As he jumped out of bed and bounded to the bathroom, he blamed himself for not gauging how tired he was. He should have set an alarm. The bathroom mirror was a source of more bad news. His thick, wavy mane was being contrary after sleeping on it the wrong way. After a couple of failed attempts to tame it, he threw his brush on the counter. He had to keep moving and get dressed. After he found a shirt in the closet, he realized it was wrinkled. In fact, none of his shirts looked presentable. They all needed pressing.

I'm going to meet William looking like hell!

Another glance at the clock told him that he didn't have time to do anything about his attire, only to grab his jacket and leave. Once outside his room, he gave the area a quick glance to get his bearings and hurried down the hall. When he got to the elevators, he gave the down button several demanding taps. He had a moment of clarity as he waited. He was holding his breath.

I'm getting myself all worked up when I need to stay calm.

But he couldn't quiet his mind or his body. He checked his watch, feeling his muscles tense. It didn't bring the elevator up any faster. As the moments ticked by, he knew that William already had an advantage. In fact, the guy was probably sitting at their appointed meeting place, serene and collected. It was William's way of handling life.

And I'm going to show up late, looking like a wreck.

His damning thoughts about his shortcomings invited more of the same. He'd already failed when it came to managing his time or looking decent. But that was the least of it. He couldn't control his temper. He couldn't control his body. And worst of all, he was letting himself go into victim mode.

Am I totally hopeless?

The ding of the elevator brought him out of his downward spiral. Its doors slid open, welcoming him into a quiet, empty space. He rushed forward, tapped the button for the lobby, and turned to face the hall.

What the hell?

Did he just see a familiar face? Tim's face? He blinked a couple of times as the doors closed. His mind was playing tricks on him. He took out his handkerchief and mopped his forehead as the elevator shifted and began to descend. Unfortunately, it stopped at the next floor down.

Oh, please, let me just get to the lobby!

The doors slid open again, revealing a group of men. Arel's breath caught as he stared back at them. They were a happy bunch, laughing and slapping each other with great enthusiasm as they crowded into the elevator. He quickly retreated backwards, but he couldn't go far before his body was jammed into a corner. He immediately had a thought that was almost crippling. He couldn't escape. He was trapped in the tiny space.

The group's loud, rowdy voices assaulted his fragile hold on composure. He hated crowds. He hated loud noise, especially when his nerves were already as taut as a hanging rope after its grim purpose was fulfilled.

I can't breathe!

His handkerchief was clutched in his hand, but he couldn't move or mop up the sweat that broke out on his forehead. A bout of panic and claustrophobia took over his world.

* * *

"Let's move!" Kevin yelled to Tim as he started to run for the elevator. He'd just seen the doors close as Arel got in. "We did it all wrong! One of us should have stayed in the lobby."

Tim reacted at once and grabbed Kevin's arm. "The stairs! They're over there. We're only on the fourth floor. Maybe we can get to the lobby in time."

Kevin was on Tim's heels and nearly collided with a cart in the hall as he rushed forward. When they reached the alternate exit, Tim threw open the door to the stairwell. They both started a mad dash downward. They were both winded and gasping for breath by the time they reached the ground level and rushed through a door to the lobby.

"Over there," Tim panted. He pointed towards the elevators just as a set of doors opened. A group of boisterous conventioneers filed out in a tight-knit group, clearly enjoying each other's company. After a long moment, Arel slowly emerged. In contrast to the group, he was all wild eyes and ashen-faced. "Good, we've caught up with him."

As Kevin studied Arel, he grinned. "Yup, that's our boy alright. He looks slightly petrified. He's not used to being in a confined place with normal people."

Tim moved towards a screened-in area where they could hide. "We're normal. He's fine with us."

"Are you kidding? He nearly killed himself with a chair the first time we met him."

"That's true."

"And don't forget that he fainted the second time we saw him."

Tim's attention remained on their target. "I hope his friend is a nice guy. Maybe he'll be like Arel, the proper English gentleman."

"Yeah, maybe," Kevin said as he watched Arel pause for a moment to collect himself and then rush unsteadily towards the exit. "On the other hand, maybe we don't want them to be too much alike. I can't imagine trying to deal with two Arels if the situation gets dicey."

* * *

It was surprisingly easy for Kevin and Tim to get a cab to follow the one Arel had taken. "We're getting the hang of this spy thing," Kevin said when they reached their destination.

Tim stood on the sidewalk and stared at the hotel. "Arel just went inside. We better hurry. We don't want to lose him now."

"Understood," Kevin said in a confident tone. "And don't worry, we've got this." Maybe he was a failure with Carol, but it wasn't that hard to catch Arel when he fainted.

Once they were in the hotel lobby, Tim looked impressed. "Geez, this friend of Arel must have bucks. This place is even classier than the one we're staying at."

Kevin gave the lobby a quick once-over, noting the elegant fountains, marble floors, and old world opulence. "Glad we don't have to pay for a room here."

Tim pointed to a sitting area with lots of large potted plants. "I see Arel at the desk, so let's hide over there."

"Great, I'll be the lookout. You better stay behind me."

Tim kept his voice low when he replied. "Keep a close eye on him. This place is big, and there are a lot of people around. We don't want to lose him now."

"We won't," Kevin said as he took cover behind a column. When he checked on Arel, he tried not to expose anything but his eyes. "Looks like Arel got a message, and he's reading it. Now he's going somewhere. He's heading towards the lounge."

Tim nodded. "Let's give him a moment before we follow him." He'd barely made the suggestion when his cell phone went off. Its ringtone was surprisingly loud when Tim retrieved the phone. A happy song, sung by a cricket, filled the spacious, hotel lobby.

* * *

Arel moved forward listlessly, a 'dead man walking' prisoner of fate. He didn't feel the need to hurry anymore. Somewhere between his hotel and William's, his mood shifted. As he approached the lounge where he was supposed to meet William, a clear message pounded in his brain.

I'm not ready!

His rendezvous with Satan's helper was at hand and everything seemed to be working against him. He'd overslept and ended up rushing around like an unkempt idiot. He was trapped in an elevator with a horde of insufferable merrymakers who nearly crushed him with their obnoxious behavior. He rode to William's hotel in a cab with a frenzied driver who cursed out obscenities at every passing car. Now, with his nerves shattered, he had nothing left. He was totally drained. If only he could get his own anger going, it would be helpful. He needed adrenaline. He needed a charge to revitalize him. Instead he was filled with a despondent dread and a horrible disappointment in his ability to cope.

Michael, I should have listened to you. I should have listened to Kell and Grace.

As he trudged forward with regret dogging at his heels, he heard a familiar sound. A cell phone's distinct ringtone stopped him in his tracks.

I know that ring. It's the one Tim has on his phone.

When Tim got a call from Peggy, his cell phone chirped out, "When You Wish Upon a Star." Tim, usually the quiet, conservative type, always surprised Arel when it came to his love for Peggy. She could bring out his playful side.

Arel glanced around the busy lobby, scanning the reception area for a friendly face. He couldn't locate where the sound was coming from. When the ringtone went silent, he shook his head. *I have to get a grip.*

* * *

William sat at a small table where he could see Arel when he came in. Many of the passersby glanced his way. He barely took note of them. His blue eyes were as serene as his thoughts. He was in charge of himself once again, enjoying his own company in spite of the fact that Arel was late. He had perfected his patience so long ago that he knew he couldn't be annoyed by such a small detail. Perhaps it was a by-product of knowing that he had all the time in the world. When he looked in the mirror each day, he was rewarded by a perpetually youthful face.

After thirty minutes had passed, he checked his newly purchased, Cartier watch. He was beginning to wonder if Arel would show. It wasn't like the man to be this late. As he continued to admire his new timepiece, his brows furrowed, and he let out a small sigh of dismay. The watch strap had a scratch. *That damnable rat from the other night, that odious rodent must have grazed it with his teeth. Now I'll have to have it replaced.*

A flashback to his night in the alley delivered another pang of irritation, but he knew he had to put the rat incident behind him.

I simply had a momentary lapse of insanity.

As he promised himself never to repeat such a foolish, rash act, he glanced up. The person he was waiting to see had finally arrived.

It's about time, old friend.

He put up a hand and gave Arel a brief wave. As he did, he prepared himself for the worst. Arel would probably be his usual tidy self, full of anger and wrath. Or would he? As he pondered their tumultuous history, he noticed Arel's appearance. His hair was unruly, his tie askew, and his face was as colorless as a corpse.

Good god, the poor bastard is worse off than I remember.

William watched as Arel stood in the doorway for a long moment staring back. When he finally began to walk towards William's table, he wasn't just clumsy. Arel moved with all the grace of an alcoholic navigating a mine field. He skirted around chairs and people with a wide eyed panic and a jerky motion.

Knowing Arel's childhood background, William understood why Arel had been nervous a hundred years ago.

But dammit, man, you're in a time warp. Let it go.

Yet he found himself cheering Arel on, caring about the way he stumbled over an outstretched foot, caring that his old friend still looked innocent and afraid and unable to defend himself, even in a simple nightclub setting.

"Sometimes I really hate you." The words came out of William's mouth in a rush. He was disgusted by his continuing weakness, angered by the feeling that he should protect Arel, instead of wanting to put him down.

221

* * *

The sight of William was a final blow to Arel's already brittle, nervous system. *Bloody hell, he looks so youthful. He looks better than ever!*

Arel might be feeling old and worn himself, but William was the picture of a man who was in his prime, who obviously had a well-used gym membership.

My take on William has been all wrong!

After Arel received William's letter, he let himself slip into the past. William had been viewed in the same way that Arel viewed his long deceased parents, as someone who also seemed dead, a ghost haunting him from his past. But he'd deceived himself. William wasn't a ghostly memory. Dressed in a trendy, grey linen jacket and a black, flowered-print, button-down, he was a dynamic, full-of-life, man of the times.

He's totally in the now, and I'm living in a delusion.

In the split-second that their eyes met, Arel was forced to accept a new truth. His ideas about hating William, about wanting to destroy him, all centered around a time that didn't exist anymore. The William who sat across the room was welcoming, not hostile. His smile was genuine, not cocky. William had moved on, and Arel hadn't.

He's matured while I'm exactly what he always called me, an idiot!

William's confident expression also exuded an aura of power, a power that Arel couldn't deny. It was a power that he didn't feel in himself. If William did decide on battle, Arel wasn't ready for it. Any grand ideas, any possibility of being new and improved and combat-ready faded. So did any remaining strength to direct or control his body.

What can I do?

Arel was facing so much more than the past, he was facing his total inability to handle life and his body knew it. As he took a step forward, it began fighting him, letting him know that it wouldn't voluntarily go along with his wishes. Instead, it went into a hyper-sensitive state. Everything around him became a threat. Clinking glasses clanged like church bells. Soft laughter became raucous and overbearing. Faces became too vivid, too harsh, with glaring eyes and toothy mouths grinning like menacing clowns at the circus.

He plodded along with two left feet, struggling and stumbling to get halfway to his destination. If he didn't stop and regroup, he wouldn't make it to William's table. Frantic to find any port in his stormy dysfunction, Arel saw the bar and made his way over just in time to slump over its padded edge. He looked like he needed a drink, but he waved the bartender off.

This is so much worse than I ever imagined. William didn't take me out. I took myself out!

Humiliation seemed like a step up from his half-frozen state. He was sinking into the icy waters of self-loathing. He was always at the mercy of forces outside his control. Even his own body refused to listen to him.

Dammit, that's it! I've had it with everything!

As he ranted silently, as he cursed at himself, his anger kicked in. It wasn't a full-blown firestorm, but there was enough fuel to thaw out his brain and let a message come through. He thought he heard Michael's voice for a brief instant.

I believe in you. I'll always believe in you.

So there it was. Michael was throwing him a lifeline. Would he grab hold of it? Would he trust an angel who had stood by him no matter what?

William has no power over you.

The second message didn't come from Michael. As Arel paused long enough to stop putting himself down, something in his core rallied. It was a part of himself that he didn't know existed, but he felt its strength nonetheless.

Could it be true? Am I really free to live my life on my own terms, no matter what William does?

The answer was there instantly.

Yes, if you believe in yourself.

It was such a simple directive, one that Michael always encouraged. Yet, until that moment, it seemed like an impossible challenge. But was it really that big a deal? William might have made him a vampire those many years ago, but he didn't stay one forever.

Michael helped me, but I was the one that broke that curse. I was the one who did the work to reclaim who I am.

It was a heady thought, one that helped him push back his sagging shoulders and stand up straighter. As he did, a physical change slowly ebbed in. His muscles began to relax enough to allow some energy to flow. He began to feel stronger and steadier.

All this time, I haven't let myself know the truth. I've been so blind about it all.

His lungs had barely been working, but now he forced himself to take a deeper breath. After several more, he turned away from the bar.

Michael has been right all along. William doesn't have the power. I do.

After a few moments, he could function. He could actually look at William and know it was alright to walk over to his table without thinking he'd keel over. Of course, it would have been nice to have his revelation earlier, to cement in the feeling that he was his own man. But since that wasn't possible, he had to wing it. He had to stay focused on himself and not let his thoughts stray or his emotions get out of hand.

Just take it one step at a time.

As he started walking, he began to encourage himself instead of criticizing. He even had a wonderful thought. Perhaps his meeting with William was a good thing, a final test to help him break free of any remaining shackles he had in his life.

After this meeting, I'll be so much more aware of the freedom I've denied myself. After this meeting, who knows what I'll do next?

As the new and pleasing ideas kept coming, his stride became more fluid. He closed the distance between the bar and his destination very quickly. When he arrived at William's table, he was actually smiling, not at William, but at himself.

William stood up and smiled too. "It's been a long time."

The sound of William's voice brought all his happy thoughts to an abrupt halt. Again, he couldn't move, but it wasn't fear that had hold of him this time. It was something so much more elusive. His entire life he'd known fear and pain, but William's voice called forth a brief interlude in his despair, a very small space when he'd known safety, when he'd known friendship. For that was what they had shared. Now, all that came back to him. It was a dizzying moment that spun him around so completely that he didn't hear the voice of his nemesis, the person who betrayed him. He heard his brother, the only person who cared about him all those years ago.

"Yes, it has been a long time," he whispered back.

That's when William's eyes met his own. They were strikingly tranquil, like pools of still, deep waters. When they settled on him, Arel could feel them seeking out his soul and wanting communion.

"It's good to see you," William said. "I hope you're well."

Arel didn't know how to answer. He couldn't think. He was suspended in a place where his mind was useless. He was floating in a never land where the past and the present all seemed unreal. For an instant, he was completely lost. He didn't know who he was or who he was with.

William's voice cut into his daze. "Arel? What's wrong?"

Arel stared at the man in front of him. He looked around at the large room of people, trying to bring himself back from wherever he'd gone. "This is so weird . . . to see you . . . after all this time. It's so hard to believe we're talking to each other."

William grabbed his shoulders and shook him gently. "I can hardly believe it myself."

Arel had almost given in to the thought that William was a comrade, but William's hands on his body jolted him out of his confusion. Even if his brain wasn't functioning well, his body was very clear about its feelings. He instantly thrust out his hands against William's chest, trying to push him away. His protest proved totally futile. William's grasp went from gentle to vise-like, and his physique was solid and unmoving.

"It pays to stay in shape," William mused, as if he could read Arel's mind. He leaned in, brushing Arel's cheek ever so lightly with his own. "Loosen up," he instructed as he remained close to Arel's ear. "You're still as flighty as a virgin on her first date."

* * *

Cautiously following Arel from a safe distance, Tim and Kevin gave him a head start and entered the lounge a few minutes later. The place was busy, and it was easy to get lost in the crowd. After Kevin saw Arel greeting someone, he quickly found a table away from Arel's line of vision. It was located in an area that was darker than most of the dimly lit bar. His eyes were wide with curiosity when he targeted Arel again.

"What the heck's going on?" he asked Tim as he watched William try to force himself on Arel.

"Shh," Tim replied. "I don't know, but we're not supposed to be here, remember? Let's just observe quietly."

"They look like they're about the same age, but Arel's buddy is a lot flashier."

Tim narrowed his gaze. "Yeah, a bit of a player from what I can tell. What could he possibly want with Arel?"

Kevin frowned. "I don't know. Our boy is a bit of a stick in the mud."

"Maybe, but at least he's not pushy."

Kevin smiled. "He's also got friends who are looking out for him."

* * *

Arel sat across from William, his eyes rigidly fixed and waiting. Any old feelings of friendship disappeared as soon as he realized he couldn't get away from William's clutches. He was barely holding in the anger that William was able to trigger so quickly. "Why did you want to see me again?"

William leaned back, scanning him. "I'm asking myself the same question. My father would have worn a jacket like the one you're wearing."

Arel glanced down and gave his gray, wool blazer a quick review. "Conservative apparel never goes out of style."

"I suppose that's an explanation. So tell me, what have you being doing all this time? Has anything changed?"

Arel crossed his arms. "Whatever I've been doing, I'm happy with my life."

"Really?"

"Just tell me why you're here."

William continued to stare at him with steady, unwavering eyes. "I wanted to see New York, and since you weren't too far away—"

"Don't give me that. It must have taken some effort on your part to find me."

William sighed. "Why wouldn't I? Aren't we family?"

Arel heaved out a breath of disgust. "If you were the last person on earth, I wouldn't consider you family."

William let his eyes drift to his slacks. He brushed away a barely perceptible bit of dust off the knee. When he looked back at Arel, he smiled. "That makes me feel special."

Arel put his hands on the table and leaned in to whisper. "You're special, alright. You're a ruthless butcher."

William's brows narrowed for a brief moment, but he began to laugh. "And I was thinking of the times when we considered each other chums. Oh, I'm sorry, I'm sure that term of endearment offends you too, just like my presence."

"The sight of you is repulsive."

William shook his head. "You're worse off than I thought. I played out the scenarios in my mind, but I never imagined that you wouldn't grow even the tiniest bit in all this time. It's almost too pathetic to think about."

"I have grown. Like I said before, I'm happy. Accept that and get out of my life."

William leaned forward too. "Fine, as long as it's true, I'll leave you to your happy life. In fact, it'll be liberating. I won't concern myself with you anymore. But first I want to make sure that you're not lying to yourself."

The remark made Arel pause. William could be an uncompromising source of honesty, and he was insisting on the same factual candor from Arel. He couldn't resist the challenge. "What do you want to know?"

"Tell me about this happy life you have."

"How could I explain something like that to you? The happiness that I feel comes from my heart, and you don't have one."

"I see." William drummed his fingers on the table for a long moment. "Maybe I need to approach this from another angle. Let's talk about how I've changed."

"Are you going to tell me that you aren't imbibing blood anymore, that you don't look at people like they're your next meal?"

"I'm simply saying that I've moved on in some respects. I've discovered more about who I am." William's eyes softened. Pushing back his chair, he relaxed into its leathery padding, crossing his long legs, getting comfortable. "Unlike you, once I got over the first rush of what I've become, I wanted to understand myself, this gift that I've been given."

"Yes, some gift!" Arel replied, hissing out the words.

His rude remark made William pause and look at him with thoughtful eyes that conveyed his unspoken disapproval. Arel felt like the kid who had no manners, but his anger wouldn't let him behave in a mannerly way. "Go on," he said in a forceful tone.

William looked away with a frown, letting an awkward silence settle over the conversation.

Arel broke it quickly. "I mean it! Tell me what you did to understand yourself." He was almost shouting the words, needing to know some secret that William seemed to be harboring.

William wouldn't be bullied. He remained still and unmoving for long moments. When he finally spoke, his voice was low and measured. "You're very judgmental, Arel. Do you know that about yourself? Do you know that you try to make others feel very small? If you're so happy, why would you have to do that?"

The pronouncement, delivered so quietly, reminded Arel of something that Kell had talked about. He said that Arel let circumstances trigger his victim mode. When he felt powerless, Arel's first line of defense was to get mad and make judgments. He used his anger to distance himself from his supposed aggressor. Was he doing it now? On some level, was he afraid that William really had changed? Was he worried about what the change portended?

"I'm sorry for cutting in," he finally managed. "Just get on with your damn story."

William maintained his unwavering position, putting his elbows on the arms of the chair and placing his fingertips together. For a moment, he could have been a contemplative monk instead of a cold-blooded killer. "As I said, I needed to know what it was that changed me from a normal human to something powerful and almost immortal."

"Almost?"

William didn't stop to explain. "You know me. I've always been the curious type. Even as a child, I needed to study and understand how things worked. When I became what I am, I was faced with the greatest mystery of my life, and I needed to understand it. I had the means to set up a laboratory, and I certainly had the time. It took years, but I persevered. I became obsessed as I studied my blood, delving into its secrets. As the tools of science became more sophisticated, my studies began to pay off. The treasure that I was looking for came to light. At least a part of it did, enough for me to realize what we've really been given." He paused. His eyes became distant and dreamy as if he was back in his laboratory again.

Arel gritted his teeth, trying not to care about what William was saying, but his curiosity overwhelmed his composure. "What? What did you find? Tell me!"

William turned and gazed at him, then chuckled good naturedly. "It was a glorious triumph to know the truth. And it was so simple. We've been given a sort of virus, a very rare virus."

"What?" The word escaped Arel's lips just before his world stopped dead in its tracks. Did he hear William correctly? Surely, he hadn't. Another question tumbled out? "Did you say 'virus'?"

William didn't seem to notice Arel now. He was clearly in his own world, smiling at his achievement, reveling in his ability as a scientist. When he did continue, he spoke with the contained voice of a researcher. "What a day that was, when I finally knew for sure. But there was more to explore. I learned about one of the side effects of the virus. It produces our extreme sensitivity to the sun. But in the end, I've learned through trial and error that it would take quite a bit for that solar orb to actually kill us."

As William went on with his explanation, Arel could barely hear him. A strange buzzing sounded in his ears. Yet, a part of him struggled to listen and to understand the information that was being offered. "Sensitivity . . . to the sun?"

William frowned at Arel's repetitive tone and let out a huff of annoyance. "Yes, Arel, that big, bright ball in the sky. Anyway, we're lucky to have survived the virus itself. There aren't that many who can become what we are. The general populace would die if they were given our gift. So congratulations, you're one of the few chosen ones."

"Chosen one?" Arel asked in a tattered, halting tone, a tone that came from disbelief. Yet a part of him understood what was happening. William's facts were dismantling his foundation. His beliefs about who and what he was, were fluttering in the breeze of a shooting gallery, and William was blasting them away.

William paused to glance at him again. This time, his eyes were sympathetic as if he realized how his revelations were affecting Arel. "I'm sorry. You survived what you were given, but you were too emotionally weak to handle the effects of the virus. I know that now, but I didn't when I passed on my blood to you. In retrospect, neither of us was mature enough to handle it back then. But it has given you an incredible lifespan. You wouldn't be sitting here today without the virus. It slows down the aging process, making it possible to live for perhaps hundreds of years from what my experiments demonstrate."

Arel sat staring into space as the buzzing increased in volume. His mind wanted to slip away, to deny what he was being told.

Looking down, he saw his hands, gripping themselves, two white-knuckled fists that wanted to fight what was happening. After a moment, he opened them and stared at their emptiness.

William noticed that he was losing his audience. He snapped his fingers in Arel's direction. "Hello? Are you still with me? What do you think? Rather interesting stuff, wouldn't you say?"

Arel blinked up at him. "I don't understand."

"What don't you understand?"

Arel's throat was closing, but he managed to speak. "You just told me that we have a virus. The curse, this thing that looses a demon inside a person, is just a virus?"

William let out an amused bout of laughter. "It's not a demon that's loosed, it's one's inhibitions. You know, one's shadow self. It's that part that's affected. Or you can think of it as your primitive brain—"

"It's too much!" Arel gasped. "After all these years, to think that I've—" He couldn't go on. He was getting sick.

William's brows lifted, and a look of bewilderment spread across his face. "Sorry, I guess I didn't realize that you'd never thought about any of this, that you'd never questioned your condition. It's kind of hard to believe from my perspective."

"To find out that all this time—"

"I know you tend to hide from things, but to totally ignore—"

"Why didn't you tell me this sooner?" Arel blurted out the words in a desperate, breathless way.

William seemed to notice the panic in Arel's eyes, the wild look of an animal that's been backed up against a wall with no way out. "You left England, remember? I didn't know where you were. Besides, the information doesn't change the facts. The person still has to deal with what they are, their demons if you want to call them that."

Arel began rubbing his temples as his face flushed. His shock was turning into a growing sense of outrage, and it was aimed at himself. "A fool . . . I'm a fool . . . a hopeless fool!"

* * *

William watched Arel crumbling in front of him and realized what a mistake he'd made. It was embarrassing to think he could still be capable of such a complete error in judgment.

I should have left well enough alone. He's in his world, and I'm in mine. Leave it at that.

But he knew it wasn't that simple, that he was letting himself off the hook too easily. Why hadn't he considered Arel's state of mind before he began spouting off? Why did he think he could share reality with a dreamer like Arel?

I never imagined that he could be so stuck in the dark ages. No, not the dark ages! He's stuck in biblical times when people consider epilepsy as a sign that a person is possessed.

He sucked in some air, narrowing his eyes. The more he let himself understand the situation, the more taken aback he felt.

Arel has a brain. Hasn't he ever thought about using it?

His mind wrestled with the thought.

You're making this too complicated. That's the point. You're forgetting that Arel is the poet, the long-suffering artist. Of course he's not using his brain to process reality. He makes his own world, and now you've crushed that world.

It was too sobering a thought.

He's not your problem. Forget it. If he's crushed than he deserves to be crushed. He's like the rest of humanity. They're all a bunch of idiots.

Yet, when William got to his feet, he couldn't treat Arel like the rest. Some part of him still remembered that they'd once been friends. Gazing down at him, he put his hand on Arel's shoulder again. With a light touch this time, he squeezed it carefully. He was partially at fault. He had asked Arel to meet him. "Go back to your happy life. Forget about everything that I've said. What does it even matter after all this time?"

Arel lifted his eyes, glaring at him with two smoldering orbs of pooled misery. "Of course it matters!"

He smiled indulgently, but Arel's presence was tiring. He'd forgotten just how tiring it could be. Or did he have more tolerance for Arel when they were young? "It's a lot to take in. But you were right. It was silly of me to contact you."

Arel blinked up at him a couple of times, flashing his wretchedness at him in a slow-paced Morse code-esque kind of way. "You should have found a way to tell me all of this. How long have you known?"

William shrugged. "I don't remember."

"That long?" Arel practically shouted the words.

William started to move away. "I've got to get going."

Arel rallied. "I want to talk to you again. Do you hear me?"

William paused, gritting his teeth.

But I don't want to talk anymore.

Turning to leave, he hesitated. He reached for his wallet reluctantly. "Fine, we can meet tomorrow night. Here's my card, call me."

Arel snatched it from his hand so fast that William moved back, feeling the tempest growing in Arel and refusing to give it any more of his time. He moved away from the table quickly.

Arel and artists! Pity the poor bastards who have to put up with them.

* * *

Kevin sat at the table with Tim, watching Arel's friend walk out of the lounge. When he was gone, they both turned their attention back to Arel. For a few minutes, Arel remained at the table. When he finally began to stir and attempt to get to his feet, he seemed too weak. He stood up only to sit back down again.

As Kevin observed Arel's behavior, he crossed his arms. "Here we go. Here's the Arel we all know and love."

Tim let out a sigh of agreement. "He looks pretty shaken up."

Kevin's gaze never faltered. He began to coach Arel from the sidelines. "Come on, old buddy, you can do it. The guy didn't look that scary. Forget him and get up."

Tim narrowed his gaze. "From what I can tell, his friend actually seemed to be rather pleasant after all, a picture of English propriety."

Kevin glanced over and gave him a warning look. "We better both stay sharp. Arel's standing up again, and I'm getting a bad feeling about what's coming next."

Tim smiled back. "You're starting to sound like Peggy."

Kevin clenched his jaw. "After all these years, she's probably starting to rub off on me."

* * *

Ignoring a peal of laughter at a nearby table, Arel kept going over William's visit. He'd felt a lot of things in his life. Fear and guilt had been his close companions, but to feel that William was more responsible than he was, that was a new one. He felt too sick to move.

I've wasted most of my life. I've been a pathetic victim of a curse that was never a curse. It's a virus! A stupid virus!

William said it affected the brain, and Arel knew that it was true. All these years, he'd been insane, a ranting, raving maniac who was fighting his own fears. He'd been living in a make-believe world, complete with demons and angels.

His next thought was almost unbearable.

Maybe Michael isn't real. Or if he is real, he isn't an angel. He's just an ordinary human being who's trying to help a friend. I've made up all the rest of it. There's no redemptive blood in me.

The idea was like a dagger being driven into his gut, making the nausea disappear. It was replaced by an excruciating, burning pain.

If Michael isn't an angel, maybe William is right about other things too. Maybe humans are just worthless vermin, victimizing each other, destroying themselves and the earth. Maybe that's all that I am.

The proof was around him. It was so easy to tune into the people in the room, to feel their emotional excesses, their underlying fears, their compulsive needs and desires. But he didn't just feel it all. His gut was beginning to pull it all in, adding their negativity to his own horrendous burden. "I've got to get away from here," he stammered, forcing himself to stand.

He almost blacked out as a tremendous flash of heat went through his body. Everything in his life was shifting and burning away, and he had nothing to hold on to. He had to use all of his strength to stay conscious and upright as the dizzying effects of William's visit solidified in his brain. He let go of the table like a toddler, hoping that he could walk on his own. He almost fell, but his hand found the table again in time to steady himself. Finally, he got underway. He hobbled along, bumping into the facts that William revealed. He also bumped into furniture and the other patrons. "Sorry," he apologized listlessly.

People scowled back at him, reprimanding him for his clumsiness.

"What the hell is wrong with you?" some guy yelled loudly.

Nobody seemed to understand that he couldn't help his wayward progress. He couldn't navigate life or a straight line. He continued to collide with passersby, eliciting more abuse from both men and women.

"Watch it, buddy!"

"What a disgusting drunk!"

Waves of anger came at him, each one felt like a slam to his core, jarring his beliefs about goodness and mercy. Where was the compassion that people were supposed to have? He was doing his best, and nobody gave a damn. "Give me a break!" he cried out as people in his path repeatedly validated the feeling that humankind and life were nothing but a screwed up nightmare.

Maybe I want to destroy myself. Maybe that's what my gut is trying to do.

In the middle of his confusion and indignation, he had a brief moment of clarity about himself. The demons were of his own making just like William told him. If he killed himself, he'd get rid of the problem. He didn't have power in his gut, he had a suicide wish.

He tugged at his tie, trying to loosen it, to get some air in his lungs as the raging heat inside of him began giving off signs of igniting. It was building in strength, a smoldering, red hot cauldron that needed venting. It was throwing off his balance even more than before. He found it nearly impossible to stay upright.

"Jerk!" an older woman shrieked when he hit her arm, making her spill her drink.

He stared back at her helplessly. He knew he was in more trouble when her escort, a big, potbellied bruiser shoved him back.

"Hey, that's my wife, you imbecile!" the man yelled.

The harsh reprimand, the loud laughter of a group of partiers, and his body going haywire made the room begin to spin. He blinked back at the gawkers around him. Not knowing what to do, he stalled, unable to move forward or backwards.

He had a final thought as he continued to vacuum up the ugly energy around him. William had succeeded. His nemesis had finished him off. William didn't do it with vampire powers or even threats. He simply held a mirror up to Arel so that he could see the truth about himself.

I am an imbecile.

His self-condemnation was interrupted when two men grabbed his arms.

"Hold him up and let's get going. Peggy's nightmare may have been an exaggeration, but if we don't get Arel out of here fast, someone is going to deck him."

Arel recognized the voice. It was Kevin's. He looked up and saw his friends. Tim and Kevin were posted on either side of him like those husky bodyguards in the movies. As his mind cleared a little, he wondered if he was having a nightmare and his friends were part of it. Whatever the truth, he heard Tim taking charge of his situation.

"It's okay, folks," Tim announced confidently to the crowd around them. "He's got a medical condition."

Arel's feet gave way when he heard the comment. William had said the same thing. Now one of his most trusted friends was repeating William's explanation. He started to laugh as he realized that it wasn't a nightmare that he was having, just a crazy dream. How could he take any of it seriously? Reality was so preposterous, and his life was so ridiculous that he suddenly let go of it all.

"Yes, I thought I had the virus beat, but I'm still sick," he called out in a hysterical voice. "Stay back if you know what's good for you."

* * *

During the cab ride back to their hotel, no one spoke. Arel was still under the influence of too much information. A large dose of embarrassment added to his distress. His rescuers, Tim and Kevin, looked slightly traumatized. He'd given them a hard time. As they practically carried him out of the lounge, they tried their best to quiet him down, but they didn't succeed. Arel was in no mood to listen to them. He yelled out the truth to everyone they passed. "I'm sick! Stay away! Protect yourselves!"

He repeated the warning and other nonsensical gibberish that flashed through his mind until he was outside. The fresh night air helped to clear his thoughts. For a moment, he thought he saw Michael. His friend was smiling at him, trying to reassure him.

When Arel got back to his hotel, Tim and Kevin took him to their room. His friends deposited him in a chair where he sat hunched over, feeling like contrite child. "I have to apologize to both of you again," he said. "I think I kind of lost it."

Kevin sat in a chair in a corner, looking confused but concerned. "We know that. Please stop apologizing."

Tim simply smiled back. "It's okay, Arel. That's why we're here. We wanted to help."

Arel looked up at him. "But you shouldn't be here. I did everything that I could to keep you out of this."

Tim crossed his arms. "Well, I'm glad we came. Peggy was worried about you, and she was right. What happened back there?"

A flash of William made Arel sick again. "The person I met tonight seems to know how to push my buttons, that's all."

Kevin grunted. "He did more than that. He lit up your whole panel. You were scaring the heck out of people. I think they were afraid you were going to give them Mad Cow disease. What was that stuff about having a virus? Are you sick?"

"I'm exhausted," Arel said quickly, refusing to think anymore. "Please, go back home and forget this ever happened."

Tim laughed. "I don't think so. If left on your own, you could piss off all of New York. We'll stick around until you leave."

Arel didn't know how to respond. A loud knock at the door saved him from further conversation.

"Hello? Tim, Kevin, it's Carey," a young, cheerful voice called out.

Arel couldn't believe it. He grimaced at Tim. "Not Carey too."

Tim went to answer the door. "Sorry, but Carey called Peggy and she sort of told him where we were staying,"

Arel felt his spirits sink even lower if that were possible. "I can't believe this is happening."

Carey walked into the room as soon as Tim opened the door, but he stopped short when he saw Arel. "What are you doing here, Arel?"

Arel barely glanced up. "According to Tim, I'm pissing off New York. I won't bother to ask you the same question. It wouldn't do any good, would it?"

Carey grinned. "I don't mind explaining. I'm visiting Tim and Kevin."

Arel stood up and started for the door. "Yes, I forgot. This is their room. I'll go back to my own." He paused. "I assume that I'll see all of you in the morning."

Carey hesitated. "I might not be able to make it. I left Annabel with my relatives. But on second thought, I'm sure that she wouldn't mind if I had breakfast with the guys."

Tim patted his back. "Be here at nine sharp."

"You bet," Carey said as he turned to Arel. "By the way, did you meet your friend?"

Arel felt his face go flush with fresh anger. "Forget my friend!"

Tim pulled Carey to the side. "Uh, maybe we should let Arel get some sleep. He looks exhausted."

Arel grabbed the door knob. "Sleep? After tonight? I doubt it."

"Wait up," Carey called out. "I'll walk you to your room."

Arel's anger drained away as suddenly as it came. He didn't have the energy to fight Carey's youthful disposition. When he arrived at his room, he stared vacantly at the door, unable to remember what to do next.

"Let me open it for you," Carey said as he took the key card from Arel's hand. "You look like you've had a heck of a day."

Arel turned and stared at the young man, rubbing his forehead. "Sorry, I'm a little distracted. I'll be fine after some sleep. Do you have a way to get back to where you're staying?"

Carey smiled. "Don't worry, I didn't drive the Mustang. I took a cab."

Arel fished in his pocket and produced some bills. "Here, get a cab back, and if you come to breakfast, you'll have money for that trip too."

Carey stepped back. "I can't keep taking your money."

"Please, at least I'll know you're safe this way."

"I didn't mean to barge in on you."

He pressed the bills into Carey's hand. "Forget it. Just be careful."

Carey came forward and gave him a quick embrace. "You really are a good friend. Thanks for everything."

"I'll see you in the morning."

"Yeah, okay," Carey replied, offering a final smile as he started down the hall.

Arel forced himself forward and into his room. Once the door was closed behind him, he hesitated. Carey's bright face remained fresh and winsome in his mind's eye. The young man seemed stronger these days, even happy.

When you helped him, at least you did one good thing in your otherwise worthless life.

He thought about his other friends, and his life in Chicago.

And you've helped a few other people, but as for the rest of it, you certainly didn't accomplish much.

He imagined William in a white coat, leaning over a microscope. William was a true scientist, discovering a new virus. He was like Dr. Jonas Salk. Well, not quite, William hadn't developed a vaccine for polio, but he was dedicated to pursuing knowledge.

Arel saw himself in a white coat too, but not a scientist's coat. No, his coat would have extended sleeves with straps. He'd be living in a padded cell and the jacket's sleeves would be drawn tight around him, to keep him from hurting himself.

That's where I belong, in an institution, where they keep the fools who can't figure out reality.

He walked into the bathroom and stared at the mirror. How many times had he felt like he was looking at a monster? And all that time, he was sick with a virus. *I have a medical condition. End of story.*

He shook his head and laughed at the absurdity of his life. He had hidden himself away all those years like some soldier holed up in a cave, not knowing that the war was over.

"Arel?"

It was Michael's voice. At first, it was a comforting sound, until he reminded himself of the truth, that he was ill, not just physically, but mentally unbalanced. Yet, when he looked out into the room, Michael was standing by the bed. "You're not real, you know. You're something I dreamed up, nothing more."

"That's not true," Michael said. "You've denied my existence before, remember? Now you're doing it again because you're upset by what William told you. But I'm always available to help you."

Arel turned back to the sink and grabbed hold, needing to ground himself in the real world. "I've denied you before? That makes sense. I've had delusions on and off for years. I'm sure of it." Shutting his eyes, he had to remain calm. His emotions were always getting him into trouble. "But now I have to maintain some measure of sanity. I have to stop this nonsense."

"You're making a very big mistake." Michael's words were delivered in a kind, but firm tone.

"No, I'm learning how to think clearly," Arel insisted. He was determined to face reality once and for all.

"Have faith in yourself, in what we're doing."

He put his hands over his ears. "Goodbye, Michael."

A moment later, when Arel opened his eyes and looked back towards the bedroom, it was empty. But it wasn't as empty as his chest. There was a hole, a terrible void of nothingness where a heart had been a few hours earlier.

* * *

Ignoring the glittering, New York skyline that lay beyond his hotel window, William sat in the darkness. He was determined to put Arel out of his mind, but he found their differences intriguing. Their reactions to life experiences were completely opposite.

Arel called the gift he was given a curse. When he found out it was a virus, he was devastated. For William, discovery of the virus was a triumph. But from the very beginning, he considered what he became a wonderful opportunity. He could be so much more than a normal human. It had been a stroke of luck to partake in his maker's rare blood, to have its powers passed on to him.

"But I had to fight for that bit of luck."

William's maker called himself Rolphe, meaning 'wolf'. He had a thick accent that William never quite figured out. Perhaps Rolphe was from the Balkans. William only spent a few hours with him. After that, Rolphe disappeared from his life. What William remembered most was Rolphe's temperament. He was a rather good-natured type for a creature of the night. Very tall, heavy-boned and slightly graying, he had a convincing smile and seemed to enjoy his own jokes. When they met in a pub, William was instantly fascinated by Rolphe's confident manner, his effortless ability to manipulate those around him. Whether it was other patrons or the bartender, Rolphe had a mesmerizing look, an aura about his person that made people want to do his bidding.

After they talked for a while, Rolphe offered to take William back to his hotel room and provide women for them both, William went along willingly, flattered to be noticed by the imposing man, eager to learn from him. But once they were alone, things changed. William could feel that Rolphe wasn't there to impart knowledge. But their time together was memorable. William knew every detail of their exchange, even now.

Like something out of a classic movie, the setting was elegant. They occupied a beautifully, furnished suite. Red flocked wallpaper added an indulgent sensuality to the room. Dark, mahogany woodwork gave it a rich, warm quality. It was a perfect back drop for what came next. William had barely sat down on the gold, silk print sofa, barely had time to take in his surroundings when Rolphe made an announcement. Coming over to William, leaning close to his face so that they were separated by no more than six inches, he smiled.

"I'm a vampire," Rolphe whispered. "What do you think of that?"

William, slightly drunk and in a good mood, had laughed. "Can I be one too?" he joked back.

Rolphe didn't react at first. Instead, he stared at William, studying him. Then he slapped William's face in a playful way and laughed too. "You are different, I'll give you that."

William smiled back, thinking about their purpose for being there. "What about the women?"

Rolphe paused and seemed hesitant at first. Then he nodded. "You're right. Let's have a little diversion."

True to his word, Rolphe arranged for two prostitutes to come to the room. But he didn't let William touch either of them. He warned William off with hard, green eyes that were definitely predatory in nature. Instead, Rolphe took charge of the women, joking with them as he had with William, plying them with drink.

William was captivated by the performance. He'd never seen anyone who could become as enraptured by women as Rolphe. He totally lost himself as he talked to each of them about their beauty, their allure. When he stroked their faces, his touch was gentle, tender. His eyes were soft when he caressed their bodies. He didn't treat them like women of their trade. He treated them with a certain respect and appreciation.

As they fell under his spell, Rolphe smiled at them sweetly. He never took advantage of them sexually, but he did begin kissing them and stroking their necks. As he did he would glance over at William, with eyes that went instantly hard.

Thinking back, William was still surprised that he hadn't been frightened by Rolphe's clear signals that he was being targeted for something. Instead, he felt an intense attraction to the control that he saw in the older man.

After a lengthy time with the women, Rolphe paid them and sent them away. Then he turned his attention to William.

"Did you enjoy the show?" he asked. "Are you ready for the next act? The whores would have sufficed, but you'll be much more satisfying."

That was when William finally realized that he was in trouble. Like any animal, he knew when he was staring into the eyes of death. His brain scrambled for something to say. He made a declaration to Rolphe. "You're everything I've always wanted to be. Tell me your secret."

William could still hear the roar of laughter that burst out of Rolphe. He laughed until he cried. But it was a dangerous laughter that ended in Rolphe grabbing William's neck and biting it passionately. Then, after a moment, he drew back, licking his lips, letting his palette evaluate his meal. "A little salty, but tasty."

William was stunned, but he was also filled with wonder. Even as a young man facing death, he wanted answers in those last remaining moments of his life. He gazed back at Rolphe with desire. "Before you kill me, tell me what it's like to be you."

Rolphe dismissed his question and bit him again, this time he didn't stop with a taste. William felt himself fading as he tried to push the vampire away, but he was helpless to stop the feeding that had begun in earnest. Rolphe let go of William before he passed out.

"I'm being a glutton," Rolphe laughed. "I won't like my overindulgence when I try to sleep."

William tried to reach out to him, but he was too weak to move his hand. "Please, tell me . . . ."

Rolphe looked back at him with wonder. It was clear that he had never encountered anyone like William. Wiping his mouth, he watched his victim struggle to voice his thoughts.

William was in the last stages of consciousness, but he held on to Rolphe's eyes with all that was left in him. "Give me something, please."

After a moment, Rolphe sneered. "What the hell! I'm in a generous mood."

William watched Rolphe take out a knife. Exposing its blade, he made a small incision in his wrist. Then he put his bleeding flesh to William's mouth. "Just a taste, enough to know me better."

But some part of William rallied. He sucked at the blood greedily.

241

S. S. BAZINET

Rolphe looked on in fascination. "You think it's mother's milk, don't you?" he asked with disbelief, even stroking William's hair with his free hand. Then he jerked away. "Enough of you," he said as he turned and put a cloth from his pocket over his wound. "Live or die, it's of no consequence to me," he said as he went for the door. He paused before he left. "But if you live, don't let your curious nature go too far. You have a bit of stupidity in you. Purge it." Then he shut the door quietly behind him.

After Rolphe was gone, William passed out. When he woke up, his body was racked with pain, but he was ecstatic. He was still alive, and he knew that something exquisite was happening to him. He was the pupa turning into the butterfly. As his body contorted, his mind took flight. He thought of Rolphe's face, his control, his power to decide who would live and who would die. William wanted everything that Rolphe embodied. He wanted his metamorphosis to transport him into a new way of being. And it did.

Afterwards, when William was well again, he knew he wasn't normal anymore. He had always loved who he was, but he hated the fact that he was a human being. There was so much wrong about the species. Now, he was a new creature, and he gloried in that fact. It changed the way he saw the world. Everything he gazed at looked new, like he was seeing it for the first time. His body was alive in a way he never expected. When he touched a flower, his fingertips were so sensitive that the smooth petals sent sensuous chills down his spine. He thrilled at the depth of the bloom's color. He felt the fragrance invade his body like a wanton woman. He was so filled with exuberance that he welcomed the thought of only coming out at night. The day would have been too much for him.

The idea of killing someone because he needed blood wasn't given much thought. William figured that nature would take its course. Like any predator, he'd simply answer the call when it came.

The call to action caught up with him a short time after his night with Rolphe, but it was unexpected. William was with a woman he didn't know very well. He'd met her in a tavern a few times. Later, she simply became one of the many whose bed he frequented. Their special night together didn't start out as a hunt. He was merely doing what he always did.

William realized afterwards that he'd been like his maker with the whores. He began his lovemaking in his normal way, as an adept lover. But in the end, he found out that he wasn't in control of his

242

carnal nature. Unlike Rolphe, he took the fair lady like a beast. Even William's usual, uncaring attitude was shaken when it was over. Control, he decided, would take longer than he thought.

Now, so many years later, William remembered those first days with a sense of pride. He'd been smart and a quick study in many ways. Sure, control took time and so did discretion, but for someone as young as he was, he did a remarkable job.

"But Arel . . . all these years . . . never moving on? How ridiculous."

Thirty-Nine

The hotel's eatery was bright with morning light. It poured into the large room from a wall of windows. Upscale artwork of oversized, abstract flowers added a spark of color to the off-white walls. Carey found the area quite agreeable as he sat at a table with Kevin and Tim. "Thanks for asking me to breakfast," he said as he glanced around the room. "This place is really fancy. And look at the fresh daisies on the tables."

"They better be fresh at these prices," Kevin protested. "How can they charge so much for a couple of eggs?"

"I was wondering the same thing," Tim added. "It's a blessing that I'm getting a bonus this year."

Carey began to study his menu again when he spotted Arel. "Hey, there's Arel," he announced, pointing towards the entrance.

Kevin shifted his attention as Arel walked towards them. "I'm surprised. He didn't seem interested in coming last night."

As if to answer his question, Arel smiled and waved as he approached the table. "Good, I found you," he said in a rested, happy tone.

"You look better," Tim observed. "In fact, you look great."

Showered and dressed smartly in a grey shirt and dark slacks, Arel beamed back at him. "It feels good to feel good."

"Where'd that tie come from?" Kevin asked. "You don't usually wear anything like that."

Arel paused to finger the silky, fuchsia tie that stood out prominently on his otherwise conservative outfit. "I was out early and got lucky. Some street vendor was already open and was selling lots of great stuff."

Tim stared back with a questioning smile.

"What?" Arel asked. "Too bright?"

"No, no, it's very nice," Tim insisted.

Arel pulled out a chair and seated himself. "I was wondering if anybody was up for a little sightseeing?"

Kevin was the first to comment. "Tim and I were looking at some of the places we might like to check out."

Arel rubbed his hands together briskly. "Well, it's settled then. Bring it on, New York. We're here to have a little fun."

Carey had to maintain his smile as he listened to Kevin and Tim's suggestions for the day, but inwardly he was concerned. When he met with Michael the night before, they discussed Arel's meeting with William and how devastated it left Arel. Michael had predicted what he thought was coming. Now, seeing Arel's altered state, Carey knew Michael had been correct. Sometime during the night, Arel's mind, unable to deal with William's news, had shifted away from reality. Now he sat in the restaurant, glowing and happy on the surface. But in truth, he was clearly in a state of very deep denial.

Forty

Carol carried her newly purchased teapot over to the kitchen table. She loved the little pink hearts sprinkled over its creamy-white ceramic surface. It was perfect for special teas. "What do you think, Peggy? Isn't it as cute as I said? I saw it online and had to have it."

Peggy glanced up from where she was sitting. "Yes, it's adorable. But I never thought about tea until Arel introduced the idea."

Carol filled Peggy's cup and then her own. "I was always a coffee drinker until Arel suggested herbal tea. I wasn't sure at first, but you know how convincing he can be."

They both giggled as Carol took her seat. She offered Peggy a scone. "Speaking of Arel, have you had any more dreams?"

Peggy's expression turned wistful. "I don't want to spoil our little party with talk about my crazy stuff."

Carol frowned. Peggy was always too quiet when something was bothering her. "Don't worry. I love the idea of dreams. I read a book about how symbolic they can be."

"Maybe, but I feel silly even talking about it." Peggy put her hands in her lap and avoided Carol's gaze. "Why do I have to have these experiences?"

"Are you kidding? You should be proud of yourself. If it weren't for you and your special abilities, where would Arel be? Where would any of us be?"

Peggy returned a shy smile. "Thank you for being such a good friend."

"Of course, now tell me what's going on."

"Well, there was another dream, a really strange one. I had this one last night." Peggy picked at the orange cranberry scone on her plate, broke off a tiny piece and ate it.

Carol leaned forward. "Please Peggy, don't keep me in suspense."

"Maybe you don't want to hear about it. Arel was acting weird in this one."

"Trust me, dreams can have hidden meanings."

"Okay, if you're sure," Peggy said. She took a sip of tea and cleared her throat. "I saw these two dogs, and they looked like they were getting ready to fight. They were both growling and circling each other. I can still feel them squaring off, but I woke up before anything happened."

Carol sat back. Peggy's dreams were usually more interesting. "Is that it?"

Peggy shot her a shy look. "This is the weird part. I feel like one of the dogs is Arel, and he's a little nuts."

"Well, let's think about what it could mean?"

"It's probably nothing. I've been worried about Arel, that's all, especially after Tim told me about last night's episode. Arel sounded like he was really upset again."

Carol reached out to her. "Then the dream makes perfect sense, Peggy. Arel can be a little crazy when he gets upset. We both know that."

Peggy's eyes softened a little. "Yes, that's so true. And he does have a tendency to get upset rather easily."

Carol took a bite of her scone and chewed it thoughtfully. "Do you think the other dog in the dream was his friend? Kevin said that Arel looked angry while they were talking."

Peggy laughed. "Probably. I know that Arel irritated everybody last night with how he was acting. Maybe I'm just afraid somebody is going to be angry with him."

"Well, he isn't alone. Our husbands are there to watch out for him. In fact, Kevin said that Arel is alright with the two of them being there with him. He was even grateful that they showed up when they did."

"Tim said the same thing. I'm happy that they don't have to sneak around anymore." Peggy sat up straighter. "I feel better. Thanks."

Carol took another bite of her pastry. "I have some encouraging news on another front. Kevin said that he wanted to find more things for us to do together. He said Tim told him about 'date' nights."

Peggy's eyes went bright. "Good. I'm glad to hear that he's getting on the ball. Take it from me, sometimes he's clueless."

"Maybe, but I think I'm at fault too. Why don't I just appreciate all the good things about him? He's a wonderful dad, and he's always happy when I buy things for myself. There's no one more generous than Kevin."

"Listen, I love my brother, but he doesn't seem to understand that women are different than men. I think you want him to take more of an interest in what's important to you."

"But maybe that's asking too much. I don't know."

Peggy looked away. "You might be talking to the wrong person. Kevin and I don't have a perfect track record either. You've seen us fight. It can get pretty brutal."

Carol giggled again. "Like the two dogs in the dream?"

Peggy smiled back. "Yes, that's true. I guess people sometimes express their differences in unpleasant ways. But I mean what I said. I love Kevin, and I know you love him too."

Carol nodded. "I do. Maybe that's why I want him to pay more attention to me. I really need to know he loves me too."

"Are you kidding? That's one thing that's for sure. Kevin adores you. He just expresses it in his own way."

* * *

After a full day of exploring with Arel and Tim, Kevin returned to the hotel moving considerably slower than he had when he set out in the morning. Tim looked tired too. Only Arel had a zip in his step. "All I want to do is take off my shoes," he complained as the three of them entered the elevator together. "They're still new. I should have brought an old pair."

Tim leaned against the side of the elevator. "I haven't caught up on my sleep. I think I'll take a nap."

"Come on, you guys," Arel cut in. His face was bright with unwavering enthusiasm. "There's so much to see. I'd suggest taking in some clubs tonight, but I have to meet William."

Kevin turned to him as the elevator began its upward ascent. "So where are you meeting this William guy?"

"He's coming to my room. It'll be better that way, private."

"Might be a good idea," Kevin said. "What time do you want us there?"

Arel frowned. "Sorry, but it's a private meeting. You know, talking about old times."

"Are you sure you'll be okay?" Tim asked. "Peggy's worried about you."

Arel let out a loud laugh. "I'll be fine. It's not like he's some mob guy with a contract out on me."

As the doors to their floor slid open, Kevin grabbed Arel's arm before he could get off. "Listen, you never did explain why you were so upset last night. Maybe we should talk about that."

"Oh, it was nothing," Arel hedged. "Remember how I acted when I first met the two of you? Last night was par for the course. You know me, I'm always overdoing it."

Kevin eyed him closely. "You're sure that this guy is alright."

Arel smiled confidently. "I'm sure."

Forty-One

William stood outside Arel's room, checking his watch. Satisfied that it was precisely nine o'clock, he gave the door a couple of sharp raps. "Let's just get this over with," he grumbled. When he thought about another tiresome meeting with Arel, he had to do a couple of neck rolls to restore his tranquility.

I want to get back to my own interests.

Maybe he'd go to Paris and explore some of the offerings in the auction houses there. Strangely enough, it was Arel who'd first tweaked his interest in the arts. Still, he hadn't become a collector until years after they'd gone their separate ways.

You didn't give me a chance to tell you that I've turned in my butcher's license. I'm an art aficionado now.

He looked at his watch again and was about to give the door another rap when it opened wide. Arel stood in the doorway looking out with a smile.

"William! Dear William, you're here!" Arel said with enthusiasm.

William stared back, slightly shocked by Arel's attitude and appearance. The man was happy and animated, almost glowing. His cheeks were rosy and his eyes were as sparkly as Christmas lights. "What's going on?"

Arel was eager to reply. "It's good to see you! So glad you could make it."

"Right." William recognized the energy that Arel was putting off. Victims who couldn't confront what was happening to them sometimes exhibited a reaction similar to Arel's, minus the rosy cheeks and Christmas-light eyes. In the face of death, they'd be smiling, looking like simpletons who couldn't cope with or accept

250

their fate. Their solution was to simply blank out. "Maybe I should come back another time."

"Why? This is perfect." Arel stepped back and grinned. "I've been waiting for you."

William knew he should resist Arel's welcoming gesture and the way Arel ushered him in with a sweep of his hand. But before he had a chance to consider his options, he was standing in Arel's room and the door was quickly closed behind him. "I can't stay, I have—"

"Make yourself at home!" Arel's voice was overly loud as he circled round and rubbed his hands together excitedly. "We can get reacquainted, not like last night, but really get reacquainted."

William glanced around the suite. The bed was unmade in the next room and clothes littered the floor. The conditions were a clear sign that something was very wrong. Arel would never allow himself to behave so slovenly if he was in his right mind. *Oh god, Arel, what now?*

Arel seemed to notice William's quick inspection of the premises and let out a loud laugh. "I canceled room service. I didn't think it was necessary."

William scowled back and crossed his arms. "Are you feeling okay? Did you get ahold of a bad rat?"

Arel shrugged. "I don't think so. I've had a wonderful day, seeing the sights, enjoying New York."

"Right." William noted a fuchsia tie that lay in the middle of the living area. Arel and fuchsia? Something wasn't just wrong. The situation set his teeth on edge, but he didn't have a chance to think about what he should do. Arel looped a hand around his arm and pulled him towards a plush, white sofa.

"Don't just stand there, Will. Sit down. Make yourself comfortable."

Arel's touch made every muscle in William's body go rigid, as if he needed to ready himself for something. He didn't know what that something was, but it felt anything but pleasant. In the meantime, he was hearing a voice in his head that told him to leave, to jump up off the sofa and head for the door. Later, upon reflection, he would curse himself for ever stepping into Arel's room in the first place.

* * *

Arel hadn't given William's visit any thought until that evening. He was too busy enjoying himself. He went out with friends, taking in exciting, new sights and finally feeling like he was on vacation. He was so totally in the moment that he couldn't think about anything else. Throughout the day, life seemed so simple, so easy.

When he heard William's knock on the door, he was still buoyant. Kevin and Tim complained of being tired after a day out, but he wasn't. In fact, he had so much energy surging through him that he had to contain himself when he answered the door. The sight of William, standing a few feet away, only revved his engines. Here was his old pal, someone to talk to, someone whose company he used to seek out when he was in trouble. The idea that William was a vampire was a mistake. He had a virus, no big deal.

After William was welcomed into his room, Arel couldn't stop talking. He rattled on about his outing with Kevin and Tim. He expressed his need to sit down and talk. When William hesitated, he felt a rush, a fresh burst of energy that compelled him to keep William from leaving. He even bodily helped him to the sofa. He was elated when William was finally seated. As he found himself staring into William's eyes, words flowed out effortlessly. "I have so much to tell you."

* * *

Michael had invited Kell to observe Arel's performance. Kell had witnessed so much when it came to humans battling each other. Michael was open to any suggestions that his friend might have in regard to the current situation. Both angels were in their etheric forms and viewed the situation from a corner of Arel's room. From Michael's perspective, Arel was behaving so oddly that Michael had cause for alarm. He tried to intervene by sending Arel a healthy dose of calming energy, but it was no use. Arel was shielded in a cocoon of manic excitement that repelled anything Michael had to offer.

Kell, who was normally very reserved, seemed mesmerized. "Arel is totally unaware of the incredible state that he's in."

Michael agreed. "He's demonstrated this kind of ability before, but he's never maintained it for very long."

"Until now." Kell hesitated. "The power that he's got going is amazing. You've done very well at helping him to integrate what you gave him. Normally, a physical body could never handle anything like this."

"Arel's body is capable, but it's his mental and emotional responses that I'm worried about."

"He's certainly safe enough with William."

"But is William safe?" Michael asked with a look of dismay.

"I agree completely. The guy looks slightly terrified."

"William is a very aware individual, especially with the unusual way that Arel is acting. William is also very capable of handling himself. However—"

"However, Arel has very potent abilities. Michael, I hate to say this, but William might be in serious trouble."

"Yes, you're right."

Kell's energy wavered a little. "If William fails to keep his distance, if he falters in the least, heaven help them both."

* * *

William's discomfort escalated when Arel sat down next to him and put an arm around his shoulder. "There's something wrong with you," he complained as he pushed Arel off. Reassessing Arel's energy, he decided his old friend wasn't in a helpless, victim mode. He was in a mode that William had never experienced before. It was disconcerting in the least, and alarming if he really allowed himself to think about it. "Go sit somewhere else," he ordered.

"I'm sorry," Arel said as he moved away a couple of inches. His eyes flashed wide and then blinked back contritely. "It's just that everything is starting to make sense. After all these years, I think you've woken me up from a deep sleep."

William crossed his arms again, maintaining a vigilant posture. "You're going to be sleeping six feet under if you don't control yourself."

"But aren't you happy that I'm happy? Isn't that what you tried to teach me when we were first friends? To have a good time?"

"I didn't want you to go around grinning like some deranged lunatic."

"I can't help it. I feel suddenly free, liberated."

"Fine, wonderful, just calm down."

Arel laughed, this time more quietly. "And I thought that you encouraged the idea of having fun. Tell me what you'd like to do. I'm game."

William froze. Arel's eyes weren't just bright, they had an eerie glow, and his body was actually vibrating. Suddenly, William felt like he was going to be the victim. Rolphe had given off a similar energy, but Arel's aura exuded a magnified force that dwarfed Rolphe's. William would have normally been intrigued by such a display, but his senses were telling him that this was different. There was something about Arel that was edging on maniacal. He stood up, knowing there was only one solution. "I've got to go. I've decided to return to London, and I have to see if I can change my flight."

As if on springs, Arel shot out of his seat and clasped on to him. "Don't leave me! Help me, Will, please!" In a split second, his eyes went from glowing to soft and fluid. "I've been lost for so long."

He stared back, astounded by Arel's instant transformation. "Do you realize how irrational you're being?"

"I'm tired of fighting, Will. Don't you understand that?" Arel's tone was pleading and sincere. Then he let go and backed away. He held out his arms in a pose of surrender. "Don't leave me like this, please."

"Just what the hell do you want?"

"I don't know. I'm confused. You told me some things last night that I never expected." Gesturing for William to stay put, Arel moved backwards to a seat across from the sofa. "Maybe I should return to London with you."

William had no reply to such an offer. Instead, he stared back with discerning eyes. There was an almost imperceptible smile behind Arel's plaintive admissions and submissive dialog. "I don't think so."

"Please, Will, take me back with you!"

"Why? You're making no sense. You can't stand to be around me, remember?"

"If I was wrong about my condition, maybe I'm wrong about other things. You could help me to get control of myself. Isn't that what you always said I needed to do?"

William narrowed his gaze. It was easy to see that Arel had some hidden agenda. He was certain of it. Arel was talking about being lost, but there was a powerful energy behind his words. Rolphe came to mind again, something about the way he fawned over the prostitutes. "I'm not buying any of this crap. I don't know what you want, but I know I'm tired of the game that you're playing." He started for the door.

"Fine, if that's what you feel," Arel said softly. His actions were hesitant and careful now. He stood up slowly, but didn't try to stop William. His face became childlike and lost. "If you have to go, let's part as friends."

"This is crazy. You don't even like me."

Arel approached him with his hand extended. "I'm sorry that you feel that way, Will. Perhaps we could just shake on it."

Backing away, he noted that Arel's hidden smile had been replaced by an open, genuine expression of friendship. His body language was completely conciliatory. William had never felt so manipulated.

* * *

From the moment that he opened the door and saw William, Arel couldn't keep up with his feelings. One minute, he was elated, like some happy fanatic. Brilliant lights flashed in his mind as he felt his world expand into the infinite. He cruised in the heavens. Then he crashed into a sea of despair. He was a frightened school boy wanting someone to take him under their wing.

Physically, his muscles were flexing and releasing. His body was a tinderbox of energy, wanting and waiting for something to set it ablaze. At the same time, his brain was being pinged with some powerful energy pulse, making him remember things, things that were hidden so deep that they only surfaced for a few brief moments before they fell back into the abyss of forgetting.

But for those few moments, he wanted to connect with William again. Theirs had been a rocky relationship. Now, he had to change all that. He and William had unfinished business.

When William announced that he was leaving, Arel acted without any hesitation. Gazing at William with petitioning eyes, he extended his hand. He had to reach out to William and put things right between them.

255

William closed his fists in defiance. He'd only been in the room for a few minutes, but the feeling of impending doom was getting stronger. Arel demonstrated many moods in the past, but he never acted this strangely.

Maybe you should be put down, but I'm tired of worrying about you. Find someone else to end your misery.

He stepped forward, wanting to finish whatever he once shared with Arel. He extended his hand as a gesture that they were parting amicably, but their bond was severed at long last. "Let's get this over with. I have a life to get back to."

Arel looked as if he'd been struck, his face going from inviting to stricken to angry. "You're right. What do I care about you? Why am I acting like this?" He paused as if he was coming back to himself. When he looked at William again, his eyes were cold. "You're nothing to me, nothing."

"Finally, the truth!" William yelled as he advanced on Arel. He stared at him with glaring eyes. As he thought about the past and what he'd sacrificed for the man in front of him, he couldn't contain his anger. "You know that I came here, went to a great deal of expense, because I was concerned about you. I wanted to make sure that you weren't still the loser you used to be. I wanted to make sure that you had moved on, but you're more pathetic than ever."

Arel laughed. "Talk about a bunch of crap. That's the biggest load ever. You came here because I have something that you'll never have. I have integrity. I have principles. And you just can't stand that, can you? Now that you've solved your little medical mystery, you're bored with yourself." He moved closer to William. "You're bored because you have nothing in here." As he spoke he poked at William's chest.

William batted away Arel's hand as if he'd been bitten by a cobra. "You ignorant, pompous bastard! What would you know? I've never met anyone more selfish than you. The whores in my bed have a hundred times more capacity to love than you."

Arel's eyes became irate slits of wrath. His voice was low and seething. "Whores are the only ones that would ever get in your bed. No one else would have you."

William's fist came up, but he caught himself before he delivered a blow. Stepping back a few steps, he had to fight for control. "I can't believe I'm having this conversation," he said, pulling in all his emotions. "It's stupid. You are what you are, and I'm what I am. We'll never get beyond that."

Arel blinked back at him and sighed. His face became placid again. "I guess you're right. I'm sorry. I really am. Like you said last night, I'm much too judgmental."

William started towards the door again. "I better leave."

Arel nodded and then laughed. "We'll have to do this every hundred years or so."

"I had that exact same thought a couple of days ago."

"Great, we actually shared one common thought," Arel said with another laugh. "That's a first."

William turned at the door, still holding himself in check. It had been so long since someone had the ability to make him lose control. Now, he'd come close, but in the end he was grateful that he didn't allow Arel that license. As he was leaving, he forced himself to once again be the adult. "Good luck. You said that you're happy. I'm glad to hear it."

Arel didn't reply. Instead, he came over and stuck out his hand again.

William took it in his and held it firmly. "You know that you're an idiot, don't you?" He was finally getting a measure of himself back, and he made sure that his tone was teasing.

Arel laughed. "Look who's talking. If you did come all this way because you were concerned, you're the crazy one."

"You were the one that called me brother at one time," William retorted quickly.

"Yes, I did, didn't I?"

They studied each other for a long moment and then Arel did the unexpected. He pulled William forward into an embrace.

William almost jumped away, more with surprise than anything, but Arel held on to him. As he did, William questioned the moment and what was happening. How long had it been since Arel had initiated such contact? How long had it been since he actually showed any sign of warmth?

As if he could tell what William was thinking, Arel tightened his embrace. "You did give me your blood, didn't you?" he whispered close to William's ear.

As soon as he said it, William was aware of Arel's heart. It was beating, loud and strong, as if the vessel wanted William to hear it. He could discern the blood flow in Arel's body. He could trace its paths as it spread out, coursing like small rivers through miles of arteries. But there was more. The blood itself was sending out an alert to all of William's senses in a way that he'd forgotten.

"Do you feel it, Will? Do you feel your blood in my body?" Arel asked in a low, soothing voice.

With Arel's breath hot on his face, William felt his flesh quicken. A deep craving began to make itself known. After all the years of being satisfied with a chilled glass of the dark fluid that sustained him, a need for the warm, living sustenance resurfaced. He tried to pull away at once, unaccustomed to being swayed by something outside himself. He was his own master. He decided what he would feel.

"Where are you going, Will?" Arel whispered. He was the strong one now. His grip was unyielding. "You gave me your gift, but I never returned the favor, did I?"

William swallowed hard, feeling the dryness in his mouth, wanting something to quench his thirst.

Arel let out a little gasp. "Yes, I know, Will. I feel your need too."

"You do?" William gasped. What was Arel saying? What was he playing at? Was his old friend baiting him? If he was, William felt himself being drawn in, and he didn't like it. But Arel was so close that William could practically taste what was being offered.

"What's the matter, Will?" Arel taunted. "Are you weaker than you thought?"

William was consumed by a rush of resentment. He wanted to punish Arel for all his bad manners, for all his judgments, for all his callousness. Letting himself go for just a moment, he lashed out. He bit Arel's cheek and let the blood pool in his mouth. An instant of joy followed, making him forget his wrath. Nothing had ever tasted so sweet. It wasn't blood that he was imbibing. He was drinking from some holy font of bliss.

But the moment didn't last. Arel's skin grew hot and fevered, breaking the spell, making William pull away as he felt his lips burn from the contact. This time Arel let him go.

Standing a foot apart, they stared at each other, joined in a strange reunion. The first time, William had given his blood. Now Arel had returned the favor.

William couldn't move at first. He had lost control. It was an acceptable failing when he was young, but not now. He knew himself completely and commanded his life on his own terms. Yet he allowed himself to cross some line that was dangerous and potentially damning.

Still red-faced, Arel smiled calmly. "Don't worry about it."

Unable to speak or understand how he let himself be bewitched, William needed to exit the room immediately.

"Promise that you'll come back in a month," Arel called after him. "I want to see you again. I have so many things to tell you, amazing things. If you think I've been an idiot before, I'll tell you about the angels I've conjured up."

*　*　*

Stationed a short distance from Arel's room, Kevin stood guard again. Tim was there too. They had agreed that they couldn't allow Arel to be totally on his own, no matter what he said. Kevin was surprised that William's visit was so short. "The guy just got here a few minutes ago, and he's already leaving," he whispered to Tim.

Tim smiled wearily. "Hey, that's good for us. I want to go to bed early."

Staying in the shadows, they watched William as he walked briskly to the elevator. Halfway there, he nearly tripped, as if he wasn't quite sure of his footing.

Kevin shot Tim a confused look. "Is that the same person we saw yesterday? He's really changed."

Tim watched William push the down button for the elevator. His hand was definitely shaking. "Maybe he's related to Arel?"

Kevin scowled. "I hope not. One guy falling down all the time is enough."

As William left Arel's hotel and got a breath of fresh air, he tried to collect himself. His anger was taking over again, but he stiffened with resolve.

I have to stay calm, no matter what.

He needed his wits to be sharp if he was going to deal with what had just happened. One fact was clear. He'd been violated. Somehow, Arel had drawn him in with some kind of extraordinary magnetism. William had never experienced anything as powerful as the ability Arel had to dispose of William's normal focus and willpower.

He had to be careful now. His instincts were close to the surface, telling him to stay away from any more emotional upheavals. His best course of action was to remain rational. Thinking things out before acting had always been his strong point. Still, there was something else bothering him. He paused, retrieving his handkerchief, and using it to wipe away any trace of Arel's blood on his lips. He could still taste the damnable stuff. It lingered in his mouth and in his mind, making him want more.

"Dammit!" he said, cursing that weak human component that Arel had activated in him. As he was voicing his disapproval, his stomach squeezed in discomfort. Once in a while, blood could do that to him.

"Like the rat's blood," he hissed. He stopped and spat out any traces of feasting that remained in his mouth. Was there a connection that he needed to consider? "Of course there is. Arel lives off the damn rodents. Their tainted blood is in his blood."

* * *

After William left, Arel put his hand on his throbbing cheek. It was already hot with fever. He went into the bathroom and washed it thoroughly. When he was satisfied that it was as clean as possible, he put a couple of bandages over the area. Looking at himself in the mirror, he noticed that his eyes looked lifeless. His face had no color.

For the past day, he'd been living in a sort of bubble. All the fears and doubts had vanished, replaced by a boundless energy. It reminded him of when Michael helped him to see things in a vision. He lost touch with his normal perception and saw with the eyes of the dreamer. The problem was that the vision often faded afterwards, like a dream. In the same way, his bubble of ease and joy burst, leaving him feeling empty.

He knew he had to act quickly. Letting himself out of his room, he felt a sense of urgency as he walked to the room that Tim and Kevin occupied. When Kevin responded to his knock, his message was conveyed very simply. "I'm driving back home tonight. If you want to come, you're welcome. I'll call Carey and tell him to bring the car. If he wants to join us, he can."

As Arel was heading back to his room, he had a very disturbing feeling. He was starting to forget where home was.

* * *

By the time he got back to his hotel, William knew that he was experiencing more than a stomach quirk. He was in pain, real pain. It took all of his strength to push it back long enough to hobble to his room.

"Hell and damnation!" His usually self-assured voice was filled with confusion as he doubled over on his bed. He hadn't felt real pain in so long. He was astounded at the devastating effects it was having on him.

What's happening to me?

For a moment, his need to answer that question was stronger than the pain. He'd always had an analytical mind. As a teenager, while others his age were reading adventure stories, William was exploring a book in his father's study, *Darwin's On the Origin of Species*. It fascinated him.

But his mind couldn't override what was happening to his body. His physical condition demanded his full attention. "Rest, I need rest," he told himself as he pulled up the covers. Twisting this way and that, he tried to find a position to ease the agony that was taking hold.

"Maybe it's not bad," he groaned as he tried to quiet his fears. The last time he felt this much misery, Rolphe had given him a wonderful gift. Perhaps this was another one.

Forty-Two

Sitting in the passenger seat of Arel's Mustang, Kevin held his cell phone close to his ear and smiled. "It's great knowing I'll be seeing you soon," he said. "Yeah ... Tim, Carey and I are taking turns driving while Arel sleeps. He can't seem to stay awake ... right ... okay ... kiss little Ariel for me. Love you too."

Tim, looking thoughtful behind the wheel, glanced over. "How's everything going with Carol and the baby?"

"They're fine, but Carol says that she's relieved that we're on our way back. If Peggy has more nightmares, you'll be there for her."

Tim sighed as he looked in the rearview mirror. "Peggy doesn't have to worry now. Carey and Arel are both sleeping like babies."

"I'm awake," Carey whispered. "I'm just closing my eyes for a few. Let me know if you want me to drive."

"Thanks Carey," Kevin said. He looked at Tim. "Can you believe Arel? He announces that he's driving back to Chicago and look who's going to actually be behind the wheel, the three of us."

Tim gave him a quick smile of agreement. "But this drive won't be so bad. We can take four-hour shifts. You guys better get some sleep so you'll be rested."

Kevin narrowed his brows. "I will, but I've been thinking about Carol. As they say, absence does make the heart grow fonder. I didn't realize how much I'd miss her and the baby until I went on this trip." He paused. "Listen Tim, you were telling me stuff about how to act around Carol. I don't mean to space out at home. I guess I just assume that things are fine with her. How am I supposed to know when they're not?"

Tim gave him a teasing grin. "Maybe you have it backwards. When you're in a relationship, don't assume anything. I find that it's better to always check in with Peggy, to ask her about how she's doing before there's a sign of trouble."

"And that works? I simply ask Carol how she is?"

"Well, you have to be genuinely interested."

Kevin stretched out in his seat. "I am interested, but what if she says she's unhappy? I don't know how to fix that kind of thing."

"It's not about fixing her problems. Just be there for her. A woman needs to feel you're really listening."

"Geez, that's Arel's department," Kevin said with a sigh. "After he talks to Carol, she always looks happier. I guess I have to ask him for some lessons."

Carey let out a quiet snicker from the back seat. "I'm learning that Arel is very good at giving out advice."

Kevin looked back and smiled at Carey. "Welcome to the club, young man. By the way, did I hear you mention something about you and Arel giving a girl a ride to New York? Is she okay?"

"Yes, she's staying with friends now," Carey replied.

Kevin glanced back again, making sure Arel was sleeping. "Most of the time I think I know how Arel's going to react, but he can surprise me. Picking up a stranger is unusual for someone as careful as he is. It's nice to know that he can be so flexible."

Forty-Three

William climbed out of bed twelve hours after he got in. His body didn't feel any better. He knew he hadn't been given a gift. The pain was a constant reminder that something was terribly wrong. When he looked in the bathroom mirror, his eyes were somehow diminished, their usual spark was missing.

His first thought was that he had been infected by something, perhaps another virus. That was it, he told himself.

Arel has a virus, and he gave it to me. That's why he was acting so crazy.

Stumbling back to the bed, he grabbed his phone off the side table and called Arel's hotel. He'd get hold of Arel and find out more about his condition. After connecting with the hotel desk clerk, he grimaced. Arel had checked out of the hotel.

I should have known he'd skip out on me.

William had to make a decision. He could go after Arel and learn more about what was wrong with him, or he could go home. The latter choice seemed more logical. William's physical condition was deteriorating. He was getting weaker. In all his years as a vampire, he'd never felt anything comparable. If the virus, or whatever the hell it was, moved this quickly, there was no time to lose. He'd have to open up his old laboratory and try to help himself.

Forty-Four

A rel arrived back home in a mental muddle. When he tried to communicate with his friends, words escaped him. He was barely able to thank Kevin, Tim, and Carey for all their help. They seemed to understand enough not to ask any questions. Perhaps they were getting used to his need to cloister himself away every so often. Yet, amid his confusion, there was a feeling in the back of his mind that he did something unforgivable. The idea was so frightening he couldn't let himself dwell on it. He did allow his view of William to shift a little. When they first met, William had been the gentleman. He was rational and forgiving, the sane one.

Perhaps William's always been the sane one. Who knows at this stage of things?

It was a difficult concept to swallow, but it made sense when he thought about their last meeting. Arel had obviously behaved badly. No, it was more than that. He behaved like a person possessed. His cheek, festered and inflamed, was proof. He remembered enough about his actions to know that he goaded William. He pushed the guy to the limits and beyond.

I think I wanted him to bite me. But why?

When he felt the answer trying to surface, he pushed it away. He didn't have the emotional resources to tackle the truth, not yet. Instead, he took to his bed. Perhaps he needed some kind of a decompression chamber to safely remember and understand what he'd done. Since there wasn't one around, he would use sleep as a retreat and pray that he didn't dream.

He wasn't given that choice. There was a knock at his door, and a man let himself into the room. Arel stared back at his visitor, noting his attire. The tall, robust man was dressed in jeans and a sweat shirt. "Damn, Michael, you look real enough."

Michael walked over and smiled. "And you look terrible."

"I'm happy to hear it. An angel would never be that negative. So, you are flesh and blood, and I've been playing my old game of pretending there's a celestial visitor in my life."

Michael's smile faded. "It's no game, my friend. In fact, it's quite serious. William is in trouble."

"William is fine. I went a little overboard with him, but he's William. He'll go back to London and resume his life."

"I'm afraid not."

"What are you talking about? You're not making any sense."

"Maybe this will help. You spent almost a century hunting rats. Then I came along. Now, you're free of all that because—"

"Stop!" Arel felt his stomach lurch. A sudden case of acute nausea joined his pounding headache and throbbing cheek. "I don't need to hear any more foolishness."

"Think Arel, you're not hunting rats anymore because—"

"Because I no longer have the virus William talked about."

"But why don't you have it? William didn't say anything about a cure."

"Are you trying to tell me something, Michael?" Even as he asked the question, he was steeling himself against an answer. He didn't want to believe in angels. He was determined to adopt William's attitude and begin living in a world of facts. "Because I think you must be crazy too. Both of us must be mental cases."

Michael put his hand on Arel's forehead. "I'm your friend."

His touch was instantly comforting. It quickly eased the pain in Arel's temples, but the effect didn't stop with his headache. A wonderful feeling of relief traveled to his chest and helped to lighten the heavy weight that was sitting on his heart.

He targeted Michael with eyes full of wonder. "How did you do that?"

"I think you know the answer. William may have certain facts at his disposal, but you have much more than that. All you have to do is stop hiding from the truth."

Michael's words were more powerful than his touch. Arel felt his mind begin to clear. All the buzzing and noise began to fade. All the muddied waters of denial dissolved into a clear pool of knowledge.

He hadn't been a mental case all this time. Michael was real. He was an angel, an angel who gave Arel his blood.

"I did it again! I denied that you are what you are, but this time I did it so that I could do what I wanted."

As Arel remembered the truth, he also realized his crime. All the details came together and formed a perfect composite of exactly what had happened when he met William the second time. He hadn't just forced himself on his adversary. He hadn't just proven that he could be the powerful one, the one in charge. He lured William into a trap.

"I've hated him for so long."

For a moment, he connected with the rage that lived in his gut ever since William forced his blood on him. For a hundred years, he wanted revenge for the heinous act. When he connected with William in New York, he finally got what he wanted. He took what Michael gave him and used it for his own petty purposes.

"Oh hell, this is the worst." He grabbed onto Michael's shirt with a shaky hand and pulled him closer. "I passed on your blood, Michael. But William never wanted that."

"No, he didn't, but you made sure he took it anyway."

"But I had to do it! William is a monster. He had to be stopped! It was the only way I had, short of killing him. You have to understand that."

"I understand that you perceive him in that way, that your actions were based on that viewpoint."

"And I'm right, aren't I?" He scoured Michael's face, wanting forgiveness and seeing only compassion. He let go of Michael and faced the wall. He was exhausted again. He needed sleep. Yet a nagging question begged for an answer. "What's going to happen to him? William is going to be alright, isn't he?"

Michael's sigh was soft, barely audible. But when he spoke, every one of his words etched themselves into Arel's psyche. "I don't know. I really don't know."

Forty-Five

Sitting on a plane bound for London, William was relieved to be going home. His body continued to suffer, but his mind was a source of comfort. He was eager to find out what was causing his physical misery. In some ways, the new mission excited him. Arel would say that his feelings proved a point. They proved that William was bored with his life. But he refused to believe such a thing. His life was perfect before his trip to New York. He wanted for nothing, and he did whatever he pleased.

Well, maybe Arel's statement had a tinge of validity.

William loved being a researcher, one who unraveled a puzzle. His skill at staying rational and quietly observant was something that he admired about himself. Now, it helped him to accept his present situation. He enjoyed being confident about his abilities to handle whatever it was that was happening to him. It's what prompted him to begin right then and there, to question what led up to his illness. He laid his head back and pondered his last meeting with Arel.

When he answered the door of his room, I could have sworn that Arel's eyes were glowing.

Arel's eyes, his frenzied movements, and his agitated speech were all indications that something was very wrong. Arel was probably in the advanced stages of some horrid disease.

He calmed down just long enough to lure me into his clutches, then he was burning up with fever.

For a moment, he felt sorry for Arel.

You've been so incapable of appreciating my gift. Now what have you gotten yourself into? What have you gotten me into?

As he questioned himself, exhaustion claimed what little strength he had left. Thinking that he'd just close his eyes, he began to doze off into a sort of waking dream. Images started to appear. He saw tall, magnificent, crystalline buildings that glistened in the sun. Intuitively, he knew that his laboratory was housed in one of the most beautiful of the structures. It looked like a temple, and it was dedicated to science and learning. He was a priest of sorts, one who had the power to extract answers from the ethers. In those ethers, he found a cure for what ailed Arel. Using the cure first on himself, he recovered quickly, his blood ran pure again. But he wasn't content to simply help himself. Wielding a knife, he sliced open his wrist. A stream of life-giving red liquid flowed freely, and he collected it in a golden chalice. The dream leaped forward, and he was presenting the chalice to Arel, asking him to drink and be restored too.

William, are you nuts? Wake up! You're having a crazy nightmare!

His eyes flew open and he mentally shook himself so vigorously that his body trembled.

Slicing myself open to help Arel? Me? Golden chalice?

He knew his thinking processes were already being affected by what he'd later call Arel's Madness.

Dammit! Whatever he gave me really screws with the mind.

It was an important observation to remember. Pulling out a notepad and pen, he started a 'to do' list. When he got back home, he had to buy a journal. He would have to keep track of everything. His method had to be precise. He'd be as scientific and orderly as possible, recording every detail. Each and every irrational thought, physical symptom, and personality change would be noted. But first, he'd commit the details of his meeting with Arel to record.

Now think, William. Go back to that night in Arel's room. Was there anything else that might be useful? Did Arel mention anything of interest?

Steadying his hand, he began to scribble down what he remembered so far. He tried to recapture every part of their conversation that night. He paused and stared at the notebook. "Oh hell, did he mention angels?"

Forty-Six

Arel leaned over the dining room table, barely able to pay attention to the cards in his hand. He'd been home a week, but he was still tired. Everything was a chore, even playing poker with Carey. He couldn't stay focused. Finally, he pushed his chips into the young man's pile with a shrug. "Sorry, I can't do this."

Carey eyed him intently. "What is it? You haven't been yourself since you got back from New York. And your face isn't healing. You said that you fell and bumped your cheek on a dresser, but the area around the bandage looks redder than ever."

Arel's hand went up to touch his cheek. He flinched.

"Problems?" Michael asked as he joined them in the dining room.

"Yeah, ask Arel what's going on," Carey insisted.

Michael smiled at him. "Would you excuse us? I need to talk to Arel in private."

Carey stood up. "Sure, I have some work to finish. I'll be out in the garage."

Arel watched as Carey left the room. "I'm glad he's visiting more often, that he's starting to think of this place as a home of sorts."

"You've made him feel needed and useful. He likes cleaning up the garage in exchange for a meal." Michael sat down and fingered the poker chips. "But Carey's question was valid. Your face is getting worse."

"Before we discuss my face, I have to ask you about something. William said we were infected with a virus. I'm sure you've known it all along. Why didn't you tell me? Why would you let me believe that

I was cursed? Like William said, it sounds ridiculous when I think about it."

"It's not my business to interpret your reality."

"Yes, but if I'd known, I would have done so many things differently."

"Really?"

"Of course! A medical condition is one thing, but a curse—"

"Would you have continued to hate William? Would you have blamed him for destroying your life?"

"No! I don't think so. I—"

"Are you sure? In New York, you knew the truth and yet—"

"What do you want me to say?" Arel stood up and braced himself on the table, glaring at Michael. "Fine, maybe you're right! Maybe it wouldn't have changed my feelings about him. But my anger went deeper than the curse or virus or whatever the hell I had!" He straightened up, trying to get a grip. He tried to touch his cheek again and gritted his teeth. "He was almost like you, Michael. He acted like I mattered, but in the long run, I just became another one of his victims." He lowered his voice. "I know you don't like that word, victim, but in this case, it fits. I was drunk that night. I wasn't in control of my faculties, and he didn't care. He didn't have an ounce of concern for my wishes. I never chose what happened to me."

"Tell me about that night. Tell me about how you became one of his . . . victims."

"I don't remember the details. I just know the outcome, the bloody facts that William likes to talk about." A sarcastic laugh escaped his lips. "Apart from everything else, that one thing was real and undeniable. I would never be the same. Virus or curse, my life changed forever."

"Yes, but there was more to it than facts, wasn't there."

For a moment, all Arel saw was a terrible darkness. He remembered pain, excruciating physical pain and even worse, the pain of finding out that his brother had betrayed him. "Strange, isn't it? It was the anniversary of Aldwin's death, and it was the night I lost the brother who pretended to take his place."

"So what did you want to accomplish in New York?"

Arel sat down, suddenly heavy with lethargy again. "I really don't understand it. In a way, I felt drunk, just like I was drunk that night long ago. I didn't have a plan to do what I did. It just happened."

"And William became your victim."

As soon as Michael voiced the words, Arel's cheek began to throb. He could feel his heartbeat in the wound. "Yes, I guess you're right."

Michael sighed. "If you don't wield power properly, with wisdom and absolute clarity, you're still cursed, my friend."

Forty-Seven

William scowled as he pushed back from the microscope slide. How could he study blood samples if his body was freezing cold and his fingers were going numb? His condition had nothing to do with his surroundings. The temperature in his lower level laboratory was above normal. At least there was good news regarding his physical condition. When he compared a current blood sample with older frozen samples he kept on hand, there was no sign of a new viral infection. His white blood count seemed close to normal. There were no antigens present. Perhaps he didn't have a virus. But if it wasn't a virus, what was attacking his body?

He stood up, walked to the thermostat and adjusted the dial. "Eighty degrees is too hot for a lab, but hell, it's science or me at this point."

In his journal, he noted that he was talking to himself on a continual basis. He could deal with his physical fatigue and achy joints, but noting that his mental health was deteriorating was cause for worry. He wasn't just talking to himself, he was losing control of his emotions. Where had his patience gone? He accidentally dropped a blood sample earlier and went into a rage.

I'm starting to act like Arel. He's infected me with something that's turning me into his clone.

A deep chill grabbed hold. The idea of being like Arel was scary. William walked over to his recliner and snatched up a cashmere blanket. As he wrapped it around his shoulders, he had a more calming thought. His outbursts had nothing to do with whatever disease Arel gave him.

I'm on edge because I'm bone-weary. That's all it is. On the other hand, Arel's always been an irrational idiot. He's always been in love with his wrath. He coveted and enjoyed his anger even before I gave him my gift.

William let his mind settle on their youthful friendship. Arel only pretended to be mild-mannered and shy. In truth, he was tough as nails when it came to defending his beliefs about how life was unfair and cruel.

Or maybe I was the only one Arel ever knew who gave him the space to express that anger. So his emotional overflow fell on me. I was the friend who indulged him too much. In the end, I cared too much. I should have—

He hesitated.

I should have what? Thrown him out in the rain?

He sat down heavily in his leather recliner. After ten hours in the lab, his mind was as exhausted as his body. Yet, it was his nature to try to understand, to question what was happening in his life.

"What the hell have you gotten us into, Arel?" The simple query was enough to set off his imagination, flooding his mind with scenes of rotting, dead bodies, black and bloated from plague. It was a disturbing sight, but he let himself stay with the vision for a long moment. Did it have any validity? Was it offering him a clue about what he was up against?

"Is my mind just going off or is it trying to tell me something?" Arel's feeding habits came to mind. "Arel was involved with rats. Could he have contracted some new type of plague and given it to me?"

Burdened by the weight of how he too could end up a corpse, his hand trembled as he pulled the blanket closer. He wouldn't let himself dwell on the negatives. It was a fruitless exercise. Besides, he didn't really think he had any form of plague. People with the plague usually died quickly. Whatever Arel had given him seemed intent on killing him slowly, tormenting him day in and day out.

"He couldn't give me something quick and merciful. Not Arel. He doesn't have a clue about mercy, the bastard!"

Clenching his jaw, he felt a bout of emotional upheaval coming on. He held tight to the arms of the recliner and tried to breathe. Others might go around ranting and raving, but he refused to stoop that low if he could help it. "Just let it go," he said in the most pacifying tone he could manage. "Don't let yourself fall into the victim trap. That's Arel's territory."

He snatched up a remote that lay on the side table next to him. He had once read that listening to certain pieces of classical music was conducive to calming the nerves and healing the body. He prayed that the theory was true as he pointed the remote at the CD player and pushed play.

"I can do this. I can beat this thing," he whispered as the first notes of *Clair de Lune* filled the room. The composition was soft and inviting. It urged him to close his eyes and let go of all the ways that Arel had wronged him. Yet, as the music played on and its passionate melody evoked ever deepening feelings, he couldn't resist indulging in a memory he had hidden away for a very long time. It slipped in between the notes and carried him back in time to a night when Arel came to visit. It was their last night of shared friendship.

The weather that evening was unfit for man and beast alike, but Arel had been out in it anyway. When he showed up at William's door, he was soaked to the bone, and he was very drunk.

I was so young and ignorant when you came to me that night. I should have never allowed you to step foot in my house. But I took you in, didn't I? I felt sorry for you.

William knew Arel was at a new low. Like a man who'd been holding on with his fingernails and couldn't hold on any longer, his mood was bleak and hopeless. He kept saying he didn't want to live anymore. He reached out to William for help.

"You had to bring your problems to me," William groaned. As he allowed himself to remember Arel's golden eyes, so filled with pain, he began to feel his anger taking hold again. "Why did I have to care about you?"

William might have been young, and he might have dismissed most of humanity as unworthy of his devotion, but on that stormy night, he knew that he did care about his best friend. When Arel clung to him and called him brother, William took his pleas to heart and did his best to live up to that title.

"And look what I got for caring about you. Gratitude? One word of appreciation? No! You've treated me like a fiend!"

He stopped himself, trying to use his breath again, trying to calm his outrage. Unwanted feelings were thrusting up from some inner depths. Powerful emotions breached the still waters of his carefully tended mind. They made him flounder in an airless, uncontrolled dimension. It was a place that didn't allow rational thought to govern behavior. But could he stop what was happening? He no sooner stilled his anger when an overwhelming shock of sadness welled up in him.

"I was your friend, Arel. I opened that heart you said I didn't possess, and I gave you the only thing I had to save your sorry ass!"

As he contemplated his attempt to do the right thing, to be a person who could put another's welfare above his own, his mind flashed to New York and his first meeting with Arel. Sitting there at a table in the lounge, Arel glared back at him with hateful eyes. He pronounced William a butcher. Arel didn't weigh any options before he spoke. He didn't consider William's well-being. He simply blurted out his bitterness, wanting to inflict pain, wanting William to suffer.

"You enjoyed your cruelty, you bastard!"

Until that moment, William had never let himself really experience the pain that came with Arel's slurs and meanness. He was strong enough to disregard it all. Now in his present, weakened condition, it punished him more savagely than he thought possible. He never felt so sorry for himself. As a sob escaped his lips, he realized how low he'd sunk. It was a shock that brought back a bit of reason.

"My god, I have to pull myself together!"

Pushing himself out of the chair, he grabbed the remote and stabbed at the buttons, needing to turn off the music. "How can some idiot call this healing?" The melody, with its sad undertones, was making everything worse. It was dredging up crap from his psyche faster than he could field it.

When the room was quiet again, he let out a gasping sigh, rubbed his brow and realized how hot he was. His body had gone from chills to overheating in a matter of minutes. It was a fact that needed to be recorded in his notebook, but he couldn't concentrate on anything but the consuming heat that ravaged his body. As he tore at the buttons on his sweater, he began to shout. "Arel has used me repeatedly and with great pleasure, with not a moment's regard for my welfare!"

It was an unbearable thought that melded with the fever in his brain and threatened to send him into another rage. When he finally got the heavy wool sweater off, he threw it sideways, not thinking about the collector's item that sat on the table next to him. The sound of his expensive Tiffany lamp crashing to the floor, made him jerk around. He sobered immediately. With a scowl of disapproval, he stared down at the mottled gold and green shards of glass that littered the tile. He'd bought the lamp in a small antique shop many years before. He appreciated its beautiful artistry, its geometric design and muted colors. Since then the purchase price of such an item had soared. It's replacement would be very costly.

He sat down in the recliner again and reached for his notebook. He held it tight in his hand as his body's fevered condition made his head throb. His emotions were still throbbing too, but he wouldn't give them another moment's attention. In fact, even the thought of Arel's behavior was reexamined from a calmer state of mind. "This damnable disease has me totally overreacting. Arel isn't a sadist. He's just immature and ignorant."

In many ways, Arel had never grown up. In fact, he seemed less capable than ever when he met William in New York. The guy was barely able to dress himself properly. Raging at Arel was senseless. It was like raging at a bawling infant.

"He's not only a child, he's a very sick one, probably half-mad. If I can't handle this illness, how can he cope rationally? He has so little to work with."

William opened his notebook, running his finger down the page, staring at the notes he wrote earlier. Sadness lingered on the edge of his thoughts, trying to gain a foothold again, trying to remind him of how hard it was to lose his brother that fateful night. But he was determined now, and he pushed the feelings aside. He could only think about the dire situation at hand. He and Arel were infected with something damning. If there was any hope for either of them, it was up to William to find a cure.

Forty-Eight

Peggy walked over to the living room window, put her hands on the wooden sill and let out a sigh of relief. Little Sara was finally down for her nap. The baby still had bouts of crying and fussiness, but she was definitely getting better about going to sleep.

I guess I'm doing okay.

As she adjusted to being a mother, she had other worries that nagged at her active mind. Staring out the window, she turned her attention to the mail boxes that stood side by side on the street. One belonged to her and Tim and one belonged to Arel. Arel was normally quite punctual about checking his mail.

Peggy glanced at the clock.

Where is he?

If she could have a quick chat at the mail box, it might be her opportunity to find out what was going on in Arel's world.

Oh no!

Michael was walking down Arel's driveway. He was headed for the mailbox.

"I knew it. Arel is avoiding me." She let the words come out in a disappointed pout.

"What's going on?" Tim asked as he came over.

She turned and stared up at him. "Don't say it. You think I'm a busybody."

Tim leaned over and kissed her cheek. "I don't think that at all."

She pushed past him and walked into the kitchen. "Why am I always the one who worries about everybody?"

278

Tim followed her. "You care about people. Maybe the rest of us aren't as thoughtful."

She paused at the counter, looking at the yellow ceramic owl. The cookie jar's bright green eyes stared back, inviting her to sample its contents. She put its large, yellow head aside and grabbed for a chocolate chip cookie.

Tim quickly intervened. "Sorry, sweetie." He had hold of her hand before she could get the cookie to her mouth. "You told me to stop you, remember?"

She frowned in spite of the fact that Tim was simply doing as he was told. "I know what I said, but this is an emergency. I have to have something to steady my nerves. I didn't think I'd ever get Sara to go back to sleep."

Tim carefully pried the cookie from her fingers and pulled her into his arms. "How about a hug?"

She pulled away from him. "You're sweet, Tim, but a hug isn't going to help."

"Then tell me what's going on? You looked a little upset when you were at the window."

"I keep trying to figure out what happened in New York with Arel and his friend. Maybe I am a meddling buttinsky, but mysteries are my weakness. I want to know why Arel is hiding himself away again."

"Honey, I told you what happened."

"I know you did, but there has to be more to it than what you said."

Tim narrowed his brows. "I'm not aware of anything. That first night, Arel met his friend. Afterwards, like I said, he seemed upset, but he wouldn't talk about—"

"This friend, was he some kind of jerk? Why would Arel be so upset if the guy was nice?"

"From what I observed, the man was very businesslike. He acted like one of those corporate dynamos, very sure of himself. Still, he also seemed genuinely concerned when he said goodbye to Arel."

Peggy straightened her shoulders, feeling confident in her questioning. Tim was wonderful, the best husband anyone could have, but he wasn't always tuned in to other people like she was. "I hate to say this, but maybe you're wrong."

Tim paused. "Maybe, but I've always been a pretty good judge of character, and this guy didn't seem like the type that wanted to cause a problem."

"I see." The words came out in a sigh. Tim was trying his best, but he wasn't telling her anything new. Yet, there was still that uneasy feeling, a neediness that made her glance at the cookie jar again. It was followed by an image of herself standing on the bathroom scale and grimacing. She turned away from the jar and headed to the coffee maker. "You want a cup of coffee?"

"Sounds good."

She took two large mugs off the mug tree and filled them with a freshly made brew. "Thanks for getting up and taking care of Sara early this morning. I really needed that extra hour of sleep."

Tim took one of the mugs and sipped some of the hot coffee. "I'm sorry that I'm not able to be more helpful about Arel." He frowned again. "But there was something weird about that last night in New York."

Peggy's eyes widened with curiosity. "Weird? What happened?"

"Like I said before, Arel was a mess the first night, but the second day, he transformed. You should have seen him checking out all the sights. He had so much energy. I've never seen him so excited. You know Arel, even when he's happy, he has that English reserve."

"Why didn't you tell me this before?"

"I didn't think much about it. I was so tired when I got home."

Peggy nodded as she ran her hand over Tim's dark grey t-shirt, noting the solid feel of his chest. Even when she was a skinny kid in pigtails, he was her hero, the person she wanted to marry when she grew up. Now, she realized some of his human frailties, how exhausted he could get after long hours with the baby. After his trip to New York, he needed a day of downtime to catch up on his rest. "I'm sorry about my dreams, visions, whatever you call them. I'm always asking you to come to the rescue."

He put his mug on the counter and took hold of her arms. "Like I said before, you care about people. I admire you for that."

"What about you? You flew to New York and made sure Arel was okay."

He smiled and let go of her, picking up his mug again. "Believe me, Arel was more than okay that second day. Kevin and I were both worn out after sightseeing. And as for his friend, William, he acted like he was really in a bad state that second night."

"What was wrong with him?"

"All I know is that he went into Arel's room looking like Joe Dapper and came out tripping over his own feet. He was very shook up."

The information pinged something deep down in the pit of Peggy's stomach. "Even so, we both know that our Arel couldn't be to blame. He's sweet." She smiled as she thought about Arel holding Sara, how his face lit up when he cooed to her. "He wouldn't hurt a fly."

Tim stared at his mug, but he didn't comment.

Peggy reached out for his hand. "Did you remember something else?"

"Maybe."

"What? Tell me."

"There was something about the way Arel looked when he came to our room after meeting his friend. There was something different about him."

"Different? How?"

"You know how you just said he wouldn't hurt a fly?"

"Yes, so?"

Tim took a sip of his coffee and frowned. "I got the feeling that if he had a flyswatter, our Arel would have used it and not thought twice about the fate of the fly."

"Are you sure? That doesn't sound like him. I've never seen him want to harm anyone or anything."

Tim shrugged. "It was probably just me. I was tired after traipsing around the city all day. Maybe I misread what I saw." He sat his mug down on the table. "I better get going. I told Kevin I'd help him put a shelf up in their laundry room. Carol says she needs a place for her soap and stuff."

Peggy let out another sigh. "Poor Carol."

Tim stared back. "Poor Carol? Kevin took her to dinner and the movies last week."

"I know, but she was hoping he'd open up a little. She said they had a pleasant meal, but he was still pretty quiet. At the movies, Kevin hardly paid her any attention. Instead he ate most of a giant tub of popcorn and two boxes of candy. Obviously, he was more interested in food than his wife."

"Yes, but didn't they go to one of those chick flicks? Kevin can't handle that sort of thing without food." Tim paused and gave her a polite smile. "Maybe a snack helps him too."

She smiled back. "Fine, I get it. My brother and I both use food to nurture ourselves."

Tim gave her a pleading look. "Honey, I know that Kevin is really trying, but Carol needs to give him time."

She walked him to the door. "Fine, if you say so. I'll try to talk to Carol and smooth her feathers."

Tim turned and kissed her cheek. "Kevin would appreciate that."

As Peggy watched him leave, she knew she had so many things to be thankful for. Perhaps she needed to keep her mind on that fact instead of thinking about Kevin or Arel.

Still, I wonder if Tim is right. Could our sweet Arel have another side to his personality?

As if to answer her own question, she had a quick flash of a different kind of Arel. He had a rolled up newspaper in his hand, and he slammed it down on a large, unsuspecting insect that was running down the sidewalk. Afterwards, as the crippled insect remained struggling on the concrete, Arel simply went on his way. The vision was a little shocking.

No, I won't believe it! I know Arel. He's not like that.

Forty-Nine

Arel grabbed the grocery bags out of Michael's hands and put them on the kitchen floor with all the others. "Thanks for helping me unload."

Michael stood in the doorway. "From the looks of all the food you bought, I have to suppose that you have a big dinner planned for this weekend."

"Yes, I do." Arel paused, almost touched his face and quickly dropped his hand to his side. He'd been distanced from his friends since his trip, and he needed to let them know that he hadn't forgotten them. "I hope you don't mind helping with the dinner too."

"Of course not."

"Really? Are you sure you don't mind all the stuff I have you doing? You're not my kitchen slave."

"I never saw myself in that role."

Arel looked down and ran his hand over the kitchen counter. "I guess what I'm wondering is if you think I treat you with respect and courtesy?"

"What are you getting at?"

"I simply want you to be honest with me. Am I a self-centered bastard like William said? If I am, I want to know."

"I've never thought of you that way."

"Then why am I constantly feeling like I am? It's like I have a subliminal news feed coming into my brain. And I keep feeling like I should apologize to someone." He went over to the table and slumped down in one of the chairs. "In the past Kevin and Tim have made comments, but I hoped they were mostly kidding."

Michael grabbed some canned goods out of a grocery bag and took them to the cupboard. "They do have a great sense of humor."

Arel looked up for a moment, but he quickly returned his gaze to his clinched hands. "I can't stop thinking about how I've done something reprehensible."

"I see." Michael stacked each can carefully on a cupboard shelf, making sure that the label was facing forward.

"Well, I'm tired of it," Arel protested.

A long pause followed as Michael continued to put away more groceries. After the canned goods were neatly stowed away, he put the vegetables in the sink and ran water in a large bowl. "After I wash the carrots, I'll make sure they're dry before I put them in a new bag." He glanced back at Arel. "That's how you like it done, right?"

"Yes," Arel grumbled. Michael was following directions that Arel had laid down, but watching the angel carry out his orders was adding to his burden of guilt. "For heaven's sake, Michael, stop fussing with all that and sit down."

Michael glanced over again. "What about the green onions, do you—"

"To hell with the onions!" Arel made himself calm down as soon as the words were out. He paused and let his gaze rest on the floor tiles. After Carey ate lunch the day before, the kid had dropped his cherry pie and tried to clean up. He'd missed several spots, and now the floor was sticky. Arel automatically added mopping the floor to his list of duties he needed to take care of before the weekend party. "I'm sorry about yelling, but you don't have to keep reminding me about how obsessive I am. I got the picture when you were arranging the place mats so perfectly."

Michael dried his hands, and looked at Arel. "Is that what you think I'm doing, that I'm trying to make you feel a certain way?"

"Yes, and it's working. I see my faults very clearly."

Michael took a seat at the table. "Let me explain something to you. You invited me to live here, and I thought that meant that you wanted me to be part of the household."

"Yes, that's right. You're my right hand man." Arel stopped himself. "I don't mean that in a demeaning way, as if I think you're here to take care of the yard and kitchen chores."

Michael smiled. "I know what you mean, and I'm very grateful that you consider me a friend."

"Of course you're my friend!" Arel fingered the bandage on his face. His cheek was throbbing constantly at this point. The pain was wearing down any patience he was trying so desperately to hold on to. "I know I'm always angry or shouting, but I don't mean it."

"Arel, look at me," Michael said in a beseeching voice.

Arel lifted his eyes and saw Michael's face brighten. "What is it?"

"You're wrong about my motives. I enjoy taking care of the garden and doing what I can around the house. I can't take away the pain that you're in, but I'd like to think that I can do other things that make your life a little easier. That's part of being a friend."

"That's very nice, but why don't I see it the same way?"

Michael paused. "My actions are seen through a filter that you've been carrying around, a filter called guilt. It distorts what you perceive."

"But I should be guilty. I used your blood for my own needs, and I don't know what to do about it."

"Perhaps you should start with your cheek," Michael said, pointing in Arel's direction.

Arel felt something wet on his face. He swiped at it with his hand and noted that his fingers were covered in blood. "Great, now the damn thing's bleeding." He grabbed a napkin off the table and patted his cheek.

"Your problem isn't going to go away by ignoring it. Help your body to heal. Let's discuss the night you lost your second brother."

"I've already remembered all that during that session with Kell."

"I know, but perhaps we could go over some of it again."

"Why, what's that night got to do with my cheek?"

"Why did you provoke William to bite you?"

"Because he's a monster! He needs to be punished!"

"So tell me about the night that you think he betrayed you."

Arel stared gloomily at the kitchen cabinets in front of him. Everything was in order on the shelves, but his life was a shambles. Now Michael wanted him to recount the worst day of his life. He didn't know where to start, but after a couple of minutes, the words began to come. He even smiled as he relived the first part of the story.

"William used to welcome me into his house with a flourish, calling me 'the tortured soul.' I guess I lived up to that title on that dismal occasion. I'd walked over in the rain, and I was almost numb

285

with cold. I was also in a horrible, depressed state. But my nickname also referred to my background. In his own way, William could be wise. He understood how I'd grown up, and I suppose he made allowances. I knew that his childhood had been vile too, but he was so strong in spite of it. Sometimes I envied the way he could put it behind him. Now I realize he hadn't put it behind him at all. He had no tolerance for people, except to use them for his own ends. But that night, he was very kind to me.

"When we got together, we usually argued more than we talked, each of us venting our frustrations from different points of view. But on that night, I was too deep in my self-pity to be roused by his taunts or his teasing. Maybe William knew me and what my bad moods could portend because he stopped joking around. He just stared at me. Then he sat down in a chair by the fire and watched the flames for a long time.

"I must have dozed off because I remember waking up and seeing him crouched down in front of me. His face was almost radiant. He started telling me how he was going to help me. He was going to give me something that would take all the pain away. When I looked back at him, with the glow of the fire behind him, it was like I was looking at one of your kind."

Arel paused, wanting to stop and knowing that Michael was right about getting to the cause of the pain he was in. "Anyway, I believed William, or maybe I needed to believe him. When he grabbed hold of me, I embraced him back, feeling like I finally mattered to someone. I began to weep in his arms, and he held me tight against him, like the father, the mother, that I never had. He stroked my hair, telling me not to be afraid. He kept repeating it over and over, like he didn't want to see me suffer anymore."

Arel stopped again. His cheek was on fire, but the memory of that night was even more painful. He closed his eyes, shutting out the light that streamed through the kitchen window. He also shut out the memory that filled his chest with desolation. "I can't do this. I don't want to think about it. I can't." He stood up from the table so fast he tipped the chair over backwards.

Michael stared up at him. "Why?"

"Because it was all a lie! William lied to me! He wasn't my friend! You understand that, don't you, Michael?"

Michael didn't answer, but his face remained calm and composed.

Arel glared back. "Dammit, Michael, tell me that I'm right, that William was a fiend who ruined my life!"

When Michael remained mute, Arel leaned over and righted the fallen chair. His voice felt spent when he asked his next question. "Why won't you say something? What do you want from me?"

Michael's tone was very direct. "It takes a lot of courage to face the heart's secrets. People fear the pain buried there. But it doesn't go away on its own. It festers in the vessel just like your cheek is festering. You need to examine more about what happened with William on that night when you felt betrayed."

"That's the one thing that I don't want to do."

Michael remained very still as he spoke. "I understand that, but it's necessary if you want to heal what's hidden inside of you. What can't you face about that night?"

"Nothing! I swear!" The more Michael probed in his steady, don't-frighten-the-wildlife approach, the more Arel felt like he was being backed into a trap. "William is the villain in the story, period."

"Really? You don't think you might be refusing to face something else?"

"What? I faced those times when my father nearly beat me to death. I'm not a coward."

"Sometimes another man's ignorance is easier to accept and release than—"

"Than what?"

"That's for you to discover."

It was a rare moment. Arel had never known Michael to behave so fixedly. He wasn't going to let the story go. Arel sat down again, stoically clenching his jaw.

Michael leaned in. "Let's go back to the part where you said that you and William were embracing."

Arel let out an overly loud laugh. "Oh yes, what a Hallmark moment that was."

"What happened next?"

Arel leaned back, and snorted out his anger. "William bit me! He sucked my blood and then made me drink the vile stuff that flows through his veins." He stopped and targeted Michael with hateful eyes. "There, are you satisfied?"

Michael stood up and walked over to him. "Would you like to know what William was feeling?"

"Why would I want that?" For some reason the question made his gut hurt. He stood up, pushed Michael aside, and moved to the counter. He stared down at the vegetables waiting to be washed. "Why in heaven would I want to know what goes through William's twisted mind?"

"Trust me, you need to know William's thoughts."

Michael moved closer, reaching out and putting his hand on Arel's cheek. "You can do this," he whispered. "Explore that night from William's point of view."

"I don't think so."

"Are you afraid?"

"No, I just think it's a waste of time."

"Really? Are you sure?" Michael asked as he took his hand off Arel's cheek and placed it on Arel's chest.

Michael's touch was usually comforting, but not this time. Instead of healing Arel's pain, it served to illuminate it. Arel could feel how heavy his heart was, how it was laboring under some great, invisible affliction.

"It's time," Michael whispered.

The statement made Arel's knees go weak. He struggled to remain in a standing position. "Time for what?"

"For the truth."

The three words pounded in Arel's ears, but a part of him knew they were the key to lifting the weight he was carrying. He'd been burdened with it for so long that he assumed it was a natural part of who he was. Now, something in Michael's eyes told him otherwise. Still he hesitated. "I lied to you, Michael. I am afraid."

"I know, but you can do this. You're strong enough to face what you've been running from all this time."

Arel offered a weak smile, knowing he had to do what Michael was asking if he wanted some measure of peace. "I wish I had your confidence."

Michael's hand grew warmer as it rested on Arel's chest. The next moment, a flash of light sliced through Arel's brain. It short circuited his consciousness, his awareness of who he was. In that flash, he was transported back in time. He felt himself become William, a younger version of the man he'd recently met in New

York. This William sat in front of a fireplace while a drunken Arel slept nearby.

* * *

William studied the flames of the fire, but he couldn't stop thinking about his only friend. Arel was in a miserable state, more intoxicated than usual. As time passed, he was slipping further away from the world, away from William. Arel was giving up.

They're going to fish him out of the river one of these days.

Why had he let Arel get close in the first place? They were nothing alike. Arel wasn't strong. He was the kid who didn't know how to fight back when others beat him up. He was the one that looked up afterwards, all bloody-nosed, wondering why it happened.

A soft groan coming from Arel made William look over. Arel's brows were knitted as if in pain as he clutched at the blanket. His fingers were slender and fine-boned, and he usually kept them hidden as much as possible. William knew it was a reflex after all the beatings he'd had from his father. Even in a slumbering state, he tried to protect himself.

"I keep explaining it to you, Arel, why don't you listen? Human beings are contemptible creatures," William whispered in a seething voice. "They don't give a damn about you, and you can't give a damn about them."

William knew Arel didn't understand such wisdom and brought his gaze back to the fire. He hadn't let himself worry about helpless creatures in a long time, not since he was a child. He learned that it didn't pay.

Put your heart out there for a second, and somebody is going to beat it to a pulp.

So what should he do? Should he throw Arel out in the cold? Should he rid himself of someone who couldn't fend for himself? "You're not my problem," he mumbled as he tried to avoid looking at his sleeping guest. Getting up and going to the fire, he grabbed the poker and stabbed at the logs, stirring up the flames, getting a little more warmth in the room. "I have to let you go."

It was the best solution. He knew it. If he wanted to stay strong himself, he couldn't afford to be soft with his feelings. As he was returning to his seat, Arel opened his eyes for a moment and smiled at him.

"Thank you, Will, for being more to me than my own brother. You're the only one who has truly cared." Arel's golden eyes were so bright, so filled with the love that he was capable of showing on rare occasions.

In that moment, William hated Arel more than he hated anyone. "You bastard," he sighed as Arel closed his eyes again. "How do you do it? You worthless bastard, how do you make me want to help you?"

That's when he decided to give Arel the gift. He knew he shouldn't. He knew in the depths of his soul that Arel would never thank him for it because he wouldn't know how to use it. But William didn't have a choice. He didn't want to lose Arel too. He'd lost too much in his young life. He wouldn't let the world destroy the last thing that mattered to him. After William passed on his gift, miserable or not, Arel would be alive. He'd have time to find his strength. That's what mattered.

For a moment, William felt his stomach grab, warning him to rethink his decision. He knew Arel so well, had studied him like he used to study a rare bird in the meadows. Arel was never aware of it. Arel was too caught up in his own world to notice William's contemplative modes.

This will be the end for us. You're too eager to judge me already. After it's over, you'll never understand why I have to do this.

His chest tightened as the pain of loss swept over him. But he pushed it away like all the other pain in his life. He wouldn't let it stop him from this last duty to something beautiful in the world. If Arel didn't value his own life, William did.

When he crouched down in front of Arel to wake him up, William broke his own rule, the one that had always been of paramount importance. He let himself care about another person more than he cared about himself. Reaching out, he ran his hand over Arel's face.

"My friend, no matter what you think, I'm doing this for you."

When Arel opened his eyes and stared at him, his gaze was innocent. "Why do you bother with me? Why?"

William didn't reply. His heart opened one last time, letting a warm glow fill him with purpose. He knew he'd pay for it later, but for that one moment, he didn't care.

* * *

Arel came back to himself with Michael kneeling next to him, shaking him gently. When he had a measure of himself, when he could let go of William's mind, he looked away, wishing desperately that he could forget what he'd just experienced. If he could be numb, it would have been so much better than feeling the truth.

"Don't try to figure it all out at once," Michael said.

Arel looked up at him. With his emotional boat ready to capsize, he clutched at the serenity that Michael embodied. It didn't help. "What's wrong with me?" he managed in a rough voice. "First, I find out that William is the responsible one, the one who took charge of his life with the real facts. Now I realize how much more capable of love he is. He was right about me. I think I would have killed myself shortly after that night if he hadn't intervened. He tried to save me, and all that I could do was hate him for it. That's irony, isn't it?"

"You did your best from your perspective," Michael offered as he helped Arel get to his feet.

Arel grabbed hold of the back of the chair. "I am a selfish bastard." As Arel spoke, a deep wretchedness flooded in. He saw William smiling at him that last time. They were both so young, but William was willing even then to endure the wrath that he knew Arel would bring down on his head. And Arel carried out that punishment repeatedly. He caned William over and over with his condemnation, but William never spoke about the sacrifice he'd made for Arel.

"You're right, Michael. This is worse than remembering my father's cruelty. This is my cruelty, my self-centered blindness. Was I any better than my father? I did the same kind of thing that he did. I made William the scapegoat. I made him responsible for my misery. Now I'm sure he feels like I've cursed him." His body began to shake with remorse. "Is that what I've done to him? Is your blood . . . . is my blood his death warrant? It nearly killed me, and I had you to help me. William has no one."

"He might have a friend."

291

"Who? I'm the only one he ever trusted. I don't think that's changed."

"You're right."

Arel studied Michael's hopeful face. "You're talking about me, aren't you? I'm that friend."

Michael smiled. "You were once his best friend."

"But not anymore, I don't know how to think in those terms."

"Then you're right, William doesn't have anyone."

Fifty

William didn't know what time it was. He was exhausted after a fourteen-hour stretch of research. Bone-weary, he battled his way from his lab to his recliner once again. The chair was fast becoming the place that he used for everything from note taking to a substitute for his bed.

Eyeing his journal on the side table, he knew he needed to catch up on his recent observations, but he was too worn. Still, his work was the only thing that kept his emotions under control. Earlier that day, he destroyed another lamp, this time on purpose. The light was too bright, and it made his eyes hurt. He only wanted to change the bulb to a lower wattage, but when he burned his fingers, he lost it. He flung the floor lamp across the room and took out one of his favorite wall hangings, an original Stones poster from 1972. The casualties were mounting.

"Dammit, William, it's a good thing most of your valuable art pieces and collectables are upstairs. As for neatness, this place is becoming a pigsty."

He liked order, but he couldn't move from the chair to straighten up the mess in front of him. He was running on empty. For a moment, he wondered if he was on his way out. Would he simply die in the recliner one day? "Oh well, if it happens, I've had a good run."

When he did a quick review, he was satisfied with his life. He had enjoyed himself in many ways. "But what a horrid thing it is to be born and have to wait to grow up." His childhood was the only part of his life that he liked to forget. "Ah well, I did finally grow up, and that's what matters."

Closing his eyes, he knew he needed sleep. He needed to put everything aside for a while. Yet his brain wanted to keep going, to go back to the lab and keep searching for answers. Finally, he lost the battle. His body was insistent. He started to drift off. A moment later, he was asleep and slipping into a dream.

* * *

The ends of William's blond, curly hair, fluttered in the breeze, but most of his seven-year-old locks were matted against his scalp. He was hot and sweaty as he ran, his breath coming in and out in gasps. He was one of the best runners when he was at boarding school, but he knew he wasn't good enough now. The sound of his father's hounds could be heard in the next field over. Their voices were raised in excitement and anticipation. He hated the sound. It meant the pack was gearing up for a kill. William knew the dogs were relentless once they latched on to their quarry.

Tears were blinding him, and he swiped them away with anger and a building fury. He prided himself in not giving in to such an emotional display. Many a cruel teacher had made it their job to whip him, to break him of his wild, stubborn spirit. They'd all failed. He could stand the pain they meted out. But one of his foxes was going to die. He couldn't bear the thought of it.

As he flew through the grasses, briars snagged at his skin, ripping at his wiry, thin legs. But he paid no heed to anything but a need to save what he loved. This was his kingdom, and the creatures that lived in it belonged to him. At least that's what he pretended. Now, it was being invaded by the enemy.

"No! Don't!" He came to an abrupt halt, falling down on his knees in despair and exhaustion as he listened to the change in the dogs' pitch and cry. They began to bay, signaling to the hunters that they were closing in on their target. He knew he was too far away to make a difference. He never had a chance in the first place, but he needed to try.

Where the school master failed, the screams of a fox being attacked and torn apart by the pack, broke his young heart. It was as if he was being torn apart too. When the screams died down, he knew the animal was beyond crying out. In that moment, rage and grief flooded William's young mind and body. He hated the dogs, but even more he hated the grown-ups in his world, those who destroyed all the beauty and life that he treasured.

"You're all bastards!" he cursed in a sobbing voice.

* * *

William was screaming as he came awake. "Someday I'll tear you apart!" he yelled in misery, still the boy kneeling in the field. The shouted threat finally brought him back to reality. As he opened his eyes and the room came into view, he had to steady his breath. He was gasping just like the boy in the dream. Lifting a hand to rub the sleep away, he realized that his face was wet. "Dammit!" But it wasn't just the tears that tore at his resolve to remain strong. His heart was still racing, still breaking as it had in the dream. Once again, the wretched screams of the fox echoed in his mind. He grabbed the handle on the recliner and righted himself, forcing the nightmare back where it belonged.

He couldn't remember the last time that he let himself get that emotional. He swallowed hard as he looked around the room and let his gaze rest on the lab area. Some unknown disease had hold of him. It had taken up residence in his body, but it was also dismantling his mind. "I'm falling apart," he said matter-of-factly. He made the words sound as clinical as possible, just a line on a doctor's report, but when he reached for his journal, his hand was shaking so hard he couldn't manage the small task. The book slipped from his grasping fingers. He was losing everything, and he couldn't stop what was happening.

Fifty-One

Arel sat in the living room, away from his guests, in the chair Michael usually occupied when he read his gardening news. It was a quiet part of the room, close to the front windows. It was the ideal setting for soothing baby Sara. Arel was hosting a dinner for his friends that evening. The baby woke up crying halfway through the main course. Now, she was cradled in the crook of Arel's arm. Pink cheeked and adorned with soft locks of golden hair, she seemed content. Her sparkling, dark brown eyes were transfixed by Arel's baby whisperings. They were finally bonding. As Arel cooed at his small charge, Peggy came over and sat down on a plush ottoman next to his chair.

"That was a yummy dessert Michael served. I just wish you didn't have to babysit while we finished," she said with an apologetic frown.

Arel gave her a brief smile before he returned his gaze to Sara. The infant could still be demanding. When someone was holding her, she insisted on being the center of attention. "No problem, Sara and I are getting a chance to know each other a little better," he said. "I found out that she likes to be told how beautiful she is."

Peggy laughed as she reached out and tied the lace on Sara's tiny, white shoe. "None of us have seen much of you these last couple of weeks." She looked up. "I'm glad to see that your cheek is finally healing."

He put his hand to his face and realized there was no pain. Once he cleared his wrathful ideas about being a victim, his body miraculously healed. "Yes, it's just fine."

"So what are you up to lately?" Peggy used a friendly tone, but her eyes were sweeping over his person as if she might find a flaw in his "just fine" declaration.

Arel's gaze quickly returned to the baby, but his mind was scrambling down a path that evaded Peggy's inquisitive nature. With the William fiasco looming over his head, he needed space, not more questions. "Michael loaned me some books on gardening. I want to learn more about flowers and that sort of thing." It was a lie, but it made Peggy's smile broaden.

"You'll be great with plants, just like you're great with children."

He carefully touched one of Sara's curls, fingering its softness. "When I look at babies, all that I see is total innocence."

"Yes, at first we are innocent." Peggy gave him a sideways frown. "But we change. You know my history. I became the skinny kid with a big mouth. I was always stirring up trouble that my brother had to sort out."

Arel smiled back, knowing how to handle the familiar relationship they often shared. Peggy liked to confess her sins, and Arel tried to help her accept her virtues. "And now, you've grown into a wonderful mother."

Peggy gave him a grateful smirk. "I do love being a mom."

"Me too," Carol said as she came over to join them. She leaned over and admired Sara. "Peggy and I are both lucky to have such wonderful children."

Arel sighed. "And your children are very lucky to have you two as their mothers. You're both very loving people."

"It's easy for a mother to love her child, right Carol?" Peggy asked.

"Yes, of course," Carol agreed. "When Ariel, Jr. smiles at me, I feel like the sun just came out. But my feelings about him are natural for a mom."

Arel responded before he could censor himself. "Not always. Some mothers have no idea about love."

Carol frowned. "What do you mean?"

"Nothing," Arel said quickly. "It's old history, that's all."

"Oh come on, Arel," Peggy whined. "You're always insisting that we tell all. Now it's your turn to share a little."

"That's right," Carol added. "Was your mother a bit difficult?"

Arel couldn't hold back a cynical laugh. "My mother wished I'd never been conceived."

"Your mother didn't want you?" Peggy asked in a sharp tone.

Carol stiffened. "What about after you were born? Did she change her mind?"

Arel gaped back mutely. Why did he mention his baby days when he knew how protective Peggy and Carol could be? His mind scurried into the first bit of underbrush it could find. "No, my mother had a busy life. She hired a nanny."

"Was she nice?" Carol asked.

Peggy's eyes widened. "Did she make up for your mother's neglect?"

"No, not exactly." As the two women queried him, Arel felt like he was under the gaze of two lionesses who'd found a stray cub in the bushes.

Peggy inched in closer. "So your nanny wasn't nice either?"

Arel muttered out the first thing that came to mind. "I think I cried a lot. I'm sure I was a difficult baby, you know what I mean, the sickly kind."

Peggy reached out for his arm. "You poor thing. You were just a baby, and you were sick and alone. How awful."

Arel shrugged. "It doesn't matter now, does it?"

Peggy glanced up at Carol. "Of course it matters, right Carol?"

Carol let out a little gasp. "Goodness, Arel, I thought I had it tough just seeing my parents go through a divorce. But to think that you never were loved from the start . . . that's horrible."

"What about your dad? Did he love you?" Peggy asked.

Arel's mind blanked for a moment. How could he field questions about his father? The guy hated him. "We were never close, but you know that old adage, right? We have to forgive and forget."

Peggy sat up again, looking confused. "I don't think it's that simple, sweetie, not if both your parents rejected you."

Carol blinked back a couple of times. "How did you manage with that kind of start in life? Weren't you bitter?"

Arel didn't answer Carol, but his mind was screaming out an answer.

Was I bitter? That's like asking if fire is really hot!

His mind was being backed into a corner and a physical change of location was his best avenue of escape. The baby was his perfect excuse. Little Sara's eyes were closing as she drifted off to sleep. "I think somebody is ready for bed," he said as he carefully gathered her up and handed her over to Peggy. Trying not to seem too obvious, he stood up. "And I better check on the kitchen and how Michael is coping."

Carol snagged his arm before he could walk away. Her eyes were kind and caring. "I'm sorry if we've been asking too many questions. Peggy and I just care about you."

"I know you do," he replied, suddenly ashamed at how easy it was to keep lying to both women. In reality, he wouldn't be taking up gardening. And he'd never forgotten a minute of his rotten childhood. Yet, he could spout off stuff about forgiveness. Did he have the courage to admit his feelings? He suddenly felt the need to put things right and admit what he was thinking. "If you really want the truth, I was bitter. In fact, I grew up hating life. When I was a young man, I wanted to end it all, but I wasn't given that choice. A person I trusted made sure of that."

As soon as he voiced the sentiment, Arel realized he hadn't given the issue of self-determination much thought. He'd been so busy hating William for cursing him, he forgot to hate him for denying him a freedom he felt he was entitled to. If he wanted to kill himself, it was his business, not William's.

Carol reached out and squeezed his arm. "I'm so glad you're here with us. Thank goodness for your friend."

Arel tried to maintain a pleasant expression as he grappled with his newest revelation. "Yes, lucky me."

Peggy looked up with expectant eyes. "Was this person the man you met in New York?"

Arel nodded. "Yes, it was."

* * *

299

Arel showed the last of his guests out the front door, locked up for the night and went in search of Michael. He found his friend getting a breath of air on the back porch. Arel was happy he'd put on a jacket. The sky was clear and there was a chilly breeze blowing. "Aren't you cold, Michael?" he asked as he stepped up to the deck railing. "You're standing here in your shirtsleeves."

Michael shook his head. "I enjoy a brisk evening. It makes my physical form feel even more alive."

Arel crossed his arms as his body started to shiver. He admired Michael's stamina, but he didn't share the idea that standing out on a cold night was fun. "I envy your take on life. I've always felt it was a burden to be alive."

Michael's brows raised a bit. "Even now?"

"Especially now. I only had myself to worry about before. Now I'm responsible for getting William into a mess."

Michael chuckled. "The mess I passed on to you?"

Arel uncrossed his arms and leaned on the railing. "How am I supposed to answer that? In fact, forget about what I called the 'mess.' I want to discuss the fact that William, who supposedly acted in my best interest—"

"Supposedly?"

"The point is that William interfered with my free will. If a person wants to kill themselves, it's their business."

Michael lifted his gaze to the night sky. "Didn't you try to do the same with Justina?"

Arel jerked back. "What else could I do? When a person is grabbing a razor and they're ready to slit their throat—"

"How is that different from what William did?"

"William didn't know for certain that I was going to do myself in."

Michael laughed again. "He made a pre-emptive strike?"

"Do you find that amusing?"

Michael sobered and shook his head. "No, but I find it strange that a human will often react negatively to an act of love, that they don't want to make allowances when it comes to other people's intentions."

"William may have had a good intention, but that doesn't mean it was the right intention."

"You tried to help Justina by distancing yourself from her. As a result of your intention, she decided to take her life."

Arel threw up his hands. "You've just proven my point. A good intention doesn't equal a right intention."

"Or perhaps you could look at it this way. Let's say that an individual believes certain things about life and themselves, and they do their best with those beliefs. When that individual decides on a course of action that involves another person, it is up to the other person to decide *how to react to* that decision. You tried to do the best you knew with Justina. She reacted by thinking she was worthless and that life wasn't worth living. "

"So the free will part is about how we react to circumstances?"

"Well, let's think about how William reacted to being a vampire. He thought of it as an opportunity. However, you thought of it as a curse. William's reaction gave him power, and your decision—"

"And my decision made me a victim. Another smart move, right?"

"You did your best with what you believed. But here's something to think about. In my eyes, the soul is immortal. It will always be part of the Creator's energy. You can only forget that fact for awhile. Once you remember the truth, you'll be free."

"Is that why you showed up on my doorstep? Are you my reminder?"

Michael's eyes sparked brighter. "I took a chance. I tried to give you an opportunity to find yourself again. I think William wanted to do that too."

Fifty-Two

William walked along the upper level hall on unsteady legs. He needed to get away from the lab and his problems. The main floor of his home was beautifully furnished and would help to shift his mood. He was sure he needed an attitude adjustment after all his rages and rants. Unfortunately, before he could admire what his old life looked like, with all its amazing paintings and exquisite collectibles, he passed a wall mirror.

Holy hell!

Bloodshot, lifeless eyes stared back at him. His once shiny, dark-blond hair was dull and tangled. With sunken cheeks and a week's worth of beard, he had a haunted look that made him gape back in shock. He knew he was spiraling downward, but now his condition hit him full force.

If someone dressed me in the garb of a homeless derelict, I'd look the part.

A couple of weeks before, he wouldn't have thought it possible to look this bad. The situation called for immediate measures. He straightened up, forced his shoulders back, and went into the hall bathroom. For a start, a shave was mandatory. It was an easy chore that he'd performed countless times. In fact, he enjoyed the ritual of personal care. When he stepped out into the world, he took pleasure in knowing that his physical appearance reflected his code of personal responsibility.

Most of the hordes of humanity have no respect for themselves. I'll do myself in before I allow myself to be like them.

He opened the medicine cabinet and reached for his straight razor. He never bothered to exchange the efficient tool for a more modern shaver. But as he lathered his face, he began to have second thoughts about that decision. His hands were shaking again. Sometimes, when he worked in the lab, they could be unsteady instruments that dropped slides and fumbled with reports. Now, in spite of that fact, he needed to persevere, to bring his body back in line with what a human being should look like. He hesitated for only the slightest moment before he brought the razor to his face and attacked the stubble.

"Dammit!"

As soon as the implement touched his skin, his hand jumped and the blade sliced into his cheek. Pain and a flash of Arel's bright eyes, staring back at him, both hit at the same time. Was Arel happy about infecting him? Was he actually smiling at William's misery?

No, he's too ignorant to know that both of us are sick.

William clutched at the razor. When paranoia threatened, he had to silence it quickly. Arel might love to play the victim, but William wouldn't allow himself to tread that treacherous path. However, as he looked at his thin, wasted face and watched the blood flow down his beard, the term "pathetic loser" came to mind. Like it or not, he was joining the ranks of the disempowered, those who were doomed to failure. It was an agonizing thought that turned into a seething resentment. His clarity and ability to stay the rational course was lost to a need for retribution.

"Arel, you idiot! You refused to take any responsibility for yourself and now we're both on our way to hell!" Even as he screamed out the words, he brought the razor back to his face. He hated looking like some neglected animal. When he arrived in New York, he was so confident, so certain about life. He loved who he was. But what was he now? Had Arel been right about curses? Had Arel been right about blame and victims? His hand shook harder as the blade hovered over his face.

Arel's pulling me into his world. It's not the disease that we share that's destroying me, it's his rotten attitude.

The thought could have made him even angrier, but instead, it had a sobering effect. As he blinked back at himself, he saw a small spark in his eyes, the spark that told him the truth about life and about himself. His hand slowly opened, and the razor fell into the sink. He was still in charge of his life. Arel would never take that away from him.

He immediately began to search the cabinets. He had an electric razor somewhere. It would have to do until he was himself again. After he located it in the back of the vanity, he used the razor's noisy hum to act as a sort of mantra. It quieted his nerves as he got rid of his beard. Once his face was restored to smooth skin, he felt better. He knew that he was working too hard, but he had no choice. Time was running out. His mind and body were rapidly failing.

Arel and I are both on our way to our graves and what is Arel thinking about? He wants me to go back to New York to chat.

His old friend was going to remain ignorant to the end.

But he'll be dead soon, I'm sure.

The way Arel acted, going from manic to depressed to burning up with fever, clearly indicated that he was in an advanced state of disease. Thankfully, William wasn't at that stage, but he wasn't getting anywhere with his research. He had approached the problem from every medical angle he knew and still came up empty.

Dammit! I'm going about this study all wrong. I should be studying Arel! He's the one that holds the key to this damnable situation we're in.

For a long moment, he let himself indulge in a sense of hopefulness. Studying Arel's condition was the fresh approach he'd been searching for.

He got me into this mess. He can get me out of it. And afterwards, when I'm on the other side of this nightmare, I'll save his sorry soul in the bargain.

He backed away from the mirror and scowled. He couldn't believe that he could still care about the person who infected him.

Am I delusional too?

Instead of an answer, Arel's face appeared again, but it was such a young face this time. When he first met Arel, William was struck by the pain that spoiled Arel's handsome features. There was no freedom in his smile. It was guarded and wanting. His eyes were always flickering under furrowed brows, as if he was about to be discovered and punished. The world scared Arel. His movements were furtive, like the young fox that knew the dogs were gaining on him and when they caught him, they would tear him apart. William sighed at the memory.

We had such a different way of reacting to our upbringing.

William knew about cruelty too, but he wouldn't let it destroy him. Every blow that he received in childhood was met with hatred. His rage profited from the beatings that were meant to break him.

He met the world head on and allowed himself to be hardened and hammered into manhood.

Yet Arel and I were both more than all that misery.

When they talked and argued, they both found parts of themselves that were hidden and waiting to be discovered. Late at night as they sat drinking under a full moon, life could suddenly become fluid and yielding, a place where wonder might be possible. William remained the solid thinker, the one grounded to the earth, who loved its ancient trees and the beasts that populated the meadows. On the other hand, Arel's spirit, once ignited, soared upwards. For all his thoughts about being a victim, Arel could reach out to the stars and bring their light to earth. His descriptions of the heavens went beyond anything William could imagine. But William was always the one who held on to Arel's astonishing visions. Arel seemed incapable of sustaining his cosmic connections. His heart, that miserable vessel inside his heaving chest, had too much heaviness to allow for lengthy flights into the realm of the cosmos.

Then William met Rolphe, and his life shifted dramatically. He was set in a new direction. Arel was also changing. He was giving up and planning to say goodbye to the weight of physicality. But William couldn't abandon his friend any more than he could abandon the fox he loved.

And look what it's come to. Arel is as mad as a hatter, raging about angels. But the hounds haven't finished him off yet. We both have a chance to beat whatever has hold of us. I just have to get him here and find a cure.

Fifty-Three

Arel's hand shook with excitement as he stared at a letter he'd just opened and read. It was from London. William had not only invited Arel to visit him, he'd included an airline ticket too. William claimed in the note that it was Arel's idea that they should see each other again. Perhaps it was true. Arel vaguely remembered saying something to that effect during their last meeting.

How brilliant of me! Now, I'm being given a chance to redeem myself by the last person I expected to help me.

He was filled with gratitude and surprise as he walked into the living room. Waving the airline ticket, he approached Michael. "Do you know what I just got in the post?"

As usual, Michael was sitting by the front window paging through a catalog on roses. His fingers stilled as he looked up. "What is it?"

Arel smiled. "This is my way out. This is my ticket, not only to London, but it's a ticket to a clean conscience!"

Michael set his magazine aside. "What do you mean?"

"William wants to see me. He should be mad as hell after what I did, but I guess he isn't."

"I see," Michael said in a quiet voice.

"Michael, show a little enthusiasm. This is my chance to be like you! I can help William like you helped me. You know how you felt responsible when you gave me your blood. Now I can be just as responsible."

"I thought you said you didn't know how to be William's friend."

"I guess I don't, but I'm not talking about being a friend. I'm taking on angel duties. I'll do what you do. I just need a little advice."

Michael sat up attentively. "Certainly, I'll assist you in any way that I can."

The angel gazed back with so much gentleness and compassion that Arel's heart sped up. Eagerness ignited those parts of him that had been stuck in remorse. His task was clear. He had to be just as compassionate as Michael. He just didn't know how. "Tell me everything! I'll stand here for as long as it takes. I'll absorb whatever you have to share. My only desire from now on is to be as wise and considerate as you."

Michael's smile broadened. "So where would you like me to start?"

"I don't know. There's probably so much to go over in these next few days." He waved the ticket again. "I better find out how much time we have so we'll tackle the most important stuff first. I haven't looked at the date to see when I'll be leaving for London." He stared at the ticket and then at his watch. When he looked back at Michael, he could feel the blood draining from his face. "I don't have any time for your advice. I have to be on a plane in four hours."

* * *

Arel's eyes darted around the cabin of the plane, paused briefly to notice a few passengers, the flight attendant walking down the aisle, and the general layout of the cabin. He was amazed and appalled that he was on his way to London. It all happened so fast. William's letter and the airline ticket came by special delivery that morning. Within a few minutes, he was trying to pack his suitcase. That didn't go well. As he tried to decide on how many shirts to take, he began to hyperventilate. Michael stepped in and helped him complete the task. Of course, his problem wasn't about shirts. When he thought about the project he was taking on, that William's fate was in his hands, he panicked. How could he steer William through the hellish storm of emotions that was a part of the clearing process? In Arel's own dark passage, he'd been a negligent captain. Without Michael's constant vigilance and enduring wisdom, Arel wouldn't be alive. He'd even

307

had a near-death experience, but Michael managed to coax his soul back into his body.

What if William dies? There'll be no angel to call his soul back to the earthly plane. If he slips away from the world, that'll be it.

Arel needed to take over an angel's job, and he had no qualifications. Instead, visions of William's last resting place began to fill his mind.

I'll bury him in a quiet place in the country. He'd like that. I'll get him the best headstone that money can buy.

It was a negative and self-serving thought, but it gave Arel a moment of respite. He forced himself to take longer, deeper breaths. This was his first test. He gripped his hands and concentrated. He had to remember Michael's parting words at the airport. "See the best working out for William. Believe in him."

Michael's right. William is nothing like me. He's probably fine.

As soon as Arel switched over to a better thought, his body responded with easier breaths and his mind delivered more positive memories.

William was still a young man when he contracted the original virus. Even though I thought of it as a curse, William never allowed the idea of being a vampire to scare him. He used it to his advantage. Maybe he'll do the same with the blood that I gave him.

Arel reached in his pocket and retrieved William's note. It was typed out and very short.

"Arel, I'm researching a problem that we share and would like your help. You suggested we meet in New York, but I'd like you to come to London instead. We'll talk about everything when you get here. PS: Bring along protective clothing, opaque sunglasses, and maximum sunscreen in case you're exposed to the sun."

William mentioned a problem, but there was no indication that William was suffering or upset. In fact, William's tone was direct and composed. When he purchased an airline ticket for Arel, he even made sure that Arel wouldn't be close to any windows or possible direct morning sunlight. Unfortunately, that meant that Arel was stuck in a middle row between an over active, five-year-old boy and an elderly gentleman who fell asleep on Arel's shoulder a half hour after take-off.

Still, William was trying to be thoughtful. If he was distraught, he wouldn't address me in such a considerate manner.

He laid his head back on the headrest, feeling a little better. He had to reinforce the idea that William was totally capable of handling what he'd been given. Their first meeting in New York came to mind. The first time Arel saw William, he couldn't believe how well William had fared. The guy was sitting in a posh night club looking like he owned the world.

The bastard will probably impress the hell out of me again.

Arel realized he had mixed feelings about believing in William. The man was still a person with no regard for humanity. The thought made him pause, but he quickly let go of the direction his mind was taking. Being judgmental wasn't part of his new role. He had to remain vigilant and not let his normal mindset take over. There was no room for any more mistakes on his part. He had to act like Michael if he was going to vindicate himself.

Fifty-Four

William decided to use Arel's visit as his motivation to clean up his living quarters. His suitcase had been lying open in the middle of the living room floor since his return from New York. Papers and clothes were scattered everywhere. He shouldn't have cared about any of it. He was in the middle of a life and death struggle. Hell, it was hard to drag himself back to the lab every day. Yet he couldn't let Arel get the idea that he'd lost control. One of them had to demonstrate fortitude if they were going to find a cure. Obviously, it wasn't going to be Arel. On the night of their reunion, the guy could barely stumble his way over to William's table.

Poor idiot will probably need a wheelchair soon.

Before long, William would probably need one too. His worn, aching muscles screamed for relief as he took a load of clothes to the laundry area and slammed down the lid on the washer. He was working ten to fourteen hours daily in the lab, his sleep was erratic if he got any at all, and now he'd been cleaning for hours. His last chore was putting away the glasses in the dish drainer. As he placed the last one in the cupboard, he realized that he hadn't had a drop of blood in days. A reliable dealer took care of his need for sustenance, but he hadn't been using what he had in storage.

No wonder I'm so fatigued.

He opened the freezer door and stared at his supply. A dozen frozen units were neatly stacked on the shelf. He reached out for one with a trembling hand and pulled back. He couldn't bring himself to care about imbibing what should have been a welcome and satisfying meal.

Was his reaction part of the disease he had? Or was he simply experiencing a lack of appetite? Depression could be responsible, but he didn't feel depressed. No, something else was keeping him from taking in the nourishment he needed. But what was it? He stared at the blood again, letting his mind wander. When had he last felt satisfied with what he ingested? He hadn't bothered with much since he'd been home.

Your body can't go on like this. Appetite or no, you have to feed yourself.

He grabbed a unit of blood and set it in the dish drainer to let it thaw. Yet the thought of coming back later and pouring some of the liquid into one of his elegant Zalto glasses was almost repulsive. He turned and walked out of the room mumbling.

"The stuff is rubbish compared to—"

He stopped himself from finishing the sentence, but he couldn't stop himself from thinking about the blood that he'd tasted in New York. Ever since coming back to London, he'd deliberately forced himself not to savor the experience. Now he couldn't deny the truth. If the gods made wine it would have tasted like Arel's blood.

The guy is a wreck, but his blood is amazing.

William's stomach growled with hunger and need as soon as he thought about having another sampling.

No, no, no! I will not go there!

He made his way into the living room, feeling weaker and more unsteady as he sat down on the sofa. Grabbing a pillow, he held it close, hoping to quiet the hollow feeling inside. It didn't work.

"Oh hell, don't tell me I'm hooked on the stuff." Even as he protested, he relived the moment that Arel's blood was on his lips and in his mouth. There was a purity to it. It wasn't like the blood of normal humans.

When William first tasted blood, he found it satisfying in a needy sort of way. It was what his body craved. Over time, his need was replaced by a more controlled approach to nourishment. He began to detect differences in the life-giving fluid that coursed through bodies. People never realized it, but their blood was a revelation, a disclosure of the failings and weaknesses that people harbored. Yet, over time, he took the tainted taste for granted. He never had anything to gauge it against.

Until now.

Arel's blood was something new. It wasn't only pure, it was unique. Just the thought of what it could do, made William hunger for more. As soon as he'd taken the first sip, the elixir instantly transported him to a place of bliss. He lost touch with codes of conduct and his rules for living. Thought disappeared. He entered a place where only joy existed. His spirit was free and unbounded. He was filled with unexplained rapture.

Now look at me. My life is in ruin after one damnable taste!

The price for that little trip was very steep indeed. He didn't dare think about trying the stuff again, but he licked his lips in spite of himself. He couldn't fight the thrill of desire that rippled through his flesh. He wanted to be consumed again by whatever it was in Arel's blood that could blot out the world and feed a part of him that was beyond it. Swiping at his brow, a hot flash of wanton need overwhelmed his body and threatened to devour his mind. He got up and almost ran to the kitchen, snatching up the frozen pint of blood and using it to cool his face. He had a horrible thought. A terrible, delicious thought. "Arel will be here soon. What if I can't control myself?"

Fifty-Five

Tim sat at the dining room table, reading his newspaper. He'd had a particularly stressful day at work, but he was trying to put it behind him. When Peggy came over, he lowered the paper and smiled. His pretty wife was holding little Sara. The baby was sleepy, pressed against her mother's chest, looking relaxed and ready for bed. "Are we going to have the evening to ourselves?" he asked in a hopeful tone.

Peggy smiled back, but a moment later, her face shifted into a frown. "I just wanted to give you the latest. Michael informed me that Arel left town again."

Tim's body went on sudden alert. He sat up attentively. Was there a possible new and unwanted adventure in his future? "Where's he gone?"

"He's on his way to England."

"Oh really?" Tim put the paper aside and studied Peggy's face. "And what about you? Any visions?"

She smiled. "No, don't worry. There's nothing on my radar yet, especially since I talked to him the other night. I feel better about his friend."

"You said Arel admitted the guy saved his life."

"Yes, all my worries about this William guy were for nothing."

"So why do you seem upset?"

"I'm fine," Peggy insisted as she swayed back and forth with the baby. "I'm just disappointed. Arel took off without a word. I thought he was going to be more considerate from now on."

Tim's shoulders eased a little. "You know Arel. You can't take his faults personally."

"You're right. I spend way too much time thinking. But like you said, we have this evening and each other. I want us to enjoy ourselves."

Tim's eyes brightened. "Would you like me to put the baby down?"

"That sounds perfect. And afterwards, join me in the kitchen."

"The kitchen?"

"Yes, let's bake cookies together."

"Cookies?"

"Yes, we're out, and I thought it might be fun if we could make that oatmeal raisin recipe that Carol uses." Peggy's smile widened. "Afterwards we can cuddle on the sofa and watch a movie."

Tim stood up and stretched. "Now that's a plan I can get into."

Peggy came over and allowed him to carefully and deliberately retrieve the baby. Sara had fallen asleep and a slow, methodical transfer usually guaranteed that she would remain in her slumbering state.

Tim smiled. "Sara is still so small, a perfect picture of what a fairy princess should be. We're so lucky."

"Yes, I know," Peggy whispered. She hesitated, looking down and smoothing out her apron. "I forgot to ask. How are things working out with Kell?"

Tim rocked Sara, keeping his voice low and quiet. "Great, he gets his point across without the hostility I've seen in some teachers. He's a lot nicer than the coaches that Kevin and I had in high school."

"So Kevin is happy with him too."

"Yeah, Kevin excels when it comes to any kind of sport, you know that."

Peggy's eyes looked up pleadingly. "I wish he was more enthusiastic on the home front. Carol says he comes back after a workout and heads for bed."

"Honey, you're worrying again."

Peggy crossed her arms. "I'm trying to stop, but I want to know that Kevin is making progress, that he and Carol are going to be alright."

Tim started for the stairs. "All that I know is that Kevin is trying his best."

Peggy let her arms fall to her sides. "That's depressing. We better make a double batch of those cookies."

Fifty-Six

Arel felt surprisingly rested after his flight to London. He'd slept for most of the journey. Not even the five-year-old who sat next to him disturbed his slumber. Strangely enough, his path to dreamland was an easy one. After he took Michael's suggestion to believe in William, he could adopt some measure of calm. In fact, as he was about to doze off, his mind came up with a dozen reasons why Michael's advice was sound. William knew how to handle adversity. He was tough and competent and smart. William was the most capable person Arel had ever known.

No matter what challenge comes his way, William will always be the one who comes up smelling like a rose.

The thought became Arel's singular focus as he went to sleep. It was there, repeating in his mind when he woke up, when he went through airport customs and when he took a taxi to William's home. By the time he arrived at William's door, he was excited and relieved that he didn't have to carry around his guilt anymore. A smile spread across his face as he reached for the brass knocker on William's door.

Michael, I hope you're proud of me. We didn't have time to hammer out much before I left, but you gave me all your wisdom in one golden kernel of truth. Thank you.

His hand paused for only a second before he gave the door knocker a couple of quick raps.

At long last, William and I can come together in peace!

As he stood waiting, he collected himself, determined to display the same self-assured demeanor that William exhibited.

In New York, I acted like a fool. Now's my chance to behave like someone who has angelic blood running through their veins.

The sound of locks being turned back on the door, made Arel come to attention. He even managed a smile as he readied himself to greet William. When the door swung open, he was ready to totally adopt his angelic role and put the past behind him, once and for all. Instead he jumped backwards in shock, nearly falling down the stone steps he'd just climbed. Luckily his hand caught the railing. He clung on to it, trying to breathe, trying to understand who was standing in the doorway. If it was William, he had the face of an emaciated wizard. There was no flesh on his hollowed-out cheeks. His skin was beyond pale.

Where are his bright, confident eyes? Where did the light go?

The William that Arel envisioned during his trip was nothing like this real-life version. Arel had been lying to himself. Now he had to face reality.

Your revenge is complete! You've destroyed William! Are you happy now?

The voice in his head shouted out the words. They were so powerful and so reproachful that his breath stopped in mid-gasp. All the while his body was still hanging on to the railing.

"Arel! Are you alright?" William asked as he stepped out of the house and quickly came over to help. He took hold of Arel's arm. "I was afraid you weren't up for travel, but I didn't expect you to fall over on my doorstep."

Arel stared up at William's dull eyes and saw his old friend's concern. He tried to mouth some words, to tell William how sorry he was, but nothing came out. Maybe it was better that way. William didn't need to hear that he was headed for the grave.

"You poor bastard," William said as he pried Arel's fingers off the rail and tried to shoulder him to an upright position.

Arel tried to help too, but it took all his willpower to make his legs carry his weight. Once he was standing, he stumbled over to the door.

William had Arel's arm and helped to steady him. "It's a good thing you got here while you can still get around."

Arel heard the kindness in William's voice.

Michael was so right about you!

The fact that William sincerely cared about Arel's welfare was doubly-damning. It added to the crushing weight of responsibility Arel felt smothering him. "So sorry," he managed.

William helped him through the door and into the foyer. "You're sick and doing your best just like I am. That counts for something. Anyway, I'll get you straight to your room so you can rest."

Finally, Arel's voice rallied. "Will, please, I'm not sick! I'm perfectly healthy!"

William continued to lead Arel forward. "What will it take to make you understand the truth? And to think I've been craving more of your blood. I must have gone temporarily insane."

Arel pulled himself out of William's guiding hands and grabbed hold of the heavy wool sweater that William was wearing. "If you think it would help, take it! Take as much as you want!" he insisted in a husky voice. He was desperate to find a way to restore William, to bring him back from his declining state. "My blood is your blood."

William scowled back. "Look at me, Arel. Take a long hard look at what I've become. Do you seriously think I need more of your damnable blood?"

Arel shook his head, trying not to look at William, but staring back anyway, like he would if he was passing a traffic accident. A ridiculous question slipped out. "What happened to your hair?" William's long, golden-brown locks were gone. Instead, he had a crewcut. It would have been an acceptable look on the old William, but it made this version look even more severe. "Why did you cut it?"

William shrugged. "Too much upkeep. I don't have the energy to waste on it."

"But it's always been one of the things women loved about you."

"Arel, please, I have no time for vanity." William's brows narrowed. "I see your mop is as thick and healthy as ever. How do you manage in your condition?"

"Will, listen to me. This is very important." Arel shifted his weight forward in a beseeching gesture. "You have to let Michael help you, like he helped me."

William narrowed his gaze and let out a heavy sigh. "Arel, a hairdresser is the least of my worries."

"Hairdresser? Michael isn't a hairdresser."

318

William shut his eyes as if he needed to count to ten before replying. "Fine, I don't have time for your barber, okay?" he said in a loud, annoyed tone. "Now let's get you to bed."

Arel's brain collapsed into a despairing numbness. He'd played his ace card, his one get-out-of-jail-free card. The situation called for heavenly intervention. It called for Michael stepping up to the plate, but William wasn't going to have it. "You're right. I need to lay down."

* * *

Arel looked around the guest bedroom. He couldn't get William's appalling condition out of his mind, but at least William's home was pleasing. The splendidly appointed townhouse could have made the pages of a design magazine. Artwork tastefully adorned the walls, and the furniture had a modern sophistication without sacrificing comfort. Plush carpets graced the polished hardwood floors. Arel's bedroom was particularly appealing. Two of the bleached oak-paneled walls had floor to ceiling shelves. Each shelf held books of all kinds, both old and new. Beautiful collectibles were carefully placed in the remaining spaces. Vases, small sculptures, and various expensive treasures accented the assorted volumes. The furniture was sparse but tasteful. In a reading area, a graceful, curved-arm floor lamp provided lighting for two elegant, brown leather chairs. All in all, the feel was contemporary, but pieces of old-world charm added warmth.

"Very nice," Arel said as he put his suitcase down.

William walked over to a wide, plain-paneled area and paused. "There's a Murphy style, pull-down bed here. I think you'll find it satisfactory. And there's a closet over there."

"Thanks. I'll be fine. I just have a little jet lag."

"I'll be downstairs in the lab if you need anything," William said as he went to the door.

After William left, Arel went over to one of the chairs and sat down. He gave the idea of thinking about the situation another shot and felt his mind flatline. He needed to rest, to shut out reality for a very long time. And if he didn't wake up ever again, he'd consider it a bonus. "Revenge! Whoever thought it was a good idea was very mistaken."

Fifty-Seven

After Arel's arrival, William felt stronger. Maybe seeing Arel stumbling around so helplessly made him more determined than ever to beat whatever disease they shared. He was able to also catch up on some sleep. While Arel was napping, William stretched out in the recliner. Hours later, his slumber was interrupted by Arel shaking him awake. When he opened his eyes, Arel was standing in front of him with more color in his cheeks.

"You look better," William said as he stretched and sat up.

Arel stared back for a long moment. "So do you."

"We were both tired."

"Yes, that's right." Arel paused and glanced around, letting his eyes rest on the work area where William spent long hours. "So this is where you do your research. It's very impressive."

One end of the large room had a hi-tech look. Glass-fronted stainless steel storage cabinets were mounted on one wall with lower level supply cabinets beneath. A workstation island was located in front of the cabinets. The layout mimicked a professional lab.

William smiled back with pride. "The microscope is new. I figured I better have something up-to-date with what we're facing. Why spare expense when one is dealing with a lethal disease?"

Arel wandered over to a sofa in the living area of the room and sat down. "I need to explain something about our situation, and I hope you can remain open-minded."

"It's why I asked you here. I need all the facts I can get."

Arel looked back momentarily, then shifted his gaze. "Good, I'm glad that we agree."

"Right, so fire away," William said eagerly. Arel was volunteering information. That was a first. It wasn't like him to deal with actualities.

Arel's brows were braced together so tightly he looked like a soulful beagle who was about to bay at the moon. "What we share is not an illness. You're not sick. It's something else."

William sat up straighter. "What are you talking about?"

"You're going to think I'm crazy."

"I already think that, so I don't believe there's anything you could say that'll shock me."

Arel scratched at the sofa arm nervously. "I ingested some blood that was a little different. I was in this alley, and I bit—"

"I knew it. You bit an infected rat with some new form of disease."

"No! I bit Michael."

"Your hairdresser, your barber guy?"

"Michael has nothing to do with hair. He's—"

William felt his body go rigid with anger. "You mean after all this time that you've been on my case, now you're telling me you drank human blood?"

"Not human in the usual sense. Michael is very special."

"Yes, he's a carrier, Arel! He's infected you and now me with some god-knows-what disease!"

Arel stood up and glared back. "No, William, he's an angel! I know that's hard to believe, but it's true."

For a moment, William couldn't move. His mind locked up in a spasm of disbelief. "Oh, I see. That's how you've justified biting someone. You've told yourself that he was an angel. And I suppose this angel gave you his blood out of the kindness of his heart."

"Well, not exactly."

William got up and went over to where Arel was standing. His patience was still holding, but he knew a fit of fresh anger was ready to erupt. "What do you mean? Did this Michael person want to give you his blood or not?"

Arel heaved out a heavy sigh, pushed past William and began to pace. "It's a long story, but I kind of begged him for it because I thought it would help. I was at my wit's end. I couldn't go on living with the curse, or the virus or whatever you gave me. The problem is that Michael's blood is very powerful. Handling it has been rather difficult."

William gave him a scornful laugh. "And why wouldn't it be difficult? It's angel blood. And you're not an angel, Arel. You're a bloody human being!"

Arel turned to face him. "I'm sorry, okay? I'm sorry for passing it on to you."

William didn't know how to respond. He'd heard a lot of nonsensical rubbish in his time, but Arel's wild tale was too much. "I knew it. I knew you did something stupid, but this takes the cake."

"Do you think I like sounding like I'm delusional? Please, Will, I'm trying to be as truthful as I can, that's all."

William went back to the recliner and sat down again. He made himself pause and study Arel. What was he dealing with? Was Arel truly insane or was he a person whose mind was affected by disease?

No matter what, he's gone around the bend once and for all.

Arel sat on the sofa again. His arms were crossed and his glowing eyes were flickering off and on like a couple of bulbs on the blink. The guy was sick, very, very sick. Cursing him out wasn't going to help.

Poor idiot is probably beyond help, but hopefully I've still got a chance.

William took a deep breath and grabbed his notebook. He needed facts for his research, but he had to be careful about how he asked his questions. He was dealing with an unstable individual. "If you want to help, just tell me everything. You said you're not sick, is that right? You haven't had any physical problems?"

Arel's hand went to his chest, rubbing it thoughtfully. "I did have a problem with my heart, but that was my fault. I kind of lost it emotionally. I was stressed to the point that my heart gave out."

William almost dropped his pen. "You just insisted that we're not sick, but you're telling me that you had a heart attack?"

"It was kind of worse than that. I guess you could say that I died, but—" Arel held up his hands defensively. "But don't worry. It all worked out for the best. Michael brought me back. Since then my heart has been fine."

William felt his face flush hot, and a feeling of madness slipped in. He gave Arel every chance, trying to be understanding under any circumstance. But Arel's ignorance went beyond anything William could comprehend. "Wasn't that considerate of Michael since he infected you in the first place? The bastard!"

Arel's eyes widened in alarm. "Will, please, I don't want you doing what I did and keeling over too. That's why I'm here. I want to keep you from making the same mistakes that I made."

William clamped his jaw shut so tight it hurt. He knew Arel was right. If he allowed himself to express the outrage that he felt after Arel's explanation, it wouldn't be pretty. Arel would be left with a very big cleaning job. He'd have to scrape William's brains off the walls after William's head exploded.

Fifty-Eight

The next day, Arel sat in a chair in the laboratory trying to appear as helpful as possible. He had to make up for his rocky start with William. First there was the arrival fiasco when he could barely speak. The episode was followed by his confession that he drank angelic blood. He probably should have skipped the fact that he'd died. Obviously it was too much for William. The man took to his bed after the conversation, using an icepack to soothe his throbbing headache. He also insisted that Arel keep his distance. William issued the warning through clenched teeth. "Listen, angel boy, I need to calm my nerves. So steer clear if you know what's good for you."

So now I can show William how willing I am to help.

Arel had agreed to let William take blood samples. It seemed like a straightforward procedure, but when William came over with a needle in his hand, Arel couldn't control his shakiness. His body remembered the first time William took his blood. No matter how cooperative Arel wanted to be, his physical being was very wary. Every time William tried to insert the needle, Arel jumped. After the first few times, William was getting shaky too.

"Dammit, Arel, stop moving!" he shouted.

"I'm trying!" Arel yelled back. His body was sending out waves of adrenaline. He wanted to believe in William, but distrust and survival needs were overpowering his thought process. "I can't help it if I'm a bit phobic about blood."

William dropped his hand to his side. "I do this to myself all the time. It's not a big deal."

"Why do you need to study my blood? I told you—"

William stared back with dismal, frustrated eyes. "Please, don't start the angel crap again. I just can't take it, understand?"

Arel sighed. "Sorry."

"I'm doing this for both of us, Arel. So let me take one lousy blood sample."

Arel noticed the desperation in William's voice, something he'd never heard before. It fit William's physical condition. Even after hours in bed, he looked exhausted. That's when a terrible thought occurred to Arel. Perhaps William was right. Maybe Michael's blood was a disease of sorts for most humans, and a fatal one to boot.

If you don't want to start looking for a headstone for William you better do what he wants.

He stuck his arm out in William's direction and looked away. "Get on with it. I promise not to move."

William frowned as he stepped closer again. "Thank you."

Arel turned his gaze to the wall. "Will, I mean it. I truly am sorry. I'm doing my best, too."

William toned down his voice to a whisper. "I don't remember you being like this. That time that sailor stabbed you in the shoulder, you weren't put off by the blood. You were very stoic about it all."

Arel gripped the arm of the chair with his free hand. "I had an experience with a woman I knew. She took her life by cutting her throat."

"Really? This woman, did you love her?"

"I don't want to talk about it."

"You're right. I know too much already." William stepped back and wiped the sweat from his brow. "The good news is that you can relax. The needle is in."

Arel glanced over, then looked away again. "I never felt a thing. I guess you are good at this."

"Please, just remain quiet for a few minutes while I take care of some notes."

Arel did as he was told. Finally, he cleared his throat and shot William a quick glance. "Again, I am sorry that you're sick."

"Right, but it's my own fault. I'm the one who just had to find you again."

"Why did you want to see me? After all this time, what difference did it make?"

"Who knows, maybe my curiosity got the better of my good sense," William said as he took the blood that he'd collected and set it aside. Next, he grabbed another syringe and started to draw out an additional amount. "I'm almost done."

As Arel watched William take more blood, he felt lightheaded. "Just how much of this stuff do you need? I don't feel right."

William glanced up. "Taking this small amount can't possibly hurt you. However, I want to take enough to study later on when you've gone back home. Now, just breathe, and you'll be fine."

Arel nodded, but he wasn't well. Seeing the blood filling the syringe set something off in his psyche. He was holding Justina again. "Blood, so much blood!" he groaned. He had his hand on Justina's bloody neck, but he couldn't stop the precious liquid from pouring out between his fingers. He began to pitch forward as the vivid memory took hold.

William's reflexes were still fast enough to help. Throwing out a hand, he stopped Arel's downward journey to the floor. "Hey, Arel, snap out of it!" he ordered as he pushed Arel's fainting body back into the chair. "What's wrong with you?"

Arel let out a soft moan as he tried to remember where he was. He fought to push back the memory of Justina's death and reorient himself. "Can't help it."

"You really amaze me. You called yourself a vampire for crap's sake."

Arel was still caught between worlds, but William's words reminded him of why he'd lost Justina, why he lived in torment for so long. He opened his eyes and targeted William with a sudden glow of anger. Rigidity replaced his recent swoon. "Don't say that word to me," he said in a raspy whisper.

"What word?"

"What you made me! No matter what your reasons were, it was wrong!" Yanking his arm away from William and violently dislodging the needle, he leaped to his feet. He had to steady himself, but he managed to stay standing. If only he'd remained a normal human being, Justina might never have died. "That night I visited you . . . you had no right to make me some monster!"

William glared back with his own anger clearly surfacing. "What the hell are you bringing that up for? That's all behind us. Now, relax and let me finish up here."

After all of Arel's plans to forgive William, some deep, hateful force began to take over his body. All he could see was Justina's blood pouring out. It turned into his own blood, and William was taking it from him again. "Stay away from me, you traitor! If it hadn't been for you, my life could have been so different."

"Yes, you would have been dead by now," William snapped back. "Believe me, I regret that night too! But here we are again, and you're as insane as ever." He paused and leaned against the back of the chair for support. "But you're also sick, whether you realize it or not. So try to calm down before you finish yourself off."

Arel couldn't concentrate on what William was saying. Old feelings of betrayal added more fuel to his adrenaline-charged body. He clenched his fists, trying to navigate his way back to a saner mindset. He managed a brief reminder that William's intentions had been good, but it was soon lost under a barrage of wrathful anger. Habits practiced for a century were deep and familiar.

William seemed to take Arel's silence as an invitation to slowly move towards him. He reached out and put his hands on Arel's shoulders. "Sit down," he ordered quietly. "You're overreacting."

Arel lost all ability to calm himself as soon as William touched him. His gut became a swirling cauldron of bitterness. When he spoke, his tone was low and seething. "Stay back! I'm warning you. I can't control what's happening."

"What now?" William asked. "What are you babbling about?"

The question was the match that ignited a madness that lived in Arel's core. He didn't even think about what he was saying or doing. The words spewed out. "Want my blood again? We'll see about that," he shouted as he grabbed hold of William. With a final enraged outburst, he hurled William across the room with a strength he didn't know he had. It all happened so fast. There was so little thought behind the violence. But the madness drained away as quickly as it came. When Arel saw William lying in a heap against the wall, his sanity resurrected itself.

Oh no, what have I done now?

He was filled with shame and remorse as he rushed over to where William lay gasping for breath.

"William, talk to me! Are you hurt?"

When William finally got his wind back, he grimaced at Arel. "If keeping company with angels did this to you, I'm glad you're not cavorting with the devil."

Arel put a hand to his own forehead and realized how hot he was. He was also having trouble focusing. "I just lost it. I'm so sorry."

"Your face is beet red. You probably have a fever," William said as he pushed himself up into a sitting position. He stared at Arel with a clinical eye. "So this is what I have to look forward to, hysteria and more ranting tirades?"

"I don't understand it. Something came over me, and I slipped back into the past."

William started to reach out and quickly withdrew his hand. "Promise me something. If I get as batty as you, promise me that you'll put me out of my misery."

Arel's stomach twisted at what was being asked. "You want me to kill you? Now you're the one that's being crazy. I could never do that."

"Of course you couldn't. You wouldn't want to soil your lily white soul, would you?" William slowly got to his feet and steadied himself against the wall. "I'm not your enemy. I never wanted to hurt you. I hoped that someday you'd believe that. Now I realize how ridiculous I've been. Go back to Chicago. I'll take care of this mess myself."

Arel shook his head. The hatred he felt a few minutes before was gone. The physical act of retribution had served as a cleansing balm. Now, he felt empty and spent, but he wouldn't give up. If he left now, he was sure that William wouldn't survive. "No, give me another chance, Will, please."

Fifty-Nine

William bent over the microscope, staring at a slide of Arel's blood. He hadn't had time to understand the full implications of what he was viewing. Still, his background in science was already filling in the facts, and they weren't favorable. William had a sinking feeling in the pit of his stomach as he pushed away from the viewing lenses.

Arel's blood is a disaster, plain and simple.

Of course, Arel would be safe from the truth. The guy never listened to William's opinions. If they gave out awards for self-delusion, Arel would be up for an Oscar. As it was, he was wearing out a path on William's rug in the living area. Since his violent episode that morning, Arel was trying to be conciliatory, acting as if he was interested in what William was doing. Maybe he was curious, like the kid who wanted to be amused by something the grown-ups were doing. William was too distracted to care one way or another. He got up from the lab stool and made his way to his recliner. As he passed Arel, he let out a sigh. "If you want to check out your blood, I'm done for the moment."

Arel accepted the invitation and quickly walked over to the microscope. After a few moments of staring at the slide, he looked up. "I don't know much about this kind of thing, but it's rather beautiful. Looks like I have snowflakes floating around with all the other stuff."

William sat back in his chair, knowing it was useless to comment, but he couldn't help himself. "Yes, well those crystalline anomalies that you're seeing don't belong there. I've studied a lot of blood, and yours is in a class by itself."

Arel went back to looking at his blood. "I guess I'm just one of a kind."

William studied him with a forlorn look of pity. "Right, and you have some malady that probably has no cure."

Arel stood up and glanced back. "No matter what you think, I can jog for miles. I'm fit as a fiddle."

"I know that you had a fit this morning."

Arel came over and stood next to the recliner. "How many times do I have to say I'm sorry?"

"I'm not looking for apologies. I'm trying to help you understand something. Have you even noticed that I'm worried about where we're headed?"

Arel crossed his arms and shifted his weight nervously. "Are there any snowflakes in your blood?"

"No, but I haven't been infected that long." William paused and stared up at Arel, wondering how much time he had left. A month? Six months? "Arel, listen, I won't sugarcoat it. At this stage, with your blood being what it is, I don't think that I can help you. Hell, I'm probably not much better off, but you're clearly in the advanced stages of whatever it is that's attacking you."

Arel's face brightened. "Don't concern yourself on my account." He walked over to the sofa and sat down. "I'll take my chances."

"So that's it?" William asked as he stood up. "You're just going to act like nothing is wrong?"

Arel grabbed a book off the side table and began to page through it. "We each have our own way of handling things."

William walked over to the couch, yanked the book out of Arel's hand, and slammed it down on the end table. "You're not going to do this!"

"What?"

"You're totally irresponsible. Ever since I can remember, you were always preaching to me about right and wrong. But when it comes to actually being accountable for your life, you bailed."

"Okay, fine, you're right. But I'm trying to change. That's why I came—"

"Change? How have you changed? You're sitting here refusing to even consider what I'm saying. You're insisting on holding on to some fantasy about angels!"

Arel stiffened. "And you always think you have all the answers. But I don't think that being Mr. Science is good enough. There's more to life than what you can see under a microscope. You took one look at my blood and pronounced me a goner. That's plain stupidity."

"You're right. I shouldn't make claims that quickly, but you're going to take responsibility too."

"Responsibility for what?"

William put a hand on the arm of the couch and leaned in. "I might have overstepped the boundaries that night when I made you a vampire, but the result was the closest thing to immortality that's possible. You, on the other hand, have infected me with a possibly, fatal disease. And I use the word, *possibly*, very loosely. Your blood is in a deplorable state, and I'm sure mine will be like yours very soon."

Arel's shoulders sagged in compliance as he looked away. "Believe me, William, I don't want that. And I know you're doing your best to help both of us—"

"Of course I am, you idiot."

"So tell me what we should do next. I'll try to be more agreeable."

William's scowl weakened as he moved away. "I think we need a break. Let's get out of here. Maybe a little amusement will help."

Arel jumped up. "Tell me that you're not hunting tonight."

"What the hell are you talking about?" William turned and stared back, meeting Arel's wide gaze with fresh disapproval. "Will I always be the person you love to chastise, the person you love to punish with your narrow judgments?"

"Sorry." Arel looked immediately penitent. "I don't know why I say things like that."

"Well, let me put your mind at ease. I find people too tiresome to bother with. And right now, I'm baffled by the fact that I care about you."

Arel returned a look of confusion. "Why do you care, Will?"

William let out a scornful laugh as he walked to the stairs. "Forget it. I need a change of scenery."

The dimly-lit local pub was usually busy in the evening. William didn't frequent it often, but he thought it might be a good change of pace after his day in the lab with Arel. Of course, he and Arel had a history of arguing in pubs. When they were both students, they drank a lot and their differing opinions were always verbalized after they had too much. Later, when their desires no longer included drinking, they still fought more than ever.

Dammit, I'm exhausted. I hope we can get through one evening without a battle.

As they made their way to a table, William recognized one of the patrons and she obviously recognized him.

"Hello, William," she said as she gave him a seductive smile. He returned a quick nod and kept going.

"Friend of yours?" Arel asked.

"She serves a purpose, I suppose," he said as he took a seat in an area that offered a little more privacy. He placed the drink he bought at the bar on the round oak table. He had no use for the ale, but it too served a purpose, making him seem like a normal customer. "How about you? Did you ever find someone special?"

Arel's eyes lit up for a brief moment. "Yes, but it didn't last."

"That's too bad." He noted that Arel's face was bathed in the sad waters of regret. "But caring for someone is usually transitory. Even if one party is able to hold onto the feeling, the other person often causes more pain than its worth."

"You're talking about me, aren't you? I've disappointed you."

"Why would I be disappointed in you?" William swirled the contents of his drink, staring at its rich, amber color. "You did call me your brother for about five minutes a century ago. That should be enough for anyone."

"About the brother thing—"

William held up a hand. "The truth is that I never expected more than that from you. Like all the others, you are what you are. I accept that. The problem is that you can't accept me."

Arel leaned in close and set his voice to a barely audible whisper. "What I can't accept is that you can be ruthless. I know you said you don't hunt anymore, but you still feel the same about murdering people, don't you?"

"People murder people all the time. They use excuses for that fact, like wars. People kill each other in the name of some deity that they've been taught is better than another."

Arel looked away. "That's true, but eventually we become more aware that such things shouldn't happen. Don't you have any conscience about taking a life?"

"No." William leaned back into his chair and let his usual focus drift. His mind went back to his dream and the horror of hearing the tortured screams of the young fox that he loved. Once he'd actually witnessed a killing scene when another fox was being dismembered by his father's hounds. His father sat astride his horse, laughing with his cronies as the fox was torn apart. "Most of humanity isn't fit to live."

Arel stared back fixedly. "What do you believe in? Is there anything that you value?"

"I believe in myself and in the physical order, not the chaos that mankind has made out of it."

"How can you be so arrogant to think that you know better than everybody else?"

"Not everyone. There are a few like-minded others."

"Obviously I'm not one of them. You don't agree with anything I believe in."

"That's right, but I tried to believe in you, Arel. Not in the misguided ideas that you aspire to, but in the person you are."

"They're one and the same. You can't separate a man's ideals from the man."

"That's the most ridiculous statement I've heard yet. You've been indoctrinated with your ideals. Don't you know that? If you'd been taught to sacrifice a sheep on a full moon, you'd think that was the right thing to do."

"I've examined my beliefs. I haven't accepted everything with blind faith. If I had, I'd be like my father was, wouldn't I?" He paused and looked away. "Maybe I put that the wrong way. Even if we do commit the sins of our fathers, we change when we see things the way they should be. Underneath all the wrongdoing, the truth is there for us."

William stared back, noting the sincerity in Arel's tone. "I'm a man, just like you, so why don't I feel any of this nonsense that you accept as the truth? Am I less than you?"

Arel reached out and took hold of his arm. "William, I'm asking you these things because I want to help you. I had a friend that did that for me. I want to pass on the favor. If you can just open up a bit and allow for more than what you can prove, I believe you'll have a chance to beat this thing, this disease you think we have. Sometimes you have to take a leap of faith and believe that there's good in humanity. You know that I've seen all the bad parts too, but I know there's more if you open yourself up to new possibilities. People can surprise you."

"By people, I suppose you mean that little family you've gathered around you in Chicago."

Arel pulled back. "What?"

"You left your laptop lying around. I saw an email and a picture from a person named Carol. She was holding a baby. There were also a couple of other people in the picture."

Arel's face instantly lost its glow. "Leave Carol and my friends out of this."

"Oh, I see. You want to talk, but on your terms."

"My friends have nothing to do with you and me."

"Why? Why are they off-limits?"

"Because they're good and pure of heart."

"And I'm the big bad wolf who's out to eat them, right?"

"Don't even go there, I'm warning you."

"So they really mean that much to you?"

"Of course they do!"

"I see."

"No, you don't see. I don't want you involved with them in any way! Is that clear?"

William stared back, noting how animated Arel was, how he transformed into some grand champion who was prepared to protect those he loved at any cost. He leaned in and lowered his voice. "If it came to them or me, you'd kill me on the spot, wouldn't you?"

"Don't push me, William." Arel paused, letting his gaze convey his lethal warning. "Don't give me a reason to fight you."

William sucked in the stale air and felt his chest tighten. "Don't worry. I don't give a damn about them. Just because you've decided that they're so wonderful and I'm worthless, am I supposed to care?" He flexed his hands, trying to calm himself. He just lied. He broke one of his own rules of integrity. But he wouldn't give Arel the satisfaction of knowing how he felt. "Just what do I mean to you, Arel? Will you ever see me as being on par with those people you like so much?"

"They're different."

"Yes, and I'm sure you've never accused them of being heartless! But you're the one who has no mercy. You came here telling me you wanted to help—"

"I do want to help—"

"No, you only think you do. You talk about seeing the good in humanity, but when I mention your friends, you stare back at me like I'm a rabid animal." He was having trouble keeping his voice even, but he couldn't hold back his feelings. "I hope that someday you know just what a total bastard you are." He stood up and threw some bills and a key on the table. "Take a cab back."

Arel jumped up too. "William, wait!"

"To hell with you!" he yelled back as he walked briskly towards the front of the establishment. The pretty woman tried to approach him again, but he pushed her away and kept going. By the time he was outside, he was trying to catch his breath. His head pounded with pain, but the pain in his chest was worse.

"You son of a bitch," he gasped as he fought the anger that was filling his mind and body. "You wouldn't have that little group of pathetic humans around you if it weren't for me. You would've been dead long ago. I'm the one that made your happiness possible, and I've yet to hear one word of thanks."

He paused for a brief moment, hating that he was talking aloud to himself again. He had to stop it. He had to stop the pain too. He didn't want to admit that he could be hurt the way he was hurting. Yet a part of him was screaming out for some shred of appreciation on Arel's part.

He's not your brother! He's your Achilles' heel. Caring about him is going to destroy you completely.

William picked up his pace, trying to outdistance the onslaught of emotions that wanted out. Earlier he told Arel that he wasn't interested in killing anymore, that he was bored with such games.

Well, old friend, you've just convinced me otherwise. I do want to kill someone, someone stupid and pompous like you.

The thought frightened him. He didn't conduct his life that way. If he took a life, it was a calculated affair. Nobody influenced him. Just the opposite, he prided himself on careful decisions. It's what separated him from the human hordes, from the bulk of fools who had no control, who were constantly at the mercy of their ignorance.

Yet the more he thought about Arel, the more he wanted to lash out, especially when he thought about Arel's connection to Chicago, to his new friends. In the past, it was one thing to be ignored and even hated by Arel. William knew that Arel was still doing his best, that he didn't have much to work with. Being a friend of any kind was a stretch for him. Now, that had changed. It was obvious that Arel had a real capacity to care for someone other than himself.

But does he care about me? Of course not. He's aligned himself with strangers. If I fell off the face of the earth, he'd probably celebrate!

Rubbing his forehead, trying to disengage from the overwhelming rage that was churning inside of him, he didn't see the people around him or even notice where he was going. He knew he was losing control, and he couldn't stop himself.

Soon I'll be another idiot who's a slave to his emotions!

Gritting his teeth, he couldn't rein in his feelings. They were coming too fast, slamming him with hard facts, just like Arel had slammed him against the wall. He didn't matter at all to the one person he chose to help.

I cared about Arel more than anything. I wanted him to mature so that he could really live and enjoy life, even if it was at my expense. Why else would I let him abuse me the way he has? Why else would I put up with his callousness and condemnation?

The facts were sharp, cutting deep into his already small reservoirs of strength, driving him on, pushing him forward at a relentless pace. Darting into the street, he didn't hear the screech of tires or the blaring horn that tried to warn him of his carelessness. But he did feel a hand grab his arm and yank him back as a car side-swiped him.

"What the hell are you doing?" Arel yelled as he practically dragged William back onto the curb. "I've been following you for a block, and you're acting like you're blind."

Shaken momentarily out of his rage, William looked back at Arel, stunned into silence. He realized that he was gasping with pain. Physical pain and the pain of loss. Looking at Arel, he didn't see a brother. In that moment, he realized that he'd held on to that concept all these years. When he helped Arel long ago, he took one more chance on the idea of family. He took down his barriers. He gave everything he had to someone he thought deserved his loyalty. Now, he knew the truth. Maybe it wasn't the truth that Arel spoke of, but it was his truth. There was no such thing as a brother. People were all bastards. But he'd been so blind, so naïve, he never understood that Arel was one of the cruelest bastards of all.

When he felt capable of speaking coherently, his voice was measured, but the horror of his discovery couldn't be entirely contained. "Don't ever touch me again," he said as he pulled away from Arel's steadying hand. As soon as he tried to step away, his leg buckled under him. He hadn't escaped the car's punishment.

"I don't have much choice, do I?" Arel said as he grabbed him a second time. "Let's get you home."

Sixty

Once he was back in William's house, Arel sat in one of the leather chairs in his bedroom. He covered his ears, trying to shut out the terrible sounds coming from the adjoining room, William's bedroom.

He tells me I'm nuts, but it's William who's insane. He was just holding it in all this time.

William had been mute the entire way home, needing Arel's help to navigate the cab and getting into the house. But once they were safely inside, William shoved him away with as much strength as he had left. If Arel dared come within five feet, he became a wild animal, snarling and cursing at him as if Arel was his worst enemy. Now he'd locked himself in his room. He continued to scream and shriek with so much fury that Arel was sure he'd gone berserk.

But he's not totally to blame for his condition. I helped bring this on. Why did I get so defensive and say what I said in the pub?

He knew why. His fears escalated when William mentioned Carol. Just hearing him say her name seemed reprehensible. He instantly went from calm to being ready to do anything to safeguard the people he loved. He even threatened William's life. Yet, now, he knew that he overreacted. William hadn't deserved that kind of behavior.

Maybe, he's right. I am cruel.

The gravity of the situation overwhelmed him. "Michael, I've really made a mess of things!" He called out in desperation. "You have to help William before he does himself in."

Another loud crash sounded from William's room. It was accompanied by more shouting. Arel swallowed hard and called out again. "Please, Michael—"

"You wanted to see me?"

Michael's voice made him jerk to attention expectantly. When he looked up, Michael was standing near the door. "Thank goodness! You have to tell me what to do," he said as he jumped up. "William's completely lost it."

* * *

It was a beautiful and expensive piece of porcelain, a French Victorian urn, and it lay shattered on the floor. William was responsible for its loss. But its value was of no matter to him. His life was just as broken. He'd been thrown against the wall, too, both literally and figuratively. He stepped out of the safety of his own world, he took one chance on trusting another human being, and he was treated like a worthless, subhuman freak.

"Dammit! How could I have been so stupid?" The question wasn't shouted, it was bellowed. His voice broke mid-sentence, threatening to go hoarse if he kept yelling. But how could he stop? He was fighting the pain that came from a place he detested, the place where he first learned that the word, 'family,' meant pain. He thought he left that place behind, but he hadn't. "I befriended Arel, and look where it got me."

The misery also came from his body being battered in the accident. He could barely stand up. His entire side was bruised to the bone. That part was screaming too, making him drag himself from bed to chair to wall, hanging on to objects as if they were lifelines. But there was no escape from his torment. As he clung to the wall, as his physical and emotional states came together, he became an abused, quivering animal, one that had let down its guard and opened itself to the cruelty of the outside world.

"Don't do this to yourself." His pleas came out in a whisper. "Rein in these ridiculous feelings."

He knew about Arel's flawed nature all along. So why was he so upset now just because Arel had moved on to embrace a new family,

340

new friends. Why should those facts make him lose all his ability to hold it together? Why was his body beginning to shake?

"Oh hell, the chills are back," he said with clenched teeth.

That's when he knew the answer to his questions.

It's Arel's damn blood that's doing this to me. I almost forgot.

A second revelation followed. It was more devastating than the first. William only had to look at the facts to understand the whole picture. Arel wanted a new life. He admitted it. That's why he infected himself with the blood of a person called Michael. But Arel hadn't stopped there. He also set out to destroy his past, to destroy William.

Arel wasn't crazy or ignorant of what was flowing through his veins. He knew that he was infected and wanted to infect me too.

"Damn you, Arel! This is your retribution! Even if you kill us both, you want payback!"

A small laugh escaped his lips. It sounded odd and too high-pitched, followed by a lamenting moan. "I only wanted to help you," he whispered as the stabbing pain of Arel's treachery hit him full force. William had decided that another human being was worthy of his sacrifice. Now he was being punished for his mistake.

"Not just punished, exterminated!" He screamed again as he picked up a lamp and hurled it across the room. It hit the top of his dresser, taking out another small, expensive French vase.

Stumbling over to a chair, he sat hunched over, shuddering, trying to fight off any more thoughts, trying to shield himself against the freezing cold that seemed to have visited the room.

As his breath eased, he sat in the stillness, feeling the exhaustion that usually accompanied the chills. His head was splitting in two, but his hearing was still adequate. He noticed sounds coming from the room next to his. He heard voices, barely audible, but he knew Arel was talking to someone.

He's probably on his cell phone, talking to his pals.

But then he heard a second voice, answering Arel. This voice was deeper and richer in timbre.

* * *

341

Arel rubbed his brow and glared at Michael. "How can I possibly help William when I don't understand him?"

Michael sat down in one of the leather chairs. "Tell me what happened."

"We were in a tavern, just talking, and then he got really angry and stomped out. The next thing I know, he's running out in front of a car. I know it hit him, that he's hurt, but he's locked himself in his room and refuses all help."

"And you don't have any idea about what caused him to react like he did."

Arel avoided Michael's gaze and stared at the floor. "Things just escalated."

"Escalated how?"

Arel hesitated, letting his mind wander to the shelves of books and collectibles. He studied a small bronze fox. It was really quite a nice piece.

Michael stood up and walked over to the book shelves. "Arel, do you remember how it escalated?"

"There was one thing. When William mentioned the group back in Chicago, I might have been a little overprotective. I said some things that he might have taken the wrong way."

"What do you mean?"

"Maybe William's jealous. But that's totally out of character for him. He's as tough as they come. He said it himself. He could care less about my friends."

"Is that how you see him, even after what you experienced from his perspective?"

"Who knows at this point?" he cried out in frustration as he began to pace. "When I went back in time and experienced William's point of view, he was a different person. The William that is here and now isn't like that."

"Or maybe you've viewed him as a villain for so long, that you still want to keep him in that role."

"Okay, that's valid. But look at it from my standpoint."

Michael stepped closer to where Arel had stopped to adjust a picture. "What are you trying to tell me?"

Arel knew what Michael was getting at, but the adrenaline was flowing again. His mind was being funneled into a small channel of facts. "William is basically ruthless. He admitted that fact when we were in the pub. When it comes to our current relationship, he's Mr. Science. He invited me here to study my blood. He wants to look for answers that go along with his narrow beliefs." He gave Michael a quick glance. "There's no room in his world for you or the thought of angels."

Michael let out a sigh. "I'm not worried about that. The important thing to remember is that William's made room for you. He's studying his condition and yours because he's trying to help you both."

Arel crossed his arms. "I think he loves being right!"

"Is it so hard to believe that he's capable of caring deeply about someone?"

"Look, Michael, for some reason he did care about me that one night, but it was a fluke. William's true nature is to divorce himself from feeling anything about others. He never cared if he was liked or disliked. He's rock solid about one thing, himself."

Another loud crash from the next room shattered his logical argument.

Michael stared at the wall as more shouts of outrage followed the crash. "I don't think that he's rock solid anymore."

"Dammit, Michael! Why did I have to start all this?" As a flush of anger surged through Arel's body, he wanted to throw something too. "I've tried to make amends, but nothing I do turns out right."

Michael's gaze remained compassionate, but firm. "Do you care about what happens to William?"

"Of course! I wouldn't be here otherwise."

"Are you sure? What if William simply disappeared? Would that matter to you?"

Arel started to answer and stopped himself. That's when he realized that he wanted Michael to be wrong about William. "I couldn't get beyond my hatred when I gave William my blood. Even now, I'm not much better off. I know I was wrong, but I can't really care about William the way he cared about me."

Michael didn't hesitate to ask his next question. "Did William ever really matter to you?"

"I thought he did. I considered him my friend, the closest thing to family that I had, but maybe it wasn't true. When I look back at who I was, even my love for Justina seems so immature." He stared down at the floor and shrugged. "It's strange, I came here with one purpose, to redeem myself. Now, after seeing William in so much pain, I want to care about him, but I don't think I can. There's a numbness in my chest, an emptiness that won't go away."

"I see," Michael said as he returned to his chair.

Arel followed him, clasping his hands anxiously. "Even if I did really care, William says that he hates me, and I believe him. He won't let me near him."

As Arel finished his sentence, the door flew open. He turned around and saw William in the doorway. For a moment he could only stare back in shock. William's face was twisted in pain, and his eyes had the wild look of an animal fighting for its life. "My god, Will, you better sit down."

William ignored his advice, holding onto the door frame to steady himself. "What the hell is going on here?"

Arel blinked back mutely, searching for an answer that was plausible.

"I asked you a question!" William yelled again, filling the space with his rage.

Michael stood up and stepped forward. "Hello, you must be Will—"

William flailed out at him, nearly falling over and grabbing the doorjamb again. "I know who I am! Who are you?"

Arel held out his hands in a pacifying gesture. "It's okay. He's my friend."

"What friend?"

"This is Michael, the angel that I told you about."

William slammed the door against the wall. "Angel, hell! You mean he's the bastard who infected us! How dare you bring him here!"

"Please, it's okay," Arel urged. Any chance of redemption was quickly slipping away.

William looked like he was barely able to stay upright, but his anger was explosive. "I want both of you out of here, now!"

"But Will, the least I can do is help you in the lab."

"Really?" William blinked back as if he had to have time to process Arel's statement. When he spoke this time, his voice went low and venomous. "That's really nice of you, Arel, considering that you wanted me infected in the first place. No, not just infected, you wanted me dead!"

"I swear, you're not infected, not in the way you think."

"So none of this is real?" William held out a trembling hand. "You're telling me that my chills, the pain I'm in, the fact that I'm losing my mind, it's just all part of a silly hallucination that I'm having?"

"It's a part of a process. It'll pass, I promise, and in the meantime, I can stay with you and—"

"And watch me suffer and die?" William had to pause to catch his breath. "You think you've won already," he hissed through clenched teeth. "When you see me like this, you're congratulating yourself."

Arel shook his head. "You're wrong."

"Oh, that's true. I have been wrong about you." William's face contorted into a sneer as he teetered precariously in the doorway. "I let myself think you were special. I forgave you for everything you did to hurt me because I refused to see what you really are, a selfish scourge on the earth, bent on destruction, like all the rest."

Arel stared back, knowing William was right about the selfish part and also about the part that had wanted William's destruction. Yet, no amount of guilt could thaw his heart or warm the icy feelings that he harbored. Still, he had to try something, anything to undo the damage he'd done. "We've both had our faults. Let's start over, please."

"Start over? I'm standing here ready for the grave, and you want to start over? Do you know how ridiculous that sounds?"

Arel got the message. It was hopeless. William wasn't going to back down. "Maybe you're right. I was foolish to think we could work something out." Walking to the open closet, he grabbed his suitcase. "I'll leave immediately."

William's face turned scarlet with fresh outrage. "That's it? Arel, the guy who can't shut up when it comes to raking me over the coals, is giving up?"

Arel shrugged, feeling as insensitive and heartless as William said he was. "It's for your best, Will, I'm only aggravating you."

"You ingrate!" William's voice reached a new crescendo as his eyes bugged out in disbelief. "One lousy offer to help and you're leaving! Is that it? Don't you have an ounce of compassion in that bloody body of yours?"

Michael moved closer to where William was standing. "William, you better not overexert yourself. Perhaps you'd like to sit down like Arel suggested."

William jerked around and stared at Michael. "How dare you speak to me, you infected bastard!"

"Don't worry, we're both leaving," Arel said quietly as he began to take his clothes out of the closet.

"Not if I kill you both first!" William screamed. He let go of the door and took a step into the room. He tried to take another, but he couldn't seem to manage it. His face was contorted with unrestrained fury and betrayal. He tried to speak, but no sound came out of his mouth.

"William?" Arel tossed his clothes aside. Even if he had no feeling in his heart, his mind was delivering a clear message that William was in serious trouble.

William tottered back and forth as he grabbed hold of his head with both hands. The next moment he went down, crashing to the floor like a felled oak.

"Oh hell!" Arel rushed over to where William lay sprawled out across the oriental carpet, totally motionless. "Will, can you hear me?" Crouching down, he didn't know if William was even breathing. He looked at Michael who joined him on the floor. "Is he going to be alright?"

"I don't know," Michael said as he turned William over. He put his hand on William's chest.

Arel's voice almost failed him as he begged Michael for reassurance. "Tell me he isn't dead! Tell me that I didn't kill him!"

Michael hesitated. "Luckily, his heart is in pretty good shape, but he's come very close to having a stroke."

"Can you help him?"

"I can't. He's cut himself off from any intervention I have to offer."

"We have to do something!"

"William doesn't have any idea about what's happening to him. His suppressed feelings are all coming to the surface at once and affecting him on all levels."

Arel studied William's pale, gaunt face. "And I've made it worse."

Michael put a hand on Arel's shoulder. "William needs support, my friend, and it's up to you to give him that support."

Arel rocked back on his heels. "But how? What can I do? When it comes to it, William was right about me. I don't know how to care."

"Power brings responsibility. If you want to redeem yourself as you say, you'll have to find a way."

"Responsibility, you and William both seem to know a lot about it, but I don't. When I first got here, I saw how frail he was. But I chose to ignore his condition. I only saw what I wanted to see." Arel stared at Michael with pleading eyes. "Now look at the state he's in. He's barely surviving at this point."

"Yes, I know. You have quite a challenge ahead of you."

Sixty-One

William opened his eyes, winced, and shut them tight again. He felt like a hammer was pounding on his brain. "I've never felt this bad before," he groaned.

Arel sat in a chair next to him, wringing out a cold compress. He placed it on William's forehead. "What got into you?" he asked as he took hold of William's wrist, feeling for his pulse. "I couldn't believe what a tantrum you threw."

William opened his eyes again and scowled back. "What are you still doing here?"

"Don't worry about that now. Your heart rate is starting to return to normal. If you get upset again, you will definitely have a stroke."

"I'm almost immortal, remember?" William started to laugh, needing a bit of levity to balance out the misery he was in. It was cut short by a stabbing pain. He grabbed his head, trying to keep it from falling off. "I've been told I have the constitution of a prize ox."

Arel let out a laugh too. "Prize ass is more like it."

William glared back. "That's it, you bastard," he said, yanking the cloth off his head and trying to sit up.

Arel's face flushed with embarrassment. "I can't believe I said that. I'm sorry, it's a habit. We've always argued about everything."

"Not anymore!" Sick or not, William wasn't putting up with Arel another minute. As he struggled to right himself, he almost blacked out. Still, he persevered. Using all his strength, he was able to sit up.

"What are you doing?" Arel asked with a frown.

William didn't answer. Instead, he swung his legs over the side of the bed. No matter what it took, he would rid himself of Arel, once and for all. With a great heave upwards, he was able to stand on wobbly feet. In a moment of triumph, he pointed to the door. "Out!"

Arel jumped up from his chair. "It was a joke!"

William tried to lower his volume so his head wouldn't explode, but his tone was unflinching and clear. "I mean it. I don't want you here."

"Will, you need me, at least for a little while. Just admit it."

"I order you to vacate my home this instant!"

Arel began to back away reluctantly. "You shouldn't exert—"

"Go!" It took all of his resolve, but William managed to remain standing. "Get out now!"

Arel continued slowly moving towards the door. "This isn't a good idea."

"Leave!" Every shout shook William's entire body. As he watched Arel retreat, the room began to spin like it had the first time he passed out. He tried to grab hold of the chair that Arel had been sitting in, but his hand missed the mark. As he fell, everything slowed down, giving him clarity of mind. It was a crystal state of awareness that replaced any former beliefs. The foolish thoughts that he could control what was happening to him were self-deceptions, lies that were swept away in an instant by reality. He understood beyond all doubt that the wondrous gift that Rolphe had given him was slipping away as surely as his ability to stop it. The new disease that infected him was a lethal malady. He wouldn't find a cure in time to save himself. Yet, in that moment of acute understanding, a miracle happened. He didn't hold Arel accountable anymore. Life was what it was. The trick was how to honor one's self in spite of what was thrown at you.

Falling heavily unto the hardwood surface of the floor again, he felt like a soldier who'd stepped on a land mine. He knew his extraordinary life was at an end. He also knew that he could go to his death with dignity, not as a victim, but as a being who could still choose how he'd confront the inevitable. It was the one gift he could still give himself.

* * *

As soon as Arel heard the crash, he rushed back into the bedroom. William lay on the floor again. "Will?" he cried out as he rushed over and knelt down. "Will, don't die on me." He stared at William's still form and imagined the worst. Another brother dead. With a neediness that had no time for caution, he quickly turned William over and began to shake him roughly. "Will, wake up!" Finally, William's eyes fluttered open and stared back at him. "Thank goodness," he gasped. "I was sure you were a goner."

"Not quite yet," William moaned.

"Should I call for an ambulance? Tell me what to do."

"Nothing." William's tone was unusually quiet, but he held out his hand.

Arel grabbed William's outstretched offering and held it tight. Something was very wrong. William's touch, his energy was different. "Are you sure you didn't do more damage to your leg?"

William tugged on him. "Help me up."

Doing as he was told, Arel managed to get William off the floor, but the ailing man couldn't get his balance.

"You're in no shape to be moving around. Your body needs to rest. Lay down on the bed."

William took hold of Arel's shoulder. "You still look like the handsome idiot I remember. I'm glad you're coping with this disease. Maybe I was wrong about you. You might be adapting to it. Maybe your snowflakes are a good thing."

"And you can adapt too. I'm sure you can," Arel insisted in his most encouraging voice.

"No, I'm the part of the experiment that ends up in the dust bin. But that doesn't matter now."

"What are you talking about?"

William clung to him for support "Did you mean what you said? Will you be there for me?" His voice was a whisper, almost a prayer.

"Of course!" Arel's eyes locked on to William's. A spark of caring broke through the icy reservoir in his chest and filled him with a great sadness. For a brief instant, he did love William. "You can't give up, Will, please!"

William smiled back with unguarded eyes. Their pale blueness wasn't hard like before, but filled with kindness and a deep compassion. "I don't blame you anymore," he said solemnly as if he was in a confessional. "I said things earlier, but I've let go of all of it.

None of it matters now. Even if you don't consider me your brother, I consider you mine. You're the only one who counted for anything in my life. Your actions were harsh and rash, but underneath I saw the real you, the person who's pure and untainted in this world of selfish bastards."

Arel could hear the sincerity in William's words. The usual cynicism was gone. William was baring himself in a way that forced Arel to do the same. "I'm sorry about what's happened. I set myself up as judge and jury. I had no right."

"It's too late to worry about it now. What's done is done."

"Just like that? You can forgive me?"

William laughed. "I know, it's strange, isn't it? But I don't want to fight with you anymore, not now."

"Why, what's so different now?"

William's eyes shifted, becoming much fiercer and determined. "Look at me. I can't go on like this," he said in a desperate, haunted voice.

Arel's body jerked as if it knew at once what William wanted. "You're giving up, aren't you? You want me to kill you." His voice was thin and ragged as he tried to back away.

William held on to him. "Please, Arel, do this for me. Please."

Arel had never heard William beg for anything, but now he was begging Arel to help him end his life. "I can't," he whispered.

William smiled again, steadying himself as he dropped his head to Arel's chest. "Of course not."

He pushed William back enough to gaze into his eyes. He could see the turmoil there and also the control, the determination not to lash out anymore. William had forgiven him, and now Arel was struggling to hold on to that virtue too. "I'm sorry."

William took several deep, gasping breaths. His eyes finally cleared again. The neediness was gone, replaced by a composed acceptance. "I'm sorry too. You've never bloodied your hands. It was wrong of me to want you to do it now."

"Even if I had bloodied my hands as you said, I couldn't kill you. It would be a waste." He shook William's shoulders with a lighthearted smile. "We're going to work together to beat this thing."

William laughed again. "I hope you can. But for me, with my gift gone, what would be the point? I could never live like the hordes again, never. But don't worry. I'll take care of getting rid of myself."

351

"No!" Arel yelled. Reeling with sudden anger and resentment, he couldn't bear the thought of William killing himself. It instantly ignited the misery and loss he felt over Justina's death. His golden eyes flared with outrage. His fingers dug into William's shoulders with the resolve of one possessed with absolute responsibility. "I won't let you do it, and that's final."

William stared back, first with surprise, then contempt. "I'd like to see you stop me."

The fires in Arel's gut burned hotter as the coals of memory were turned over and exposed. Once again, he found himself rushing after the woman he loved, trying to reach her before she could get to his razor. "Justina, stop!"

As William struggled against Arel's painful, grappling hands, Arel barely registered the man's response. He was watching a nightmare. Justina had the sharp blade to her throat. "God, no! Don't do it! Please—"

William grimaced. "What the hell are you talking about? Who's Justina? Arel!"

William's shout broke through Arel's temporary spell of wretchedness. As he came back to himself, his hands clamped down tighter on William's shoulders. "I might have failed her, but I won't fail again! I can't! I won't!"

"Arel! Those snowflakes are affecting your brain! Calm down! Talk to me!"

Arel let his mind reel backwards again. Regret and sorrow were powerful reminders that bound him to the past. "Justina! I failed you!"

"Who's Justina?" William shrieked. "Tell me!"

Finally, the answer trickled out. "A person who loved me. She killed herself."

William's face wasn't serene now. "Why? Did you infect her too?" he bellowed as he continued to fight to free himself.

The words were like a violent slap to Arel's face, adding more fuel to his already explosive feelings. "She took her life because she didn't think I loved her! It was my fault!"

William stopped resisting and glared at him. "So I'm not your first victim, am I? You're not as pure as I thought. What else don't I know about you?"

Arel felt something shatter inside of him, something hard and brittle that should have kept a baser part of him contained. He growled out his next words. "I . . . won't . . . let . . . you . . . die!"

* * *

An alarm went off in William's mind. Arel's voice was measured and slow, so deep and ominous that he almost didn't recognize it. As Arel backed him against a wall and continued to snarl at him, he felt like he was in the hands of a maniac. Arel's eyes were proof that he was going mad. They were glowing again, more brightly than ever.

"Okay, you win," he said quietly. He kept his voice carefully contained, almost light and cheerful. If Arel was pushed the slightest bit, he might crack completely. The guy suddenly had the strength of two men, two heavies that could easily go berserk. He tried to smile. "No need to worry. I'll keep trying for a cure. Just let me—"

"That's a lie," Arel seethed back. "But what am I going to do with you?"

William's smile broadened. Why was he trying to appease Arel? He needed to do just the opposite. If Arel's hand was forced, he'd lose control. It would be curtains for William.

I'll get you to kill me in spite of yourself!

The thought was a triumphant one and made him lunge for Arel. "You're right! I am lying! I will kill myself!"

"Never!" Arel's shout went up like a battle cry.

As they struggled, William's chance at a new kind of victory was so exhilarating that his own body rallied. Strangely enough, he felt better, more physically capable. As Arel bounced his body repeatedly off the wall, he was able to perform a sudden, frenzied, counter-movement. He got an arm free, then the other arm. "I'm not making any more mistakes either," he yelled as he grabbed Arel by the throat. "If you won't kill me, then maybe I can put you out of your misery!"

William felt reserves of strength coming online. It bolstered his determination. He had a grand purpose that needed fulfilling. No matter what, one of them was going to die then and there. The feeling was revitalizing. The harder he squeezed Arel's neck the more he wanted this one last go at power, the power to end a life. All his kills would culminate in one final and glorious fight to the death.

Arel wasn't prepared for William's counterattack. Yet as his opponent's dark, malicious cravings poured out of him in a black field of combat, Arel's gut sucked in massive quantities of the stuff. It overpowered his own feelings, his own emotional chaos. It fed the already blazing fires, turning them into a raging inferno of wrath that had one function, survival. But that was only the first step. Things soon spiraled totally out of control and a new directive surfaced.

The broiling energies in his core raced through his blood, through his tissues, and hit his brain. A nuclear blast of pent-up rage drove out all responsibility, all caring and concern. William would get his wish. Arel would gladly tear him limb from limb.

* * *

As the two assailants, Arel and William, geared up for a lethal climax to their long association, as they each began to unleash all their animosity, the sprinklers in the ceiling went off. Torrents of water sprayed in all directions, not as advertised in the literature that was passed out with the system, but with double the force and triple the amount of water.

One sprinkler head, located to the side of Arel and William, blasted their bodies with an icy, pummeling downpour so fierce that it nearly threw them off their feet. Feeling like they'd been hit with a fire hose, they sputtered and choked on the water that they were breathing in as they tried to remain standing. It brought them both out of their personal war at the same time.

"Dammit!" William gasped as he came back to himself and glanced around. His practical concerns immediately came to mind. He'd already lost several objets d'art in his previous rampage. He wasn't pleased afterwards when reason reinstated itself. Even if he wasn't going to be around to enjoy them, he couldn't bear the thought that all of his possessions, his priceless books and paintings, would be destroyed.

For Arel, the dousing was accompanied by Michael's stern face staring at him through the flood. "What am I doing?" he asked as he released William and backed away. His face was red with mortification as he stared vacantly ahead, but William was frantically trying to get his attention.

"Don't just stand there! There's a shut-off valve in the lab downstairs. Go turn off this blasted water!"

Sixty-Two

Hobbling about with a cane that he found in his closet, William went from painting to painting, letting out moans of distress. "Ruined, all my beautiful paintings are ruined."

Arel was down on his hands and knees with a large sponge and a bucket, sopping up water from an expensive, oriental carpet. "At least your library is safe and most of the books in here were behind glass doors. You should be happy about that."

William turned and stared at him. "It's my bedroom, the room that houses my most cherished possessions. Do you have any idea what some of these paintings are worth?"

"Then why in the hell did you install sprinklers?"

William limped over to where Arel was working. "To protect my collection, you idiot. When the damn things were put in, I made sure their spray wouldn't hit the artwork, but something went wrong. The damn nozzles should never have delivered that much water to that large an area."

Arel wrung the sponge out and continued working. "Well it's a good thing they did, isn't it? Or you and I would have killed each other. Then what good would any of it be to you?"

Instead of an answer, William let out a great sigh and moved off to inspect more of his injured paintings. He was so devastated by his losses, he couldn't appreciate Arel's wisdom.

Arel threw the sponge in the bucket and stood up. "What got into us? I didn't think I could ever let myself get so carried away."

William gave Arel a fierce scowl. "Look at this. Look at what the water did to the canvas," he moaned as he tilted the frame. Water had collected in the molding, and now it spilled down on the floor.

356

"When I asked you here, I had such good intentions. All I wanted was a little help from you. And if I was going to die, I wanted to leave this life gracefully."

Arel wiped his hands on a towel. "Is that how you still feel?"

"No, I think I feel better. While I was strangling you, my energy started to return. I don't think I'm as bad off as I thought."

Arel grabbed the handle on the pail. "Glad I could help. Now, if you'll excuse me, I have to dump this out."

William turned and softened his tone. "Thanks for cleaning up. It's not what I asked for, but it's something."

Arel's frown slipped away. "Admit it, Will, aren't you glad that I didn't kill you? I promised that you'd get better, didn't I? You'll see. It's all going to work out."

"Just go empty the pail."

"Right," Arel said as he left the room. His voice was quiet but somewhat audible as he issued several words of thanks in the hallway. William could make out a few.

"Thank goodness for you, Michael. You saved us both with that dousing."

Sixty-Three

The day after their attempted fight-to-the-death skirmish, Arel was relieved to see that William continued to feel much stronger physically. He was even agreeable to Arel doing some energy work on his injured leg. Happily, it worked. William was able to get around without his cane. He had even returned to his laboratory.

"Nice to see you working again," Arel said. He sat alongside William, taking notes as William dictated.

"Your 'woo woo' magic seems to have some scientific basis. I did some research on the internet while you were sleeping."

Arel kept writing. "Your leg is almost back to normal. I'd think that would be proof enough."

"Fine, you have a point."

"For what it's worth, I wanted to help."

With caution uppermost in his mind, Arel hadn't acted without first checking in with Michael. Under the angel's advisement, he hadn't actually touched William during the healing process. He took a more long-distance approach with Michael's advice clearly sounding in his mind. "Someday, I think scientists will be able to measure the energy that comes from a healer's hands."

William made an adjustment to the slide he was studying. "Yes, maybe so, but right now we have other problems. Take this down. Subject B's blood has changed. In a little more than twenty-four hours, the crystalline structures are more disorganized."

Arel threw his pen aside. "What? Subject B is me, right? Let me see what's going on," he demanded as he pushed William back from the viewing lenses.

William was right. Arel's blood had changed. The day before, his snowflakes, as he liked to think of them, were clustered in tiny groups that formed symmetric patterns. Now some had strayed away from their groups and become loners who seemed rather lost. "I wish you wouldn't look at my blood," he complained. "I never thought about any of this in terms of my body. I have enough to think about. I'm trying to stay on track emotionally too, you know."

"You?" William let out a contemptible laugh. "Do you seriously think that you can keep track of your emotions? That's like a fish saying that he keeps track of the water that he's swimming in."

"Why would you say that?"

"Because you love your emotions, especially the ones that make you feel like a victim. You treat your constant drama like it's gold bullion that you have to fondle every moment of every day."

"At least I know that I have emotions, but you're the fish that acts like he doesn't ever dip a fin into the water. But admit it, Will, you're swimming in the stuff just as much as the rest of us. You just don't know it."

"Is that how you see a rational, level-headed individual? I'm the guy who looks before he leaps. I'm the responsible one here."

"That makes it worse. You've killed people in cold blood."

"Would it be better to kill them like some crazed maniac? I sized up every person I ever killed beforehand. And every person I killed deserved it. Every one of them was a self-serving, worthless human."

"You think that about everyone, that the entire human race is selfish and self-serving."

"Well it is. They've screwed each other and the planet to boot."

"What about you?"

"I'm including myself. Humanity's created a dog-eat-dog world, and instead of complaining about it like you, I accept it. I pride myself on knowing the truth."

"What if we were all like you? Have you ever thought about that?"

"Yes, actually, I have. If people all owned up to who they were, at least they'd stop acting like victims. Each would have to face facts and realize that they're not innocent."

"So you chose me as a friend because you thought I was the exception. Is that right?"

"Yes, but you proved me wrong. You were as bloodthirsty as any of us before the sprinklers cooled your jets."

Arel got up and walked over to the sofa. "You make me wonder why I'm even here, why I'm alive. If you're right, then I should be shot like all the rest."

"Why did you come?"

"What does it matter? Like you said, I'm worthless, just another one of the hordes that you detest."

William smiled. "Good, you've admitted that you're no better than me. I like that. It's a first for you."

Arel was about to sit down, but changed his mind. He started for the stairs. "I'm glad that you're pleased. I feel like slime, but if you're happy then at least one of us has achieved something."

"Where are you going?"

Arel paused. "Look William, nothing has been achieved by my visit. Just the opposite. We almost killed each other. Now, after the conversation we just had, I'm taking my bloodthirsty hands back to Chicago where I won't be tempted to go into a rage again."

"What about finding a cure?"

"Why would I want a cure? Like you said, humanity deserves to die. When my time comes, you can celebrate. There'll be one less selfish individual in the world."

"You're being dramatic again. You don't have to run off just because your feelings are hurt."

"My presence isn't adding anything of value to your research. And we'll never agree about anything of substance. So there's no reason to stay. It'll be better for both of us to part company while we're still able to be civil with each other."

William waved him off. "Fine, do whatever you want, but don't expect me to call you if I crack this damn disease we have."

Arel started up the stairs again. Without looking back he yelled out a final comment. "For the last time, it's not a disease!" What he didn't voice was his next thought.

I gave the guy my best shot. So the hell with him.

As he walked to his room, he didn't want to admit it, but William had been right. His feelings were bruised. Now his only thought was to pack his bags and get a flight back to the States. When he opened the door to his room, he was stopped in his tracks. "Michael! I didn't expect to see you here."

Michael sat in one of the leather chairs, stretching out his long legs and smiling. The angel looked different. He was wearing a classic, Norwegian fisherman's sweater and dark slacks. His blond hair was loose, framing his strong features, and his eyes were as pale as blue topaz. "I thought you might be glad to see me."

"You look good."

"I thought a little change would be nice. Maybe your sophistication is rubbing off on me."

"I've seen you in your more formal, otherworldly attire once or twice. I don't think I'll ever come close to that. Wings are hard to compete with."

"Each world has its elegance."

Arel went to the closet and took down his suitcase. "Well, right now the only world I want to think about is one that doesn't include William."

"So you're leaving?"

Arel threw his suitcase on the bed. "Yes, there's nothing for me to do here."

Michael looked around the room and let his gaze settle on the book shelves. "William has a very nice collection of volumes, just like you."

"Yes, it's rather strange, we both like to collect things."

Michael got up and went to the shelves. "There are so many stories here, so many dramas, adventures, and even comedies."

"Yes, well William and I have our own horror story coming to a close at long last."

"You're not leaving him with much, you know."

"He doesn't want anything that I have. We seem to bring out the worst in each other. You saw us fighting. We were like a couple of savages."

Michael laughed. "Yes, but William doesn't want to kill himself anymore."

Arel let out a huff of annoyance. "He really had a grip on my throat. I guess I gave him a reason to fight again, but now we're back to square one."

"Not completely. You may not have noticed, but William gave you a gift today."

"A gift? I don't consider a headache and a severe bout of depression a gift."

"He said that you admitted that you're no better than he is."

"Right, I guess that's true. I mean I haven't murdered people like he has, but I can see that I have the potential."

"That's not exactly what I'm getting at. You have to be careful not to get a man's actions mixed up with the man himself."

"Thanks a lot, Michael. That's William's line."

Michael's eyes lit up, but he didn't reply.

Arel walked over to the other leather chair and sat down. "So he's right?"

"What do you think?"

"I don't think I realized that I clumped his actions and his person together, but maybe I did." He grasped his hands and stared at the floor. "William said I've always judged him. He's right. But he did so many horrible things. How could I separate who he is from all that?"

"But in his mind, his actions weren't horrible."

"So you agree that each person lives by their own truth and that's okay?"

"I'm not saying that their actions are right, or good, and I'm not excusing actions that harm another person. But there's more to each life than beliefs and actions. At the basis of every being, there remains a soul. And that soul is waiting to be discovered and honored. When that happens the soul is free to love, to create from a place where everyone is connected, where there's nothing to fight or fear."

Arel stared back at him. "Is that why you took a chance on me? Is that what you always see when I do stupid things?"

"Of course."

Arel's gaze shifted with concern. "A few minutes ago, you said I wasn't leaving William with much. Do you think I could explain any of this to him?"

"Maybe you need to take some time to integrate it more fully into your own way of thinking first."

Arel's jaw tightened. "Are you suggesting that I should stay?"

"You have an opportunity to help yourself and William."

"If I only believed that I could."

"Search a little deeper," Michael said quietly.

"Search deeper? But what am I searching for?" Arel asked as his brows came together in confusion. When he didn't get an answer, he looked up, but Michael was gone. "Great, I'm left to figure out what to do when I haven't the slightest idea."

He got up, put his suitcase back in the closet, and went to the door to lock it. He might have to stay for a while longer, but he didn't have to talk to William while he was soul-searching.

He stretched out on the bed and closed his eyes. He could feel his mind resisting Michael's advice. He started to run through a list of his failures, reasons why he couldn't help William. Michael was expecting too much from him. Staring into the ethers, he tried to give Michael a mental message.

I don't know how to keep my own life on track. How can I do anything for William?

At the same time, he knew that he was making excuses. If Michael believed he was capable, he had to believe that too. Or did he? Michael seemed to have a lenient attitude about William's choices.

So why shouldn't I give myself a break? I'm doing my best, that's enough.

The statement ignited a flush of shame. He was lying again. The truth was that he was doing a very poor job of using Michael's blood. He was allowing his own self-centered desires to dictate his actions.

Bloody hell, I need a nap.

* * *

William climbed the stairs to the upper level of the house with relative ease. His leg was functioning well. Unfortunately, the rest of his body was flagging. He'd been on the internet for hours, trying to find something that related to the condition of Arel's blood. Nothing he found came close to looking like what they were dealing with. Still, he was starting to feel more optimistic about the situation. Arel seemed healthy as a horse most of the time. The only time he looked really bad was when he arrived on William's doorstep. Of course there was Arel's mental and emotional instability, but Arel's body was doing quite well. "So how will *I* end up?" he sighed. "That's the question."

He stopped outside of Arel's room and listened. Had Arel left without saying goodbye? He tried the knob. The door was locked.

363

When he listened again, he could hear soft snoring coming from the room.

Still here and sleeping. He's probably worn himself out thinking about being as fallible as the rest of us.

William was looking forward to having the place to himself again. In the meantime, he went to his own bedroom and glanced around. The space looked almost normal after its dowsing. Arel had done a nice job cleaning up the floors. Two ceiling fans were helping to circulate the air and enable the paintings to dry.

He walked over to one of his favorites. It pictured a forest of towering trees with deer browsing in the foreground. Inspecting it closely, he sighed. The color didn't seem quite the same as before. It would never be perfect again.

Who cares at this point?

He took off his clothes and climbed into bed. With the house quiet, he'd try to get some rest. He needed a respite if he was going to continue with his studies. A clear, focused mind was his true friend. If there was a solution to be found, his mental acuity needed to be sharp and ready for the job.

After he got into bed, it felt good to simply lie in the quiet. Thankfully, his mattress had escaped harm. He'd had a protective cover put on just in case the sprinklers ever went off. Now as he pulled a soft, satiny sheet close, he was pleased with himself and the way he generally handled life. The sprinkler incident wasn't his fault. He took every precaution. On the other hand, he wasn't obsessive like Arel. He maintained a positive view of his life. Worries and regret served no purpose. Those attitudes depleted the energy he needed to carry on. After a few minutes, his mind was still, and he fell into a deep sleep.

Sixty-Four

Arel smiled proudly as he walked through the open field and approached the edge of a woodland area. The vast, grassy meadow that surrounded him was gloriously green and vibrant. In the distance, neat squares of thriving farmland provided a splendid backdrop. He paused to inhale the fresh, clean air. He knew he was dreaming, but it was lucid dreaming, and he was the creator of this perfect world. All that he had to do was picture what he wanted or even generalize his desires and the scene adjusted itself. His present creation was a bit like the English countryside, without the dreariness that he remembered from childhood. This was a place where he could relax.

As he continued on, his pace was leisurely. His body was at ease. This was his playground, a world of endless possibilities. A short distance ahead, he noticed a wild rose, covered in blooms. Spread out over some mossy outcroppings, it was a mass of pinkness. It reminded him of Michael's roses. Going over to enjoy the fragrance of one of the flowers, he wondered if the earth had been a dream in the beginning. Was the Garden of Eden real or simply the Master Creator's lucid dream?

No matter. Real or not, whatever possessed Adam and Eve to eat from the forbidden tree? Why would anyone want to know about good and evil? Why would anyone want to spoil something so wonderful?

As he pulled back from the rose bush to resume his wandering, he accidentally pricked himself on a thorn. His blood oozed out and formed a small droplet on his skin. Even when he knew he was dreaming, he seemed to bring in the element of blood. Did his dreamy blood have crystals in it too?

As soon as he thought about it, he thought about William. In fact, he could see William. The tall, thin man was walking through the meadow, looking totally mesmerized by its lush beauty.

Arel knew that he had invited William into the dream. But now, seeing him, he almost wished he hadn't. He had a moment of angst. He knew that he was responsible for damaging William's real-life dream, his small hope that there was still purity and innocence in life. And when he went back to Chicago, Arel was leaving William in a more hopeless state than ever.

"Show William that he was right about you," whispered a voice that was carried on the breeze. "Let your light shine bright again."

The voice was a deeper, wiser part of himself. He often heard it when he dreamed. Still he had to reflect on its advice. His sense of failure with William was so great, it wanted to overshadow everything.

"Don't go there. You have to believe in yourself, for his sake," the voice advised.

"It's not that easy," he responded.

Still, being in this magical place, he felt a kind of dispensation, a relaxation of the rules that usually structured his life. Finally, he smiled to himself. This was his dream. He could make this his Eden.

Forget about right and wrong. Enjoy the moment.

* * *

William had never had a lucid dream before. He'd read about people being aware that they were dreaming, but it was new for him. He found himself in a broad, grassy field that seemed to go on for miles in all directions. Overhead, the sun was newly risen.

It's so beautiful, and its warmth feels so good. It's not burning my skin!

To be able to bask in the bright, warm presence of the golden orb was a miracle for him.

I didn't realize how much I missed the light.

He spun around in joy. Everywhere he looked, every blade of grass was illuminated by the brilliance that had been denied him for so long. Stopping to regain his composure, he wondered for a moment how he'd been strong enough to be content with only the moon.

But I've been compensated.

He contented himself with the thought.

You can't have everything.

As he began to walk towards the area ahead, he noticed that Arel was a short distance away. He hadn't noticed him before.

"I should have known that you'd be here," he protested, not wanting any problems to spoil the perfect day he was enjoying.

Arel's smile was wide and welcoming as he spread his arms out in a wide arc. "Will, look back at the meadow! Have you ever seen so many wildflowers?"

As he spoke, William noticed that where he'd seen green fields, there were suddenly thousands of flowers blooming. Violet, pink, yellow and countless shades of color lit up the landscape.

"Did you do that?" William knew that some people could manipulate their dreams. "Did you just change the grass to flowers?"

Arel grinned back. "I'm so glad that you could make it."

"It's not like I tried to come here. It just happened."

Walking up to him, Arel's face was almost playful. "I'm glad that you're here."

"So tell me, am I in your dream or mine?" he asked as he tried to add a few trees to the landscape. When nothing happened, he pulled back. "Oh, I see."

"Would you like something different?" Arel snapped his fingers and turned the surroundings into a forested setting. Tall, stately trees stood guard where the fields had been.

William inhaled deeply, taking in the smell of pine and loamy earth. A deer, fifty yards away, took flight in order to join its companions in the distance. William felt like he was standing in his painting. "You're very good at this. It's beautiful. It reminds me of the place where I grew up."

Arel motioned to a small, ornate gazebo in a clearing close by. It sheltered a small table and a set of chairs. "Can we talk?"

"About what?"

"We can talk about our lives. This is a good place to discuss things."

"I think we've done enough talking. It always ends up in an argument."

Arel shrugged. "I know. Which makes me wonder why you wanted me as a friend in the first place?"

"What difference does it make now?" Sleeping or not, William suddenly felt tired. "Besides, it's too long ago to delve into all that."

"But I want to know. I want to know what I missed when I thought about who I was."

William stared back for a long moment. In this dreamy landscape, Arel looked so young again, and he had a lighter, brighter energy that made him look like one of the angels he talked about.

"Please, Will," Arel pleaded with a broad, winning smile.

William walked over to the gazebo, checked out the rustic, wrought iron table, pulled out a chair and sat down. "Why do I bother? But I suppose this is your dream, and I have to indulge you."

Arel sat down across from him, settling back in his seat. He stared at William and laughed. "I never noticed this before, but now, in this dream, your eyes can look like those of a sailor searching for land."

"I'm tired, that's all. I'm looking for a good night's sleep."

"I think I'm responsible for that feeling."

William swore quietly as a fleeting memory surfaced. It came from a time long past, but the feelings it resurrected were still fresh and inviting. "I'm going to hate myself for this, but maybe I owe it to both of us to tell it like it is." As he spoke, he gave Arel a quick glance. It seemed enough to take him back in time. "When I first saw you, I thought you were the most incredible creature I'd ever seen. I knew at once that you didn't belong in this world. Great art is the same way. It's almost like it's a gift from somewhere else. It transcends the ugliness that we find around us. So when I saw you, I was captivated." He laughed softly. "I wanted to be your friend, your family, someone that you'd love as I was prepared to love you."

Arel pulled back with disbelief. "I had no idea—"

"Just listen, because, I swear, I'll never let myself go here again."

"I'm sorry. Please, continue."

"Anyway, it wasn't easy to get to know you, because of course, you were aloof, detached, the ultimate loner. But I didn't lack self-confidence or patience. I took my time, letting you get used to me, like I did with wild animals I'd studied in the woods." He paused to look at the beautiful landscape, to enjoy the blue, sunny skies. "Eventually, you allowed me to get closer to you. And I was secretly thrilled at my small victory. Of course, we began to argue at once. We seemed to be on the opposite sides of every issue. I believed in the natural world, and you believed in a world beyond any that I could imagine. I was the druid who believed that everything was sacred. I worshiped the earth and believed in its creatures. They made sense to me. And you, Arel, were the priest of the one god. The only thing you cared about was some unseen force that you claimed was all about love. But you didn't respect the world around you. The way you treated your body was disgusting. Your perfect vessel was maligned, something to contain your thoughts, nothing more."

"How can you say that you held anything sacred?" Arel asked with defiance. "I remember what you used to say. You told me that you hated people."

He smiled. "I did, and I still do, because people are self-consumed parasites. What I held in awe was the perfect way that nature works. It makes sense to me."

Arel frowned. "Whatever."

William held up his hand. "Be patient, I'm trying to explain. As I was saying, you were always talking about the way things should be, that people should care about one another, that sort of gibberish. When in fact, you didn't allow people to care. I wanted to be there for you, with you. In return, I just wanted you to acknowledge that I was more than a sparring partner. But you were so caught up in what things were supposed to be and how unjust they were."

William took a breath of the woodsy air and felt the wistfulness of where they were. It softened his thoughts and made him laugh. "What a complainer you were and still are. But I put up with it. I listened to you moan about your abusive father, your selfish mother. I sat there as you spouted off about how much you hated them. You were always talking about how people should love, and all you could do was hate. There wasn't room in your heart for anything else.

"I look back and wonder why I wanted you as a friend, but under all your foolishness, I thought there was something more. That was my failing. I was still hoping that someone in this world was worthy of my respect. I thought I could make you see reason and take some responsibility for your life."

He stopped, letting his eyes get hard as he stared at Arel. "You had so much potential. But only I saw that potential, only I believed in it. That's why I fought so hard with you, argued so vehemently, because I had plans. If you could have let go of your precious judgments about who had wronged you and how you were now a failure, you could have been glorious. We could have been glorious." He paused, weighing his next words carefully. "You would have never believed it, but I did have a vision. I imagined the two of us and what we could accomplish together. I, the man of science, would delve into nature's secrets and add a human's touch. I would try to be something that nature could be proud of. I'd give something back after all that humans had destroyed. And you, Arel, the man of God, would do what you talked about, show me how to love enough to take another chance on mankind. What I didn't realize was that I was so much more capable of taking a chance. In fact, I already had, with you." He let out a sigh of disgust. "But you cared nothing about me. I came to realize that in the end. That last night that I was still an ordinary human, we'd been arguing over something. I asked you to stay instead of storming out like you usually did. Of course you claimed I was to blame for your ill mood and left. After that I met Rolphe. But I don't regret it. He gave me more in one moment of sharing than you could have ever given me."

Arel's mouth was hanging open, and he was taking short gasps of air. "You're saying that if I hadn't—"

"It doesn't matter. I don't know why I even agreed to tell you about it."

Arel went pale. "To think that you would have never met that monster—"

"That's not the point!" He tried to stop Arel from going down the guilt path, but it was hopeless. At the same time, the fair skies were vanishing. A storm front was moving in, bringing gloom and a dreary cold. The brilliant heavens and the sun were lost to rolling, ominous clouds, traveling so fast that the blue was swallowed up in moments.

"Get a grip, Arel! *I* was enjoying the nice weather even if you weren't."

Arel's gaze became distant and removed from the scene. "All of this misery, all these years, if I had been there for you, neither of us would have become a vampire. I could have loved Justina forever, married her and had a family. What a wonderful life that would have been." He stopped and brought his attention back to William. "All the people who have died at your hands, none of it had to happen. And it's my fault. It's all my fault!"

"Oh hell, don't do this," William sighed. "It's all in the past, Arel. Let it go." But Arel wasn't listening. He was totally engrossed in his sad, increasingly volatile lament. William knew it was hopeless to argue with him. He stood up and pushed back from the table. "Dammit, let me out of this nightmare!" The order was delivered in a loud commanding voice. "I want to wake up now!" The order worked. He came awake with regret. As he looked around his bedroom, a question came to mind. Did he really tell Arel how he felt? "I hope not. If I did tell him what happened, we're both going to have hell to pay."

* * *

Arel might have been standing in a dreamy landscape, but his pain was the worst he'd ever experienced. William's story was responsible for his misery. It might have been told in a matter-of-fact way, but its implications were disastrous. Arel wasn't just responsible for passing on Michael's blood to William. His ignorance, his own blindness, had propelled both their lives into darkness to begin with. "It's all my fault! How many have died because of me?"

No lie, no self-deception could save him this time. The truth filled the air, polluting its purity. His rampage of blame became a suffocating sickness that invaded the trees and flowering plants. Everything around him started to wilt and die. Arel's own body grew heavy and weak. Soon his shouts turned into harsh whisperings. "I can't go on knowing what I did."

As he spoke, the light began to dim. Overhead, the sun gave way to black, menacing clouds. Thunder cracked open the sky, releasing a great wind. Its powerful gusts grew in power, fed by Arel's overwhelming self-loathing and guilt. It quickly became a hurricane, a swirling vortex that began to pull him in.

Even as he was buffeted and battered by the storm, Arel's attention remained laser-sharp. Focused on his failed responsibility, he welcomed destruction. He needed it. There was no way to reverse what he'd done. Annihilation was his only choice.

"Not even Michael's blood can help me now!"

371

He was sucked into a treacherous whirlpool that spiraled downwards. Then it let him go. He began to fall from some great height, as if the bottom dropped out of both his real world and his dream one.

He descended into a fiery world where flames surrounded him. Was it hell? If it was, he welcomed it. He wasn't afraid of the fire anymore, not if it would destroy him. Anything was better than his remorse and hopelessness. He didn't want to have a heart that could feel. He forfeited his right to life. He hungered for oblivion.

"I hate it all! I hate every damnable form of existence!"

He woke up screaming. Grabbing at the covers, he felt like he was still in the flames. He opened his eyes and saw that he wasn't in hell, but the room was spinning, and his body felt like it was on fire.

"Kill me once and for all!" he shouted. "Kill me!"

A minute later, there was a pounding on his door.

"What the hell is going on in there?" William called out from the other side. "Open up!"

He tried to respond. "No," he shouted back. "Go away!"

"Dammit," William snorted in a muffled tone. "I think I have a spare key in my bedroom."

After a short wait, there was the sound of the lock being turned. The door swung open, and William stood in the doorway. He was in his robe, rubbing the vestiges of sleep from his eyes. "What are you shouting about now?" As he walked over to Arel's bed, his brows narrowed in annoyance. When he got a good look at Arel, they quickly arched with surprise and distress. "Why is your face crimson?" He put his hand on Arel's forehead. "You're hot as Hades."

William's hand on Arel's brow was a cool, comforting balm in the midst of a punishing inferno. He realized he was still only half-awake. A part of him was still caught up in the dream. But his mind wasn't the only component involved. Even if Arel thought he wanted annihilation, his body fought for life. A base survival instinct pulled him back into the real world. His gaze settled on William's face and voice, using them as beacons in a firestorm. "Why do you keep bothering?"

William's alarm was evident, but his voice was even and tempered. "You were yelling so loud, you woke me out of a sound sleep."

"You were in my dream."

William averted his eyes. "I don't remember dreaming," he said as he took his hand away. "The truth is you have a fever. You must have been hallucinating."

"Don't you remember any of it? You told me about—" he paused. "I guess it doesn't matter. It's too late."

"Too late?" William frowned. "Too late for what?"

Arel blinked back, searching for a way to explain a lifetime of pain. The blinding heat wasn't coming from hell. It was coming from his gut. The sickness that killed the trees in the dream state had traveled back with him. It was a consuming disease made up of despair and grief. "I understand why you wanted to kill yourself. Why should a person go on when they've lost everything that has meaning and worthiness in it? My life is nothing but failure and shame."

"I see. You're the ultimate victim, aren't you?" William asked with a scowl.

"No, that's not the point." When he tried to sit up, William helped him. The movement was enough to disorient him. His brain reeled in and out of a deep confusion, but a part of him was fighting to be heard. "It's the opposite. I understand that I'm the one who's been the monster all along. I've been blaming you when I'm the one who's made all the mistakes. Forgive me, William."

William stepped back. "Oh no, not more of that. I refuse to get involved in any more of these discussions. Besides, I've already forgiven you. I'm not going through that foolishness again."

"Listen, Will, if I die—"

"Oh please, you have a fever, but for the most part you're in good shape. So don't talk nonsense."

Arel sighed. William wasn't aware of Arel's gut and how quickly it could burn him out of existence. Maybe that was just as well. William needed to concentrate on the positive side of Michael's blood. Still, there was unfinished business between them. Arel reached out a shaky hand, but his action made William retreat even further. He let his hand fall back to the covers. "I want to give you something, something that might help you in the future."

"What? What could I possibly want from you?"

Arel's glowing eyes flitted over the soft, downy comforter. He felt like what he was about to say could help William in some way that he couldn't fully understand. "You need more of my blood," he said in a firm, steady voice. He thought that his heart was dead or at least numb, but now he truly wanted to help William. That was the one redeeming part of the dream. He saw William in a new light. William had the capacity to exhibit a nobility of spirit. "When I'm gone, you'll find a way to use what you've been given in ways I could never imagine."

"Don't talk gibberish. But I agree that another blood sample might be useful."

"That's not what I mean."

Instead of listening, William's eyes widened. "My god, I've never seen someone look as flushed as you. I swear, your skin has turned purple. I better take a blood sample right away. I want to see what's going on. I also need to get your fever down. I'll get some ice too," he said as he turned and started for the door.

As he waited for William to return, Arel knew he had to think fast. He had to put his need for oblivion on the back burner and figure out what he could do to help William. Hell would have to wait until he got William out of limbo. William was stuck, thinking about curing a disease instead of unleashing his soul from the darkness where it was jailed.

He has a potential for the greatness he once imagined.

"You look a little better," Michael said.

Arel jerked back, grabbing his chest. Michael had appeared with no warning at the foot of his bed. "Dammit, Michael, why do you keep sneaking up on me? Do you want me to keel over on the spot?"

"I thought you wanted to die."

"I do. I can't go on after finding out what I've done."

"You seem very calm about it all."

"Before I go, I have to do something for William, like you suggested. I've decided that my last act on this earth is going to be a grand and generous one. It won't make up for all my failings, but at least William will have something good to remember me by."

Michael ran a quick scan over Arel's body. "You're learning some control. That's very good."

Arel glanced at himself in the mirror on the opposite wall. "I don't look purple anymore. I'm more of a deep pink. What happened?"

"Your focus on William and his happiness helped to tone down the negative feelings in your core."

Arel looked away. Normally he'd be happy to know that his internal furnace was powering down. But what if he wanted to use it to self-destruct? "So if I want to get it going again, I can—"

Michael held up a hand. "I only have a few minutes before William comes back. So perhaps you can tell me what you want to do for him."

"I'm not quite sure, but I feel like some part of me knows." Arel recalled an early portion of his dream when he talked to a wiser, more inspired part of himself. "What I do know is that William would love to bask in the sun again. Deep down, I think he also wants to be a grander version of himself."

"So you're seeing him in a better light?"

"Yes, and I don't want him to have to suffer through this process like I did. I want things to be easier for him."

"That's a wonderful intention, but don't forget about free will. It's the something that you didn't consider when you damned yourself in the dream."

"What do you mean?"

"You didn't force William to go with Rolphe. It was what he decided he wanted."

"He needed a friend, a person who supported him when he was down. I refused to give him that. I was too self-centered and ignorant."

"Still, it was William's choice. That's what you have to remember."

"Thanks, that's somewhat comforting."

"You're both very strong individuals, Arel. And strong people can make some big mistakes when they get passionate about what they believe."

"Maybe that's the real problem about living. I'm always going to make mistakes."

"That's earth, my friend. It's a place where things sometimes turn out tragically, but the opposite is also true. Think about Kevin taking a chance on being a father. Think about his son, Ariel, Jr. and what a wonderful life that child can look forward to with Kevin being there to guide him."

"It's hard to think about my friends. Chicago seems like worlds away right now."

Michael put his hand on Arel's heart. "Or maybe it's in here."

Arel blinked and was instantly transported to Carol and Kevin's suburban house. He sat on their floral sofa. He was chatting with them as he held little Ariel Jr. The baby's large, blue eyes were bright with mischief as he reached out for Arel's finger. It was obvious that it would soon become the baby's teething toy.

The scene disappeared as quickly as it appeared when Michael stepped back. Arel glanced around the guest bedroom and then at Michael. "How did you do that?"

"I simply interfered with the part of your mind that filters out multiple perceptions of space and time."

"Multiple perceptions? Please, I already have a splitting headache. I don't need another mystery thrown my way."

Michael smiled. "It's just that you're only thinking about the down-sides of life. I want you to understand that there's so much more for you to experience."

"Name something easy."

"Your heart is an amazing portal of sorts."

"A portal? You think that's an easy subject?"

Michael's form shimmered as it began to fade, but his voice was still clear and audible. "You can use the vessel creatively. And it's not hard if you'll let go of what you consider your failings. Instead, focus on what you want. Give your desire the same attention you give normal reality. You might be surprised at what happens."

"Interesting," Arel mumbled back. If Michael was right, and his heart was a vehicle for his desires, it might be useful when it came to giving William a gift.

Michael's voice began to fade too, but his last words had a sterner tone. "Just remember that everyone has free will, Arel. When taking any actions, the key is to always honor that freedom in yourself and others."

"Of course," Arel called out, but Michael was gone, or more accurately his physical form disappeared.

Don't go too far, Michael. I may need you!

Alone again, Arel went back to his original intention, the idea of giving William something amazing.

If the guy could have the best Christmas present ever, what would he ask for?

Arel's brain pounded with strain and came up empty. He had to relax and start over, letting that wiser part from his dream take over.

AREL'S BLOOD

Oh my, I know what it is! I just have to get William to agree to accept it.

* * *

William had never been so confused by anything as Arel's condition. One minute his one-time friend looked fine. The next, he was screaming out like a maniac and burning up with fever. William's former conclusion about Arel being healthy was rapidly giving way to a new thought.

If I can't control his fever and whatever else is going on with him, he may not make it.

As he hurried back to Arel's room, he prepared himself for the worst.

We don't need two irrational people in this type of situation.

His short pep talk helped him walk into Arel's room looking confident. But one look at Arel destroyed his resolve not to react to Arel's condition. "What the hell? I was only gone for a few minutes," he gasped. "How did you recover so quickly?"

Arel stood by the bed with his hands behind his back, looking better than ever. With shoulders back, and his head erect, he was the picture of vibrant health. All signs of fever had vanished. As Arel stared at William, his face eased itself into a broad smile. "I have a few tricks you don't know about."

"Tricks?" William didn't know how to respond. He felt his own forehead wondering if he was the one who had the problem. Was he hallucinating?

Arel laughed in a good-humored way, as if he knew exactly what William was thinking. "It's okay. We're both fine."

"Sure we are," William said a little breathlessly. He couldn't get enough air with all that was happening. He went to the dresser and placed his medical supplies down. He needed a moment to clear his mind, to remember not to get caught up in Arel's dramatic mood swings and his ability to go from ailing to vital in the space of five minutes. When he turned back to look at Arel, he was feeling better until he saw what Arel had in his hand. He was holding William's switchblade.

Oh hell, what now? Is he going to kill himself? Is he going to kill me?

He advanced a few steps. "Where did you get that?"

Arel's gaze remained steady. "I found it after you talked about doing yourself in. I thought it was safer if I held on to it."

"Is that right?" William almost let out a nervous laugh, but he stopped himself. Arel was clearly unstable. Better not to agitate him. "Give me the knife, Arel. Hand it over immediately." He tried to keep his voice steady, but it had a slight tremor that couldn't be helped.

Instead of doing what was asked, Arel grinned back. His golden eyes took on an unnatural brightness, filled with passion. Facing William, he extended his open palm while his other hand gripped the knife blade tightly. "We can be brothers, Will. It's something we've both wanted. Now it's time to make it so."

"Brothers? After all the hell—"

"That's behind us," Arel said as he raised the knife. In a swift, fluid sweep, he sliced it across his palm.

For a moment, William could only stare at the blood dripping from Arel's hand. "You're insane."

Arel didn't seem to hear William's conclusion. He held out the knife to William. "Now it's your turn."

William's mouth was hanging open. How could he stay composed when everything about Arel was freaking him out? "Do you realize how irrational you sound?"

"What do you mean? I'm being your friend, Will. For the first time, I'm thinking about your welfare and nothing else."

"Just stay where you are," William said as he stepped forward. He reached out and slowly removed the weapon from Arel's hand.

Arel's eyes were getting even brighter as he leaned in. "I've worked it all out. We can finally have a new start. If we're joined in blood, we'll be real family."

"We're already joined in blood! And the damn stuff is killing me!"

Arel laughed off William's anger. "So if you're already infected, what would it hurt to be real brothers? Think about it, you and me, working side by side, just like you wanted all those years ago."

William retreated a few feet. If his body had its way, he'd have fled the room. But he wasn't a coward. He never backed down before, and he didn't plan on it now. Still, he would remain prudent. "If you think I'm going to engage in some primitive bonding ritual, you're more deranged than I imagined."

"Would it be so horrible to seal our ties with the gesture?"

"There are no ties, no bonds, nothing between us. Get over it."

"Do this one thing for me, and I promise to leave immediately."

"I said no. I'm not into self-mutilation."

"You told me to trust you, remember? Now I'm asking the same of you. Trust me this one last time."

William tried to back away, but there was something about Arel's eyes that had hold of him. They'd gone from overly-bright to hypnotic orbs. Their golden color radiated an intensity unlike anything William had ever seen. He tried to blink, to break the connection, but he couldn't move. Arel had turned into some kind of Svengali. There was one major difference. Arel's eyes were compellingly benevolent and caring, not treacherous. They were the eyes one saw in a painting of saints and men who embodied godliness. Just the thought made William stiffen. Men like that wanted followers, and those followers often ended up martyrs. But he couldn't make himself look away.

Arel closed the gap between them. "Please Will, listen to me. In the dream we shared, you bared your soul. Your vision of what could have been was so amazing. Tell me that you remember it too."

William nodded automatically, like a marionette that had to do what the puppeteer wanted. Still, as he gazed into Arel's eyes, a part of him never felt so free, so unencumbered by rules of conduct or rational thinking or any of his usual ways of handling life. For a brief moment, his mind took flight and the vision he had as a young man felt real again. "We could have discovered so many ways to work together, ways that could have been a model for others."

"Maybe there's still a chance," Arel whispered in William's ear.

William nodded again, hating that he couldn't stop himself from being pulled into Arel's mesmerizing world.

"But it's up to you, Will," Arel said as he looked away.

As soon as Arel broke the connection, William came back to himself. All of his normal thoughts returned. "No, I don't think so."

Arel remained very close. "Maybe not, but we can have this last and final exchange, one last time when we join together and make peace with all that's come before. Please, don't be afraid," Arel urged, still keeping his eyes to himself.

William knew what was going on. Arel wanted him to freely choose what was offered. He stepped back, wondering if he was afraid. The next moment, he knew he wasn't. Why would he fear a ritual that little boys acted out? "Fine! If it will get you out of my life forever, what the hell."

Following Arel's example, he made a quick slicing motion across his hand and let out a cry. "Dammit, that really hurts!"

"We'll always be brothers now, Will, just like you wanted, bonded by blood," Arel announced as he grabbed William's hand.

As soon as Arel brought their bleeding palms together, as soon as their blood was joined, William felt his world fly apart.

* * *

Arel was about to reach out for William's hand when he felt a sudden rush of excitement. William didn't know it, but Arel was going to help his old friend in a way that would change his life. He'd snatch William from his dark existence and bring him into the light, just as Michael had reclaimed him. And it would be so easy. He knew who William was now. He had glimpsed William's soul just minutes before William came back to the room.

In a flash of understanding, as he brought his attention to that part of himself that Michael called a portal, everything began to make sense. The heart had stellar connections to a place where light resides. It was Michael's domain and the domain of the soul. At first Arel almost turned away from the portal. The limited, unworthy role he played for most of his life didn't have a place in the vessel. But a vision of William's once bright and caring face wouldn't let him give up. If he had to forfeit his failings to enter the heart, then so be it. After that, he saw the truth of who he was. He wasn't Arel, the irresponsible victim. He was a timeless being standing next to another like him. He instantly recognized William's soul. In that wondrous place of brilliant light, they were more than brothers, more than family, more than definitions and names. They were pure light, pulsing and alive, existing in a place that was beyond anything that was bound to the earth. Yet they both had a powerful connection to the planet and to their lives as humans. In their earthly bodies, their challenge was to remember their greater soul-selves and bring their light into physical form.

The vision faded once Arel's normal thinking returned. Though he quickly forgot most of what he'd understood, one important facet remained. The feeling of brotherhood was the earthly representation of how a soul functioned, how it related to another soul. That's when he decided on a plan of action. When William came back into the room, Arel had a singular intention. He would convince William to join him, to connect in a way that reminded each of them of their greater selves. William's reluctance was ignored as Arel's heart continued to pulse out the feeling of unity and acceptance. The more Arel stayed out of judgment, the more he connected to his heart. It began to fill with joy, the same joy that baby Ariel evoked. The difference was that Arel allowed his past to slip away. He was anchored in a present moment. When he looked at William, there was no need for revenge. There was no mistrust or desire to resurrect old hatreds. Arel's heart was pulsing out love and a desire for expansion. If he embraced William with true acceptance, both would benefit.

As he realized their potential to leave their limited lives behind, Arel's joy was so great that he felt a small explosion in his chest. There was no pain, just the strange sensation that he now had two fires burning within. The flame he usually felt in his solar plexus wasn't the raging inferno he'd known before. With the negativity banished, it was pure and steady and safe. The second one in his heart was more ethereal. Together, working in tandem, they sent a tremendous energy surging through him. It was similar to the energy he felt when he assumed a healing role with Carey. When William finally agreed to join their blood, it was the go-ahead that Arel needed to let all limitation fall away. He gave himself up completely to the energy that waited for him to connect fully. A last thought went through his mind just before he touched William.

I want to give him back the sun!

"Arel, stop!" Michael's voice came out of the ethers as Arel grasped William's hand, but it was too late. An incredible flash of light, a great discharge issued from his body. Like a bolt of lightning, it hit William with a violent force that lifted him from his moorings. William flew across the room, crashed into a heavy side table, and came to rest in a heap on the floor.

* * *

Just a fleeting moment before Arel grabbed William's hand, Michael materialized in physical form. He immediately grabbed Arel's shoulder and acted as a grounding rod for Arel's energy. He was able to draw off the worst of the powerful discharge, but the blast was too extreme. He couldn't totally save William from its effects. The uncontrolled surge that came from Arel was enough to send William sailing across the room.

Afterwards, Michael wasn't in the best shape himself. He hadn't had time to prepare his physical vessel for such an explosive event. Arel had gone beyond simply tapping into his power. He had amplified it exponentially. Now William lay still and motionless.

Michael stumbled over to the stricken man as he tried to clear his own fuzzy faculties. After he checked William's pulse, he breathed a sigh of relief. It was weak, but at least William had a pulse.

"Where am I?" Arel moaned as he began to regain consciousness. "Where's William?"

"Over here," Michael called out.

As soon as Arel was able to focus properly, his eyes widened in panic. "Oh no, are William's clothes *smoking?*"

Michael nodded, but he was giving his full attention to William's condition. He had to act quickly to reduce any possible internal injuries.

Arel struggled to get to all fours. As he slowly crawled over to where William lay, his breath was fast and shallow. His eyes weren't glowing anymore. They were dull and leaden until he let out a shriek. "Michael, what have I done now? I asked William to trust me!"

Sixty-Five

With the curtains shut tight against the light of day, Arel maintained a vigil close to William's bedside. Michael was there too, just in case he was needed again. "So you think there's a good chance that William escaped permanent harm?" Arel asked as he dusted a piece of lint off the bed cover. William always said that it was prudent to remain impersonal. Now Arel was sure it was true. After the initial shock of knowing he almost killed the person he was supposed to be helping, he needed distance. He would have loved to transport himself to another planet, but shutting down his emotions would have to do. Even his old habit of groveling in failure was off limits. William hadn't opened his eyes yet, but Michael explained that even in an unconscious state, the ailing man was still open to the energy around him.

Michael's message had been clear. "That word, 'trust', is key for both of you. It's important that you demonstrate that William can depend on you while he's recovering."

Arel glanced at William and winced. Detachment might be a nice concept to bandy about in conversation, but to actually embody it was hell. For a moment, it slipped through his grasp completely. "I hate this, Michael! How can I look at William and stay hopeful. His face is so flushed, his breathing is heavy and every time he moves in the slightest, he groans."

"He's been through a lot. Give him some time."

Arel gritted his teeth, trying to reel in his fears, trying not to pollute William's air with his own misgivings. "I don't understand how this happened. My intention was good. I wanted to do something special for William. What went wrong?"

383

Michael hesitated. "You might have gone overboard when you wanted to give William the sun."

"That was just something extra I threw in. I didn't mean it literally."

"Yes, I understand, but when you're working with the powerful energies that you're accessing, you have to be very careful about those extras."

"But I don't even know what I did, except I let go. I got really happy. Is that my crime?"

Michael smiled. "When great desire is coupled with unbridled joy, one must be prudent in how to direct that power."

"Great, so now I have to be careful about getting *too* happy?"

"No, of course not. But in this case, your focus was on righting a lifetime of misguided acts. In releasing all your negativity, you became a conduit of pure, unrestrained creative energy. The problem was that you directed it all at William. His body couldn't handle it."

Arel went back to the moment when his blood joined with William's. He ran a shaky hand over his brow. "I did experience this extraordinary flash before I passed out."

"Give yourself time to learn more about your power. In the meantime, try not to take what happened too personally."

"Tell that to William. I know I'm being overdramatic, but I have this reoccurring vision that his body could have become a pile of ash, and that his spirit was screaming at me from some heavenly cloud, calling me an idiot."

Michael sucked in a breath as he walked over to a chair and sat down. "I suppose that was a possibility given the circumstances," he said in a barely audible voice.

"What?"

"Nothing, I was just talking to myself."

"Well stop it and get back over here. My hand is bleeding again. The bandage is soaked and the blood is wrecking William's Persian rug. He'll go nuts when he sees the mess I'm making."

Michael rushed over, grabbed a towel from the side table and wrapped it around Arel's hand. "You need to take a break. You're worn out and—"

"I almost killed William! Who cares?"

Sixty-Six

Propped up in his bed, William didn't remember much, but when he tried to use his hand, it became a painful reminder of the folly he'd been privy to. He had taken part in another of Arel's crazy stunts. But how did he end up in bed? "What's going on?" he asked, noticing that Arel was close by, trying to tuck a blanket around him. "Why are you fussing over me like this?"

"I'm just trying to make sure that you're comfortable."

"Comfortable? With this hand?" William held up the wounded body part and winced. "Why in the hell would you want to do something so foolish?"

Arel clutched his own injured limb. "I'm sorry about all this. I didn't know—"

"That's the problem. You're rash. You don't think ahead."

Arel offered a weak smile. "I thought it would help us to stay connected. I wanted to cement our friendship."

"Friendship? We'll probably both get some god-awful infection next." He fought his way out of the covers and started to get up. He swayed unsteadily, trying to adjust to the room going in and out of focus.

"William, don't exert yourself. You need to rest." Arel's voice had a pleading, panicked edge to it.

"If there's something wrong with me, I have to investigate what it is. Lying around isn't going to help." William held on to a chair with his good hand until he could get his balance. "What I don't

385

understand is how I ended up here. Our hands touched and then poof, I don't remember anything."

"Maybe you're more squeamish than you think. Maybe when you saw your hand and your own blood—"

"I'm not squeamish." He paused and glared at Arel. "Why are you avoiding eye contact? What aren't you telling me?"

"Please, William, just leave me alone."

William glanced at himself in the mirror. He looked pinker than normal. "Did I have a fever too?"

Arel remained close-mouthed, busying himself with making up the bed.

"So you're not even going to try to explain what happened?"

Arel returned a furtive frown. "There's nothing to say."

"Easy for you. I feel like somebody's been beating me with phone books."

"Then come back to bed," Arel pleaded again. "I know a little about the lab. Let me check things out."

"You? In the lab? My god, what chance would either of us have?" As he moved to the door, William used his functional hand to protect his sore ribs. "But you can give me a blood sample. Let's see if anything's changed."

Arel rushed to get in front of him. "Please Will, be careful on the stairs."

* * *

Arel paced the length of the lower level as William manned the microscope. After a few minutes his curiosity couldn't be contained any longer. "You're pretty quiet over there. Has anything changed?"

William looked up, but he didn't reply.

"It can't be that bad, can it?" Arel asked as he walked back to the lab area. "Come on, let me see too."

William gave him a kindly look, the kind you offered an orphaned stray being hauled off to the pound. "No, it's better that you don't. Believe me, it's . . . not good and you're emotional enough already."

"I'm sure I'll be fine," Arel insisted. "Just let me see what's going on. It is my blood after all."

386

William finally gave in when Arel pushed him aside. Staggering over to his recliner, he sat down heavily. "Fine, I tried to warn you."

Arel adjusted the lens to a higher magnification. "What could possibly be so bad?"

William didn't answer. His gaze was directed upwards as if he needed to study the ceiling.

"Ohhhh!" Arel held on to the word as he stared at the sample. "My blood's changed a bit. Those strange little flakes have multiplied a lot."

William closed his eyes. "Changed? Your blood is totally screwed. You should be dead." He paused, letting out a heavy sigh. "Now look at mine."

Arel stared over with concern. "Will, are you sick?"

"Just look at my blood."

Arel switched out the slides and studied the new one. "Oh no, you have them too, don't you, but not that many."

William returned a scathing glance. "I can hear you so clearly. What were your exact words? Oh, yes, you said, 'Trust me like I trusted you. Be my blood brother.'" He glared at Arel. "I gave in to you, and now I have no chance at all. You might as well shoot me now."

"Will, don't go there, you have to admit that we didn't look like we were dying when we were fighting."

William remained mute. When he finally spoke, his words came out through chattering teeth. "Have you seen my cashmere throw?"

Arel quickly walked over to the sitting area, grabbed a blanket from the sofa, and handed it to William. "How are you doing?"

William clutched at the warm cover. "The chills are back, my head is pounding, and my body feels like I've been on the rack. Other than that, I'm fine."

Sixty-Seven

A rel walked around the lab in a t-shirt. He had the heat turned up to ninety degrees and was sweating profusely as he paced. His nerves were in shreds. No matter how many blankets he piled on, William continued to shake violently. His teeth were chattering so hard, he'd given up trying to talk except to manage a swear word occasionally.

As Arel made his rounds, his thoughts were repetitive. How long could William go on like this? What if he did have a massive stroke? He stopped at the stairs, paused and glanced over at William. "Excuse me for a few minutes. I need to get a breath of air."

As soon as he got upstairs, he went to his room and shut the door. After the suffocating heat in the lower level, he needed several deep breaths before he began to cool down. When he turned around, Michael was sitting in the leather chair. "Thank goodness, you're back."

"William seems quite despondent. That's unusual for him," Michael said.

"I know. But it's worse than that. At one point just an hour ago, he shuddered. He went from shaking to stillness. For a few moments, he stopped breathing. I thought that was it." Arel stumbled over to his bed and sat down. "It's such a shame. William's soul is so bright. As a person, he's just lost and searching like I was when you found me."

"But William paid a price for that glimpse into the truth. I'm afraid that your exchange has accelerated the process."

"But why? He's already tasted my blood. The deed was done in New York."

"I'm not talking about the blood. I'm talking about your energy. You tapped into and unleashed a tremendous charge. William wasn't prepared for anything like that. He had problems before, but now—"

"How will he survive?" Arel's breath caught as he imagined all of William's pent-up feelings, all his deep and dark history of pain and torment erupting from the bowels of his subconscious and crashing against him like a tsunami. "Did you come here to tell me that it's hopeless?"

"I would never tell you that."

"But what can I do? What if I try doing more healing work on his body, maybe—"

Michael quickly held up a hand. "I don't think so. Besides, William is very wary now. His shields are in place."

"Then what?"

"You can be understanding. Remember when your emotions came to the surface?"

Arel did remember. He'd been hit with a tsunami of his own. "I was a maniac. I hated you. I hated everything."

"Yes, you might try to avoid anything that causes William to direct his anger your way."

A loud, halting voice yelled up from the lab below. It was William's voice. "Arel! I'm freezing!"

William's plaintive cry affected Arel so profoundly that he felt his temperature drop instantly. He wasn't hot anymore. As he started to briskly rub his arms, his injured hand sent out a painful signal to be careful with it. Again, he ignored the pain. He had to put his bodily concerns aside. He had bigger problems. Still, the frigid state that invaded his body wouldn't be denied. He went to the closet and retrieved a sweater. "I don't think I've ever been this cold."

Michael watched Arel button up the wool garment. "The exchange works both ways. You've opened a door, so to speak, between the two of you."

"Wonderful. First it was a portal. Now you're talking about a door. I can't keep up with all of these concepts that you're throwing at me."

"You're very sensitive to each other's energy. You'll find it easy to take on whatever William is experiencing and vice versa."

"I see. You're saying that we'll be in the deep freeze together."

Michael came over and smiled. "There is an upside. If you can truly believe in yourself, if you maintain an open heart and no judgments, nothing and no one can affect you."

"Are you kidding? With my track record?"

"Believe me, even with your track record, you can do this."

The conviction in Michael's voice made Arel stare back with a glimmer of renewed hope. He remembered the first part of his lucid dream. Standing in the flowering meadow, he'd felt so capable of creating something beautiful. What if he could be that kind of positive force in real life? "Michael, if you're right, maybe I can do more than free myself. Maybe I can convince William to hang in there and find that person inside who's in touch with his heart." He walked over to the door. "I'll go talk to him."

"I don't think William is ready to talk."

Arel paused and looked back. "I'm beginning to understand what you meant when you said I opened a door. It's strange, but I suddenly have more clarity. I feel more than William's chills. I feel like I know why he's stuck and can't move forward."

"It takes time for people to move forward."

"William doesn't have time. He could check out physically or simply give up. I have to do what I can while I have the chance."

* * *

William glanced up as Arel came down the stairs. "You can turn the thermostat down. The chills suddenly stopped. I'm better," he announced with relief. He actually felt warm enough to throw off some of the blankets. "But what's going on with you? Why are you wearing a sweater? I thought you were hot."

Arel walked over to the computer desk and took hold of a chair. He slowly dragged it over to William's recliner and sat down.

William felt a sharp chill again. "What now? Why are you sitting so close?"

Arel reached out and took William's uninjured hand and squeezed it firmly. "I'll stay here and continue to help if you want. I don't have to go home."

390

William recoiled from the touch. His senses were keen, and Arel's icy hand relayed information he didn't need. Arel wasn't just frozen to the bone, he was frightened, even horrified about something. "You look like you're staring at a corpse! Which would be fine if I were dead, but in case you haven't noticed, I'm still breathing."

"Yes, I know, but—"

"But what?"

"I'm worried about you, the way you reacted when you saw our blood samples. You can't give up."

"I'm fine."

"How can you say that when it's not true?" Arel asked.

"Why should you care?"

"Because we're connected now." Arel began to mindlessly flex his injured hand. Soon the bandage turned red with fresh blood. "We're brothers, Will, don't you feel that?"

"If you cared for me, tell me, why am I sitting here like this, feeling like somebody dropped me from two stories up? Is that what brotherhood is about? I always had the crazy concept that it strengthened both parties."

"I agree. I want that too."

William let out a laugh. "You are so full of it."

"What are you talking about?"

"I know exactly what's going through your mind." William sat back heavily. "Maybe you're right. Maybe we are connected or maybe you're just easy to read."

"What are you getting at?"

"Are you sure you want to know?"

"Yes."

William shut his eyes, letting something surface that he'd tried to ignore for a long time. "When you asked me to do the blood-brother thing, I think you believed what you said to me. You were sincere about wanting a brother. That lasted for about five minutes. Now, things are back to the way they've always been. Your heart is off-limits again. When you look at me, you're scared, but there's no genuine feeling for me behind it."

Arel's eyes flared as he continued to flex his hand. "I don't understand why you're saying that."

William reached over and grabbed a box of gauze. He thrust it at Arel. "Let me make it clear. When your brother died, something inside of you died too. Now, you believe you can resurrect that dead part, but every time you try, you fail. Your heart opens and almost lets in a breath of fresh air. Then you find some excuse to close it, to shut out life again. You think you're afraid for me, but you're afraid for yourself. You're afraid that you'll always be that little boy who couldn't bear the idea of being left alone, who couldn't change what happened."

"You're wrong," Arel insisted. "My heart's fine. I have people I love—"

William smiled. "Yes, you've told me that before, but your friends in Chicago aren't enough, are they? You're always wanting more than they can give you, admit it."

Arel's eyes became desolate and remote. "If I'm stuck like you're saying, help me to find some way to change."

"Deep down I don't think you want to change. Your anger is all-consuming when it comes to what you lost. It destroys everything in its path. It's nearly destroyed me."

"I'm sorry."

William let out a sigh. "Go home. You promised that you'd leave if I did the blood brother nonsense, now keep your word."

Arel pulled back, letting his eyes glaze over with the forlorn look of someone in a churchyard, grieving. "Even if you're right, I've tried, I've really tried to do the right thing."

After his recital on Arel's inability to truly care, William heard the pain in Arel's voice. Why was it there? Normally, Arel would be shouting back, distancing himself from the truth. Instead, it was one of those rare times when Arel's golden eyes were those of the boy who desperately wanted someone to believe in him. When they first met, William tried to be that person, but Arel was already too bitter. He'd been beaten down too many times. He was too broken, too damaged.

"I tried too, Arel. I hope you believe that." William reached out and ran a trembling hand over Arel's cheek. "My god, if only your brother had lived, if only that bastard who called himself your father hadn't beat your heart to a pulp, I think you could have been such a magnificent example of what a man could be."

"It's not too late for either of us—"

"Yes, it is. Look at who we've become. Believe me, it's too late."

"Maybe that was true a couple of days ago, but things have changed." Arel's shoulders straightened a bit. He smiled. "I've changed. I have your blood now, Will."

"You had my blood a hundred years ago."

"No, that's not true. What you gave me wasn't your blood, it was some contaminated crap."

"What you're calling contaminated crap enabled you to stay young. It kept you going all this time. It set you above the rest of humanity."

"That's only your perception. What that vampire gave you looked great because you had already given up on yourself, Will."

"What are you talking about?"

"I always saw you as the strong one, but I missed the point."

"Oh, here it comes, your newest discourse on my failings."

"No, give me a chance, please. You just told me about the child I was. Now let me tell you about the boy that you were, that free-spirited, gentle boy who loved his creatures, who loved every tree and flower in the field."

William steeled himself at the thought, but Arel had a point about both of them expressing their views. "What about him?"

Arel looked away wistfully. His focus seemed to move to distant places and times that only he could access. "The boy that you were was fair and handsome like my brother, but he was more than that. He was brave and courageous. He had so much love to give to every stray and injured animal that came his way. Yet everything he loved was desecrated. Everything he tried to save was destroyed."

"How do you know any of that?" William growled out.

Arel looked at his bloodied, bandaged hand. "I don't know. I just do. Sometimes I see things. I see events in people's lives whether I want to or not."

"Well, forget all that nonsense. We live in a world of men. Children have no place in that world. So let it go." William made the announcement in a firm, forceful voice, but his injured hand was throbbing. He was remembering too, whether he liked it or not, memories from when he was a young boy, too young to change what was happening to him. As he saw flashes of his life unfolding, his ears pounded with his quickened heartbeat and the sound of a child screaming. It was everything he could do to push back the cries, to keep them behind locked doors that could never be opened.

Arel didn't seem to notice the change that was coming over William. His eyes were still searching and withdrawn. "My father wasn't the only bastard, Will. Your father was dark, steeped in some unfeeling attitude about life. You tried to escape, to seek solace in the woods, but you couldn't get away from his monstrous ways. He did things, unspeakable horrors that broke your heart."

"Shut up! Don't say another word!" William's shout filled the room with a deafening cry. Arel was relentless. His words were feeding the fires of an inner hell that William thought he'd left behind. That part of him had been closed off for a reason.

And it has to stay that way.

He paused, refusing to contemplate what would happen if too many memories resurrected themselves. Instead, his hand went to his forehead. He realized he was hot and feverish. He wasn't himself. It was the disease talking, the disease that Arel passed on.

Arel blinked back, looking confused and unsteady too. His mouth started to move, but then he fell silent.

William sat back, reaching for solace in the familiar setting. His notebook, carefully kept and updated, lay on the side table. His lab was a few feet away. It was a place where he could find answers. It was a place where he could make order out of seeming chaos. There was only one element that didn't belong in his world. He stared at Arel. "Why do you always torment me? You can never leave well enough alone. You're always wanting to pull off the scab and rub salt in the wound, aren't you?"

"Is that what you think?" Arel let out a little laugh. "The truth is that I care about who you really are, and you're rejecting me because of that fact. Still, it's not only me that you want to purge, is it, Will? You rejected the boy that you were, that part that still lives inside of you. You keep him hidden and out of view."

"That child doesn't exist anymore!" William yelled out, but in the next moment, he made himself calm down. Giving in to his emotions wasn't helping anything. "There are no children here, just two adults sitting across from each other."

Arel's face flushed with fresh emotion. "You'd like to think that, wouldn't you? But neither of us can be happy until we make peace with ourselves."

"I made peace with myself a long time ago."

"Maybe you think you did, or maybe you joined the rest of the defeated men who grew up to become cold and calculating."

William waved him off. "Whatever. Think what you want."

Arel held his bandaged hand close. "I'm grateful to you, Will. When I came here, I thought I could help you. Instead, you've helped me."

"Obviously you're not talking about the condition of your blood."

"I'm not. I'm talking about something much more important. I'm also connected to that boy that you were, that you still are. He's the one who cared about me, who made me his friend when I had no one. And I swear, I'll find a way to resurrect him. Someday, he'll be free and brave again, not hidden under that tough shell you keep around you."

"You won't let it go, will you?" William's eyes froze, hardened by a need to set things straight. "I don't want to be that child. I may be cold in your estimation, but I'm happy to be a man who can decide his fate. You cling to the idea that we can be these idealistic kids again because you can't move on. You can't grow up. You don't have it in you. You're too weak, and I'm tired of it. Now go upstairs and pack your bags. Leave this house and never come back. Is that clear?"

"It's clear." Arel stood up and began to walk away. He stopped at the base of the stairs. "I have just one thing to add. Maybe I have been weak until now, but I'm not the same person I was when I arrived. I can feel your strength coursing through my veins. You might reject your true self, but I won't. I'll use what you gave me. And someday, you'll understand how powerful our blood can be when it's joined."

"No, I won't. We are done." William didn't move this time. Nothing Arel said was bothering him anymore. Maybe Arel couldn't comprehend the idea of growing up, but it made perfect sense to him. Once he stepped back into the role of the confident, capable man he knew himself to be, his jaw relaxed into a sneering smile. "If I ever see you again, you'll understand how easy it is for me to finish you off once and for all."

"Do you even hear yourself, William? There's no feeling in your voice. You talk about killing me as if I'm a pest running along your baseboard."

"Yes, Arel, I can assure you that I hear myself, and I mean every word." William shut his eyes and sighed. It felt good to finally know he was on his own again. "So don't plan on any more visits. If you come back, you're a dead man."

* * *

As Arel walked to his room, he wouldn't let William's threat bother him. William had always seemed like a self-centered type before, but not anymore. The truth was running through Arel's veins. When they joined blood, it wasn't in the ordinary way that little boys became blood brothers. Their connection was an explosive, life-changing event. Arel caught glimpses of who William really was deep down. As time passed, more and more of William's memories were becoming accessible. Arel could understand how William came to be the man he was. There was an added bonus. Aspects of each of them were exchanged. William's courageous approach to life was added to Arel's own less-confident attitude.

But what did I give him?

In their final conversation, William was able to maintain his usual, logical manner. He almost cracked for a few brief moments. He seemed affected when Arel mentioned his childhood, but he quickly recovered his usual impersonal mode. He didn't exhibit any behavior to indicate that he had changed, too.

I hope my gift was something that will help him in the days ahead. Or have I given him something negative? Oh hell, what if I got one of his virtues, and he got one of my faults?

It was a disturbing thought that haunted him all the way back to Chicago.

Sixty-Eight

When Arel's plane touched down, Chicago was rainy with blustery winds. Once he collected his luggage and got through airport customs, he clutched at his overcoat as he hailed a cab. He shielded his book from the gusts and the weather. It was his solace during his travels, a ticket to mindless study, a distraction that shut out London. William looked so fragile and worn when they parted. It was too painful to think about his condition. Arel read from his book instead. It was a large, boring volume on hematology that William had given him. It contained a recital of facts, everything the scientific mind wanted to know about blood. Weighty and cumbersome, its contents were less exciting to Arel than a pamphlet on toasters. It was the perfect tome to keep his mind occupied. When the cab pulled up in his driveway, he was still attached to the book. It would remain his mainstay until he had the energy to think about what to do next. His life had become something suitable for a daytime television series, a continuing saga of people battling for life.

I have the lead role in my own afternoon soap opera.

As he climbed out of the cab, the thought of a long hot shower was somewhat reviving. After the shower, he'd climb into his bed and sleep. His plan might have worked if somebody had informed Peggy about it.

"Arel!" Her voice rang out as he stood at his front door. He tried desperately to let himself in before she managed to cross their adjoining lawns and catch up with him.

397

"I saw the cab pull into the driveway," she said as she hurried her pace. The weather was between storms, but she was careful about the wet grass, making quick little leaps as she darted forward.

Arel's fingers were fumbling with the house key. He couldn't manage the lock before Peggy joined him, throwing her arms around him and squeezing him tight.

"I knew you were coming home. I could feel it," she said enthusiastically.

He squared his jaw. With Peggy's sixth sense, she could track down a lost polar bear cub in an Alaskan whiteout. When she looked at him, that's what she saw, someone lost and helpless. How could he make her understand that he was the opposite? He was someone with too much power, a person who nearly hurled William out of existence. He didn't need Peggy worrying about him. He turned to face her, ready to rebuff her efforts, when a strange feeling came over him. It was so calming that he said the first thing that came to mind. "Peggy, how wonderful to see you."

She released him and gave him a scowl. "I was really annoyed when you ran off, not saying a word. You know that I get these horrible feelings about your safety. Remember New York?"

Of course he remembered New York. It was the pilot for a series called "Days of Doom and Other Misadventures." But when he went to respond, he surprised himself again. Instead of thinking about how to defend himself, he looked at the facts. Peggy was right. He ran off without considering her sensitive feelings. "I'm very sorry about what I did. I had to take off in a hurry. It was completely irresponsible of me not to let you know what I was doing." He leaned over and kissed her cheek. "Can you forgive me?"

She backed up, letting her brown eyes soften. "Of course I can, sweetie. I'm just happy that you're okay."

He gave her a broad smile, one that showed his dimples, the kind that Peggy liked most. It seemed out of character. He usually saved such smiles for very special times, like the birth of a baby. But he felt generous and open for a change. "Would you like to come in for tea? I'd be happy to—"

"No, you just got home. I'll let you get settled. I just wanted to make sure that you were safe and sound."

"I know. You're always thinking of others." Unexpected statements were pouring out of him, but he meant what he was saying. Still, he wasn't used to such conversations when he was exhausted. Maybe he was dreaming or maybe he really was starring in his own soap opera. Whatever the truth, he realized he was enjoying himself. "You're very thoughtful and a dear friend."

Peggy's shoulders sagged a little as she latched on to her shirt and twisted a button. "I hope I'm not too forward with my concerns."

He tipped up Peggy's chin. "Stop that right now. You're perfect."

"Sometimes I'm afraid that my worries might be misinterpreted. Do I come on too strong?"

"If people don't always appreciate you, it's their problem, remember that."

"Are you sure?"

"Absolutely."

For a moment, Peggy hesitated. A slight frown crossed her brow, but then she rallied and smiled again. "Your trip must have agreed with you. You sound more relaxed than usual."

"I'm glad to hear that."

"Anyway, I better get back to Tim and the baby."

As Peggy turned to leave and started down the stairs, he called after her. "Give Tim my best and hug little Sara for me!"

Arel was still smiling as he let himself into the house. He didn't feel as tired as he thought. A crack of distant thunder rumbled outside, but it barely registered. For a moment, he felt so at ease that his mind blanked. He stood in the foyer, staring at the walls, but there were no thoughts about what he needed to do next. It was such a foreign feeling that he panicked. His anxiety grabbed hold so quickly that he began to frantically search the house, calling out as he went. "Michael, help! There's something wrong with me!"

When he got to the kitchen, he grabbed the doorjamb with relief. Michael was standing at the back window, gazing out. "Michael, thank goodness you're here. I need to talk to you."

When Michael turned around, his blue eyes were filled with a reassuring warmth. "Welcome home."

Arel's shoulders settled a little. "Home . . . I almost forgot I had a place of my own. Being in London with William is like being in a different world."

"You look relieved to be back."

"I am. I just spoke with Peggy. She was happy to see me."

"And were you happy to see her?"

"I didn't think I wanted to talk to anyone yet, but we had a very pleasant conversation."

Michael smiled. "Are you surprised?"

Arel pulled out a chair and sat down. "You know me, Michael, when I've been through upsetting events, I'm usually on the defensive or else I hide myself away. Yet, in this case, when Peggy told me I'd been negligent about keeping her informed, I smiled." He glanced up, narrowing his eyes. "Nothing bothered me, and that's weird." He squeezed his bandaged hand into a fist. "I thought William's blood gave me more confidence, but now I'm afraid that it's gone beyond that."

"What do you mean?"

"This blood business is out of control. First I get your blood and go completely crazy. Then I give my blood to William and just about destroy him. Now I've forced William to do this blood brother ceremony and the two of us are all mixed up. Some of his childhood memories are almost as clear as my own. I can feel the way he handled life. He never let himself back down. It's such a foreign response compared to my take on it all, and yet—"

"Go on, what are you getting at?" Michael angled a chair from the table and sat down too. His face was open and serene, looking like he was ready for a good story.

"William wasn't afraid all the time like I was. When I imagine myself being that way, it's very liberating." Arel let his fist open a little and fingered the gauze. "Is it wrong to simply enjoy feeling confident and at ease with life?"

Michael's eyes sparkled even brighter. "Life is supposed to be that way."

"What about responsibility? William is in London barely hanging on, and I'm to blame. How can I smile at people when I should feel just the opposite?"

"When you talked to Peggy, you were in the moment. You were able to react appropriately. I think you knew she needed that smile."

"Maybe, but what about William?"

"Perhaps you can use the strength you feel, that part of him that you carry inside, to help you relate to him in the days to come."

"Really? I never thought of it that way." Arel raised his eyes to meet Michael's piercing gaze. "So I can use what he gave me to help in some way?"

"Yes, exactly."

Arel opened his injured hand and stared at the blotches of dried blood on the bandage. The wound was still bleeding off and on. "I have another question. William's strength is adding to my own, and that's great, but what did William get out of the deal?"

Michael pulled back and sat up straight. "That's a good question, and I don't know quite how to answer it."

Arel stiffened and made a fist again. Michael's tone and the confused look on the angel's face made his panic come back. "Don't tell me he got one of my flaws. It'll finish him off for sure."

"No, of course not."

"Then what? Have I contributed anything good or helpful?"

"It all depends on how William looks at your gift. It could be very helpful if he allows it to be so."

"So what are we talking about?"

Michael smiled. "The only clue I can give you is that your contribution can expand his view of reality. However, William might reject that view completely given the circumstances."

Sixty-Nine

Peggy closed the refrigerator door and went back to her guest. Carol was sitting quietly at the table. She was picking at her chocolate chip cookie, wistfully sampling a stray chip. Peggy put the pitcher on the table and sat down too. "Would you like some cream for your coffee?"

Carol glanced up, retrieved the pitcher, and poured a generous amount in her mug. "Thanks."

"You're welcome. And thank you for bringing over the cookies. Tim will be thrilled when he sees them this evening."

"Kevin will be happy too. He loves it when I bake."

Peggy took a sip of coffee. Should she ask the big question or not? After a moment, she decided to be brave. "How are you guys doing lately?"

Carol returned a frown at first, but then she smiled and shrugged her shoulders. "We're okay."

"So things are better?"

"I think they are, but sometimes I wonder if we're right for each other."

"I thought you two were in love."

"We are," Carol said as she played with a crumb on her plate. "But is that enough? Do you know what I mean?"

Peggy hesitated as she observed Carol's somber face. She wanted to make sure that her brother and her best friend were happy, but now she understood the old adage that ignorance was bliss.

Carol reached out and squeezed Peggy's hand. "I'm sorry. I'm upsetting you."

Peggy swiped at her nose, trying not to give in to the hopeless feeling that usually came up when she wanted life to be perfect and it wasn't. "I guess I was wrong when I thought love was enough."

Carol sat back and crossed her arms. "Maybe not. I'm just not sure anymore, that's all."

"Are you saying that you're not happy?"

"It's not that exactly. I have one of those minds that's always asking questions. I wear myself out sometimes. So it's no wonder that Kevin is confused."

"What kind of questions?"

Carol shrugged again. "I guess I wonder why Kevin needs so little to be content. On the other hand, I'm always wanting more, emotionally that is. That's why I question our compatibility."

"Maybe that's where the love comes in. It's that constant part of us. It's always there no matter what our mind is doing. Whether we're asking questions or not, love sustains us through it all, if you let it."

Carol blinked back as if she was trying to digest what Peggy was saying. "So you think it's okay for us to be very different and still be together?"

"Yes, of course. I know you think that Tim and I are perfect for each other, right?"

Carol broke off a section of cookie and chewed it with a scowl. When she answered, her voice was very firm and direct. "Yes, I do think that. In fact, I'm quite envious."

It was Peggy's turn to reach out, maybe not with a touch, but with more confidence in helping Carol. "I think so too, but that doesn't mean that Tim and I are alike. Like you and Kevin, we're practically opposites too. I get all flustered, and Tim's the unruffled, steady one. That's what makes our relationship strong. We try to be there for each other."

"Yes, but Tim talks to you a lot more than Kevin talks to me."

Peggy laughed. "Kevin needs time to hone his communication skills. He's still suffering from all the times when we argued. I was such a loudmouth that he simply clammed up instead of fighting back."

"You have a point," Carol said, letting her green eyes spark a little brighter. "I guess I just get afraid about life and start wondering if everything is going to work out."

Peggy sighed. "Well, I can tell you this much. People can change. When Arel got back from his trip, he was so different. I've never seen him look so confident."

"Really?"

"Yes, instead of being all upset with my worries, he was a complete lamb. He was the picture of composure. It was really strange. He even smiled, really smiled."

Carol laughed. "Wow, that is a change. He can be pretty uptight, especially when one of us is upset."

Peggy laughed too. "I know. That's the point. If Arel can do a one-eighty, there's hope for all of us."

Seventy

William slumped over his desk, trying to ignore his throbbing hand. His eyes were focused on the monitor, but the text was getting blurry. He'd spent too many hours searching the web for new information. When Arel finally left, William promised himself to get back on track, to forget the debacle that took place, but it was hard to keep that promise when his research kept hitting dead ends. A cure seemed like the wish of a pauper wanting a windfall.

He got up and took a deep breath, hoping to clear his head as he headed for the stairs. A long soak in the tub might help to ease the soreness in his muscles.

But what can I do about my hand?

No matter how he tried to cope, pain remained a sharp, insistent reminder of how foolish he was during Arel's visit. He allowed Arel to undermine his emotional stability. As a result, he made some god-awful decisions. Yet, those hard lessons wouldn't be forgotten. He would never go down that path again. In fact, he wouldn't go down any path if he didn't find a way to address his wounded limb. It was sapping his strength. Just climbing the stairs was a challenge. His once energetic footsteps were now heavy and labored. He had a superficial cut that should have responded to his meticulous care. Instead, it continued to bleed with the slightest provocation. A careless movement could result in a new outpouring of blood that soaked through the bandages in mere moments. His shaving cuts were quick to clot and mend, but his hand refused to heal.

"Arel has probably passed on an infection that will finish me off." He wheezed out the words as he reached the upper level. He'd barely caught his breath when the doorbell rang. The unexpected intrusion made him scowl as he made his way to the foyer. Who could be calling? He wasn't expecting any deliveries. When he got to the door, he opened it quickly, eager to send his caller on his way.

"Hello, William." A man with dark blond hair stood on the stoop.

William glared back. "How do you know me?" His edgy voice reflected the constant pain he was in and his new irritation at being disturbed. "Are you a neighbor?"

"No, I'm a friend."

"Really? That might be true if I had any friends." When it came to strangers, he could quickly recognize personality types. He found it easy to read mannerisms, the set of faces, and the way people held themselves. The man in front of him refused to be categorized. The guy had the kind of face that one saw in a dream. His features seemed to change from moment to moment. There was also something very eerie in the way the man's eyes almost glowed a bright, sparkling blue. "You're no friend of mine."

"I assure you that I am," the man responded in a determined but friendly tone.

William let out a contemptuous laugh when he realized what was happening. The infection in his hand was affecting his mind. "You're nothing more than a hallucination. You're a clear indication that my condition is getting worse." He started to shut the door.

The man was too fast for him. Before the door closed all the way, the man reached out and held it ajar. "I could help you with your hand."

William didn't reply. Instead, he leaned his weight against the door. There was no way he'd listen to an apparition.

"Please, William, I can help you," the man said as he countered William's actions. He held the door open with seeming ease. He even managed to reach out and connect with William's bandaged limb. "You're missing something, the whole picture."

William was stunned at the immediate effect of the man's touch. All the pain in his hand was gone in an instant. For an apparition, the man was seemingly able to manipulate the physical world. After days of mental and physical torment, he was liberated and able to breathe easier. As he enjoyed the moment, the man smiled back.

"You think there's only one way to live, but that isn't true. If you let me help, I'll show you another way." The man's tone was as soothing as his healing touch. "Trust me."

"Trust you?" William jerked back, breaking the connection. He was being lured into another trap, this time by a ghostly visitor. He almost laughed at the idea, but the pain in his hand was back and throbbing miserably again. He held it close to his body in a protective gesture. If someone thought they could invite themselves into his life, they were gravely mistaken. When he glanced up to reprimand his caller, the man was gone. "What the hell?" William stared out at the darkness and the empty street in front of his home, but there was no sign that anyone was around. His brows were narrowed as he quickly shut and bolted the door.

"It's just more of Arel's madness, so keep it together." He issued the order in a firm tone. He was exhausted and his health was shot, but excuses wouldn't help. He had to maintain his control, even if he was taking a last breath.

Anxious to clear his mind, he walked wearily to the bathroom and turned on the taps. As the tub filled, he looked forward to shutting out everything. When he saw the bath salts sitting on an adjacent shelf, he grabbed them and added a generous amount to the water. They were always a revitalizing, yet calming element that he enjoyed. He wasn't disappointed as a satisfying, resinous aroma began to fill the room. With each deep inhalation, he felt better, more serene than he'd been in a long time. He shed his clothes with some effort. It was a simple but tedious chore with his hand screaming out in protest. Thinking about the tub's steamy, welcoming waters helped a little. Once he was seated in the fragrant waters, he was finally able to let go.

Still, he noticed that he hadn't bothered with the bandage on his hand. It was saturated with blood. As he stripped the covering away, he saw that his palm was bleeding. Droplets of blood fell into the water, tainting the liquid with a filmy redness. What else was new? He lowered himself deeper into the bath and let his thoughts drift. His unexpected visitor came to mind. For a hallucination, he seemed very solid when William tried to close the door. Was there any chance that he was real?

"Of course not," he scoffed as he closed his eyes. He was rewarded with a vision of the man at the door. This time the face was clear and unchanging. The man's every feature was defined in exact detail.

William sat up and blinked a couple of times, but the vision was still there. The man was still staring back. "What the hell is going on now?" He was looking at himself, but it wasn't the William who was a man of science. This was the version of himself that he left behind in childhood, the boy who cared about foxes and meadows and keeping his beautiful world safe. Now, the boy appeared in grown up form, but his innocence was still there.

"I thought I made myself clear when I talked to Arel, but maybe you need to hear this again. You have no place in my life. This world isn't suited for your kind."

The man's smile faded as he continued to gaze back, but his eyes were brighter than ever. "Are you sure? Do you really think I'll stay hidden forever?"

"Get out, and don't come back!" William's shout filled the room, and the man disappeared. Still, it took a few minutes before he could breathe easier. "Damn you, Arel! This disease that you gave me is as damning as you. Now I'm haunting myself."

Seventy-One

Arel sat down heavily in the kitchen chair and began to take the bandage off his hand. Ever since his conversation with Michael and the possibility of helping William, he'd been trying to come up with a constructive idea about what he could do. So far, nothing came to mind. When the last of the bandage was off, he stared at the wound. As he opened and closed his fist, blood began to pool in his palm. Just when he thought it was getting better, the injury would bleed again. He looked up at Michael who sat across from him. "I know we talked about William before, but I keep thinking about him. I know he insisted that I leave, but I didn't have to. I could have kept my mouth closed and tried to help him."

Michael's brows raised a little. "Do you really think that would have worked?"

"I guess not, but I can't just sit here and do nothing."

"You are doing something. Haven't you noticed that as you integrate William's gift, you're letting go of some of your anger."

Arel leaned back, furrowing his brows in concentration. "I guess you're right. The more I let myself feel William's kind of strength and courage, the less my anger flares. Instead, I just feel sad about the whole thing. So how does that help?"

"Perhaps it allows you to approach your problems with more clarity, even wisdom."

Arel let out a mocking bark as he dabbed up some of the blood in his hand. "Wisdom? If William heard you, he'd have that stroke for sure."

"No matter what, you seem more capable of handling the sight of blood."

"I refuse to give into my phobia anymore. From now on, every damnable drop of the stuff is going to be a reminder of what a mess I can make of things."

Michael reached out and took Arel's hand in his. "May I offer a little advice? Perhaps it's time to let William do what he has to do. If necessary, let him go."

Arel pulled his hand away from Michael's grasp. "You never let me go."

"I was always there for you, but I respected your decisions."

"Oh come off of it, Michael. Remember the time that I wanted to run off, and you refused to give me the car keys?"

Michael smiled. "I didn't say that I didn't try to give you other options."

"Anyway, I won't have to worry about William for very long."

"What do you mean?"

"You know exactly what I mean. William is going to die." As soon as Arel said it, an overwhelming feeling of gloom took over. He let his hand drop to his side. "I went to London to help him, and by the time I left, I managed to finish him off. One of these days soon, he's simply going to stop breathing."

"How do you know that?"

Arel leaned forward hopefully. "So it's not true?"

Michael paused and stared back, pinning Arel down with his clear, crystal gaze. "The future is fluid. Nothing is certain."

"Fine, let's deal in probabilities. What do you think his chances are?"

"That's not my job—"

"How about a chance in a million? Does that sound about right?"

"Arel, I can't—"

"You messed up, Michael, big time. You believed in me. Now I have the power to kill people by touching them. What advise can you give me about that?"

"You didn't kill Carey. When he had that motorcycle accident, you helped him."

"Is that how my life works now? I save Carey one minute, and then I kill William the next?"

Michael ignored his question. "Speaking of Carey, he stopped by the house while you were in London. I think he needs a place to live."

"Oh hell, I completely forgot to ask about the kid. He's not on the street, is he?"

"I'm sure he's safe, but you do have that extra bedroom that he could use, at least for a little while."

"Are you crazy? My life is in the toilet. He doesn't need to be around that."

"Do you think shutting out the world is a good thing? It didn't work before."

"At least I didn't hurt anyone."

"That's true, but since you've taken a chance on resurrecting yourself so to speak, you've been there for your friends. That's why Peggy cares so much about you. Plus, the babies love you. Carol and Kevin don't call you the baby whisperer for nothing."

"Right, I've helped everyone but William." He glanced at the floor. With his wounded limb dangling, a puddle of red was spoiling the tile. He lifted his hand and put it back on the table.

Michael offered a compassionate smile. "You tried your best, remember that."

Arel couldn't help but notice the light in Michael's eyes. It was so bright, so full of warmth and kindness. Occasionally, when Arel looked in the mirror, he saw that same light in his own eyes. So why wasn't he more like Michael when it came to taking action? "Maybe people aren't equipped to handle angel energy. You've helped me countless times with the stuff, but when I try to use it, it backfires."

Michael reached out for Arel's hand again. Cradling it in his own, he carefully pried open Arel's fist. "The energy that you're talking about is always there for human or angel. However, in your case, you might say that you have a more powerful connection to that energy than the normal person. When you tried to give William a gift—"

"I know what you're going to say, that I didn't give William options. I thought I knew what was best for him."

Michael began to cleanse Arel's palm with a sterile pad. "Your intention was good, but—"

"I wanted to repair the damage I did, that's all." Arel stopped himself and sucked in a guilty breath. "That's where I went wrong, isn't it? When I tried to help William that last time, it was still about me. What was best for William got mixed up with me atoning for what I did to him in the first place."

"That's part of it."

"There's more?"

"There's always more when two people are involved. When you talked about being brothers in blood, you gave William a choice."

"Yes, but then I bullied him into doing what I wanted."

"Did you bully him or inspire him? For a few minutes, I think William saw and wanted what you offered."

"Then why didn't things work out differently?"

"You wanted to give William the sun, but why? Have you ever thought about the reason that solar orb exists?"

"Finally, something easy. Without the sun, we'd be dead."

"That's true, but it's also a beautiful reminder for every person on this earth. You didn't have to give William something he already has inside of him. You're each a small sun from my viewpoint."

"Sorry, Michael, but I see a couple of bumbling idiots."

"Exactly. Perception is one of the biggest ways we differ. Angelic beings see everything and everyone as part of one perfect source energy. When I gave you my blood, you might say I gave you the opportunity to see things from my vantage point. However, you have to clear away your fears and all those feelings that tell you that you aren't worthy of that vision."

"But how? Am I supposed to keep making these horrible mistakes until I get it right?"

"Learning the truth about oneself takes time."

"In my case, it could take forever."

Michael laughed. "How about this? I see what is, and you see what isn't."

"What does that mean?"

"It's rather simple. You're trying to fix something that's not broken."

"William is definitely broken. I know. I broke him."

"Someday, I think you'll feel otherwise about William and yourself."

"Does that mean that William has a chance of making it?"

Michael began to bandage Arel's hand. "Every moment is a new moment."

"Maybe, but those moments are ticking away too quickly in William's case." He fingered the roll of gauze with his free hand. "The bottom line is that I've finally learned my lesson. I'm not ever using my power again."

The doorbell rang as Michael finished putting the bandage in place. He looked up. "I think that's Carey. He said he might stop by this afternoon."

"Carey, now? I can't face anybody with my brain feeling like it's been through a bark mulcher."

"What do you want to do? Is it too much to let Carey stay here?"

"I can't just turn him out." Arel stood up. "Tell him he can use the spare room. Oh, and one more thing, make it clear that if he hurts himself on that blasted bike of his, he'll have to find someone else to patch him up. I am officially out of the 'healing' business too."

Seventy-Two

Passing clouds hung low in the night sky, but the silvery light of the moon couldn't be denied. Its bright rays peeked through the vapors every few minutes, illuminating the deck where Arel was gazing skyward. He glanced over at Carol who stood next to him. "It's cold again tonight."

She pulled her jacket close. "Yes, winter will be here soon."

"Maybe you should go back inside."

"I have to get some fresh air. Whenever you or Peggy host a dinner, I eat too much. I'm not complaining. Everything is always delicious. I just wish I had as much talent in the kitchen as the two of you."

"But your baking skills are unsurpassed from what I hear."

She blushed. "I know you object to too many sweets, but I can't help myself. I guess I enjoy people going crazy over my triple-chocolate cookies."

He smiled back. "While the cat is away? Peggy says she gained three pounds while I was gone."

"Don't blame that on me. Peggy has been baking her own cookies."

"I see."

"Enough about sweets. I want to talk about you. How's your hand doing?"

Arel gave his bandaged limb a brief inspection. "It's better."

"I don't understand something. You always come back from your trips with an injury."

"A bit of clumsiness."

414

Carol took hold of his arm. "Anyway, it's great having you back."

"Really? As soon as Peggy saw me, she let me have it for not letting her know I'd be gone."

"I'm sorry, but I agree. Thankfully Michael let us know your whereabouts."

Arel ran his good hand over the smooth, wooden banister. "I don't always think things out, but that's going to change. I promise."

"We care about you. We don't want anything to happen to you."

"But I was only gone for a little while."

Carol gave him a sideways glance. "Did you have a nice time?"

"Not exactly."

"Tell me more about this man, William. You've been very close-mouthed about him."

"He's an old associate, but we really don't have too much in common anymore."

"You must still have some kind of a tie the way you rushed off to see him."

"I thought he needed help, that's all, but I wasn't able to do much."

"Maybe you have more in common with him than you realize. Remember when we first met? You were very reluctant to let us do anything for you. We all felt pretty helpless at times."

"I never thought about it that way."

"Perhaps he's shy, like you."

"You think I'm shy?"

"Yes, it was months before you smiled enough to let your dimples show."

Arel flushed with embarrassment. "I don't think I had dimples back then. I was quite thin, but you have a point. Maybe I can be a little introverted."

"Whatever, we were happy when you finally let us in. It's hard to watch when someone's in pain and you can't do anything about it."

"In William's case, everything I did seemed wrong."

Carol squeezed his arm again. "You're a total sweetie pie. William must have a problem accepting help."

A sweetie pie? Carol's appraisal of him would certainly make William roar with laughter. Of course, at this point, William was lucky to be drawing breath.

Carol tugged at his arm. "What's that face you're making? It's the same one Peggy has when she's worried about you."

He quickly changed the subject. "Don't pay me any attention. Tell me, how are you and Kevin doing?"

Carol let out a great sigh. "You were right about the martial arts lessons. Kevin likes his workouts with Kell, but to tell the truth, they haven't changed anything. He just sleeps better on the nights that he works out."

"I'm sorry. I hoped he'd get some benefit—"

"It's not your fault that Kevin is afraid of intimacy."

"Is that the problem?"

"I think it is. I've given it a lot of thought and realized that he has trouble going beyond a certain point. We're having more fun together, but he'll only go so far when it comes to opening up. I guess I'll have to learn to be content with what we have. It's just that I—" She hesitated.

"Go on."

"It's just that I have this idea that a couple should be able to share everything. And Kevin—"

"And Kevin what?" Kevin asked as he stepped out onto the porch.

Arel glanced over at the tall, young man as he came over. "Carol and I were just chatting about your sessions with Kell."

Kevin returned a questioning smile. "I feel like you're talking about more than that. Should my ears be burning?"

Carol quickly let go of Arel's arm. "No, of course not," she said insistently. "I just love you, that's all. Now, if you'll excuse me, I better see if Peggy needs anything."

After Carol hurried past Kevin and went back inside, Kevin turned to Arel. "Let me guess. I'm doing everything wrong again."

Arel smiled sympathetically. "Join the crowd."

Kevin's brows shot up. "What are you talking about? What's going on with you?"

Arel let out a grunt of disgust. "You've seen me in action."

"Give us both a break. You can do some crazy stuff, but you always come through in the end. I'm proof of that. You've saved my butt on a number of occasions."

"And you've returned the favors."

Kevin stiffened his jaw. "I can't please Carol. I try, but she's never satisfied with me."

"What do you mean?"

"She won't give me a break. I don't know what more I can do."

"I get this sense that something besides Carol is eating at you."

"It's that damn dream. Remember?"

"The one where you're the old man?"

"Yeah, that's the one. It's been coming up again."

"I think it was more than a dream, but—"

Kevin shrugged. "I still don't know if I believe in all that bull about us having other lifetimes together."

"It doesn't matter. Dream or past life, I remember that you were our wise teacher. You did your best to give us something to believe in."

"Listen Arel, the way I see it is that each person has to come up with their own truths about life."

"I agree. So what are you upset about?"

"If the dream, or that lifetime, had any validity, I'm not making the same mistake twice. You and Peggy ended up being burned for what I taught you."

Arel paused and patted Kevin's back. "We wanted what you had to offer. Our lives would have been hopeless if we believed in the ignorance around us."

"Still, there's a feeling inside of me. I don't want that responsibility this time."

Arel flinched at the 'R' word. It seemed like everyone was having the same problem with accountability. "I'm sorry that you still feel like that, but believe me when I say I understand. I guess it just takes time to work things out."

"All I know is that Carol should have her own ideas, but she's always wanting to grill me. Why do I have to tell her what I think? Why can't she do her thing and leave me be?"

"Have you tried to explain how you feel?"

"Are you kidding? You know Carol. She'll be in tears, and I'll be in the dog house."

Arel smiled. "Talk to her. More than anything, she needs to know that you care. I think with her background, she's afraid you're deserting her when you won't confide in her."

"I love her. Why isn't that enough?"

"When's the last time that you told her that?"

"It's hard. I don't want to tell her that and get her all stirred up. We'll start to get close again, and that's when she'll want to talk about stuff."

"Just talk to her. Then, even if you do stir things up, at least she knows that you care."

"Why are relationships so tough?"

"You're asking the wrong person. Take Carey for example. Now that he's living at my place, I worry about him every time he takes off on that bike of his. With his devil-be-damned attitude, I never know if he'll come home in one piece."

"Yeah, he's pretty independent. He's kind of Carol's opposite. Want some advice from a guy who was a little like Carey?"

"Of course. Fire away."

"He's old enough to be on his own, so let up on the reins. My dad had to do that with me, and it worked. If Carey screws up, then he did it to himself."

Arel laughed. "You're still the wise person when it comes down to it, old friend."

"Dammit, you're trickier than Carol is. You always manage to bring out that part of me."

"I know you love Carol. You're just afraid of making a mistake with her. However, with me, you seem to take more chances."

Kevin's eyes brightened. "I have to. Remember when you were so out of shape? Somebody had to take you in hand."

"You made a hell of a drill sergeant."

"And you were a hell of a complainer, but in the end, we accomplished a lot." Kevin took a deep breath of the fresh, night air. "I guess that's the trick, hanging in there."

"More wisdom, Kevin? You haven't hidden your light totally under a basket, have you?"

"Just with Carol."

* * *

Kevin stayed out on the porch for a few minutes after Arel went back inside. He enjoyed the brisk breeze and the night sky as he let his conversation about Carol sink in.

Maybe I'm too emotionally retarded to be married, especially to someone as sensitive as Carol.

He wanted to hold on to the thought, to excuse his failure with the woman he loved, but his next thought made his chest cave.

If I don't smarten up fast, I'll lose her.

He had to shape up, but how? How could he put aside all his fears, especially when those fears even haunted his dreams? His hands tightened on the hand rail. If only it was just a game of football, he'd be okay. When he was on the field and the score was tied with only a few minutes left in the game, his old football coach made it easy. "Don't think how you're going to win, just do it!" And Kevin did. When someone fumbled the ball, he didn't hesitate. A few times, he even scored a winning touchdown.

Now, as he headed back inside, he prayed for enough confidence to restore Carol's belief in him. But when he got to the living room and saw her sitting on the love seat, looking so small and so beautiful, his brain froze. He couldn't think. Instead, he forced himself to walk over and sit down beside her. She barely glanced over at him before she turned back to the conversation that Carey and Tim were having.

Carey's voice was excited and full of youthful optimism. "Living for a while in the Big Apple, what a blast that would be. Think about all the things I could try if I go back there on my own."

"Sounds like fun," Tim agreed. "We should all be so footloose at some point in our lives."

Kevin looked over at Arel. When he saw the scowl on Arel's face, he tried to send him a silent message.

Take my advice, old buddy. Don't get involved.

Unfortunately, Arel didn't seem to get Kevin's advice. With squared-off shoulders, he targeted Carey with a totally reprimanding stare. "Some of us have tried not to be so footloose that we nearly kill ourselves, but if that's what Carey wants, it's his life."

Carey wilted a little. "Aw, come on, Arel. I know I made a mistake, but can't we forget about it now?"

"You almost died," Arel shot back. "Later, I got hell from you when I minimized that night."

Carey started to say something, but Arel was already out of his seat and waving goodbye to the group. "I have to be going."

"You're leaving already?" Peggy protested loudly.

"I have some things I need to do before I turn in."

"I'll go with you," Michael said, getting up from where he was sitting.

"No, stay here," Arel insisted as he walked towards the door. "You don't get out enough."

Carey jumped up and followed him. "I think I better come with you, Arel. You look like you need a little cheering up."

Arel didn't reply. Instead, he quickly let himself out.

Once Arel and Carey were both gone, Tim shook his head. "I think those two have a few things to discuss."

Kevin smiled as he thought about the times he went up against Arel's wrathful side. It made playing sports look like a tea party. "Arel does have a bit of a temper when he feels strongly about something." He paused and reached out for Carol's hand. "Of course in my case, I'm really glad I listened to him."

Carol looked at his hand over hers. "I'm glad you feel that way."

Kevin knew the ball was in play, and his mind went blank again. Happily, another part, the part that couldn't lose the game, took over. He squeezed Carol's hand, determined that he'd never let go of what they had. "I may be a little dense at times, but I know when I've hit the jackpot."

Carol blushed, leaned over and kissed his cheek. "Me too," she whispered in his ear.

* * *

Once they got back to Arel's house, Carey followed Arel to his bedroom which also served as Arel's study. Arel ignored him, settled into his desk chair and grabbed some mail. Carey lingered in the doorway, letting the situation cool a little. Finally, he let out a youthful sigh. "Are you mad at me?"

Arel remained focused on the bill he was studying, but he returned a clipped, one-word answer. "No."

Carey moved a few feet into the room. "Really?"

Arel grabbed his checkbook, glanced at the bill and began to write out a check.

Carey crossed his arms. "You look upset."

420

Arel paused, still not looking up. "Why should I be angry? If someone almost kills themselves, then plans on taking off on another potentially dangerous excursion, it's their business. And if that person has a reckless attitude—"

"Arel, please." Carey walked over to the desk and leaned in. "You don't have much faith in me."

When Arel stared back, his eyes were hard and accusing. "And you have no respect for my opinion. So just go and do whatever you need to do."

"Wow, you are angry." Carey picked up a blown-glass sphere and started tossing it from hand to hand as he contemplated what Arel needed from him.

Arel gave him another scowling look. "And stop playing with that."

Carey carefully placed the collectible back on the desk. "Look, I am sorry. I did something stupid, that's all. I'll try to be more careful. In fact, if you think I shouldn't, I won't go to New York."

Arel dropped the pen he was holding. "Really? Why?"

"Because I respect you. And I appreciate all that you've done for me."

Arel sat back in his chair and rubbed his face wearily. When he looked up, there was only concern in his eyes. "I've never had to think about a son. You're the closest I've come to having one. I know I have no right to tell you anything—"

"I'd be proud to have you as my father. But you're too young for that."

Arel smiled. "That's a very nice compliment. Thank you."

"You're my friend."

"I'm sorry, Carey, but you don't want a friend like me."

"Why?"

"Because underneath it all, I'm selfish. You might think differently, but you don't understand—"

"Is this about that William fellow? What happened with him and why is your hand all bandaged up?"

"It's a very long story. There's no way I can explain it to—"

"You really like William, don't you? When we drove to New York you said you didn't have much in common, but you rushed off to help when he needed you."

Arel's jaw tightened. "Yes, I did, but I don't know if it was because I cared. It was more of an obligation."

"So is he still a friend?"

"He doesn't want me to be his friend at this point."

"Well, I do. And I appreciate you giving me a place to stay."

Arel smiled and picked up the glass ornament. He slowly turned it in the light of the desk lamp, letting an array of rainbow colors dance on his desk blotter. "Am I too hard on you? Tell me, because I want to do whatever a friend does."

Carey let his grey-blue eyes sparkle mischievously. "Friends look out for each other, but at the same time, they try not to be too pushy."

Arel replaced the glass sphere on its holder. "Thanks for the reminder."

Carey laughed again. "We're all in this together, right?"

"Yes, I guess we are, but I wish I had a better handle on how to react when people do things that scare me."

"Have some fun. Take a real vacation. I don't think that trip to New York or London counted. Get away from everything for a while."

"A vacation? I don't know about that."

Carey walked to the door. "Maybe you can give it some thought."

Seventy-Three

Over the next couple of days, Arel's mind kept going back to Carey's comment that Arel must really care about William. He answered Carey's observation with an excuse, something about how their relationship was more about duty. Now, as he stared out the living room window and watched the last few leaves falling from a maple tree, he didn't want to think about William, period. Every time he did, his palm throbbed with pain.

"Are you okay?" Michael asked. He was sitting in one of the recliners studying the book on blood that Arel had ferried home.

"I don't know. I feel rather numb at this point."

"Are you going to ever let your hand heal?"

Arel turned to face Michael and shrugged. "The pain strengthens my tie to him."

"A painful hand isn't the best reminder of your tie to William."

"I guess you're right."

"Do you really want to stay connected? If your guilt was suddenly washed away, would you still worry about William?"

"I think I've been using my guilt so I don't have to think about the truth. That last day when I knew William was dying, I saw things so clearly. It nearly did me in. Unlike my real brother, Aldwin, William was there for me. He stuck by me no matter what. I was often a drunken idiot, but he tried to protect me just like he tried to defend those young fox kits that he loved."

Michael put his book aside. "Yes, I know."

"Dammit, what am I supposed to do for him? I know William's been misguided, but when I felt what was in his heart, I knew his bitterness was the only thing that could shield him from all the pain he endured growing up. As a boy, I never noticed much except for my own misery, but William was different. Even though he was abused himself, he still cared about what happened to the world around him. Every bird that fell from the sky during his father's shooting parties affected him deeply. In a way, I think all the death and ignorance around him drove him slightly crazy. When I tuned into the burden he's carried, I couldn't bear it. I think that's why I'm numb to him. I can't let myself feel what he's going through."

Michael stood up and came over. "You need to get away from everything for a bit or else you'll be slightly crazy too. Carey said he mentioned a vacation to you. It's a good idea."

Arel smiled. "Carey's a bright spot in the middle of all this mess."

"Take him with you. He'd love to see more of the world."

"I can't just go off—"

"Arel, I'm trying to help you. As you've said, on some level, you and William are connected to each other. He needs you to believe in him. That means going beyond his past and his pain."

"You really think that's the most helpful thing I can do? I'm trying to have faith that he'll get himself through this thing. I'm trying to remember that he has choices too."

"Absolutely."

Arel carefully opened and closed his hand. "Carey said something about all of us being in this together. Is that how you think about what we're doing? Do angels feel that they're connected to humans?"

Michael paused and stared back for a long moment. His eyes were even brighter than usual. "What do you think?"

"I know that if it hadn't been for you, I'd still be lost. For your part, I can only suppose that you truly love human beings no matter how imperfect we are."

"Yes, but remember, it's easy to love when you only see a person's true essence." He patted Arel's shoulder and turned to leave. "Give the vacation some thought, and if you go, choose someplace bright where the sun is shining."

"I think I could use a little sun. Like you said, it's a reminder of what we have inside."

Later, that night, Arel lay in his bed thinking about the lucid dream he had with William. In that beautiful world, they had shared a few minutes of peace and wonder.

I know that you don't believe me, Will, but I'll find a way to make it all up to you. I promise.

He sent the message out on the telepathic airways a few times with the hope that William would hear him. Finally, he turned out the light and closed his eyes. He was tired and ready to sleep.

Time to dream.

He would have good dreams, lucid dreams. The sun would be shining and every flower in the meadow would be radiant. William would be walking through glorious, shimmering fields. He would still be a man of science, but one who could enjoy vaster vistas. He would feel the joy of being able to walk in the light again.

You believed in me, Will. Now it's my turn to believe in you.

Even if William didn't get the message, it was okay. It just meant that Arel had to believe for both of them.

Oh hell, what am I doing?

Arel felt his heart quicken and his throat go dry. He had sworn off getting involved, but wasn't that what he was doing? Yes, unfortunately, it was. Still, he knew Michael was right. He couldn't become a hermit again. He'd come too far. The blood in his veins was too strong to be ignored. He had to carry on, no matter what he had to face in the future. He also had the present moment, and in that moment, he had a hopeful vision of what could be.

The story continues in book three, William's Blood!

Thank you for taking the time to read *Arel's Blood*, the second book of my series, THE VAMPIRE RECLAMATION PROJECT. If you enjoyed it, please consider telling your friends. Word of mouth is an author's best friend and much appreciated.

Thank you. – S. S. Bazinet.

BOOK THREE: WILLIAM'S BLOOD
The Vampire Reclamation Project
By S. S. Bazinet

In book three of The Vampire Reclamation Project series, William continues to struggle with the devastating effects of Arel's blood. When he fails to rally physically, he finds peace. He accepts that he's going to die. However, his tranquil state is short lived. He soon discovers that Arel's powers over him extend beyond this world.

In order to regain any sense of freedom from Arel's obsessive needs, William is forced to seek out the assistance of Rolphe, the person who passed on the vampire virus to William.

William discovers another ally when he meets a woman named Annabel. He's immediately attracted to her, but he doesn't realize that he's falling for an angel who's taken on human form.

Will he survive further interference from Arel? Will Rolphe turn out to be a lethal threat rather than a savior? Will William open his heart to Annabel only to have it broken? Find out the answers in book three of The Vampire Reclamation Project series, William's Blood.

To visit S. S. Bazinet's website, go to SSBazinet.com

www.ingramcontent.com/pod-product-compliance
Lightning Source LLC
Chambersburg PA
CBHW070349260626
47161CB00001B/84